T0161910

KING OF THIEVES

by

Shea Godfrey

2017

KING OF THIEVES

ISBN 13: 978-1-63555-007-8

THIS TRADE PAPERBACK ORIGINAL IS PUBLISHED BY
BOLD STROKES BOOKS, INC.
P.O. BOX 249
VALLEY FALLS, NY 12185

FIRST EDITION: DECEMBER 2017

CREDITS
EDITOR: RUTH STERNGLANTZ
PRODUCTION DESIGN: STACIA SEAMAN
COVER DESIGN BY SHEA GODFREY

Acknowledgments

Thank you to you, the reader. I hope you like it, and I hope it provides you with a brief escape from whatever your worries may be. Thank you to Ruth Sternglantz for your infinite patience, and thank you to Sue Reese for being such an exceptional bluestocking.

This is dedicated to all of you who provide compassion, kindness, and the strength of a helping hand to those in need. The resistance against what's happening in America now is not only the resistance of marches, protest signs, and voices raised in defiance of injustice and hatred, it is also the rebirth of equality, empathy, community, and free thinking. Your compassion gives aid and comfort to those who are most in need. Your kindness replaces fear with love. Your strength protects those most vulnerable in our society against the indifference and cruelty of power. #TheResistance

CHAPTER ONE

San Michele di Serino, Italy
Present day

The breeze moved like an animal within the leaves of the oak tree, familiar and certain of its path. There were a dozen other trees clustered upon the natural terrace of land, but for the moment, the wind had chosen only the tallest. Its lofty branches were heavy with foliage and the wind spiraled downward into the rich chaos.

Finnegan could almost feel the roots of the tree far beneath her feet, the ropy veins living proof of the last two hundred years. When she closed her eyes, she imagined she could hear it through the thick soles of her boots, a primitive pulse unlike any other.

The air smelled different here than anywhere else she had ever been. It was the earth itself, she'd been told once, the soil lavish with sorrow and the touch of God's leisure, when the afternoon sun hit the hills just so. And it was Italy, after all, still caught within the fading embrace of summer. There was nothing else like it in the world.

She could taste only sadness at the moment, however, as she took another step closer to the stone that marked the grave. The words carved within the granite were a dark silhouette upon the surface and they held no structure within the darkness. The only purpose they served was to show that the smooth rock had been made uneven by an impossible truth.

Finn turned her head to the left just a bit as her muscles tensed.

"It is only me."

She recognized him, though his whisper bore no mark of the rough, distinctive qualities it usually held. The echo of Italian was thick within his English, and her eyes found him within the shadows cast by the long clouds that passed beneath the moon.

"It's too late for you, Papa Piet," Finn replied softly. She smiled, though; she couldn't help it. "And so far from the house…How did you know I was here?"

"You think I don't know when you are close? You think I am so rich in love, that one feels like another?"

"If you trip and break a hip, I'll be pinched for sure."

The old man laughed beneath his breath and moved closer to her. "I know this land better than any man ever will. I do not trip." Finn caught sight of the cane he used, and a small push of anxiety warmed her chest. "I know all the stones here as I knew the crown of my son's head the day after he was born. So and warm beneath my hand. He smelled of peaches."

Finn smiled, not expecting the words.

She turned away and looked past the grave that had drawn her halfway around the world. There were others, and from the corner of her eye she watched as the cane moved through the air. She followed where it pointed.

"He lies over there…and the brother of my heart is just there. It is his blood that runs through your veins." The cane gestured to the right and then struck the ground as he took a small step for balance. "And his son there, your father. My mother and her people, beyond. My sisters and my brother Emilio, who was a great fisherman." He was quiet for a time. "He looked like our mother."

"Technically…" Finn teased in a gentle voice. It would pull him back and she knew it. "We aren't actually related. You do remember that, right?"

The old man stepped close on her left. She was taller than he was, but it still felt as if she looked up. "The heart's blood is different—you know this."

Finn tried to see his eyes in the darkness.

"You are close, then?"

"Yes."

"You would still see justice done?"

Finn said nothing.

"Good. Revenge is better. I have stood where you stand. I know what I'm saying. They took everything from me…but I made them pay."

"I haven't forgotten," Finn acknowledged.

"Then you should not have risked coming here. They will kill you if they see you."

Finn's eyes returned to the gravestone.

"You received your package?"

Finn smiled, surprised. "Yes, thank you."

"It must be a woman."

She tried not to laugh. "What would you know?" Her tone was filled with affection, for she knew damn well that he knew everything.

"I know enough." His response was amused.

Finn watched the shadows slide across the cold granite. She heard him move, and then she closed her eyes as the warmth of his fingers brushed in a fleeting manner across her cheek.

"Is she wild and beautiful?" His voice was filled with respect, for the size of the gesture she would make had not been lost upon him.

The darkness that clung to the headstone began to swim and sway, no match for the tears that filled her eyes. For just a few seconds the moon slid free of the clouds, and she could read the marker, its elegant swirl of letters pushing the air from her lungs.

"Is she?"

Finn remembered the words he had once spoken. *Find a woman who is wild and beautiful, with a will that will match your own.* Her voice was a ghost. "Yes."

"Then don't fuck it up."

Finn laughed. She hadn't seen that one coming. She met his shadowed gaze as she wiped at her eyes. "You're a pain in the ass, you know that? I'm pretty sure no one would complain when you don't show up for dinner. All I need is a rock and a shovel."

The old man laughed in return, his frail shoulders going back. He took a breath and spoke in a happy rush of Italian.

Finn turned to him at last and lowered her head. He slipped a gentle hand into her thick dark hair and claimed a generous handful. "I miss you, too," she whispered.

Near Bergerac, the Dordogne, France

Cassandra Marinos shut her suitcase and threaded the lock through the holes in the tabs of the main zipper. She knew that, at best, such a paltry attempt at security would only preve her things from flying free down the runway. As for keeping them saf from human mischief, she had no illusions.

She dragged the bag from her d and it dropped to the carpet as she glanced about the shadows of h bedroom. The suitcase followed her down the long, wide hallway un she reached the main room.

The curtains were closed and he shadows were thick as they swarmed upward in the fading light f the early evening.

Her bookshelves were in ord and the furniture was covered. Janine would stop by every other ᴠ to make sure all was well, and that the alarms were working prope . *And to use the pool if it gets hot enough*, she thought with a wry s le at her beloved housekeeper's expense, *and drink my wine*. She'd l t several bottles of a rather lovely Spanish wine on the kitchen table, a ⅼ she had no doubt they would be gone when she returned. The expa ive kitchen swept away into the darkness of the dining room beyond. nd for a moment, she thought she saw a shadow of movement.

Her gaze skipped to the firepla on the opposite wall.

The urn sat at the center of the ⅼrved mantelpiece, surrounded by framed photos she could not make o from where she stood, and a few tokens she could not bear to hide aᴠ y.

The ceramic vase was rich wi colors that had lost their names without the light, but she knew eve dense turn of paint as it moved, intense eddies of midnight blue tha washed over indigo. There were greens and splashes of gold as well, ke swirling stars that might jump free and land upon the stones of the ᴇarth with a hiss.

Casey set the suitcase up and ᴠalked to the fireplace, her hand lifting as she neared.

The brushstrokes beneath her f gertips were like Braille, and she closed her eyes as she read the mem ies. They raced across the insides of her eyelids like words spoken toc ast.

"One last adventure," she whi ered, and her palm moved like a breeze across the smooth curve of tl urn. Her throat was tight and she wiped at her eyes as she turned awa

She retrieved her suitcase and ᴇcked for her tickets and passport before she set the alarms, and then s ᴇ closed the door behind her.

CHAPTER TWO

Baia Mare, Romania
May 1986

The .45 caliber semiautomatic looked expensive and shiny against the faded and beat-up surface of the kitchen table. It was silver plated with red maple wood stocks, and scrollwork that wound down the barrel. The smooth etch was either a dragon, or flames, or both—Asher James couldn't tell. He didn't think it mattered, though, since neither flames nor a dragon would do him in. A bullet from the clip *inside* the gaudy weapon might make a mess of him, but the weapon itself did not impress him.

The words that were spoken as Asher stared across the table were foreign to him, but they sounded vaguely insulting, nonetheless. He recognized the words *pistol* and *thief* in Croatian, but that was all.

"In English, if you please," Asher responded. He struck a match upon the surface of the table and lifted it to his hand-rolled cigarette. He suspected his companion didn't speak French, so he didn't bother asking.

The young man smiled as his left hand dropped slowly to the table. His fingertips tapped lightly, but an inch or two from the weapon. "You like my gun, yes?"

Asher picked a piece of tobacco from his tongue with his thumb and ring finger. "Yes, it's very pretty." His eyes narrowed against the smoke. "Where is Ketrin?"

The young man tossed his head to the side and smoothed back his long black hair at the same time. He wore stiff dark blue Levi's and black boots laced up tight. He did not, however, wear a shirt. The reason for that was a show of strength, and while Asher recognized the

Madonna and Child tattooed upon his chest, the tiger's head, the Tao, and the dagger that started on one side of his neck and came out the other, Asher didn't care.

"You're dealing with me now, Mister Ash, Ash, Asher. I am Pavel, and I speak for Ketrin. Ketrin does not track with a common thief."

Asher let out a small chuckle of surprise and searched behind the pale young man.

The woman in the kitchen wore a sleeveless paisley dress that had seen better days, her blond hair pulled back from her face in a severe ponytail. She had quick eyes and a strong face, and though she was thin and pale, she appeared to be full of spirit. She couldn't have been more than thirty years old. "Does he speak for Ketrin?"

The woman eyed Pavel and gave a sniff of amusement before she stepped back to the stove. Her arms were covered with bruises.

Pavel slammed his fist against the table and leaned forward. "You don't speak to her! You don't speak to Magda."

Asher gave another soft laugh. I speak to you, right?"

"That's right."

"So you're the one who deals with common thieves, yes?"

The young man stared at him for several moments and then he sat back in his chair. "Whatever you think, you are not knowing anything." He made a face with his lips pursed out.

Asher took a long drag on his cigarette and considered his options. It didn't take him long, however, for there was only one path to what he wanted.

Pavel said, "Ketrin trusts me, I am his own bl—"

The cigarette hit Pavel in the face, just beneath his left eye. It exploded in a spray of sparks and burning tobacco, and Asher filled his right hand with dark, greasy hair as Pavel flinched up with a hiss of surprise. He cracked Pavel's head repeatedly against the table until blood ran from his nose and he stopped his shouting.

Asher stepped back and Pavel was pulled unconscious from his seat, his upper body limp against Asher's leg. The weight of the flaming dragon .45 was heavier than Asher thought it would be. Pavel was not. "Put it on the stove, please."

Magda stared down the barrel of Asher's newly acquired weapon, and then met his eyes.

"Why do you think I am here, in the middle of fucking nowhere, Magda, asking for Ketrin in the last place on earth he should be?"

She lowered the cast-iron pan slowly and deliberately. Her eyes hadn't lied. She was quick, and she was smart. "Because he asked you to come." Her voice was also rather lovely, and Asher favored her with a smile. He turned his hips to the right and swung Pavel by the hair. The young man landed unconscious at her feet. "If he has been unkind to you, tell Ketrin that I grabbed the pan and hit him with it." Magda's eyes filled with subtle suspicion.

"If he asks me, I will say that I did," Asher offered. "Take your swing."

"Why?" Magda demanded, her right hand still holding tight to the handle of the pan.

"Where I come from, you treat a woman with respect."

Magda's grip eased slowly as she let go of the pan, but she said nothing.

Asher lowered the gun to his side. "Where is Ketrin?"

"There is a barn, round back of the house."

"Thank you, Magda."

They looked at one another.

"You're not going to hit him?"

"If I hit Pavel with my good cooking pan," Magda answered, "the wound will be filled with bacon grease, and he will know that it was I who hit him."

Asher tried not to smile. It was a good answer. "Fair enough."

Asher tucked the gun beneath the waist of his pants and turned away from her. He moved from the open kitchen and through the front room, eyeing the huge console television that sat near the fireplace. The screen door creaked when he pushed it open, and as he took the front steps, he moved his newly acquired weapon to the small of his back. He aired out his brown leather suit jacket with a snap and ran his hands through his hair, smoothing it back.

The hills surrounding the farmhouse were green and lush, and though it was still early summer, the temperature was warm. He had traveled for two long days to reach the wooded area just north of Baia Mare, and while the country he had traveled through was beautiful, Eastern Europe had never been the location of his choice. He didn't like the food, and the wine was not sweet enough for his liking.

The wind moved through the black walnut and red cedar trees, and it filled the air with a clean scent that did not seem to touch the farmhouse and the buildings around it. It passed over them and around them, and perhaps even through them, but it did not stay. As Asher walked around the back of the house and onto the path which led to the weathered barn, some thirty meters away, he wished he were the wind, blown clean from this place, and with no memory of it once he was gone.

Ketrin Arshavin walked toward him in the distance, and even though Asher could not see his eyes yet, he could feel them.

Arshavin was a large man, several inches over six feet and square in just about every aspect of his physical appearance. Square, wide shoulders, and a square jaw. Huge hands that were hidden within a dirty towel as he walked and wiped his blunt fingers free of whatever annoyed him. His head was blocky as well, his thick graying hair too heavy to stay put, despite the cloying pomade that he used. It flattened out on top and pulled to the sides like an old Christmas box no one had wanted to open.

"Asher James," Ketrin said as he neared. He tucked one end of the stained towel beneath the wide leather belt on his worn jeans. It might have been oil, and it might have been blood on the towel. Asher didn't care to know.

He braced for the bone crushing grip that was to come and met Ketrin's outstretched hand. "Ketrin Arshavin."

"Did you meet Pavel?"

"Yes. He's a nice boy."

Ketrin chuckled, the sound deep within his chest. "You didn't kill him, did you? That would be bad for you."

"No. I'm wearing my good shoes."

Ketrin glanced down. "Oh yes. Very nice. Italian."

Asher reached into his pants pocket and pulled out a soft drawstring bag that fit fully within his hand. The velvet fabric felt like an opportunity that would never come again, and one that he would always regret missing.

"It was good of you to come all the way here. I appreciate it."

Asher placed the bag in Ketrin's hand.

Ketrin pulled the bag open and dumped the contents into his other hand.

The Cartier diamond choker tumbled into the light of day and he smiled, his lips still oddly full despite his wide mouth. His violet eyes were bright with excitement. "You pulled it off."

Asher held up his hands. "We are good, then, yes?"

Ketrin's eyes narrowed a fraction, but he nodded. "Of course. This settles your debt to me. That was our deal, Asher James."

"Good."

"I will call on you again, I think."

Asher's heart was beating harder with each second he stood there. He was well aware that his odds of leaving Romania alive were not the sort of odds that a seasoned betting man would favor. "I'm going to America," he lied. "I'll send you a postcard."

Ketrin pondered his words with a dark, penetrating gaze. "I see." He slipped the choker back within its pouch and held out his right hand. "Then I wish you good luck."

Asher put all his strength into it, as they shook hands again. He could feel his knuckles groan in protest. "You, too."

"War is coming. War is good for business."

Asher waited for Ketrin to release his hand. "I've heard talk."

"I will keep an eye out for you, just in case." Ketrin finally released him. "A man in my position always has need of a good thief. There will be opportunities for many things."

Asher turned his back and walked away. He kept his stride in check, but the hair upon his arms tingled with a chill despite the warm air. It was bad enough he had to turn his back, but it would be a tragedy if he just flat out broke down and ran. He was in no way a coward, but Asher understood the precarious reality of his current situation. He wasn't stupid, either.

"Have Magda give you food for the road," Ketrin called after him. "It is a long drive back to Baia Mare, and Firiza has no good food there."

Asher glanced back with a wave and noted two men had emerged from the barn. One of them carried a shotgun, the barrel set upon his right shoulder in a casual manner.

Asher lengthened his step, but he did it smoothly, and a small sound of relief slipped from his throat when he saw his rusted silver Renault. It wasn't pretty, but he knew when he turned the key, it would start without a hitch, and it would take him to Zagreb and then Zadar without incident. From there he would take the ferry to Ancona, and Italy would welcome him with open arms.

He dug the keys from his pocket and cursed himself beneath his breath. He bobbled and dropped the keys as he rounded the front of the car, but he did not stop as he tried to pick them up. They fell a second time, and he stepped back with a hiss in order to complete the job. He chose the square key, threw the door open, slid onto the seat, and then slammed the door shut beside him.

The key was in the ignition when the passenger door opened.

Asher's eyes were wide and he expected the shotgun he had glimpsed in the distance. He thought it might have two barrels, though only one was needed.

The little girl could not have been more than six or seven years old, at least that's what he figured, though he didn't have any children of his own. He didn't know any children, either, so he really wasn't sure how old she might be. He knew nothing about children, and this fact was partly by design and partly by sheer luck.

She had blond hair that was tied behind her head, and it wanted to curl, but it wasn't clean enough to indulge its own wish. Her face was heart shaped and her eyes were a rich and lovely brown, and probably far too large for a child her age. Her dress was made of the same material as Magda's dress, and her blue coat was dirty and far too small for her, though she wore it zipped up tight, nonetheless.

Magda held the girl's right hand, and before Asher knew what was actually going on, the girl was sitting in the passenger seat. Magda leaned into the car and grabbed the safety belt.

"Close your mouth, Asher James," Magda said in a very calm, but hurried voice. "Her father was Greek, and his name was Zahl Petinos. Her mother was French—her name was Marrin. Her father hid something important, but Ketrin did not break them. They are gone now."

Asher sat back in his seat. "Wait, *non*, you—"

"Shut up," Magda ordered without raising her voice, and Asher obeyed. "That was a few years ago. She is six years old now, I think, and her name is Cassandra." Magda clicked the belt, and her eyes were fierce. "She has another year of being a house slave, and living on scraps, maybe two. If she cannot give Ketrin what he wants, when that time comes, it will all change for her. She will be sold—do you understand?"

Asher stared at her.

"Or Pavel will take her. And a year after that, when he is bored with her, he will pass her around to his friends. If war comes, as Ketrin is preaching, then I should put a bullet in her head right now."

Asher continued to stare.

Magda knelt down beside the car. "Cassandra?"

The girl lifted her eyes from the ragged stuffed cat that she held.

Magda smiled. "This man"—Magda glanced across the seat and then back to the girl—"this man comes from a place where girls go to school, and they may have a real kitten to play with, if they want. He will take you there, and he will find you a new home."

The girl returned to her stuffed cat and began to pet its head.

Magda met Asher's eyes. "I don't know what language she speaks, but she understands very well what goes on around her. Her parents both spoke English. She has never answered me, not ever. For almost three years she has not said a single word, not even to her cat, who she loves."

Asher felt his shoulders go, and he sank back against the seat. Pavel's gun dug into his ribs. "Magda, please, I know nothing about children."

"This place, this world, has no need of another victim. This place needs a strong woman, who takes what she wants and does not ask for a man to say she can. You are a smart man. I know this." Magda tapped a finger against her temple. "Because you are walking away alive, from the hooks that hang in Ketrin's barn. Do you have a sister?"

Asher made a face of complete surprise and he knew it. "Yes, but no, no, I haven't seen her in almost ten *years*."

"So you know women."

"Yes, but—"

"Take her to your sister."

"Magda, *please...*"

"This girl watched her parents walk into that barn and never come out. I do not know what she saw before that, or heard over the three days he kept them, but I am thinking something. She has taken the back of Pavel's hand and the devil within Ketrin's eyes while he waits for her to grow, and she has said nothing."

Magda turned to the girl and lifted her face with a gentle hand. "Be strong." Her voice was filled with emotion. "Live your life, yes? And when you are afraid? Be afraid with a fire from your soul, and burn down the world around you." Magda stood, but leaned over as she reached into the car. "Give me Pavel's gun."

Asher made a face, but he leaned forward and pulled the weapon free. It was a relief, though he didn't want to admit it.

"Pavel will not notice the girl missing for days. For this gun? He would hunt you down and make you into little pieces for a pie, and that is no joke."

Asher set the heavy weapon into her hand.

"Drive now, and do not stop. Do not go into Baia Mare. Go to

Prague. Just north of Baia Mare, ta the E58 to Satu Mare. You will know from there where you shoul go." With her free hand Magda handed him a small package wrapp in brown paper that she pulled from the front pocket of her dress. Those are papers I had made for her. From Prague, you might go any here. There is some little money there, to help. New clothes, perhaps and some food for a while."

Asher took the packet.

"The one who steals her heart om the silence, Asher James, will be the King of Thieves." Magda's e es were desperate and filled with an abundance of hope at the same ti e. "Do not ever come back here."

"I wasn't planning on it."

Magda leaned down and kisse the girl upon the cheek. "Forget this place," she whispered in a thick nanner. "And forget me, too."

The door slammed shut.

"Start the car, you fool."

Asher obeyed.

Magda leaned down and smile through the open window. "Your sister was older, yes?"

"Yes."

"You listen to a woman very ell. Now start driving, for God's sake, and do not look back. A week two of trouble, and you will save the life of a child. It is not such a bad ing to have in your pocket, when you go to meet your God."

Asher felt the question within t e pit of his stomach. "What about you?"

"Do not look back."

She walked away from the r with a straight back and her shoulders squared, and Asher obeye her one more time. He put the car into drive and they moved forward. her followed the gravel drive as it curved back around, and when the h se went by on his left, he caught a glimpse of Magda as she opened t screen door and disappeared into Ketrin Arshavin's house.

His eyes were on the road as the passed beyond the small clearing, and the gravel turned into a well-wo dirt road that passed between the red cedars. Asher went as fast as he ared, and thankfully, the Renault seemed to move as if it had wings. did not look back.

CHAPTER THREE

San Francisco
Present day

Finnegan Starkweather watched Cassandra Marinos step from the limousine, the shadow Casey cast along the pavement lengthened further by the slant of the lights along Stockton Street.

Finn was fairly certain that should Ms. Marinos be in need of a weapon, even her shadow might come in handy, like the Prada heels Casey wore. Not that Casey was known for her violence, but she had raced to the top of an extremely exclusive roster, with very little sympathy for the people left in her wake.

Casey spoke to the driver briefly and offered an easy smile as her dark blond hair brushed across her face. The style was reminiscent of Veronica Lake, and it spilled onto the shoulders of her fawn-colored cashmere coat in a dreamy manner. The driver nodded and closed the door as Casey walked toward the Campton Place Hotel.

Finn leaned against the railing of the fire escape two flights up and one building over, and her upper body tipped into midair as she tried to see Casey all the way into the hotel, despite the awning that blocked her view.

"Maybe you'll fall down her dress."

"Maybe, but I wouldn't have time to see much on the way down," Finn cracked as she found her feet and spun about.

"Are you sure this is going to work?"

"Of course not, but I think maybe it's time I introduced myself."

Malik Kaseem pushed back the brim of his Manchester United hat. "You're going to get your ass kicked."

Finn wanted to laugh, but her nerves refused to oblige. "Speak for yourself."

"We could just step up the surveillance, Finn. Let's call in a few of Aaron's people. They're solid, and he already knows we're in town."

"Yeah, but then what?" Finn asked. "We need a better view of things, period. When this all goes down, at the very least we need to be within spitting distance, as they say."

"Who says that?"

"*They.*"

"Who are *they?*"

"The opposite of us?" Finn asked with a grin. "Don't get me all worked up, please."

"Let me call Aaron."

"Fine, go ahead." Finn gave him a hard look. "Let's just do this, though, all right? I'm all grown up, in case you haven't noticed."

"Yes, but are you wearing your clean knickers?"

"Shut up."

"Yes, sir."

"Did you pick out the waiter?"

"Yes, his name is Marcel. He seems extremely practiced."

"At what, being French? Are there brined cheeses involved?"

"No, at not asking any questions."

"How do I look?"

Malik took a step back and appeared to give her an honest once-over.

She wore a dark navy Jil Sander suit with bluish-gray lapels, over a pristine white shirt that Malik and his wife Aiyla had gotten her for Christmas. Her matching trousers were cut low and fitted, and her silver buckled belt offset her low-heeled Steve Madden boots that added a rough edge. Her thick black hair was spiky about her face and she felt that for the moment, at least, it was behaving itself.

"Don't make me repeat myself. You know I hate repeating myself."

"Sex on a stick," Malik answered.

A flash of regret moved through his eyes after he spoke, and so she smiled, stepping into the punch. Her fist landed against his right bicep with a thud.

He winced as he pulled his shoulder in. "Go with God."

"Just don't mess anything up while I'm gone, okay?" Finn stepped from the fire escape and maneuvered smoothly through the open window. "Two weeks of surveillance, and it all goes up in smoke because you can't remember to put a thumb drive in your pocket."

"That one wasn't actually my fault, you know."

She smiled and kept moving.

❖

Finn stood just beyond the arch that led into the restaurant and watched as Cassandra Marinos claimed her reservation by one of the blue-tinted, etched windows. Casey's dress was cut low between her breasts and wonderfully sleek, draped along her body as if the black fabric had spontaneously combusted along her skin in a burst of silk and sexuality. It was Carolina Herrera, and Finn knew it would be a match for Casey's dark eyes.

The headwaiter caught Finn's attention for a brief instant and she gave him a nod.

Casey accepted the menu and ordered a drink, no doubt the 1998 Clos des Goisses that Finn knew was her favorite at the moment. The waiter would bring a '47 Cheval Blanc instead. The damn thing had cost Finn ten grand, and Pietro had called in a very old favor besides, but it would be worth it just to see her take that first sip.

Only the best of everything for one of the top thieves in the world, and that's exactly what Cassandra Marinos was.

She had never been caught, and as of yet, no charges had ever been leveled against her. A few private firms had investigated an alias she used, but not a single piece of hard evidence had been discovered. She had yet to make Interpol's Red Notice list, and barring a disaster of epic proportions, Finn doubted she ever would. When a rare work of art went missing, though, one of Casey's fictitious names could always be found on someone's short list of possible suspects.

The name Cassandra Marinos, on the other hand, had rarely seen the light of day.

It was a bauble of diamonds and white gold that had turned out to be the final piece of the puzzle, and it had landed Finn in France, just beyond the backyard of Casey's home outside of the Dordogne. A trinket worth thirty grand that had been stolen in Amsterdam, though the *what* of the theft wasn't nearly as telling as the *when* of it.

The bracelet had been stolen in 2002, just hours before the theft of two Van Gogh paintings, and in Finn's mind, it had never been a coincidence that Casey just happened to be in Amsterdam at the same time the museum job had gone down.

The theft of *Scheveningen* and *Nuenen* wasn't all that shocking in the end, but what was surprising was that it took so long to recover them. They'd shown up over a decade later just south of Naples, with the Italian Mob on the hook. While Finn would not have chosen those particular paintings as Vincent's best work, taken together they were worth well over a hundred and twenty million dollars.

At least fifteen million had fallen into Casey's coffers from somewhere, and the timing had matched intelligence reports on the original sale of the stolen paintings, even though it appeared as if Casey hadn't done much of the heavy lifting. The fact that Finn was fairly certain of who *had* planned the heist was the picture on the cover of the box.

It had been almost three years since Finn had started her search for Casey, working from a swarm of haphazard clues and savory bits of information she'd gathered over a very long time. Casey was calling herself *Alyssa Stavros* when Finn had finally found her, and her papers had been beyond reproach. It had taken Finn several months after that to expose the hidden woman upon the elaborate canvas, though when she did, the person underneath was everything Finn had imagined she would be.

The truth had been a revelation in more ways than one, and Finn was not oblivious to the power the knowledge now held over her. There were small things, of course, and there were things that shook her right down to the ground and back again.

She had learned what Casey's favorite breakfast food was, and how she took her coffee. Finn knew what movies she had given her time to, and that Casey loved to read. Finn knew she loved dogs, but what Casey really had a weakness for were fat cats that liked the sun and too much food. She preferred the BMW, but when it came to speed she went with the Aston Martin, and she had a Vantage GT2 that proved her commitment to the edge. And Finn knew when she was heartsick, Casey would go to the sea and bide her time until her pain eased.

Such things were random, perhaps, but they added life to an incomplete canvas that had long been lacking in color.

A man named Eric Werner was the conduit through which Vincent's paintings had passed, and he had also fenced several items from that rather well-timed Amsterdam jewel heist, including a bauble of white gold and diamonds.

Werner was the number-one fence in Central Europe, not only for a Van Gogh or a Picasso, but for any work of art that suddenly found itself looking for a new home. For the past twenty-five years, he had dealt almost exclusively in the underground art trade, and Finn knew that his operation was impressive, and extremely well financed. Eric Werner had arrived in San Francisco less than a week ago, along with a multitude of possible buyers from around the world. Combined with Casey's presence, it was the moment Finn had been waiting years for.

There was a private auction about to happen, and Finn had every intention of either being there or getting what she really wanted from Eric Werner himself. Casey was in town to cash in on a Rembrandt sketch that would fetch her a cool three million, but Finn knew for a fact that the world-class thief was in possession of something much more valuable and far more dangerous than just a wayward Rembrandt.

Finn's endgame was in sight, and the man she wanted, the man she had been hunting for over a decade, would come for what Cassandra Marinos had to sell.

Casey checked her phone, and Finn smiled at the smooth fall of her hair as Casey looked down. Finn was amazed that such a small thing could affect her so easily, and amused that it had done so right from the start.

CHAPTER FOUR

Monte Carlo, Monaco
September 2012

Finn stood in the Salle Renaissance of the Casino de Monte-Carlo and leaned her left shoulder against one of the arches. She pushed at the earpiece nestled within her right ear and felt thoroughly fine in her deep blue Armani suit and black silk shirt. "This thing doesn't work."

"Of course it works, I can hear you just fine."

"Well, I can't hear *you* just fine."

"You just heard what I said, didn't you?"

Finn smiled, her eyes taking in the room beneath the warm glow of the wall sconces and the bluish lights of the slot machines. It was an interesting combination, and she felt as if she were somehow underwater. "What?"

"You just heard what I said, didn't you?"

Finn cringed a bit at his raised voice through the pristine sound of her earbud. "Are you there, God? I in need of forgiveness."

"For fuck's sake."

Finn was pleased. "Hey, I know your mother, remember? If she finds out you're using that kind of language, she will *so* kick your ass."

"Quit fucking around, Finn, please. Vakken is here. Security just saw him in the Salle Médecin. He's dropping a ton of cash at the wheel."

Finn shrugged away from the arch and entered the Salle Renaissance, the sound of the slots ring through the sea of light with a bit more aggression as she neared. She reined in her focus. "Just another bread truck left in his wake." Finn was unimpressed. "This guy totally mystifies me, and what sort of a name is Viking, anyway?"

"*Vakken.*" Malik sighed through her earpiece. "You're doing that on purpose."

Finn chuckled as she turned through the crowd. "You're so easy, Malik, it's almost no fun. Whatever his name is, it's going to be a nice payday, and I haven't even broken into a sweat."

"Security just cleared you for the private rooms, if we need entrance. I'm switching over to their channel."

"Thank you. Where is he, please?"

"The table near the bar, closest to the outside doors. Come in from the Salle Touzet Sud."

"Am I going to get lost again?"

Malik's affectionate laughter filled her head. "Probably."

"Ask…what's his name again, the insanely beautiful guy with the nice eyes?"

"Luc Angelos."

Finn maneuvered around a group of patrons as they toasted with champagne. "Great name. Ask Luc where we can get some authentic Italian pizza, preferably something that will put me into a coma."

"Are you actually asking about food?"

"I didn't eat lunch, okay?"

Finn eyed the hand that touched her elbow.

"If you wish a good pizza that will put you into a coma, only my wife's mother can make that," Luc Angelos said with a grin. His black tuxedo was impeccable and so was his smile. "She is from Sicily."

"Good Lord." Finn was pained at the thought. "With the sweet peppers?"

Luc Angelos chuckled as he guided her smoothly beneath an archway and into a common area. "Yes…Go through the west door just there, and you will find the Salle Touzet Nord, another common area, if you will, and this will lead to the Salle Touzet Sud. Turn to your left, and at the opposite end, you will find the Salle Médecin."

"I wasn't out of line, calling you insanely beautiful, was I?" Finn asked, feeling a bit like an ass. "I didn't know you could hear us, so, you know, you weren't supposed to hear that."

"I told you they could hear us." Finn could hear Malik's happy smile.

"I don't really listen to him."

Luc laughed, a slight blush beneath his perfectly trimmed five o'clock shadow. He was only an inch or two taller than her own height of five-ten, and his brilliant blue eyes were filled with warmth. "I am far from offended, and if I may say, I find you to be the same. I am wishing I were not Luc." Finn's brow went up in surprise as he took her right hand in a practiced move and leaned forward. "I am wishing I were my cousin Esme, perhaps, yes?"

"Esme Angelos?"

Luc placed a light kiss upon the back of her hand. "*Oui*, yes, she would wish to meet you very much, this is my thinking."

"And I am thinking I need to come to France more often."

"I think you do."

"Oh, man, I don't believe you," Malik moaned. "Are you flirting by *proxy*?"

Finn laughed, and Luc winked as he let go of her hand.

"Let's all just take a breath," Finn said, and followed his directions. "Even if this guy ends up stabbing me in the neck with a cocktail fork, he's going back to Paris tonight, *and* I'm getting my pizza…and Luc is giving me his cousin's number, maybe, possibly. I don't know, I feel pretty confident in this suit."

"Your shoulders look really good in that, it's true."

"Thank you, Malik."

"There's a space at the bar, on the near side as you enter. You'll have a good view."

"The Salle Médecin has the veranda, correct? Can he jump?"

"The veranda's covered. If he jumps? He won't get far."

"That's what you say *now*, Malik, but what's your excuse after I end up running across all twelve of their manicured courtyards and then ruin my suit because I was forced to tackle him into a garbage pile? That would only be fun if he turns out to be Liam Neeson. The veranda has B movie action sequence written all over it."

Malik laughed. "It's covered."

"Thank you."

"And if I may say"—Luc's deep voice echoed within her earbud—"there are no garbage piles at the Casino de Monte-Carlo."

Finn almost laughed. "I'm just giving him a hard time. He likes it."

"I'm still here, you know," Malik replied.

The common space was exquisite, plush blue chairs with television available and waiters that moved through the area. Champagne was flowing and the smell of something delicious had found its way from the restaurant at the heart of the casino. Finn's stomach tightened and she sighed as she walked through a cloud of perfume. It smelled expensive and heavy, though despite that, or perhaps because of it, it was strangely appealing.

The Salle Touzet Nord was filled with people as Finn stepped beneath yet another massive archway, and the light was rich and golden. She wandered to her left as she surveyed the art, the huge and heavy frames rolled with plump gold scallops. The renaissance women portrayed were caught within peculiar, uncommon poses that only renaissance women had ever held, though she thought they did it rather well. The curtains in the room were an arcane shade of red and tasseled on the ends, opulent beside the healthy green of the strategically placed plants.

There were five gaming tables and Finn considered the patrons, curious and filled with a great amount of interest. She saw Texas Hold'em and blackjack, and if she remembered her James Bond correctly, baccarat. She had never been sure how that one worked, but she understood that you could make a boatload of money in a very short time, or lose it, as well.

The sound of a singular laugh was soft, but loud enough to reach her from across the room, and her eyes were drawn to its source. It was startling and filled with warmth, and not one bit out of place amidst the luxury of the casino.

Finn's gaze tumbled along the fall of blond hair as the woman looked down, the light caught within her long, loose curls.

Finn was surprised, though she wasn't sure why, and her attention was fierce as her eyes drifted. Her skin appeared to be soft, and the curve of her neck was like an invitation written upon silk. Finn's concentration was lost then, pulled through the black crepe of her dress.

The dealer spoke and the blond woman reacted, her interest sharp and her expression alive with anticipation as the cards were pulled from the shoe.

Finn's mind spun a bit as she studied the lines of her face, swayed by the high cheekbones and full red lips. Her movements were precise and certain, and the confidence she displayed was unquestioned by those around her.

Finn felt a bit weak in the knees, and it was a lovely feeling.

A redheaded woman in a flowing green dress stepped close and set her hand upon the blond woman's bare right shoulder, her long fingers and pink nails possessive in their touch. The woman turned, and the redhead leaned down and whispered in her ear. She stood as if they were lovers, and when she touched those lovely blond curls, it was with a familiar ease. It was a gesture that caused a pang of anxiety, and Finn had to check herself before she stepped forward.

A wave of emotion rolled through Finn's chest, and the unexpected reaction caused her to tighten her shoulders. There was a clear violation in progress, but the offense was given only within Finn's mind, and not reality. And though she knew it she could do nothing to stop the feeling.

"He's moving. He's moving to the veranda."

Finn tried to place the face, the generous mouth and the beautiful line of her jaw. She felt certain that she'd seen her before, though in the sudden, hard beat of her heart, Finn knew that it couldn't be true. "I'd remember you," Finn whispered, and a shiver skimmed along her spine.

"Finn?"

Finn blinked and her focus shifted to her left, into the distance.

"He's moving to the veranda. Where the hell are you?"

Finn moved with a purpose, but she didn't rush. "Does he have a drink?"

"Yes."

"He's taking a breather, trying to decide how much he has left to lose. I'm almost there."

The Salle Médecin was a much larger room, with at least a dozen roulette tables. The crowd was good, and the noise level was higher as she moved through yet another archway. She spotted the door she wanted and glanced to her right. Luc Angelos was at the other end of the room, and he waited until she saw him before he moved to one of the veranda doors farther down.

Finn took a cleansing breath and walked with confidence about the crowded table.

The handle of the door turned easily, and she saw Tobias Vakken near the high railing, his attention lowered to the expansive grounds as they flowed to the sea.

"Place your bets! No more bets, please!" the nearest croupier called out.

Finn stepped onto the veranda.

Chapter Five

San Francisco
Present day

Casey Marinos felt a smile pull at her lips as the tall butch stepped away from the bar.

She had known she was being watched but she hadn't returned the attention, biding her time for the right opportunity. She found the woman utterly gorgeous, though she supposed that some might not agree. The woman's features were strong and clean, and from the stark cut of her suit, Casey could see she had the lean, well-built body to back it up. There were a lot of women who would never find such a masculine energy appealing, but Casey was most definitely not one of them. She seemed familiar, actually, although Casey couldn't quite place her. *And I think I'd remember you.*

She stared beyond the window once more, though with considerable effort. *Another time, another place perhaps*, she mused, *and we might play.* She closed her eyes, and the storm within her head seemed to ease at just the thought of finding a respite within the strong arms of such a lover. The soft authority of the right lover could sway her like nothing else, which was why women like that were far too dangerous.

Casey turned back to the table in genuine surprise as the woman pulled out the empty chair across from her and sat down.

She favored Casey with a sweetly crooked grin and leaned back as she crossed her legs. The waiter arrived but a second later and set two wineglasses on the table. A second server placed the ice bucket beside her, which held a dark, heavy bottle.

"It's not what you ordered, I'm fairly certain, but I have it on good authority that it's just as good as anything you might find here."

Casey couldn't help but smile the confident statement, and her mind filled with curiosity as she st lied the woman's face close up. Healthy, slightly tanned skin with st ng features and classic lines. Her hair was an amazing tousled mess f black strands, and her amber-colored eyes were filled with warm . Casey wasn't sure if she'd ever seen such a color before in a person eyes, but then she thought, *I must have*. They held challenge in their epths, but it was their heat that Casey found compelling. So much , that for a moment, it threw her completely off her game.

The waiter pulled the bottle fro the ice and poured them each a glass with an expert hand.

The woman leaned forward a took up her glass as the waiter returned the bottle to the bucket, an then promptly disappeared.

She held her glass out. "My na e is Finn Starkweather."

Casey laughed, delighted at th sheer audacity of the unexpected scene. She took hold of her g ss, and they clinked together. "Starkweather? Doesn't that have s ething to do with the strength of a wolf?"

"I'm not sure, it's all Irish to m " Finn replied. "All I know is my grandmother had a feud with Thon s Angus Boyle across the fence. They used to curse in Gaelic and th w small red potatoes that would dent your skull if you weren't fast e ugh."

Casey took a drink, liking the rd, quick feel of her pulse. "*Póg mo thóin?*"

Finn laughed, a flush of heat vi le along her neck. "Kiss me arse, yes."

"Good God!" Casey spoke i shock and eyed her glass with pleasure. "What is this?"

Satisfaction shone from Finn' mber eyes. "Tell me your name first."

Casey wanted to laugh again, b t she held her unexpected joy just out of reach.

"Too bold?" Finn asked.

"I'd say a more subtle appro h has probably left the station without you."

"Yes, but if I'd waited for you, d still be standing all alone."

"Do you think so?" Casey let t a small breath as another grin slid across Finn's luxurious mouth. t was one of the loveliest things Casey had encountered in a very lo time.

"I do. Tell me your name."

Samantha Drake, Casey thought but didn't say it. It was on the tip of her tongue, waiting and ready, but she couldn't do it. She liked Samantha. Samantha was always in charge and never at a loss, never in doubt. Samantha was always in control and would not relinquish her command over any given situation. *Control is an illusion. But that's not what you see, is it, Finn Starkweather.*

"Okay, how about this." Finn set her glass down and leaned forward a bit. "I buy you dinner and we finish the wine. We could go dancing then, if you'd like, or at least we could find some decent music. There's a place not too far from here, Biscuits an—"

"Blues." Casey smiled as she finished Finn's sentence. "And if I were to tell you that I'm waiting for my husband?"

Finn reflected on the question. "I'd say…"

Casey waited patiently and enjoyed the careful expression on Finn's face. "Yes?"

"No."

"No?"

"No. You're wonderfully gay. I could feel it from across the room."

"And you're never wrong?"

Finn smiled. "Frequently, I'm sorry to say, but not about this."

Casey sipped her wine and was distracted by its taste yet again. She glanced at the bottle but the label was turned away from her. The glass was old, and it sent part of her brain down a different path in search of a vintage.

"Are you ready to order?"

Finn heard the waiter well enough, but she did not look away from Casey. "We'll start with the Trumpet Mushrooms, and then we'll pick from the Spice Route menu, please."

"Very good, sir."

Both Finn and Casey smiled, and Casey looked down to keep from laughing. It fit, actually, but from the startled amusement in Finn's eyes, it had been unexpected.

"Perhaps I should venture a guess?"

"Perhaps you should." Casey's gaze came back up, rebellious.

"I'd say Veronica, but that would be too obvious."

"Perhaps for some, but not as many as you might think."

"And it looks so beautiful." Finn's eyes were bright. "I mean, the way you have it."

Casey was surprised by the subtle change in Finn's tone. Her confidence had slipped thoughtfully into something else entirely, and it was delightful.

"And besides"—Finn took a breath, and Casey could see her shift gears again—"hers was a sad fate that I don't see in your future."

"Perhaps you should just give me a name."

"Rachel?"

Casey frowned.

"You're right. I knew a Rachel once. It was unpleasant."

"First girlfriend?"

"No, that was Paula," Finn corrected her.

"What happened to Paula?"

"Too much of a top for my taste."

"Ah, yes, the old conflict-of-interest conundrum."

"I like what I like, and besides it all worked out in the end."

"Really?" Casey asked. "Don't keep me in suspense, please. What happened to Paula?"

Finn said nothing, but her eyes were alive with enjoyment.

"Top secret?"

"Highly classified. However, I can tell you it involved balls flying at her face."

Casey stuttered in the midst of taking another drink, swallowing awkwardly as she choked back a surprised laugh.

"Sorry...she worked the pro tennis circuit."

Casey cleared her throat and took up her napkin. "Of course."

"Football was always more my sport."

"American?"

Finn's eyes flashed happily. "Yes."

"What position?"

"Tight end."

Casey resisted the urge to lean forward, the unexpected desire to be closer welling up and sending a pleasant wave of heat through her chest.

"Tailback?" Finn offered instead.

"No, I'd say tight end is more than fitting."

"Juliette."

"Juliette?"

"Your name," Finn said through her grin. "Tell me your name."

"Is that what you want, Daddy?"

Finn let out a faint sound and reached for her glass.

Casey chuckled and watched her take a drink, enjoying the telltale blush of color along her neck. She knew somehow Finn was aware of the blush, and she disliked the reality of what it revealed so quickly. Casey leaned forward and reached for the bottle, in search of its label. Finn caught her by the wrist before she could get there, gentle for the most part, but firm enough to establish control. Their eyes met and Finn changed her grip, letting the tips of her fingers find the underside of Casey's wrist. Casey could feel her pulse beat hard beneath the touch.

"Don't be naughty."

Casey pulled her hand away slowly, her fingers sliding along Finn's until they parted.

"It's not such a high price to pay," Finn challenged her.

"It might be dangerous for you."

"Your name?"

"Perhaps."

"I was thinking the other might be more dangerous." Finn's tone was playful.

"The other?"

"What if you *do* have a husband? Here I am making my play, and the next thing I know, someone is punching me in the throat."

Casey laughed. "That doesn't seem like such a high price to pay."

Finn sat back again and graced her with a highly critical look. "Have you ever been punched in the throat?"

"Not that I can recall."

"It hurts."

"Well, you know what they say, the trick is not minding that it does."

"So you're saying that you're worth it?"

"Am I?"

"I wouldn't be sitting here if I didn't think so."

"You look as if you can take care of yourself."

"It's the boots, right? Too butch?"

"Butch, yes, but they work."

Finn leaned to the left a bit and considered her feet. "I just polished them, actually. When I was finished, it felt like a betrayal." She glanced across the table. "All those years to break them in properly and cultivate some character, and then I go and ruin it."

Finn, Casey thought, and a start of recognition followed upon the heels of the name. *Finn Starkweather.* "Who punched you in the throat?"

"Rachel's husband."

Casey felt a pleasing ache within her cheeks, uncertain of the last time she had smiled so much. "Was ␣ big?"

Finn's brow went up. "How bi␣ do you have to be?"

"A big, bad daddy such as you␣elf? I'd say pretty big."

Finn said nothing, but neither ␣d she look away. The sounds of the restaurant filled the atmosphere around them, though it did very little to invade upon their quiet ␣nnection. Several conversations could be heard—one that concern␣ local politics, and the other… Casey wasn't quite certain, though s␣neone was sure to be out of a job the next morning. The music was M␣hler, playing low, but it was still loud enough to be heard should any␣e care to listen.

"He wasn't that big," Finn res␣nded at last. "But he caught me by surprise."

"Didn't know, or didn't expect ␣m?" Casey asked gently, and she thought that perhaps Finn told the tr␣. Her eyes were too open and she had no reason to lie, even if they we␣ playing.

"I didn't know, actually." Finn␣s expression held regret, with a touch of embarrassment. "I was step␣ng out of the shower at the time."

"Ouch."

"Not one of my better moment␣" Finn agreed.

"Then my name won't be Rach␣l," Casey acquiesced.

Finn's eyes acknowledged th␣ tenderness beneath her words.

"Thank you."

"You're welcome, Finn."

"Tell me your name," Finn der␣nded with quiet authority.

Casey was about to say it, the l␣ers tumbling and sliding together upon her tongue and pressing eag␣rly toward her lips. *Casey*, she thought, willing them into life after ␣eping for so very long. *My name is Casey.* She was about to speak, bu␣ another name intruded before she had the chance. *Finnegan.*

"What?" Finn asked. "What is ␣?"

"Finn…is that your full name?␣"

"It's short for Finnegan, actual␣."

Casey considered the name in ␣lence, never looking away as the fingers of her right hand caressed th␣ stem of her wineglass. *Finnegan, bloody hell. You're Finnegan Star␣eather. Holy shit, I thought you were a man.*

"I didn't pick it."

"Don't worry, I like it."

"I wish I could return the favor."

"Is this your usual scene, Finn?" she asked softly. "Because if it is, it's very good. And you're very good at the game."

Finn seemed to seriously consider the question and before she looked down, Casey was absolutely certain that she saw a rush of vulnerability move through her expression. Finn sat very still, and then the index finger of her right hand pushed at a small knot in the weave of the tablecloth. Casey's heart beat faster as the energy Finn gave off began to change. Everything about her unexpected companion seemed to slow and take on a new weight, and it was as charming as it was surprising.

When Finn lifted her face, Casey caught her breath as smoothly as she could at the intensity which greeted her. Whatever she was going to say, Casey was fairly certain it would be the truth. *Or perhaps you're just hoping for that much.*

"I was wondering what your perfume would smell like." Finn's voice was quiet and filled with an unexpected intimacy. "Would it be subtle and simple, something with a touch of musk? Or perhaps it would smell like the frangipani flower, full and too heavy with its own importance." Finn's smile was barely there, but it reached her eyes well enough. "And how different would it be, against the skin of your neck, when compared to the bottle?"

Casey sat as still as she ever had, her fingers quiet upon her glass.

"I thought about these things before I came over here…but now I'm here, and I can just barely smell your perfume, and it's unlike any perfume I can recall. It's moved things about in my head, and my curiosity has changed completely."

Casey watched as a slight blush colored the skin of Finn's neck near the banded collar of her shirt. She could feel the heat within her own cheeks, and she couldn't stop it.

"I'm wondering other things instead." Finn took a breath, and for just an instant, Casey thought she would explain further. "And so everything has to be fair if it can be."

Casey considered the statement and then asked for clarification in a soft, careful voice. "What does that mean?"

"It means there's no scene, there's just you."

Finn's face was guileless and her eyes showered Casey with a sincerity so natural it affected her entire body. Casey's pulse thickened even further and moved south with surprising ease, the vibrant and unexpected emotion from across the table both mysterious and delicious as it wrapped around her. It was the ruth, and she could see it, though it made no sense whatsoever.

Finnegan Starkweather was former Interpol and a private investigator who had given up the game about five years ago, as far as Casey knew, at least. It was always good idea to keep an eye on the other team, and though they had never actually crossed paths, in the end they were hunter and prey. She'd been a bounty hunter for a few years, Casey remembered that much, but he had dropped off the grid and Casey had stopped paying attention. *Though I see I was remiss in that.*

Showing her hand like this and stepping into the open—it was completely illogical. And though h guard was now firmly in place and the game would change by morning, Casey could not deny that she wanted more. More of what exactly, she wasn't sure, but more was definitely on the menu. *More of you Finn Starkweather.*

"And you're wrong. I'm not very good at this at all." Finn pulled the wine from its resting place within a tumble of ice and set it on the table between them.

"I beg to differ," Casey said, feeling an odd twinge of panic. Finn was throwing in her hand, and Casey had never been so disappointed or curious in all her life. *Finally, a woman worthy of the game,* she acknowledged. *Don't give in so easy, Finnegan.*

"I don't lie very well." Finn reached into her suit and pulled out a business card. She placed it beside the bottle, a simple white card with nothing but a phone number printed in dark blue ink. "Not about this."

"This?"

"You."

Casey blinked in surprise at her answer, though she pushed it aside as quickly as she could. "You're not staying for dinner?"

Finn smiled. "No."

"Why ever not?"

"Because what I really want isn't on the menu," Finn answered smoothly. "And the wine was for you, Cassandra Marinos."

Casey buried the shock of her real name being spoken aloud, and then she was torn between relief and protest as Finn stood and walked away. It took her a moment to recover her focus, but once she did, Casey reached out and turned the wine bottle.

Her eyes went wide and her gaze shot up, landing hard on Finn's back as she disappeared beneath the arch which led to the bar. Casey didn't know whether to be more impressed by the vintage, a rare '47 Cheval Blanc, or by the fact that Finn knew her real name.

Casey stared at the wine label once more and tried to decide just how much danger she was actually in, and how much dancing might be required in order to get away clean with what she'd come for.

❖

Casey rolled her eyes in exasperation as she walked to the table and pulled out the chair with her free hand. She was in her bare feet, and she had exchanged her dress for baggy, faded Levi's and a soft white T-shirt. "Colin."

The voice on the other end became just a bit louder as the words came faster.

"Colin?"

There was silence on the other end of the phone as Casey sat down and studied the screen of her laptop. "Just send me what you have, okay? I don't need a Ken Burns documentary—I just need some facts." The lock on the hotel door clicked and Casey leaned forward. The light had turned green and the handle turned downward. "I have to go. I'll call you tomorrow."

Blackjack Vermillion pushed the door open with his hip and turned into the room, carrying a grocery bag in his left arm and a very large coffee in his right hand.

Casey smiled as she set her phone down. "Did you bring treats?"

"That would depend on your definition of the word *treats.*"

"Did you bring information?"

Blackjack walked into the hotel suite as the door closed behind him. He was dressed in his usual black jeans and button-down shirt, with his worn black leather jacket. His hair was long and combed back, resting against his shoulders. Over the past ten years it had begun to turn gray, and it was now a salt-and-pepper mixture that was just about picture perfect. His face was weathered and tan and he sported a scar on his chin that stood out as old and deep. He was a good-looking man, and Casey had been witness to his charm over the years. So had four different wives.

"Probably nothing you don't already know."

Casey reached out and he handed her the coffee.

"It's from the street cart."

Casey groaned. "For the love of God, Jack...you're killing me."

"The love of God had nothing to do with brewing that baby up, I assure you," Jack said with a smile. Casey took a tentative sip as he set the bag down and pulled out a six-pack and several sandwiches wrapped in paper. "She has a loft here in the city."

Casey was surprised. "Really?"

"Yeah, and you've got more than one tail."

Casey sat back slowly.

"And no, I didn't get made." Jack sat down and pulled a beer free. "I'll pick him up again in the morning. It looks like he's settled in for the evening. I gave Caleb a call, and he'll pick up Starkweather in—"

"No," Casey said quickly, and she knew her tone was too forceful. She made a face. "No, Jack, I'll take care of her."

Jack smiled as he twisted the top off his bottle and grabbed a sandwich. "She's a tall drink of water."

Casey's eyes narrowed just a tad.

"I'm just saying."

"Saying what?"

"Just…saying."

"You don't think I can handle her?"

Jack chuckled happily. "I'm just curious as to how much actual handling you'd end up doing, that's all. She looks like a bit of a badass, and I think she is."

"Really?" Casey knew that Finn looked the part, if only by the masculine energy she gave off, a distraction that often led to more than a few misperceptions. Jack knew his business, though, and he knew people even better.

Jack stopped what he was doing and met her eyes across the table. "Now's not really the time to be messing around, is it? I mean, the fact that she's here, and she knows who you are, those things right there…I don't know, it makes me think we should just quietly slip out of town and wait until next time. Let's find out who the hell she really is."

"No. No, Jack. I want this over with. And I know who she is."

They stared at each other for several more seconds, and then Jack unwrapped his sandwich, unconvinced.

"Her record is out there, at least most of it." Casey defended her decision, even though she knew it had been a strange and foolish thing to say. She didn't know Finnegan Starkweather at all. She wanted to, though, and she couldn't deny it. She could still feel the heat of Finn's grip against her wrist, and it felt good. The whole thing had felt good, and in that brief moment of contact, Casey had known she was in trouble. And that had felt good, as well. "She's an independent player now."

"Sure, but who's paying her at the moment?"

"I don't think she's working for anyone, actually."

"How could you possibly know that?" He took a bite of his sandwich.

"I don't know."

"That's not like you."

Casey took a drink of her awful coffee and let it heat up her insides as she contemplated his statement. "I know."

"Let Caleb take care of her."

"No." Casey denied him yet again. "I'd like to know what she wants."

Jack took another bite of sandwich, and then reached for his beer. "Why?"

"Because she bought me that bottle of wine."

Jack followed her gaze. "And why the hell not?" He turned back to her. "Seems like standard operating procedure to me."

"It's a '47 Cheval Blanc, one of the rarest bottles of wine there is. It had to have cost her, I don't know, fifteen grand, maybe twenty, depending on who she might know."

Jack stared at her.

"It's a message."

"It's *bait*."

"Maybe," Casey said quietly, studying the bottle from afar. "But I took it, Jack, and she walked away. I even asked her to stay, and she still walked."

"A manipulation," he countered before he took another bite. "A gamble."

Casey remembered the warmth of Finn's eyes, and her strong hand as it rested on the table. Finn had pushed at a stitch in the linen tablecloth with an uncertain touch, and it had signaled a change in her entire demeanor. She'd been trying to decide something, and she'd been unable to hide her emotions while doing it. She had changed her mind. "She gave me her name, Jack. I've got enough information now, as basic as it may be, that she might as well have worn a sign around her neck telling me to stay the hell away. She broke cover. She didn't have to do that."

"Maybe she thought it would get her somewhere."

Casey smiled. "If by somewhere, you mean closer to me than she already was, she didn't have to try so hard. If you must know, she was already there."

Jack waited a moment, and then he picked up his beer again. "I knew she was a badass."

"I'll take care of her, at least for the moment," Casey told him. "Colin is digging deeper. Give him what you have on the second tail as well. Both of you, find out whatever you can. Text if you find something I should know about, but otherwise, wait until I call."

"Do you want backup?"

"No, I'll be okay. I'll check in Colin's app."

"What are you gonna do?"

Casey took another sip of coffee. "I'm going to see if Finnegan Starkweather has anything interesting to say."

"And how do you plan on doing that?"

"By going shopping and getting my hair done."

"Are you getting those frosted tips again? Those were just simply divine."

Casey laughed. "Shut up."

CHAPTER SIX

Finn opened her eyes as she gasped for air, and the ragged sound against her throat filled her head like a scream. She lay perfectly still, and though her lungs were suddenly full and on fire, she needed more. The sheets clung to her skin and the sweat stung her eyes, but she didn't move, nor did she blink. The shadows within her bedroom were well known, but they held a coldness that was alien and it filled her with fear, like the frozen waters of an unfamiliar lake, ready to break apart with unexpected life if she offered them too much weight.

Breathe…

A flash of light, harsh and empty, washed across her vision and she reacted. She kicked free of the sheet, stumbled from the bed, and fell to the floor on her hands and knees.

The sound of the gunshot exploded inside her head and she tipped back onto her heels. Her bedcovers pulled within her fist and she staggered to her feet. The darkness closed in as she moved, and she threw her right arm up against its approach, certain of her destination. The bathroom light was like a hammer against the side of her head, but it dispelled the shadows rather neatly. That was all she knew, that the shadows were gone.

The cold porcelain of the sink was beneath her hands, and then her stomach rolled and her shoulders tightened. There wasn't much for her stomach to reject, but what there was, her body found offensive. Her muscles pulled as she threw up, the cough that followed coming from deep within her body. Her right hand trembled as she turned the water on.

She shivered as she stepped back from the sink, avoiding the mirror with a deliberate turn. She looked down the short hallway that led back into the bedroom.

The darkness she had left behind seemed to move, taking long, deep breaths as it waited for her r arn. She saw the glow from the clock on a far bookshelf, but her visi was blurred. She wiped the back of her left hand over her eyes and pu hed the hair from her forehead. Time.

She still couldn't read the clock The numbers hovered beyond the rise and fall of the air, oddly splinte and bleeding when she blinked, a taunt in slow motion. She would ave to brave the darkness if she wanted what it could tell her.

It didn't matter what time it wa It was just that time.

The floor was ice-cold against e soles of her feet but it felt good, and she took the few steps necessa to close the bathroom door. The heavy surface bolt was more seriou han most, and the thick brass rod slid past the edge of the door and tightly into the plating that was mounted on the frame.

Finn stepped back to the sink a cupped her hands together. The water was cool, and she spat the ur taste from her mouth several times before she cleaned the sink w a washcloth, shut off the water, and turned to the tub. She pushed th curtain back and spun the knobs.

Her T-shirt and boxers peeled way from her skin as if she had already been in the shower, and Fin moved in a stilted manner as she tossed them into the laundry basket.

The sound of the water was so hing, and as Finn turned back to the tub, her left hand slid along her s and over her stomach. The two scars to the left of her belly button re about two inches apart, and as each patch of rough tissue passed be ath the palm of her hand, she felt her stomach roll with nausea. The pa she felt throughout her abdomen was a ghost, but she recognized its f iliar presence as if it were an old acquaintance she had no interest in eing.

She stepped into the shower w the help of the tub and stood on shaky legs as she pulled the curtain ack around. The firm spray of hot water jolted her thoughts to the side nd pushed them into a no-man's- land between reality and memory. It vas not the worst place to be, and she knew it.

Paris
December 2009

Asher James took the cigarette from iis mouth and contemplated what he saw.

The lights along the Seine were golden, and the reflections they left upon the water moved with the current, the cresting wake of a westbound barge still pushing in waves against the built-up banks that contained them. It was late, even for the Left Bank, for though the Montparnasse was still home to artists and musicians, it was not so much the cauldron of freedom it had once been. People tended to work for a living these days and ply their loves with hope after earning their wages.

The woman was tall and beautiful, though her beauty was fierce and unique among those women he had thought beautiful in the past. Her hair was covered by a loose-fitting stocking hat at the moment, but when she had ordered drink after drink at the Café de la Rotonde, it had been a wonderfully wild landscape of rebellion. Her clothes were very American, her jeans dark and her boots buckled loosely. Her jacket was wool and warm, but the T-shirt beneath it showed her allegiance to a Boston baseball team.

She was not given to drink—Asher could see that after her third one, for her complexion had begun to pale and her strong personality had dimmed. The natural confidence she wore began to fade as her demons awoke, and she did not seem so at home within her skin.

It wasn't until she had left the bar and he had followed that he began to suspect what she might finally be about. He'd been following her for almost a week in order to take her measure, and what he'd discovered was when left to her own devices, she would become a ghost.

She had indulged in drink, but it was not her vice of choice. She had spent three of her nights at the Atelier Charonne, where the jazz leaned toward the manouche and devotees of Django Reinhardt. She had mingled with an older, more dangerous crowd and smoked from several water pipes, hashish most likely—her reaction had not been overly dramatic. She had taken absinthe as well, though whether the thujone had affected her, Asher couldn't tell. She had gone home with several different women, and then escaped into the early morning like a thief.

She walked along the edge of her world with no apparent concern for whether she fell, or not, into the emptiness that waited.

She'd been sitting on the bench for well over an hour and she had barely moved, not even to stamp her feet or to warm her hands with a breath. While it was not what she might be used to in America, a Paris winter could be gloomy and wet and just plain annoying.

When she finally stirred, Ash · cursed beneath his breath and pushed away from the unlit street l np he leaned against. He hurried across the wide walkway as he to ed his smoke to the ground, no longer able to see her hands as he ne ed. He coughed as he approached the bench, and though her shoulders erked in surprise, she did not turn around.

Asher stepped about the far nd of the bench, and without invitation, sat down several feet fro her. He spoke to her in French, but there was no reaction.

He glanced at her amiably and hen toward the river, her weapon held between her knees with some all attempt at discretion. A burst of adrenaline moved through his sy em and he narrowed his eyes at the buildings across the way. He wa ed a hand at them as if in disgust and spoke again.

From the corner of his eye, he watched as she pulled her hands back and put them in the pockets of er coat, the handgun disappearing into the black wool. Asher looked a her openly for the first time. "Do you speak English?"

She wiped quickly at her face b fore she found the bench between them. "Yes, I'm sorry." Her gaze lif d, but she had turned back to the river.

"Do not apologize," he said in gentle voice. He reached into his pocket and pulled out his tobacco a l papers. "All of this attitude—if you don't speak French, you are a p ce of shit."

She let out a breath of laughter nd glanced at him.

"I'm telling you, I am French m self, and they look at *me* like I am a piece of shit. I was born in Lyon, r Christ's sake."

He caught the surprise in her xpression, her eyes still swollen with tears. She pulled her jacket shu as her shoulders came in.

"But then, maybe they know so ething that I do not."

She smiled a very small smile.

"I said before that I am sick of is cold and rain…and they have not even turned on the festival lights t is very beautiful if the lights are on, even if it is cold."

"It's beautiful anyway."

"Yes, you are right. It is the Se e. You can't really go wrong."

Asher filled the paper and clos his tobacco pouch with a pull of his teeth before he let it drop into his ap. He gave the paper a practiced shake and rolled his smoke with sk l. With a touch of his tongue he sealed it. "Do you smoke? It is a ba habit, but it calms my nerves."

"Thank you," she said, and took it.

He leaned over as he pulled the gold Zippo lighter from his jacket pocket. "My name is James. I do not bother you, do I?"

She met his gaze for just an instant as she sought out the flame. Her words were almost lost within the smoke she exhaled. "No, it's okay."

Asher retrieved his tobacco pouch from where he had dropped it and began to roll a second smoke. "Do you know this place, where we are sitting?"

She pulled at her smoke but did not look up from the water.

"This place, in the 1930s, it was the best place to be. Writers and painters, and beautiful women looking to be someone's muse, they were everywhere here. Picasso and Chagall, and even your Hemingway, they all lived here."

For the first time, he caught her smile.

"That would have been a good time to sit on this bench, eh?" He put his new smoke between his lips and lit it.

"Yes."

"My daughter…" Asher let out a sniff of affection. "My God, when we were in Paris, she would be here at all hours. She was not so much loving trouble, but she liked the romance of it. *I stood where Modigliani stood*, she would say, and then laugh. *Your curfew is foolish.*"

Her eyes held his for the first time. "She was right."

Asher laughed, but he felt a wave of sorrow move through his chest, for her eyes couldn't hide the pain she was feeling. They were eyes he had seen before, and it was like a punch in the stomach. "I know," he agreed. "But she would not call, and she would just disappear into the Paris night at sixteen years old. My God, it gave me gray hair, you see?"

She smiled, still looking at him. "That's our job."

Asher willed all his love for Casey into his expression. "Yes, just so. I did not scold her. I would have done the same."

"What's her name?"

Asher debated for a few moments how he might answer the question. He had pondered it before, and he had never come up with a satisfactory solution. One's true identity as a thief was more precious than any work of art. Such information was worth more than its weight in gold, and Casey was even more cautious than most. She was an artist herself, and he had no wish to ruin the fine canvas of anonymity she had created with such care. He did not forget for a second, however, how precarious the current moment was. ⟨H⟩e could feel the veil pulled back, within the fog and darkness, and it ⟨deserved⟩ served respect.

"I have called her Domino sin⟨ce⟩ she was a girl." He smiled and gestured with his hand. The ash fro⟨m⟩ his smoke fluttered to the bench between them. "She has that power⟨.⟩ tip over the rest, you know?" He chuckled, certain of his words. "A l⟨itt⟩le turn of her head?" He made a soft clicking sound with his tongue⟨.⟩ "They all fall. I call it Domino's gravity."

Her tears returned. "My name⟨ is⟩ Finn."

"It is good to meet you, Finn⟨,"⟩ Asher said with a genuine smile and then glanced away. He did not ⟨w⟩ish her to be embarrassed. "Will you join me for a coffee, Finn? I an⟨ t⟩oo old for this wet and cold, and I have had a strange day. I am lone⟨ly⟩ for my family." He looked back at her. "Just to talk, I promise you. ⟨S⟩ometimes, it is good to talk with a stranger, and if you would permit ⟨m⟩e, I have a story I think you will like."

Finn stared at him, and he wait⟨ed⟩ for her to focus. "A story?"

"Yes, my new friend. I think y⟨ou⟩ will find it interesting."

"And why is that?"

"Because it starts in Nuenen, i⟨n⟩ the Netherlands. It starts with the sketch of a church and a spire and a ⟨y⟩oung Vincent van Gogh, who had not yet discovered the joys of a colo⟨rf⟩ul palette."

He watched as she fought despe⟨ra⟩tely to clear her mind of whatever influence she was currently under. ⟨He⟩ smiled, satisfied he had her full attention, or at least, as much as she ⟨w⟩as able to give him. "And it ends with a man named Ketrin Arshavin."

CHAPTER SEVEN

San Francisco
Present day

Finn sat down at the table, glanced at her phone, and felt like a fool.
The foot traffic on the other side of the window was steady, but it was fairly tame for a Wednesday. The sun was bright and the sounds within the small restaurant were pleasant—the rise and fall of conversations and the noise of dishes and silverware from the kitchen were familiar and safe. The smell of apples and bacon hung in the air, leftover from the breakfast crowd.

Her attention had been elsewhere for just an instant, or so she had thought. Apparently, it had been long enough for Casey to slip away and disappear rather easily.

Casey had been efficient with her time since she had left the hotel, though she had browsed at several shops along the way. Finn had laughed and watched with pleasure as she had walked slowly through a custom jewelry store and chatted amiably with the salespeople. She had tried on a bracelet, as well as what appeared to be a sapphire ring. She had purchased nothing, though, nor had she liberated anything expensive that yearned to be free.

When Casey had finally emerged, she had smiled as she put on her aviator sunglasses, and though Finn had been absolutely certain she was out of sight, she could've sworn Casey looked right at her.

Cassandra Marinos knew she was being followed, and she did nothing to deter it. In fact, she seemed to be having a wonderful time.

Finn was tired and slightly off her game, but from the moment she had watched Casey leave the Palace Hotel, as bold as a life well-lived and looking delicious in just a⋯ ⋯out every way, Finn's nerves had eased. The painful heat that had sw⋯ ⋯med in the tense muscles of her back and shoulders was gone, repla⋯ ⋯d by minor twinges that were far less distracting. She had no real hea⋯ ⋯iche to speak of, and she actually felt hungry, which was new but not ⋯nwelcome. Perhaps she had slept better than she thought, though that ⋯ould be something altogether rich and strange, so she had her doubts. ⋯ie had counted on her adrenaline to keep her sharp, but it appeared n⋯ ⋯v, sitting alone in a strange diner with her target nowhere in sight, th⋯ ⋯this had been a rather poor plan of action.

Finn dialed Malik and waited ⋯hrough the third ring for him to answer.

"Did you lose her?"

Finn smiled and glanced across ⋯ie main room of the old-fashioned restaurant. "I'll have you know I'n⋯ ⋯better at this than you are, and I don't appreciate your apparent gle⋯ ⋯it the possibility that I might've misjudged my current abilities."

Malik's laughter was decidedl⋯ pleased on the other end of the phone. "You just used about thirty⋯ ⋯vords when you should've used three. You fucked up. You did, just a⋯ ⋯mit it."

"I did nothing of the sort."

"If it makes you feel any better⋯ ⋯ou're the first one to lose her. It's ⋯ght?"

Finn narrowed her eyes and g⋯ ⋯bbed a menu. "We really should ⋯ have a longer conversation abou⋯ ⋯your theory, using our critical ⋯ thinking skills, but I see your poin⋯ ⋯Do you have to be a dick about this?"

"But I'm really good at it, and⋯ ⋯arely get the chance." There was ⋯ laughter in his voice. "Where are yc⋯ ⋯?"

Finn was amused by his resp⋯ ⋯se, despite that she'd blown the ⋯ simplest tail she'd had in years. All ⋯inn had to do was spend the day ⋯ with her, albeit from a distance. Her ⋯itigue was a terribly poor excuse. "I'm in a nice little diner just off Ge⋯ ⋯y, where I fully intend to enjoy a ⋯ bacon sandwich, I might add."

Malik let out a startled soun⋯ ⋯that turned into an odd giggle. "That's so wrong."

"Doesn't she have an appointn⋯ ⋯nt later today?"

"Yes, actually, I do."

Finn was startled by Casey's vc⋯ ⋯e as Casey answered her question before Malik had the chance.

"Two o'clock, at David's Salon," Casey provided in a helpful manner.

"I have to go," Finn said into the phone. "Something just fell into my lap."

"Was it your greasy bacon sandwich?" Malik demanded. "Asshole."

"Perhaps we should just have an early lunch, and you can escort me on my errands," Casey suggested as she took off her sunglasses and set them on the table. She pulled out a chair, sat down, and set her bag at her feet.

Finn almost sighed, and though she didn't, she wondered if the repressed urge to do so might lead to an aneurysm at some point later in the day.

Casey was beautiful at a distance, but up close, Finn really didn't have the words to describe what Casey did to her. Her hair was a lovely dark blond about her face, and it fell in soft curls onto her shoulders. It was darker than it had been at the beginning of summer, and Finn liked it. Her clothes were sharp, a Stella McCartney blouse of black silk with embroidered lilies on it worn beneath a cropped forest-green biker jacket that set off the stitching. It lent an air of sophistication to the faded 501s and polished Docs she wore. She sported very little makeup, and Finn liked that as well. She liked everything.

"Am I breaching some sort of predator-prey etiquette?" Casey's attention was pulled to her right as the waitress approached. "I'll take a raspberry lemon ice, and one for my..." Casey turned smoothly and considered Finn, her expression filled with interest. "What is it I should call you?"

"Whatever you would like," Finn answered with a grin.

Casey smiled and her cool demeanor wavered beneath the flash of humor that warmed her eyes. "Make that two, if you would, please. We'll take a few moments and then we'll order," she told the waitress, who glanced at Finn and smiled as she walked away.

"Finnegan Starkweather." Casey set her elbows on the table and laced her fingers together. "You left without finishing your wine."

"The wine was for you."

"But you were clearly invited to stay."

"Staying wasn't in my best interest."

Casey's gaze was extremely focused. "And why is that?"

Finn slipped her phone into the inner pocket of her jacket. "Because you knew who I was, Casey Marinos."

"But you told me who you were," Casey disagreed easily. "Now, what would be the point of doing that if you didn't want something as a result of it?"

Finn had nothing much to say to that, other than the truth. "I didn't want to lie—that was the point. I didn't know I couldn't do that before I sat down, and once I did *that*, I couldn't do the other."

Casey narrowed her eyes slightly. "Do which?"

"Lie to you."

"Why couldn't you lie to me?"

"Would you prefer I had?"

"Not really, no."

"Are you used to people lying to you?"

Casey appeared to give the question serious consideration. "Yes. Aren't you?"

"That depends on where I am."

"Where do people usually lie to you?"

"Mostly to my face."

Casey chuckled and pulled her chair closer to the table. The waitress approached and set their drinks down. "Thank you," Casey said and picked up her straw. She pulled the wrapper off, dropped the straw into her drink, and stirred the ice. "You must be in a curious business, Finnegan Starkweather. I can't even imagine."

"You should give it a try. I'm betting your imagination is more creative than mine is, and mine's fairly wicked, as those things go."

Several heartbeats passed between them and then Casey looked up from her glass.

Finn held her gaze and Casey could not have been more thrilled at the tease she saw within those camel-colored eyes. She was about to respond, but she looked to her right instead. "Are you waiting for us to order?"

The waitress dragged her attention away from Finn. "What?"

"Would you like us to order?"

The young woman didn't blink and then she seemed to register the words. Her cheeks turned red as she glanced at Finn yet again. "Sure, what would she like?"

"I'm not sure yet, but I intend to find out," Casey responded as she eyed Finn. "What would you like?"

Finn's smooth, sexy smile was a slow burn of invitation that Casey felt all the way to the bottom of her feet and back again. She'd half expected something of the sort with the opening she'd given her, but she hadn't expected it to rip through her defenses with quite so much ease and good-natured gusto. She held Finn's eyes for as long as she dared. "We'll take two cheeseburgers, both with a side of fries, please."

"Right...right away."

Casey watched her walk away and then returned to Finn, assessing her options. In keeping with the spirit of their encounters thus far, she decided to stick to the straight and narrow.

"Finnegan Starkweather, formerly of Interpol, though only for five years. You achieved the rank of detective superintendent in the organized crime unit after just three, followed by almost two years of something mysterious, without any records I could access. I'm assuming it was something black-ops-y, with tactical hoodies and knee pads. Either that, or you were stuck in a budget meeting."

Finn's charming giggle of laughter caused a slight stutter in Casey's thoughts before she found the one she wanted. "When your request for a transfer into the division that handles antiquities and stolen art popped onto the radar, and you were subsequently turned down, you resigned and dropped out of sight. Within that same year, however, you were found collecting bounties on criminals the official system couldn't quite seem to catch on its own."

Finn reached for her drink. "When you put it like that, I sound like I'm a really poor sport. And vaguely creepy, in a pouty, Jason Bourne sort of way."

Casey laughed into her straw and her raspberry lemon ice reacted. She set her glass down and reached for her napkin as gracefully as she could.

"No one likes to be the pissy antihero of their own story."

Casey laughed into her napkin, and there was a heated spark within Finn's eyes that Casey remembered quite well from the night before. She cleared her throat, wiped at the last drop of cold drink that tickled her cheek, and met Finn's gaze head-on. "My question is, what is it that you want from me, Finnegan Starkweather? I'm not a criminal. And if you do really want something from me, why alert me to that possibility? Why not just play me for it?"

"Once I sat down, it was pretty much over. Not very smooth, I suppose," Finn admitted, clearly amused. "But I was able to get some sleep."

"I wasn't."

Finn lifted an eyebrow.

"Everyone has a plan until they get hit, is that it?"

"Maybe," Finn answered and s red at the table. She tried to hide her grin, but it was a poor effort.

Casey sat back, crossed her leg and reassessed. Finn was rougher around the edges than she had been at the Campton, but Casey liked it. She liked it a lot. Her button-down was a crisp white and her charcoal wool jacket was a fine cut. Steve Madden, if she didn't miss her guess. Not overly expensive, but some thought clearly went into the purchase. Her jeans fit well and in all the right places, the faded, low-cut Diesel denims worn and soft looking. Her hair was a brilliant mess and no matter how Casey looked at it, she wanted to run her fingers through it.

"Do you think I've committed a crime?" Casey asked. "I'd be curious to know what that is, if you think I have."

"No, not that I know of."

"Is there a bounty on my head'

"Not that I know of."

"Then what do you know, Finnegan Starkweather?"

"If I answer that question," Finn replied, "we'll end up going our separate ways, and if we do that…"

Casey held her breath just a b as she waited for Finn to finish, but she didn't.

Casey had told the truth—she had barely slept at all. After Jack had left and she had gone to bed, she had replayed their encounter over and over again, and she had imagined what might have happened if Finn hadn't walked away. It had been wonderful to fantasize about a woman who was bold and appeared to embody all the things that aroused her so completely about a strong butch woman. It was a dangerous game her mind had played, but at the time she seen no harm in it. She wasn't so sure of that at the moment.

"If we do that?" she asked soft .

"It won't be what I want."

"And what is that?"

"Well, now that we're here, I' ike to spend the day with you. It was a good suggestion, and I'm glad you spoke up."

"Are you going to be my escor "

Finn's expression was one (pure magic, and her insanely charming smile promised all sorts things Casey assumed couldn't possibly be good for her, though o y in the best possible way. *Holy shit.*

"I could do that, yeah," Finn agreed.

"You might get bored."

"Do you think I will?"

"Maybe."

"Here's your burger."

Finn turned her attention to the waitress and reached out for the plate. "Thank you."

"You're welcome, I'm, I mean, my name is Brett."

Finn waited patiently for her to let go of the plate. "Brett, like the Lady Brett Ashley?"

Casey noted the easy grin and the honest interest on Finn's face, and it threw her a bit. She wasn't actually flirting, she was just...*being totally sweet, for the love of God. Asher would've loved this one. I'm being tracked by a Boy Scout.*

"I don't know who that is," Brett responded, and a look of embarrassment flitted through her eyes. "I mean, I don't—"

"It's from a book." Finn interrupted with care, finding the pause. "Don't worry, though, it wasn't very good. Not many people finished it, at least that's my guess. Lady Brett had short hair like yours and she knew what she wanted. She was the best part about it."

"Oh, cool, thanks. I just got it cut."

"I like it," Finn replied and gently pulled her plate free.

Brett let out an embarrassed laugh, her left arm swinging out toward Casey. Her eyes did not leave Finn. "Here's yours."

Casey had an extremely hard time not laughing aloud as she took her plate. "Thank you, I think..." She glanced at her food as she set it down. *An extremely hot and charming Boy Scout, I get it, thank you, Miss Brett. You can go away now.*

"Yeah, okay. If you need anything else, just, you know, ask for Brett."

"I will," Finn said as Brett lingered just a moment before she walked away.

Casey watched her leave, somewhat amused by her own unexpected irritation.

"That was fast."

"I'm pretty sure she hijacked the seniors at table three so the anxiety of the wait wouldn't burden you," Casey cracked as Finn organized her plate. She moved the pickle to the edge and made a space beside her fries.

When Finn reached for the ketchup, her hand stopped halfway. "Pardon?"

"Nothing." Casey's chest filled with a wicked heat, and she willed it to stay exactly where it was. "So you're not a Hemingway fan?"

Finn's eyes flashed happily, and Casey felt for a brief second as young and out of sorts as their waitress appeared to be. "Not usually," Finn answered and then chuckled as she squirted ketchup beside her fries. "I fall on the side of the adjective, for the most part, and I like my clauses separated by a nice, fat comma. It keeps me from running out of breath."

Casey laughed within her throat and took up a clean napkin. "Was that really what you were thinking, though?"

"No," Casey admitted. "I was thinking that this day is turning out far different than I imagined it would."

"Well, Cassandra Marinos," Finn said and lifted her burger, "take heart. If at any time I begin to induce a feeling of ennui or annoyance, taking a quick step to the left while I'm looking elsewhere should do the trick." She took a bite and then spoke through the side of her mouth. "Apparently, I'm not very good at my job."

Casey laughed yet one more time, uncertain of what would happen next and loving it. Finnegan Starkweather was altogether pleasing, and in every sense of the word. Casey had the impression that Finn's quick tongue and unexpectedly kind demeanor hid a suitcase full of secrets, and though that wasn't ideal, it satisfied. She liked the danger of a situation, just as she always did. The woman sitting across from her might very well be instrumental in stealing away the prize she'd spent years waiting for, and that was sauce for the goose.

Casey wanted more, though, just as she had the night before. She liked their outrageously easy banter and the way her pulse quickened with heat. Both things were extremely rare for her, and she wanted them to last for as long as she could reasonably indulge her pleasure. It was all strangely familiar in the loveliest of ways.

"At least you're polite," Casey quipped.

Finn tried not to laugh while she chewed, and she turned her face to the side until she had swallowed. Her eyes were bright. "I'm not all that polite."

Casey picked up two long fries, reached across the table, and pulled them through Finn's pool of ketchup. The look she received for her trespassing caused her heart to hold hands with her stomach and sprint down the street. "You also like doing things the hard way." Casey brought the fries back as she leaned over her plate. "Are you good with hard things, Finnegan?"

Finn's expression was amused and filled with life. "I know you just lobbed that one out there, but I'm not gonna swing."

Casey laughed happily. "Do you want your ketchup back?"

"No, but you're buying me pie now."

CHAPTER EIGHT

Near Bergerac, the Dordogne, France
May 2016

"It's a good location," Luc Angelo said over his shoulder as he led Finn up the stairs.

The house was old, but the upkeep had been consistent, and Finn noted that the railing along the stair was new and smooth as she ran her hand along it. There were plenty of windows, and the dark green shutters were freshly painted. They hung upon new hinges, and they were open to the late morning sun. It bathed the landing at the top of the stairs with a clean light, and Finn stepped to the window as Luc pointed into the distance.

The house smelled of magnolia blossoms, and though it was a sweet smell, it did not overpower the scent of the chestnut trees and pines that surrounded the smooth stone and oak farmhouse.

"The room above us has a clear line of sight. Any cars arriving, the drive comes to the back of the house. The land in back—there is a heated pool and a studio. She has access to the river and a dock with a boat. A nice boat, too."

"Are you sure it's her?"

"Yes," Luc answered. "All your information, it checks out. I did not ask in town, for it is not so big a place for such inquiries, but the taxes she has paid, they lead here. It's a small, ah, *empreinte*?"

"Footprint."

"Yes, footprint. It is a small footprint that she has left on the world. Very, very clean." He stared down the hill. "I do not know what she is hiding, but she has many names, and very few of them will connect her to the woman who lives there, though they are one and the same."

Finn gauged the distance, and it was not so great a span, but it would be enough to mask the surveillance she would need to set up. "I'd like to keep her out of the system, okay?"

Luc nodded. "Of course. Sometimes, a woman hides for a very good reason, and I respect this right. There is just me, and my old partner, who found the tax records. I trust him."

"Then so do I."

Luc held out his hand. "It is good to see you, my friend."

Finn smiled and shook his hand. "And you. How is Manette?"

"She is wonderful. She sends regards, and an invitation for as many dinners as you may stomach." Luc still held her hand. "You will be missed if you do not come to us often. Our home is your home, for as long as you are here. The train ride is not so long at all, you see?"

Finn let go of his hand. "Yes."

"She will not invite Esme."

Finn laughed. "Oh my God, Esme. She broke my heart."

Luc had the good manners to blush, and Finn touched his arm in friendship. Her heart hadn't really been broken, but Finn would've enjoyed a few more weeks of her company. "I'll have help in a month. I'll call ahead and warn Manette."

He was pleased. "Good, good, this makes me very happy."

"It makes me happy, as well. Thank you for your help, Luc, truly. This is the lead I've been waiting for, for a very long time."

"Good." He stepped back and gestured to the second set of stairs. "Go up and look around. I will bring in the supplies." He moved past her and descended the stairs they had just climbed. "You will have more than enough for many weeks, if you will need," he called back. "And the garden will be full with the summer weeks. There is also a grocery in town that will deliver. There are many rich people here."

Finn took the second set of stairs two at a time.

There were two smaller rooms beneath the peak of the roof, and she stepped to the one on her left. She had to duck beneath the door frame, but once inside she could stand tall. It was a clean bedroom with a good-sized bed and windows upon each end of the house, and the temperature was cool and comfortable.

The window to her left was the focal point, and Luc had set up and prepared for her needs with expertise and forethought. There were the cameras she had requested, and several computers sat upon a long table. The dish outside would provide all the online access she could want, and there was a SkyMaster military scope on a tripod that would allow her an incredible field of vision. He had provided a long-range parabolic microphone as well, still packed in its box.

Finn shrugged out of her black leather coat and tossed it onto the end of the bed.

Luc had been right about the view. It offered the best line of sight that she could've hoped for, which included a long bank of windows at the back of her target's house, near the pool.

The owners of the farmhouse had rented to her for a year, and she had paid the price, though it had been dear. She could opt out within the first month, however. If the woman at the bottom of the hill was not Cassandra Marinos, there would be no reason to be there. *In which case, I'll have a quiet little vacation in the French countryside for a month while I figure out how I'm supposed to start all over again.*

She stepped to the SkyMaster, bent down, and peered through the scope.

The house in the distance was exquisite, as were the grounds, and the tan stone of the house stood out against the young green of spring. The region was filled with orchids, and where the landscaping stopped, the long grass and flowers would begin. The inner property was surrounded by Japanese maple trees, and though they were still young, Finn could only imagine the color they might provide.

The back of the house supported several additions, and the terrace beside the pool was amazing, with a fire pit and guest house but a short distance away by a path paved with flat stones. The shutters were a purplish red, and Finn wondered if they would match the maples when their leaves were in full bloom. It would make a beautiful pairing and Finn was impressed.

One of the glass doors along the terrace caught the light as it moved, and Finn nudged the scope to the right just a bit. Her target emerged from the house, and Finn held her breath as she adjusted the focus for a closer view.

The woman below had been running, her clothes formfitting and black. She had thrown a towel over her shoulders and her hair was in a ponytail. Her face was hidden as she spoke on the phone, but she moved with grace and strength as she walked along the edge of the pool.

Finn's heart beat within her chest like a drum, and she took a breath.

Cassandra Marinos turned around, holding the phone with one hand and freeing her hair with the other. She stepped around a chaise lounge and set the phone on a small table as her hair slid down and covered her familiar face.

Finn stood up straight, stepped back, and stared down the hill without the advantage of the scope. Her steps were small as she moved away from the window, and when the backs of her legs touched the bed, she sat down.

Finn could picture her at the baccarat table in Monte Carlo, and she could still see the fall of her hair as she had smiled and looked down at her cards. The black crepe of her dress was still vivid against the bare skin of her left shoulder, as dark as her eyes when she had lifted her face.

Finn had never forgotten her or the feelings that had crowded her chest, attraction and appreciation, coupled with the peculiar sensation that a closed door had just been opened. The woman in the black dress had been Cassandra Marinos, and for the moment at least, Finn had absolutely no idea what she was supposed to do about that.

Alyssa Stavros was Samantha Drake, and Samantha Drake was Evangeline Wright. And Evangeline Wright was Marie Anne Broussard, and Marie Anne Broussard was Cassandra Marinos. Cassandra Marinos was the woman in the black dress, and the woman in the black dress was gay, but the woman in the black dress was—

"Finn?"

Finn heard the voice and turned, surprised to see Luc just beyond the doorway.

"Are you all right?"

Finn reassembled the words he had spoken and put them into the proper order. "Yes."

"You're very pale."

Finn forced a smile. "No, no, I'm fine. It's just..." What could she say?

"Just what, my friend?"

"Just, the world."

"The world?"

"Yes, the world." She paused as her thoughts took shape. "It's a truly messed-up place, and yet there are Japanese maple trees the color of purple fire, and dreams that have a life of their own, with or without you."

"Yes," he acknowledged, and she knew that he was most likely giving her a pass. "I met Manette on the day my father died. She was wearing the same color shirt that he [h]ad worn that very morning, with the same black buttons."

Finn held his gaze and then sm[il]ed.

"Is she the one?"

"Yeah," Finn answered, and [he]r eyes found the window once again. "She's the one."

"Good. Come downstairs whe[n y]ou're done here, and I can show you the kitchen and the fuse box. Th[er]e's a trick to the alarm system—it is very old."

"I'll be there in a minute."

"This is a good thing, yes?"

"Yes. It's very good."

"But it's been a long time in co[m]ing."

"Yeah. I wasn't sure, but now I [a]m."

"I'll make us some lunch. Ta[ke] your time, my friend. I'm not going anywhere."

She listened to his footsteps a[s h]e took the stairs back down and noted that she had not heard his a[rr]ival quite so clearly. She hadn't heard a thing. Nothing but the tip[p]ing over of all the days between Monte Carlo and the weakness in h[e]r knees as she sat upon the edge of the bed.

It wasn't just her knees, eithe[r.] She could feel the weight of her wonder as if it were a house built o[n a] thousand errant daydreams, and flashes of regret. She had gone bac[k,] of course, but the woman in the black crepe dress had been long go[ne]. Daydreams of what might have been, and regrets that life was neve[r v]ery fair, were surprisingly heavy building materials.

The tickle within her stomach [se]nt a wave of goose bumps along her arms and Finn could feel the l[ac]k of strength within her thighs, as well. She set her hands upon he[r] jeans, and the potent memory of cherry-scented tobacco caught with[in] her nose.

She let out a startled breath of [la]ughter. "Domino's gravity."

CHAPTER NINE

San Francisco
Present day

Finn stared at the ceiling as she lay on her bed.

She had changed the sheets, but the coolness of the fresh, soft cotton did little to soothe her. She had put on her favorite T-shirt from a Foo Fighters concert at the Orpheum in Boston, and her softest pair of boxers, but they didn't help, either.

She glanced at the TV on the wall across the room, but she couldn't remember where she'd left the remote. She remembered she'd been reading Havel's *Open Letters* when she had turned on *Casablanca*, and she'd marked her page with the remote, but she couldn't find Havel now, either.

She imagined that she could still smell Casey's light cologne in the air around her, but she knew it wasn't true and so she tried to avoid even the idea of it. Casey's presence seemed to float about her, though, like the fog that rolled in from the Pacific, invading every crack and crevice she happened upon.

Her phone buzzed and she let out a startled grunt as she grabbed it and glanced at the screen. She accepted the call. "Yes?"

"Did that bacon upset your stomach?" Malik asked.

"No, actually, it enhanced the flavor of all things."

"I talked to Aiyla. The baby's kicking, every day now."

Finn smiled and lifted a knee into the air. "You're going to be a father."

Malik's voice was filled with joy. "Yes."

"You need to be with her at home, not here."

"I still have time," Malik argued in an amiable manner. "The auction shouldn't be more than a week away. Werner would never stay longer than that."

"Maybe this whole thing...maybe it's all wrong, and I'm making it too hard."

"Maybe," Malik responded. Finn couldn't tell if he agreed or disagreed. "But you're very good at this. My son has a trust fund for college now, you know?"

"I'm glad for that."

"Or my daughter."

"She'll need an excellent school. A place that will challenge her."

"Yes. Maybe Harvard."

"Wellesley is good."

"That's what Aiyla says, too."

"You should listen to your wife."

Malik laughed. "That's what Aiyla says, too."

"She's smarter than both of us."

"Yes...but hey, I wanted to ask you something."

Finn cringed, sensing his purpose. "Yes?"

"How was your day?"

"It was fine."

"She didn't really fall into your trap, did she?"

Finn laughed and covered her eyes with her free hand. "No."

"Because that would've been, you know, really cool."

"I'm hanging up now."

"Hey!"

"What?"

"You're an honorable person."

Finn stared at the ceiling again, but a response refused to form within her brain.

"Our cause is just. Dimitrovan and Arshavin will come, and they'll be held accountable for their crimes. I wouldn't be here now if I didn't think you were right."

Finn's left hand slipped under the soft hem of her shirt and fingers skated lightly over her scar. "Go to bed—it's late. She's not going anywhere tonight."

"Do I take point to—"

"I've got it," Finn interrupted. "Keep trying to track down Werner. If we can tag him in any way at all, I won't have to worry about everyone else. He's the center of the wheel. If we find him, we'll find the auction.

And if we find him sooner rather than later, maybe we can get him to give up Arshavin before the whole thing even goes down."

"All right, tomorrow then."

Finn slid her thumb over the screen and ended the call. She studied her spot on the ceiling for a minute or so, and then rolled and dropped her legs over the side of the bed. The phone buzzed within her hand before she could stand, and she answered it.

"I told you to go to bed, okay? It's the middle of the night. I don't sleep, but you should. Aiyla will blame me if you pass out on your first night home."

"I have two questions in response."

Finn dropped her face into her left hand and shut her eyes as tightly as she could.

"Why don't you sleep, and who are you keeping up?"

"I thought…" Finn began and then stopped. She sat back with a frown and studied her screen for a moment before she remembered. "I gave you my card."

"Perhaps your lack of sleep has made you slow," Casey responded drily.

"I don't sense a question mark at the end of that statement."

"Did I interrupt something?"

"No. Just a friend, right before you."

"Why don't you sleep?"

"I don't, I mean, I do. Sleep."

"That wasn't exactly a ringing endorsement, *and* it's past one in the morning, Finnegan Starkweather," Casey countered smoothly. "I plan on being out the door by eight o'clock. How am I supposed to make it to all my appointments on time if I have to drag your exquisitely fine but sorry ass with me?"

Finn smiled and flopped back onto the bed. "Why are *you* still awake, Marinos?"

Finn closed her eyes at the sound of Casey's sexy laughter. "Do you want me to lie, or tell you the truth?"

"Do whatever is safest for you."

After several moments of silence, Finn opened her eyes.

"Why would you say that? Why do you care what the safest thing is for me?"

Finn let the question sink in, but she had no idea how she should answer it. "Do you want me to lie, or tell you the truth?"

"Why would you lie?"

"I don't know," Finn answered. "Maybe that would be safer for me."

"Then tell me the truth."

"I don't want anything to hurt you."

"Are you planning on hurting me, Finn?"

"No, I'm not, but…but sometimes that's what happens, no matter how hard you might try and stop it."

"How long have you been following me?"

An intense discomfort moved through Finn's entire body at the question. She'd been expecting it, and though she had prepared a thousand different answers, none of them were the truth. *And none of them are good enough.* "For a while now, I guess."

"You guess?"

Finn chased after the words, but her heart kept digging in deeper.

"Never mind," Casey said in dismissal, and her voice was content. "Would you like to know why I'm still awake?"

"Why?" Finn asked in a whisper.

"I keep thinking about how you looked in those jeans today," Casey explained softly. "And that where it starts, and then other things push their way in, and I can't sleep. You were right. I have a good imagination."

"Would you like to know what else I didn't say?"

"Yes."

"Today was the best day I've had, in a really, really long time."

"Even the salon?" Casey's tone was playful, pleased and sweet all at once.

Finn chuckled. "Well, it's an unfamiliar blood sport for me, the salon waiting area. I think I held my own, though."

Casey laughed with approval. Just so you know, you were *the* talk of the afternoon."

"I'm sure there was weeping and wailing over my hair."

Casey made a hiccup of sound. "Your hair is made of fallen fucking angels and you know it," she declared with laughter. "Don't you dare pull the butch card—*I'm just a boy and I don't know what I could possibly do with my hair.*"

Finn laughed with her, her stomach vibrating with a righteous happiness that echoed down into her legs. The silence that followed was quite lovely and Finn rolled full onto the bed. She pulled the sheet over her legs and then grabbed one of the pillows.

"Thanks for making me queen for a day," Casey said, and Finn could hear the smile within her voice. "I'm not sure that's ever happened before, especially at David's. Sometimes, even though I fit, I don't. Today, though, I really liked it."

"You're welcome. Thank you, Casey, for a lovely day."

Finn waited, but the silence through the phone was peaceful and soothing. The sheets felt so soft, though she wasn't sure why. They hadn't felt that way an hour ago. They hadn't felt like a thick cloud of promise that she could sink into and be safe. The lamp on the bedside table was warm and low, like the sky just after the sun goes down.

The pillow was glorious, and the back of her head no longer ached.

"Close your eyes," Casey said gently.

Finn obeyed as her muscles relaxed in a warm manner, and her legs felt almost weightless after she stretched them out. The echo of her heartbeat no longer thrummed within her ears, and the pressure had eased in her shoulders. She felt the drift of sleep arrive, but it was oddly quiet and faint as time lost its hold upon her thoughts.

"Are you falling asleep yet?" Casey's faraway whisper tickled at Finn's senses.

CHAPTI ꞁ TEN

"So what's next on your agenda?" nn asked as she put the last bag onto the pile and closed the trunk. " ꞁur efficiency is impressive."

They had shopped, and they ha eaten lunch at the Fringale bistro, and they had spent the afternoon at e California Modern Art Gallery. It had been a marvelous day, agai and Casey had yet to discover Finn's secret, whatever it might be. ꞁ ꞁe had to admit, however, that she hadn't tried very hard to figure it ou She was having fun, and she was in the company of a woman who m; e her pulse race and her thoughts spin. She didn't know how long the ꞁ ell might last, but she had learned that such things were fleeting at bes

It was Thursday, and Eric's auc on was on the following Tuesday night. She had arranged a late-night ꞁartered jet to Tokyo within a few hours of the last bid, and after that' ꞁhe had to admit she was having a hard time trying to envision what ould happen after that. Her plans had most certainly not included a ta gorgeous butch who could shake her good sense loose with just a sma ·ass comment. *Maybe, possibly...* *probably*, she thought with amusem ꞁt, *I'm out of my fucking mind.*

"Hold on," Casey said as she w ked to the passenger window and leaned down. "Go ahead, Trevor, I'l ꞁe okay."

Casey returned to Finn as Trev started the car and they watched as he put on the blinker, waited for s moment, and then pulled away from the curb. The black car eased ꞁoothly into the oncoming traffic and left them behind.

Finn put her hands into her poc ets. "Is he coming back?"

"No."

"Your hotel's a good walk fron iere."

"We're not going to my hotel.'

"Where are we going?"

"Wherever you'd like to take me."

Finn met and held Casey's gaze.

"You've been an extremely good sport for two days, Finnegan Starkweather," Casey complimented. Finn looked even better today than she had yesterday, and Casey realized she had spent much of her time wondering how on earth she might find the middle ground. How *they* might find it. She had yet to figure that out. "Now it's my turn."

Casey had not ruled out that Finn might work for Eric Werner, though that particular thought sent a cold tentacle down her spine. Eric understood full well what she had to offer at the auction, and he was one of the most dangerous men Casey knew. She would not have put it past him to pull a double cross. No matter how she considered that scenario, however, she could not honestly see Finn working for Eric. Finn would hate Eric. She wasn't sure how she knew that, but she did. Despite the possible payoff, Casey just couldn't see it.

"I would've had to go to those places anyway—you get that, right?"

Casey enjoyed the wry tone. "Yes, but you wouldn't have had to carry my bags, which was nice of you, by the way. Thank you."

"You didn't have any textbooks." The wind blew at Casey's curls and Finn reached out and hooked a dark blond strand about her fingers. She tucked it behind Casey's left ear with exquisite care. "We could go to a movie at the Castro Theatre, have you ever been there?" The back of her fingers caressed Casey's cheek in an intimate manner, down the length of her face and whispering beneath her jaw before they disappeared.

Casey felt the caress like a jolt of electricity, and she watched as Finn realized what she had done. Casey couldn't help but smile, for while Finn's expression held surprise at her own actions, there was a second reaction that showed itself quite clearly. It was desire, and there was nothing Finn could do to hide it.

"If you apologize for that," Casey warned her, "I'm not sure I'll ever forgive you."

Finn stepped close and Casey held her ground. "I wasn't going to."

Casey pulled in a breath and her head tipped back as Finn's fingers moved within her hair at the back of her neck. Finn's lips brushed against her mouth and their breaths mingled together for just an instant, and then she was being kissed.

It was a kiss caught between need and tenderness, and Casey took hold of Finn's shirt at the waist, pulling slowly but firmly at the material. Finn's lips were full and sinfully soft, and Casey's heart thrashed within her chest. Her pleasure flew down ard and filled her thighs with a shiver of weakness as Finn's tong opened her mouth, delicate as she explored. Casey welcomed her. nd for the sweetest of moments, everything changed into something holly perfect and complete...and then, like a waking dream, was go . The heat and pulse of Casey's own desire throbbed between her le s, her flesh aching as Finn pulled back, as gentle and easy as their firs kiss had just been.

Finn's amber eyes were dark nd smoky, and Casey wondered how intense they might actually get hould they share more than just a kiss. Casey let out a slow, controlle breath and went about collecting her scattered thoughts.

Finn smiled down at her. "Cas ."

Casey swallowed and licked r lips. "You seem to know the city." Her voice was a bit rough, an she cleared her throat. "Take me to your favorite place."

"You might get bored."

"Do you think so?"

"Maybe."

Casey still held on to Finn's irt as she stood against her. She didn't want to let go, and so she indu ed the rush of warmth and stayed exactly where she was. "I don't thin I will be. I mean, could it be any worse than sitting in chairs at the sa n?"

Finn laughed, and her eyes lit u as her hand slipped along Casey's arm. Casey let go and Finn gripped er hand with an easy confidence. She glanced down the street. "We'll eed a cab now."

Casey looked down at their jo ed hands, and it felt both strange and blissful. She couldn't remembe he last time someone had wanted to hold her hand. She took the pho from her pocket. "Easy enough, Starkweather."

❖

Casey touched the plain wood ookshelf. "What about this one?"

Finn stepped close behind her nd Casey swallowed and let out a careful breath. She wanted despe tely to lean back against Finn's body, but she held tight to her resol .

Finn's left hand came forwar touched the top of a book, and tipped it toward them with just a fin r. "Flannery O'Connor."

Casey's head dipped to the side as she read the spines of the books beside it. "I've heard of her, but I've never read her."

Finn's voice was close beside her ear. "You should. You might not like her in the end, but that doesn't mean you shouldn't read at least one of her books. She has a wonderful way of giving even the meanest character an odd sense of grace. She's a good example of Southern Gothic style, a slice of Americana that appreciates the existence of people no one seems to appreciate."

Casey turned her head to the left. "Have you read Muriel Barbery?"

"*The Elegance of the Hedgehog?*"

Casey's gaze found Finn's mouth with pleasure. "Yes."

"Not yet. Is it good?"

They had been exploring the Green Apple Bookstore for some time, and Casey was so far on the opposite end of the spectrum from bored, she really couldn't describe what she was feeling. Finn stayed close to her as she had all day, but since their kiss, the closeness had taken on a new energy, one of absolute presence and sexual promise that Casey couldn't deny, and she didn't want to. Beyond that, however, she noticed countless little things that Finn did, and they were slowly driving her mad with a different sort of enjoyment.

Finn would touch the small of her back, not as a guide or a representation of her own will, but as support or an acceptance of Casey's wishes. This row of books, not that one. She was being given the lead, and not as part of some elaborate seduction. It was almost protective in nature, but in the best sort of way. She had sought out that discreet shelter of strength in the past, but she had always abandoned the search. She had come to the conclusion that it wasn't possible for a top to hold her close and let her go at the same time, and yet surprisingly, at least for now, here it was.

Their hands would brush together, and Finn's fingertips would skate with warmth on the underside of hers, just barely touching her skin, a light but intimate caress that sent shivers along Casey's arm. The tickle of contact went beyond her skin, and she felt her arousal low within her abdomen. An honest, undeniable roll of physical pleasure that had flipped her equilibrium on its head and left her at the not so subtle mercy of her desire.

Finn's lips were full and ever so slightly wet, as if at any moment Finn might kiss her. Her scent was understated and unknown to Casey. Finn's cologne was fresh and refined, and yet it held a nostalgia within it that made Casey think of the past, a distant past which she had played no part in, where soldiers came home from the war and there were four shades of lipstick, all of them red.

"I think it might have suffered a bit in the English translation. I liked it," Casey said as her eyes st I followed the small movements of Finn's mouth. "She seemed to ke the same route, in a way, an appreciation for characters who are usually castoffs in the narrative. I'm not sure I agreed with her philosophy on some things, but I liked it."

Finn smiled. "A tangent, perhaps, but I held a hedgehog once."

"You didn't."

"I did. It was very small and ange, like an alien creature with eyes that knew exactly what was h opening, as if he was doing tiny math calculations about the angle o mpact, should you turn out to be stupid and drop him."

Casey laughed softly and met nn's gaze. *Oh…oh my God.*

"I love the sound of your lau h," Finn confessed with a grin.

"Cassandra Marinos."

"I love your favorite place," sey whispered, each breath she took a bit shallower than the last. nn seemed closer with each one of those breaths, and Casey knew he had endured as much as she could take. "But if you don't kiss m again, Finnegan, I'm going to be supremely disappointed in what—"

Finn heard the words and her drenaline gave a hard push. She ached for another kiss, even thoug she knew it might be the worst mistake she could make. She hadn't neant to touch her earlier, but she had taken hold of Pandora's box re rdless, and she had yet to let go. There would be no plagues unleashed upon the world if she threw it open now, but a broken heart would be just as devastating, and Finn knew it.

Finn had accepted a long tim ago that she was on a collision course with many things that were ot of her choosing, but she had always thought her heart would be rs to give. When she had looked through that scope all those mon s ago and discovered the real Cassandra Marinos on the other side of it, that quaint idea had been refuted rather easily. One way or a other, Casey was standing at the end of Finn's road, and what she cho se to do with Finn's heart would be entirely up to her.

"—has otherwise been the best fternoon of—"

Finn's hand slipped beneath Ca y's cashmere coat and turned her at the waist.

Casey pulled in a breath at the same time, and Finn drew her close without hesitation. Casey's dark brown eyes were filled with anticipation and welcome in equal measure, and Finn grabbed at the emotions before Casey might rein them in.

Something warm and soft broke within Finn's chest and spilled free in a weighty manner. It was luminous and molten and it filled her to the brim as she kissed her, Casey's lips supple and eager. Finn tasted the faint flavor of vanilla as their mouths joined, and she was careful at first, a sliver of fear the only logic that hadn't jumped ship. The scent of Casey's skin filled her nose, and Casey took hold of her jacket, holding tight to the leather. Her body leaned against Finn's and Finn opened Casey's lips with her tongue, in search of more.

Casey let her in, Finn's arms going about her as she leaned down. Finn heard a startled but pleasing sound and it filled her mouth as the collar of her coat pulled hard against the back of her neck.

Finn had never wanted to kiss anyone so deeply before and, though she knew she should temper her desire for discretion's sake, she opened Casey's mouth further. They had taken a step farther into the row of books, and Finn's hand found the back of Casey's neck, her fingers opening within the thickness of her hair and taking hold. Casey went on her toes and Finn's arm tightened and lifted her closer, and even through their clothes, Finn could feel the insane heat of Casey's body. It was close to overwhelming, and her body reacted, a heady wave of arousal pulsing painfully between her legs, profound and without relief.

Finn hadn't known that a kiss could hold such promise, such a ripe and delicious pledge of want and need, but then she had wanted Casey for such a very long time. The disparity between what lived at the heart of Finn's desire and what Casey may or may not have been feeling struck her, and she pulled back slowly, easing away from the haven she had found. Her hand opened within the curls that she held and she let her touch float along the soft skin of Casey's neck until she held her face, her thumb touching the side of Casey's lips as she finally pulled free.

Casey's face was flushed and her lips were parted as she met Finn's eyes.

Finn held tight to her words as the reality of their situation rushed back to her.

"Don't," Casey whispered.

"Don't what?"

"Don't you dare say you're sorry…I can see it."

"No, it's not that. I'm not sorry us and Finn let out a small breath Casey's eyes sharpened their focus and Finn let out a small breath as Casey touched her cheek. "Then what is it?"

Finn didn't know how to answer her. *Be careful, Finn, remember?* Casey's smile was slow and filled with such a clear invitation that it threatened to break her completely. That was it. That was all it took. Just a smile. "You should just tell me what this is all about, Finnegan Starkweather, and then you can take me back to my hotel. The room service is second to none…and their breakfast menu is quite good."

Finn's heart was beating much too fast and she knew it, and the pressure within her head threatened to drown out the sound of Casey's voice.

"Is there someone else, then?"

Finn blinked in shock at Casey's question and leaned back.

Casey laughed quietly in response, and she took hold of Finn's jacket with both hands once more, to put an end to her retreat. "Of course not, I'm sorry I asked that."

The vibration of a phone startled both of them, and by the fourth buzz, Casey reached inside Finn's jacket. She pulled the phone from Finn's inner pocket, glanced at it, and then held it out to her. "Saved by the bell, so to speak."

CHAPTER ELEVEN

Casey sipped at her wine and watched the traffic as it moved along Montgomery Street. The corner room had cost her, but the view at night was worth it, and she would've paid double if she'd had to. She had showered, and the thick hotel robe was soft and cool against her skin.

The '47 Cheval tasted just as spectacular now as the night it had been opened, and she savored it, letting the flavor sit in her mouth before she swallowed. It held an essence that she had never tasted before, and no doubt, it was one she would never taste again. It was a beautiful gift on several levels, but the true mystery behind it was the message Finn was trying to give her. After spending time with her, Casey had no doubt that some hidden part of Finnegan Starkweather was trying to speak up, whether the rest of Finn knew it or not.

The phone call had been a relief, in retrospect; and now that she was alone, away from Finn's immediate presence, she could admit that to herself.

She needed to catch her breath. She needed to step back and consider all that was happening with a dispassionate eye. Her amusement at that thought was significant, as she tried to catalog the rush of emotions that threatened to swamp her.

Their kiss in the bookstore had been beyond compare, and she remembered the feel of Finn's tongue against hers, gentle at first, and then not so much, as she demanded everything that Casey might want to give. It had been more than just desire and Casey knew it, and she had returned the sentiment quite willingly.

Finn had brought her back to the hotel, and before Casey had gotten out of the cab, she'd been unable to resist a kiss good night. A part of her had done it on a dare, to prove to herself what had happened, what she'd been feeling for almost three days now, was nothing more than lust. A hunger that had not bee[n] satisfied in a very long time, that needed to be shut down again and lo[ck]ed away. Either that, or indulged until it was sated and out of her syst[em].

But Finn had destroyed her all [ov]er again, and rather easily at that.

The taste and heat of her mo[uth], and the scent of her skin. The strength of her hands, and that hair. [C]asey had yet to bury her hands in the crazy goodness that was Finn's [ha]ir, and she was suddenly annoyed at the omission.

"Break it down," she said al[o]ud, before she enjoyed the last swallow in her glass.

Finn kept a loft in San Francis[co], which was no mean feat in any metropolitan city, but San Francisc[o e]specially. Was this her home, or was it just a base of operations?

Eric Werner had held at least [te]n of his last fifteen auctions in San Francisco, and so Finn's prese[nce] [migh]e might've been a coincidence, though she couldn't be certain of tha[t]. Perhaps it was nothing but highly convenient for Finnegan Starkwea[ther] to find her prey in her own backyard. Perhaps it was something [m]ore. Perhaps she was a hired gun after all, as Jack had suggested. Per[ha]ps what she wanted from Finn, at this point in their relationship, was [f] different than what Finn wanted in return. *Relationship...for the love [o]f God, Casey, get a grip.*

She couldn't deny, however, t[ha]t her every instinct was on high alert. Her gut told her she was sud[d]enly caught up in something far bigger than she'd expected, and sh[e] [ha]d expected quite a lot in the first place.

Her phone rang and she stepp[ed] about the table and grabbed it. The number was blessedly familiar. [C]olin, my lovely genius. What do you have for me?"

"Where did you get that numb[er]?"

"Never mind where, whose is i[t]?"

"Agent Thomas Hanson, Natio[na]l Security Agency."

Casey let out a harsh breath, tr[ul]y shocked.

"Listen," Colin said, "I'm sh[utt]ing down here, and I'm moving to a secondary site. I'll have a new [s]etup. If you don't hear from me by Sunday, look for a Paris packag[e] with my new specs. If there's no package, assume I've been grabbed.

"What is there, I mean…" Cas[ey] tried to process the possibilities of Colin's information, only she h[ad] no idea what those possibilities might be. "What do you have on thi[s] guy?"

"He works for the *Nationa[l] Security Agency*," Colin said, emphasizing each word. "That's what I have on him. Listen, Casey, these guys don't fuck around, not after Snowden. I think I tripped a door finding him, so I'm setting up fresh. Sunday, okay? By noon, your time. If I can't reach you, I'll call Jack."

"Did you get a location?"

"Yeah, he's in San Francisco. I sent Jack everything I could find on her partner, Malik Kaseem—that's all I've got for now. I've still got a few hacks running on Starkweather. I'll send whatever I might get. Get rid of your burner phone. Do it now. I'll reset the app, which will take about an hour. It'll wipe your iPhone, so snag any information you might need. Good luck."

Casey started to speak, but he was already gone. "Fuck."

She dialed Jack and he picked up on the second ring. "Yeah, I'm on my way."

"Maybe you were right, Jack."

"I'll let you decide that," he replied. "I never took her for a spook, and I still don't. You've got a second tail tonight, Malik Kaseem. He's in the lobby, actually. One of the clerks is keeping an eye on him for me. Take the stairs on the south end down to the third floor, and then take the service elevator to the basement. It's in the maintenance room behind the vending. I'll meet you there in thirty minutes. Can you make that?"

"I'll be there."

Casey hung up and moved toward her suitcases when the phone rang once more, and the number stopped her cold. Her adrenaline was high, but her thoughts were catching up. She took the call. "Are you having second thoughts, Starkweather?"

Finnegan's surprised laughter on the other end of the call slapped her upside the brain, and she stepped to the bed and sat down.

"I'm sorry about that call. It was…"

Casey was careful with her tone. "It was what?"

"It was really bad timing, and totally unexpected. It was also something that I thought was over with, almost two years ago, I guess."

Casey could hear a hard edge of nervousness in Finn's voice, a sharpness that Casey had definitely not heard from her before. It was damn close to fear, and that was a surprise. She didn't know much, but she knew Finn didn't scare very easily. "Are you okay?"

"Yeah, I just…it's just a life I used to live, and I don't live there anymore."

Casey wished that she could see Finn's expression. She had

already learned there wasn't much nn could hide that wouldn't find its way into her eyes rather quickl "What exactly does that mean, Finn?"

"It means I used to be a cop, re ember?"

"I remember."

"It's okay, but, listen, I won't s ; you tomorrow." Casey had not expected to hea hat. "What's going on?" "I'll find you, okay? As soon a [can."

Casey waited for more, but sl received only silence. It hadn't really occurred to her that Finn's hone call might've been about something else entirely. *Perhaps yo re not the center of the world just yet, you idiot.* Casey closed her ey . "Who should I be looking for, then?"

"Well, in the spirit of transpa ncy, and goodwill in general"— Finn sounded extremely tired, Casey could almost feel it, but she could hear the smile in her voice—"his na e is Malik Kaseem, and he's one of the best people I've ever known. on't give him a hard time, okay? He's not as tough as I am."

Casey's thoughts adjusted to th information. Malik Kaseem, just as Colin said. "I'll be gentle."

"Don't be gentle, just be carefu "

Casey searched across the ro n, and her eyes stopped at the '47 Cheval Blanc, which sat beside er empty glass. In her own way, Finn was asking her not to shake hi loose. "What is it you think will happen to me, Finn, if someone isr keeping an eye on me?" Casey waited far longer than she thought i vas possible for her to wait, until she couldn't take it. "Finnegan," she vhispered into the phone.

"I'm afraid I won't see you aga 1. Just promise me, please, okay? You can trust Malik."

Casey thought about Finn's stat nent, and the idea of never seeing Finn again was not a scenario she ished to contemplate. "But can I trust *you*, Finnegan Starkweather?"

"Yes," she answered simply. But that decision isn't mine to make—it's yours."

Casey wished Asher were still ve, and not for the first time. She was a better thief than he had been ut he could get to the bottom of any given situation faster than a grav digger with a new shovel, as Jack liked to say.

And I have a vested interes n you, Finnegan Starkweather, whether I like it or not, she thought, l r emotions fighting it out between a definite sense of want and a good deal of well-founded anxiety. Finn's energy was an amazing thing, and when it was focused on her, she felt safe and wickedly reckless, two emotions that rarely felt at home in the same room, much less familiar and honest as they sat together on the couch.

Asher whispered through her thoughts, and at least for now, that much was enough.

There will be a time, Domino, when you must make a choice between the heart inside you and protecting yourself against what you know to be true of the world. And the world has no concern for such things. It does not give a shit about you and what you want.

Your moment? You will have precious little time to make up your mind—you must trust me on that. Either you cross the tracks before the train passes, kicking the world in the balls, or you stand and wait, and count the cars like everyone else.

What can you live with? What can you not? An easy question, that is what I say. Better to choose for yourself than to have that choice taken away from you. Better to be crushed down, every now and then, than to spend your life afraid to make a fucking decision. When I look back? My heart has always won out, and I have no regrets.

She could hear the echo of Asher's laughter, rough from cigarettes and cursing the horses at Vincennes, though she had never seen him bet more than fifty francs on any given day.

And if you choose the wrong thing? There is always another train coming at you, yes? The train from Paris to Marseille runs four times a day. Move faster next time. Choose better.

Casey smiled. "All right. I'll be careful, and I won't hurt him."

"I have to go now."

"Finn?"

"Yes?"

"Watch your back, whatever it is."

"Always." Finn's reassurance did very little to reassure her.

"And, Finn?"

"Yes?"

Casey bit at the corner of her lower lip as she debated her next words. She could demand to know why Finn was following her, but she knew it wasn't the question she really wanted to ask. She'd find that out on her own, anyway, and Finn had just opened the door for her. No, what she really wanted to know had nothing to do with such mundane details. "Do you always kiss so deeply?"

Casey closed her eyes while s ; waited. She could feel the heat within her face, and she felt like a t(nager, hopelessly at the mercy of a single word.

"There is no deep enough wi you, Cassandra Marinos," Finn said in a quiet, seductive voice. "I)und that much out, anyway. I'll always want to be deeper inside yo ..and you can take that any way you'd like."

Casey smiled, her eyes still shı as her phone went silent.

CHAPTER TWELVE

Casey sat in the old high-backed chair, her shoulders pressed against the thin cushion that still remained. Her arms were crossed and she held herself, the strength of her own embrace some small defense against the riot of emotions that raced through her. Her right leg was hooked over her left knee, and she sat as still as a marble statue.

The lamp beside the chair gave off a full golden light, and she had tipped the shade slightly so as to illuminate the matching chair that faced her, as well as its occupant.

Each breath she took was slow and even, and her eyes were focused and clear as they followed the brushstrokes. Deep gold, cupped and holding a lighter tone, with a splash of orange here and there. Short brushstrokes layered on top of each other as they moved up the canvas, until the fall of a man's shadow dropped over them, green with threads of blue pulled through it.

The man who walked upon the road was dressed in workman's clothes, most likely wool with button fasteners, which befitted the time when he would've walked the road. Blue and black as he followed the path, a box of paints in one hand and a canvas under his other arm, his easel strapped to his back. His straw hat was gold, the color a match to the wheat fields behind him, and a beautiful contrast to the triangle of green grass that cut across the land. The trees that framed him on the road were simple, but the leaves looked as if they would fall if you shook the canvas too hard, bubbles of green and black that might catch the breeze and blow away.

The horizon was a pure sort of blue that depicted a town, perhaps, in the distance. It brought out the blue of the rocks and pebbles that littered the top of the road he walked. The sky was a thousand spots of pale blue and green, the green becoming lost among the leaves of the trees in the foreground.

Casey took in a deep breath and let it out slowly between her lips.

She imagined the colors as they were meant to be seen, thick and bright and filled with the afternoon sun. In reality they were faded, with years and with time and with the vagaries of fate that had named the painting a miracle, just for having survived intact. There was some damage to the lower left side of the canvas, smoke and heat. Someone had put out the flames as they had touched the paint. It made perfect sense.

The painting was *Painter on the Road to Tarascon*, created by Vincent van Gogh in the year 18_. And while that was a game-changing fact, it was not the most interesting one.

It had been seized and labeled degenerate art by the Nazis, and somehow it had wound up in Magdeburg, stored away and waiting to be destroyed. Or at least that had been the plan. As far as the rest of the world knew, it had been turned to ash when the Allies bombed the city in 1945.

Someone in the Kaiser Friedrich Museum had seen the wonder of it, though, and had most likely risked their life to pull it from the flames. Who had saved it, and where it had been since 1945, Casey had absolutely no idea.

What she did know was it had sat in Mabelle Babineaux's attic since Asher had stored it there. When and where he had come by it, she didn't know that either, but he'd been expecting her to retrieve it. He had left it for her, and the letter attached to the back of the frame, tacked beside the edge of the canvas, had told her as much.

Along with the letter, there were papers of authentication, signed by Sir Verle Dandemount, who at one time had been the world's foremost authority on Vincent van Gogh. He was dead now, but the papers had been signed, witnessed and notarized. His reputation and expertise were beyond reproach. Why he had kept silent about the survival of the painting was a question that Casey had tried to answer for three years, and she had yet to come close to an answer. She knew that Asher and Sir Verle had known each other for many years, though, and Sir Verle Dandemount had not been the cloistered scholar the world had considered him to be. This did not, however, negate his expertise.

Mabelle Babineaux had been a talented jewel thief in her time, and she had taken some part in Asher's education when he was young.

Her well-kept Victorian home near Duboce Park in San Francisco had always been a safe house, not just for Asher and herself, but for Blackjack Vermillion and many others throughout the years. Its upkeep and restoration had been financed by any number of people who owed Aunt Mabelle a debt of gratitude, and the house was spectacular in just about every way. This included state of the art security, and two separate escape tunnels that would lead you to the far side of the park. They had been constructed during the Roaring Twenties, apparently, and Mabelle had seen to their safe restoration. Asher had a permanent room on the top floor, with access to a private attic, and since his death three years ago, the room had belonged to Casey.

Asher's last message to her had sent her here, and she had found the painting just as it was at that very moment, waiting to be discovered.

Casey glanced at the table to her right.

Asher's letter still sat there beside the lamp, safe within the envelope she had found it in. She knew what it said, and at the moment, she wasn't sure if she could handle seeing his handwriting. Everything was wild within her head, and seeing the proof that she was all alone in the world was not something she felt was a good idea. Asher had possessed beautiful handwriting, slanted and with strange flourishes that made a letter from him not only a message from the man who had been her father, but a reminder that he was truly gone from her world.

She closed her eyes and took a deep breath.

She smiled suddenly, and she let out a soft breath of surprised laughter, her eyes drawn to the porthole window and the lights of the city beyond it.

She could smell Finn's cologne.

She hadn't been wrong, when she had first watched Finn at the bar of the Campton. Women like her were far too dangerous. But then again, she had already made up her mind that she had never met a woman quite like Finnegan Starkweather.

Her eyes returned to the painting.

"Maybe she wants *you*."

She didn't really believe that, though, and the fact that she could still feel Finn's mouth against her own was proof enough for her. She'd been caught up in more than a few games in her line of work, and no matter how much someone might want, there were no lies in a kiss such as that.

"The sort of kiss…" she whispered, though she didn't finish her sentence.

Eric had told her he had a spe al buyer, and though they would run the auction as usual, he had n doubt his new client would pay whatever outrageous sum was neede to obtain Vincent's lost painting. They were surprisingly scary words

She could retire on this one. Sh :ould be done with it all, and only dabble if the fancy struck her or sh couldn't resist. She could attend university if she wanted, which wou l make Asher chuckle and laugh, that such a thought had finally enter l her head. She could…

"I could stop running," she w spered again, and still her voice felt too loud.

She blinked and wiped at her c eeks.

"I could start clean."

She had no idea what that wou l feel like. To start fresh, with no restrictions on what she might want o do, or where she might wish to go. She had money already, yes, ar plenty of it. But money ran out, and with one bad investment, or a s igle wrong move, it could be cut in half. It could even disappear if sh were truly careless. The house in the Dordogne, and the land, had tak almost every bit of her available assets. A superb investment, to be ure, but years of jobs, years of planning and risk, and with one fe swoop, her budget for living a retirement of ease and comfort was oking a bit pinched.

But not with this one.

This one would give her freed beyond any and all attachments and limitations. This one would ; ve her power. And power was something she had never really had t fore. Power over her own destiny, and the ability to keep what she love , no matter what life might bring.

She picked up Asher's letter ai brought the envelope close. The fact that she could smell Finn's colo e as she thought of Asher did not seem out of place, though she had n idea why.

He had wanted her to have it. I had left it for her.

This was the life she had chosei She had no idea if there was room enough for the promises Finn had ade with her kiss. Casey wasn't even sure if Finn had been aware f them, the taste of that fleeting dream she'd not had since she was girl. A dream of being safe and warm, and surrounded by…by what

Casey swallowed over a tight tl at and wiped at her cheeks again. She tucked the letter in the inner po et of her jacket, pushed up from the chair, and clicked off the light be re she made her way in the dark.

❖

Orléans, France
August 1997

"But I don't *need* it."

"Of course you do. Do you think I will give my secrets over to a girl who cannot keep track of her own accounts?" Asher exhaled smoke toward the half-open car window. His French accent was still evident in his English, but it was not as heavy as it once was.

Casey pulled her left foot onto the seat and cast him a glance as she laced her fingers against her shin. "Is this the part where you lament your lack of education and explain to me how it's kept you from polite society?"

Asher chuckled, and the sound hit a lovely high note that always amused her. "You see? I never used such words when I was your age. And I went to school. If I had gone to university, we would be living a different life."

Casey smiled, irritated but still entertained. "I think you went off the track a bit with that one. Should you try again?"

Asher gave a scoff and pulled lightly at his smoke. "Yes, okay, you're right. Who wants to live like those rich pricks, in houses that all look the same? Dinner at seven and then"—he made an odd, somewhat sinister digging gesture with both hands, and scrunched up his face—"tuck, tuck my little rat children, who will whine and sneer and click their teeth, and who will forget you in twenty years because you are old and you shame them."

Casey laughed. "Well, those rich pricks and their spoiled whiny brats are going to pay for our trip to Provence."

Asher smiled, but his eyes said something more. "Only after you finish your exams."

Casey groaned and dropped her head back.

"What?"

"I'm so *bored* there, *Oncle*."

Asher nodded. "Yes. You are seventeen years old—of course it bores you. So then you take your graduation exams early, yes?"

Casey narrowed her eyes at him, caught off guard and wary of his statement.

The headlights of a car flared within the rearview mirror and they both stilled, Asher's eyes quick and alert. The black Volvo passed them by just as Asher turned his face away. His eyes met Casey's. "Take them, and you are done with school."

There was a long silence between them as Casey tried to decide if he was serious or not. She had tried in the past to convince him that she should test out and move on, but he had always refused to sign the papers. "Do not fuck with me," she warned.

"Why would I fuck with you? And watch your language, please."

"Why would you agree now?"

"Because you are a young woman. There is nothing else they can teach you if you pass their exams." He made a face of acceptance and pulled on his cigarette once more before he flicked it out the window. "I see the logic in this. You have not asked me since the last time, however, and I have changed my mind since then. So now I say, if you pass? We will move on. Get me the papers and I will sign them."

Casey's heartbeat quickened and she sat up straighter. "Don't mess with me, please."

Asher pulled in his shoulders with a shrug. "What is that? I am not messing with you. I promise, my little Domino."

Casey's smile was slow to form, but it was heartfelt when it arrived.

"Listen," Asher replied, and his tone was gentle, "maybe this is not the time, but since we are talking of big things…" He wore a serious expression within the shadows of the car, and she steeled herself for what he might say. "I tell you now, what I know."

Casey held his gaze for a long time, and her smile faded just as carefully as it had arrived. "You know what?"

"I know what you're hiding from me. I know, my sweet girl."

Casey's words left her completely and she swallowed upon a tight throat.

"Do not be afraid, Cassandra, I don't care about such things, my darling. I care only that you are happy." His expression contained genuine warmth, and his eyes were filled with love for her. Despite that, she felt the blood beneath her skin become hot and panicked. "Love is only love, isn't that what they say? Love is just love."

Casey felt the blush burn its way down her throat and into her chest.

"But what I do care about is that those girls at school, they are worthless. I am seeing that, Domino, and they are not good enough for you." He made a face. "So you pass your exams and we have a party, a lovely party, and then we go to the coast." His grin returned. "There are girls there, Domino, who will appreciate a young woman such as yourself, brilliant and beautiful. We will go, and we will have ourselves a grand summer, yes? We will have another adventure."

Casey reached for her voice, but when she closed her thoughts about it, her tongue came back empty. *A grand summer, yes, Oncle*, she wanted to say, scarcely believing it.

Despite his words, which were filled with love and goodwill, her oldest fear rose up from the pit of her stomach. She could not name what it was, but then, she was never certain she needed to. It was fear, and it was bright and terrible, and it brought with it the loss of her voice.

She had a vague memory of being a child and not being able to speak, even though she had wanted to. She would dream about it sometimes, and she would wake up sweating and cold and filled with panic. She would turn on the lights and try to read, but her mind was never right until she had slept again. Sometimes, Asher would knock on her door, and he would make crepes on their small stove and they would watch old Belmondo movies. He would talk and she would listen, and he would tell her stories of when he was young and lived in Paris.

Asher pulled his pouch of tobacco from the inside of his worn brown leather jacket and began to roll a new smoke.

She had thought about telling him so many times, but that was as far as she had ever taken it. What was she to say? *Oncle, I love girls. I want to kiss them, I want to touch them, and I want them to touch me.* How in the hell did you wrap that one up with a pretty bow and slide it across the breakfast table? There had always been a deep feeling of shame in the truth, though Casey had understood it was the shame of disappointing him somehow. She had kissed Yvonne Lambert in the music room closet, and she had slipped her hand past denim and silk. Yvonne had not minded in the least, and there was no shame in the happiness that had resulted. There was no shame in her heart.

"We will buy some of those dresses you are always looking at, in those heavy magazines." He took the string of his smoke pouch between his teeth and pulled it shut before he tucked it back in his jacket. "And I've always wanted an Armani suit. There is nothing quite like a man in a well-tailored Armani suit. I would like to be that man."

Casey nodded as he tightened the fragile paper and evened out his tobacco.

"If we happen to stumble upon something shiny, here and there, what can we do but pick it up? We must be good citizens."

Casey let out a breath with he ;mile, and she turned away from him. Her vision blurred as her tears ⟨ ⟩lled up and slid down her cheeks. "There," Asher said softly. "Th re's the night guard." Casey wiped at her eyes and sa forward. The guard moved down the Rue de Changelin just as he had ⟨ ⟩ery night for the last three weeks. She pushed back the sleeve of her b ck cotton jacket and checked her watch.

"As soon as he turns the corner nto Vivier, you will have twenty-one minutes to do what you came fc "

Casey turned with a jerk of her houlders. She felt the word form and then explode within her chest. l burned along her throat before it left her mouth in a flame of sound. ' 7hat?"

"There you are, Domino, welcc e back." He touched the cigarette to his tongue and sealed the paper ith a practiced ease. "You know the security systems as well as I d⟨ Can you bypass the alarm? The cameras, as well?"

Casey stared at him.

"Can you, Domino?" he dem ided in a hard tone. "Find your voice once and for all, for I do not j⟨ e around here."

Casey's heart hammered withii her throat. "Yes."

"You are in better shape than I n—that's for certain. Can you get over the wall and to the second floo ⟩alcony?"

"Like the farmhouse, back in I on. Yes."

Asher let out a grunt of agre nent. "We should go up for the weekend soon. The place has probal y blown away by now."

Casey raised an eyebrow at hii

"You picked the painting, Don 10, not I. You have been begging for a job of your own for months nc . So this one is yours. Orléans is as good a place as any to decide wh you will do with your life."

"But I don't—"

"You don't what?" Asher inter ipted her. "You don't want to be a child, so then don't be one. Our nd, we are strong, Domino. You and I, we are not victims. These pc ple do not even *know* what they have, they just take everything and l ve those who are less fortunate to drown in their wake. Or they destro hem and take what little treasure people have, because they can. We wn who we are, and there is no need to apologize. Can you open a s e?"

Casey's blood raced through h⟨ veins. "Better than you can."

"Can you strip the painting fro the frame?"

"Yes."

Asher smiled. "Do you remember what it looks like?"

Casey grinned back at him. "Yes. She is beautiful. I know her."

"And the plans to the house? How high is the balcony?"

"Five and a half meters."

"Which room do you enter?"

"The study." Casey closed her eyes for a moment to gain her focus. "The study is five meters by six meters, with the door on the north wall. Down the hall to the left, and twelve meters more. The double doors."

"And so you are wearing black," he mused and Casey opened her eyes. "You packed my kit, so if you forgot something, it will be on you. Do you have your gloves?"

"I didn't forget anything, Oncle."

Asher peered into the distance. "I would get going, then, if I were you."

Casey spun to the right and grabbed the door handle, but she didn't turn it.

The silence was thick and it bound her like a rope, until she heard the ping and scrape of Asher's gold Zippo. She heard the crackle of the dark tobacco, and then his breath as he exhaled. The faint scent of cherry tobacco whispered through the car.

"When did you know?" She closed her eyes against his answer.

"I knew…when you kissed your first girl, Domino."

Casey frowned and glanced over her shoulder. She couldn't see how that was possible. "But…Yvonne?"

Asher smiled into the darkness beyond their '76 Jaguar. "Ah. There he goes, Domino, very close now."

Casey turned, her eyes focused. "I'll see you on Place de Vivier."

"Yes. Twenty minutes from his turn, no more, understood?"

"I know," she said with a quick smile. She watched as the guard turned the far corner, and then she opened the door. It closed behind her with but a click of sound.

Asher pulled the lever for the trunk as she rounded the back end and she grabbed up his kit. She closed the lid in silence and then slipped across the road like a shadow, his duffel bag slung across her back.

CHAPTER THIRTEEN

San Francisco
Present day

Casey had spent the latter half of the day engaged in a game of tag with Malik Kaseem, and though he didn't have Finn's presence, or her edge, he was good at his job. She had lost him once just to spice things up, and then she had allowed him to resume his surveillance. While this amused her, she had the horrible feeling that she was wasting valuable time. And not just her time, but Finn's, as well.

According to Jack, Finn had spent the day in her loft and had left only when the sun went down. She hadn't done anything unusual that Jack was aware of, but Casey couldn't shake the anxiety she felt. Perhaps it was everything. Perhaps it was waiting for the auction. Perhaps it was being entangled with Finn and not knowing what to do about it, or how it would all turn out. Perhaps it was a painting by Vincent van Gogh that had ceased to exist in 1945, sitting in an attic less than an hour away.

Maybe you just need to find some answers.

It was past ten and she had shaken Malik loose for a second time, doubling back on him and finding his car, a rather nice BMW X3. The security was tight, but most people didn't bother with the upgrades beyond what the dealer supplied, and so she took her chances.

She was able to bypass the alarm with a code grabber key that Jack had given her, and though she felt somewhat conspicuous waiting for the slim box to snatch the combination, once it had, she was in the car. She waited for a minute or two to avoid any curious bystanders on the street, and then she slipped between the bucket seats and into the back. She smiled through the rush, pulled the handgun from the back of her jeans before she leaned back, and then waited.

She only had to check her watch once before she heard him approach the car as he talked on the phone. He was efficient if he was anything, and he wasn't going to waste his time once he'd truly lost her—she'd known that much.

He punched in the code, yanked the door, sat, and then slammed the door shut. "I don't know, Aaron, can you get someone to the Palace Hotel? She'll show up there at some point."

Casey let out a slow breath and adjusted the grip on her weapon.

"Thanks. I'll check back in twenty. I've got one place I can look yet…yup, thanks."

Malik Kaseem hung up his phone, tossed it onto the passenger seat, and flipped his keys around. "She's gonna kill me."

Casey sat up and reached around his seat with her right arm.

His startled intake of breath sent a shiver along her spine, and she placed the muzzle of her 9 mm against his right temple. "Put your hands on the wheel, please."

Malik was very still, though his eyes lifted to the rearview mirror. "Wait…"

"Should I say please again?"

Malik did as he was told and opened his hands on the steering wheel.

"Malik Aariz Kaseem, born June 16, 1980, in Colchester, England. Your family came to the States in ninety-seven. You currently live in Pittsburgh, Pennsylvania." Casey's tone was curious as she leaned between the seats. The weapon felt strange in her hand but she held it with confidence. "Two sisters, both teachers. Your sister Sanaa teaches college prep English at Fox Chapel, and Haleemah teaches third grade at Kolfax." Casey tilted her head farther to the right and felt a twinge of guilt at the panic in his eyes. Her hand, however, stayed exactly where it was. "I'd have chosen third grade, myself. Dealing with teenagers on a daily basis? I'd have to take the stovepipe."

"You don't need the gun," Malik said with care.

"How long have I been under surveillance?"

Casey waited through his decision-making process with polite patience.

"Six months, give or take a few weeks."

His words shocked her, but she moved around it. "What's the setup?"

"I'll tell you whatever you want, Ms. Marinos, but please…you don't need the gun."

"Why would you tell me whatever I want?"

"Because you deserve to know."

"Not because I have a gun?"

"No."

Casey frowned. "But I went all this trouble. This is terribly unsatisfying."

"Okay," Malik responded. "It's because of the gun."

Casey wanted to laugh. If his tone had been any drier, she could have poured his words into a long-stemmed glass and served them with a steak. "Don't be a flirt," she cracked.

Malik swallowed and Casey watched as a line of sweat rolled along his neatly trimmed sideburn. "And because…and because I love Finn, and she'll never tell you."

Casey blinked at his words. "Why won't she tell me?"

"Because she's trying to protect you."

Finn had been right, he wasn't as tough as she was. "I don't need protection."

Malik turned his head to the right, slowly, and slightly, as if his life depended on it. "Maybe, maybe not. But she's very good at what she does, and her judgment is spot-on. You're not the one who's being hunted, at least not by us."

Casey's brain switched gears as quickly as he said the words. They could debate the finer points of what one human being hunting another human being might entail, or they could spill some brass tacks and take off their shoes. "I know a shop a few blocks from here that serves the best Qahwa in the States. Shall we indulge ourselves?"

"Coffee?"

Casey smiled at the surprise in his voice. "Yes, very *good* coffee."

"Coffee. Coffee would be nice."

Casey pulled the gun back and opened her hand. The matte black Bersa 9 mm spun down around her finger until she caught it by the barrel. "It's a replica, an airsoft," she explained as Malik sank back against his seat and a small sound slipped from his throat. "I have my moments, Mr. Kaseem, but I'm not a complete ass."

Malik stared at the weapon as he tried to regain his balance. "It looks real."

"If it didn't, there wouldn't be much of a point."

"Pellets?"

"Yes, but not loaded." Casey turned her wrist, pleased at the illusion she held. It felt better now that it wasn't scaring the shit out of someone. "Putting pellets in it would imply intent, and accidents do happen, you know. I just want answers, Mr. Kaseem, not a guilty conscience."

Malik met her eyes, and Casey saw he had reclaimed a good portion of his composure. "Perhaps that's not the best game to be playing."

"There are all sorts of games being played at the moment, the least of which is my use of a toy gun. Shall we walk?"

❖

Malik lowered his handleless cup onto its saucer. "You're right, it's the best coffee I've had in a very long time."

Casey watched him from across her favorite table and leaned back, the soft cushions of the booth as comfortable as she remembered. "So tell me."

Malik paused for a moment and then took a breath. He let it out slowly and she could see the tension ease in his shoulders as he accepted the situation and honored his word. "Straight surveillance," he began. "I wanted you wired, but Finn wouldn't have it. Basically, we just watched you—where you went, who you met."

"No taps or PPM kit? Did you hack my security?"

"Finn said a wire wouldn't give us anything, and in the end, I agreed with her. We started with a parabolic mike, yeah. Finn put a stop to that after the first week or so in June. We didn't even try a hack on your system. I'm good, but I'm not that good."

"Finn dumped the mike?" She'd done the math as he'd spoken, and she was fairly certain she knew what the answer would be. "Why?"

"She didn't say."

Casey studied his face. He definitely had an opinion. "And your best guess would be?"

"You took a lover," Malik answered. "An Englishwoman, Abigail Stanton. The morning after she showed up, the mike was gone. It never reappeared."

Thank you for that, at least, Finnegan Starkweather. Casey remembered the night Abigail had shown up, and how little sleep she'd gotten during the first few days of their three-week long reunion. "Did Finn do a hack?"

"That's not her specialty."

"What is her specialty?"

"You haven't figured that out y ?"

Casey made a bored face and ⟨w⟩aited him out, annoyed that he should ask such a bitchy-sounding qu⟨e⟩stion about what she did and didn't know about Finnegan Starkweather. *⟨F⟩uck you, Malik, I know enough... Goddamn it, I totally don't know eno⟨u⟩gh. This is so unacceptable.*

"Finn sees the big picture."

"And you don't?"

Malik smiled. "Not like she d⟨oe⟩s. I've never seen anything like it, ever."

"You were in the Dordogne, a⟨s⟩ well?" Casey felt the edge in her voice, and it felt like a precision bla⟨de⟩ within her throat. From the guilt that flashed through his eyes, touch⟨ed⟩ with a splash of panic, she was pretty sure it didn't do much for hin⟨m⟩ either. "For how long?"

"I arrived at the end of May. It ⟨w⟩as just Finn before that."

"Just you and Finn?"

"Yes."

"Were you inside my house?"

Malik frowned. "No."

"Why not?"

"Because it's your house."

His answer was utterly unexpe⟨ct⟩ed and Casey laughed. "You can watch me from afar for six month⟨s⟩ and some change, but you can't break into my house while I'm at th⟨e⟩ grocery and take a little peek?"

"Of course not."

There was a touch of confusior⟨ i⟩n his tone and Casey could see he wanted to say more. She waited yet ⟨a⟩gain, but when he didn't continue within a reasonable amount of tim⟨e⟩ she offered him a prompt. "And your next thought was…?"

"I thought you saw her for wh⟨o⟩ she really is."

Casey let his words sink in a⟨nd⟩ slap her ego around for about three whole seconds. She cursed in ⟨Fre⟩nch and then clicked her tongue, giving herself a mental shake bacl⟨ i⟩nto English. "That's it, asshole, okay? Let's not be so condescendii⟨ng⟩, or too dramatic either, because as much as that might be fun? It's ⟨no⟩t. And I'll have you know, I *do* know—"

"No." He leaned forward and ⟨m⟩et her heated emotion with his own. "Please, Ms. Marinos, I just. ⟨⟩ Casey. I just thought, I mean, I thought you two…"

"I thought you two, *what?*"

"I thought she spent the night, and I'm sorry, I didn't mean it that way." He looked down and adjusted the brim of his hat. "I'm sorry." The words hit Casey hard.

Casey had been about to say that she *did* know Finn for who she really was, but that had been wounded pride, and the fact that she wasn't getting what she wanted, which was more. More information, more of anything where Finn was concerned. Just more Finnegan, plain and simple.

But she wouldn't have been lying, exactly, either, and that realization caused her heart to skip oddly as she reexamined the situation.

Finn, who couldn't even get through ten minutes without revealing herself in some quiet way. Finn, who was so filled with humor and quick wit that Casey could barely get through the same amount of time without wanting to kiss her, without wanting to run her hands through that lovely mess of hair, which she still had yet to do.

Ten minutes, really, without wanting to give Finn everything she might wish to take. And maybe five more after that, without becoming desperate for Finn's weight on top of her. Finnegan, who was the loveliest of mysteries, yet might tell her everything with just a glance.

Oh God. No. Absolutely not, Casey, don't do this, not now...

Casey reached for her coffee in an abrupt manner and her cup tipped to the side, though she caught it neatly before it could fall from its small saucer. "Shit."

Malik didn't look up, but Casey could see his sudden smile.

"Don't be so smug, Kaseem." She wiped at her hand with a napkin. "You two can play cat and mouse, that's fine, I'm game," she challenged. "But the smart money says as soon as I walk out that door? Neither one of you will ever see me again."

"We have nothing on you, that's true," Malik countered, and he met her eyes with sudden confidence. Behind it, however, Casey could see her words had made him panic. "We can't prove you've committed any crime, except maybe your fondness for changing lanes in the intersection. Finn says you have the Rembrandt sketch for *The Prodigal Son*, but we can't prove it, and that's not why we're here anyway."

Casey reined in her smile before it could reach her lips. "Yes, of course not, the money is of no interest to you. How much would that be, anyway? A paltry two hundred thousand for you? Two fifty?"

"That would be great, but it would be a bonus. It's not the prize."

There it is, thank you, Malik.

Casey calculated the angles in an efficient, logical manner.

He really had no idea that she was in possession of a Van Gogh, and not just any Van Gogh either. If they weren't after the Rembrandt bounty, then they were playing a much deeper game, a game that most likely had no connection to Eric Werner. If Finn knew she had the Rembrandt and had followed her track because of it, instead of cashing out, she was after the auction itself.

"You're after one of the buyers." He didn't confirm her suspicion, but his expression was close enough to an affirmation for her to make the leap with just a stretch of her legs. "How can she be certain they'll show?"

Malik's eyes gave a defiant flash. He knew what he'd said. "Who?"

"Whoever you're after."

"That's Finn's call. That's her magic, the magical big picture."

Casey made a soft sound within her throat, unable to stop her grin. "Don't be too sure about that. Maybe you don't know her as well as you think you do."

"You don't think she has magic?"

"That's not what I said."

"Listen, we can dance around the—"

"Who are you after?" Casey could almost hear the debate taking place within his head.

He didn't answer her.

"Are you in love with her?" Casey already knew he was married. She knew, as well, that he had a child on the way. Her sources were very thorough and she had no reason to doubt her information.

"Good God, no, she's family." His tone was amused but sincere.

"Who are you after?"

"The details of a job are not for me to say. But I wanted you to know…"

She liked him, and she could see why Finn did. He was trying to help Finn and yet not betray her, and while trying to protect her from someone he really didn't approve of. *Well, I did hold a gun to his head. I did that. He's got a point.*

"I wanted you to know, that for the past six or seven months there's been—"

"A boring lack of naughtiness?" Casey cut in smoothly.

It wasn't the first time she'd been tracked, although she was extremely disturbed she'd never caught on. One of her greatest assets was a sixth sense for knowing when she was in danger, and she hadn't felt a damn thing, no warning at all. It was time to get out while she still could. She'd been right about that much, anyway.

Malik's earlier words came back to her as if he'd described a sin she could not atone for. Finn had heard her making love to Abigail, and Casey's stomach churned in an ugly, slow burn sort of way that made her regret the coffee. *Although I suppose* fucking *Abigail would be a more accurate description. Richard Burton in a bloody goddamn rowboat.*

"I wanted you to know she's been your friend." He countered her acerbity with quiet conviction. "I know the idea of being watched, of having your movements tracked if even for a short time, it can feel like a dark thing, a violation."

"That's one way of putting it."

"But there wasn't a day that went by when I didn't see Finn consider that, and how it might affect you."

Casey waited several seconds. "So she's your cousin, right?"

"My mother's sister's daughter, yeah," Malik answered, keeping up.

Casey's attitude softened at his response. "I'm going to get up now and leave, Mr. Kaseem, and you're going to wait about ten minutes before doing the same. Finn will know where I am. There's no need for you to waste the rest of your evening."

"Where are you going to be?"

"Well, I won't be calling my pregnant wife, like you should be. I won't be asking her how she is, and telling her how much I love her for carting my progeny about for nine months."

Malik's face registered shock at her statement and the blush was furious upon his cheeks.

"Have you bought her something yet? Something sweet and romantic? Something just for her, and not the baby. Something for your lover, Malik, and no one else."

Malik was truly stricken, though she was uncertain as to the exact cause. She certainly owed him one or two—she knew that much.

"It doesn't feel very nice, does it…someone prying into your business, someone knowing where your soft spots are. Someone knowing things about you and your life, which they have no right to know."

"No," Malik answered, and his voice was tinged with warning. "It doesn't."

"Or are you just pissed that yo[u] forgot to buy her a present?"

"Can it be both?"

Casey slid across the seat, stoo[d], and pulled a pen from the inner pocket of her leather jacket. She le[an]ed over the table and grabbed a clean napkin.

"Man, she's gonna kill me." H[e'] d given up the goods, or at least a significant part of them, and he w[a]s fully realizing what that might mean. "She's gonna bloody well kil[l] ne."

"No, she won't." Casey glance[d] up. "She won't, don't worry. Go here," she added as she wrote. "Ask [f]or Gretchen, tell her your wife is pregnant." Casey held out the napk[in] and he took it. "And take your wallet. You're going to need it."

"My wife, she won't like anyth[in]g, um, anything that's too—"

"Wicked?" Casey smiled. *Peri[sh] the thought.* "Tell her Samantha Drake sent you. She'll fix you up. Ju[st] trust me on this one, okay?"

"I didn't mean—"

"I know what you meant," Ca[se]y said as she turned away. She adjusted the airsoft 9 mm at the sm[al]l of her back and then aired her jacket straight with a snap. Her smil[e] felt dangerous as she moved, and she liked it. "You weren't wrong."

CHAPTER FOURTEEN

"Christ, Jack." Casey's face contorted at the bitter taste. "How can you *not* find a decent cup of coffee in San Francisco?"

Jack smiled before he took a sip from his own cup, careful not to burn his lips as he did so. "Everyone has a special skill."

Casey let out a snort of laughter. "I didn't know making women cry was considered a skill these days."

"We travel in different circles."

"At least you always manage to pinch a lovely ride." She ran her gloved hand along the soft leather interior of the door. The Shelby GT350 was a thing of beauty, and Casey was extremely curious as to how it handled at a high speed.

"I can make men cry, too."

Casey laughed. "I thought you—"

"There she is." Jack gestured with his coffee. "The tall one with—"

"I know what she looks like," Casey interrupted, and her gaze was intense as she scanned the parking lot across the street. The fire doors of the Flores Club were open to the colored lights for a few moments as five men and Finnegan Starkweather exited into the back lot. Casey leaned forward. "A busy Friday night."

Finn wore a pair of faded Levi's and a white T-shirt beneath a long leather duster that brushed against the backs of her calves. The cuffs of her jeans were caught on the turned-out collars of her combat boots, and her hair was a hot mess that made Casey smile.

"The one in the really shitty suit, that's Ammon Richter," Jack informed her. "He's on half a dozen watch lists for suspected domestic terrorism. Those are his goons—the big one is Joseph Edmons. As far as I could find out, he's a convicted felon currently wanted for murder in Alabama. I didn't have much tin , though, so I'd say he probably has more up his sleeve."

Casey digested his words, an then disagreed with spirit. "The hell you say, Jack! I've only been g᷍ ᴇ for a *day*."

His expression was amused. ᴐon't ask me, Casey." His eyes returned to the lot and he nodded in the distance. "Ask her."

Casey's pulse revved into a ha᷍ ᴇr beat as she followed his gaze.

"She seems to have superior ᴦganizational skills. Sort of like throwing together the perfect tea pa ᴠ at the last minute."

Everything was in motion bef ᴇ she could even respond to his comment, and a small push of air b ᴡ through her lips instead of the words she'd been planning to say.

Edmons had grabbed Finn froᴦ behind, but his assault didn't last long as Finn used his weight again᷍ him. His scream could be heard as he went to his knees and his riᵷ t elbow bent the wrong way by about ninety degrees. Finn yanked h ᴀ forward and her knee connected with his chin. He hit the pavement l ᴇ a bag of cement, and the others reacted.

Finn was already on the moᴠ as their bodies converged on a central point, which happened to be ᴇr, and the violence that followed happened far too quickly for Casey ᴠ follow.

"Finn," Casey said in a startlec ᴠoice, unable to stop it.

A muffled gunshot popped intᴏ he night, followed by two more.

Casey's shoulders jerked and ᴏffee spilled onto her glove. She was vaguely aware that Jack took tɦ cup from her hand, but his touch seemed a thousand miles away.

Time spun much too slowly fo the music her heart played, and a dense wave of emotion washed oveᴦ ᴇr. She knew right then and there that it was a dance she would never ᴦn down, no matter what she told herself. The fear that came with that ᴢalization, as Finn's jacket swung to the side and she stepped free of thᴇ ɴelee in a sleek arc of movement, was held tightly within the hard, wᴏ ɪless sound she made.

Finn stood with her right arm ᴏutstretched, the muzzle of what appeared to be a 9 mm resting agai᷍ ᴛ Ammon Richter's forehead. His entourage was in tatters, Edmons dᴏ ᴠn along with two others. One of them crawled toward the apparent sᴀ ᴇty of the Flores Club, though the doors were closed against him.

"Drop your cocks and grab yoᴜ socks," Jack whispered.

Casey's mind shifted beyond ᴇ immediate shock of the truth, and the angles tipped out before hᴇ a map of neon lines that hissed beneath the collision of electrons. She glanced over her left shoulder and down the street.

There were two vans parked a block away and very little foot traffic—none, in fact, in the immediate area. There were several parked cars, including Jack's new Shelby, though for a Friday night within walking distance of a decent club, the empty spaces she saw belonged more to the realm of fantasy than reality.

She turned back to the action and Richter's bodyguard had opened the trunk of a black Lexus. He pulled a bag out, turned, and tossed the heavy canvas at Finn's feet.

Finn took a step back, shoved the gun beneath the waistband of her jeans, and reached into her jacket.

Richter stared at the small bag Finn held out and then he grabbed it with a greedy hand.

He moved quickly and so did the remaining bodyguard, both men getting into the Lexus with very little fanfare and even less concern for their fallen comrades. Finn waited as the car started and the brake lights flooded her in red before they pulled forward with a jerk of horsepower. Finn picked up the duffel, turned, and walked away, stepping over Joseph Edmons without a second glance. The Lexus cleared the lot with a push and fishtailed onto the street.

Casey moved the rearview mirror and watched as both vans came to life, the one facing east pulling out first. "You have to dump the car."

"Yeah." Jack found the side mirror. "Good thing it isn't mine."

Finn buttoned her coat with her left hand and rounded the corner of the club. She was alive, but Casey could see she wasn't finished. When Jack reached for the door Casey grabbed his jacket sleeve. "Wait."

Finn wiped at her face, and though she was still a fair distance away, Casey could see the blood as she stepped into the street and stopped.

The black SUV that peeled around the corner appeared to be more of a danger to Finn than Joseph Edmons had ever been, though Finn didn't shy away from the vehicle, either. The SUV came to a hard stop but a few feet away from her, all four doors swinging open in unison as the car jerked into park.

"We're not gonna get outta here," Jack said in a tight voice. Sirens wailed in the distance and he glanced back between the seats. "Colin's NSA goons are everywhere, and there's gonna be an assload of cops here in about two minutes."

"Give it a second, okay?"

The man who approached Fin was shorter than she was but he was broad and beefy in a way that m le up for it. He smiled and spoke, but Finn's only response was to toss e bag at this feet. The man cocked his head to the side and they stared one another.

"A pissing contest," Jack mum ed beneath his breath. "Lovely." Finn was livid and Casey coulc ee her rage even from a distance. Whatever had gone down, for wha ver reason, Finn had been left to fend for herself.

The man reached into his nav blue suit and pulled an envelope free, the manila packet thick within s hand.

The entire scenario didn't sit w l with Casey, but she knew a bad play when she saw one. If he was c ering Finn her promised payday, she should grab it and not look bac . "Take it, Finn," she whispered, her nerves more frayed by this new ncounter than they had been but a few moments before. The sirens v re getting louder, maybe three or four blocks south, perhaps a bit mor

Finn wiped at her face again, to k the envelope, and walked away without saying a word.

"Wait for the ambulance," Cas said to Jack. "Wait until they're right on you, and then move. We'll leet up at Mabelle's. I'll call you with a time."

"Roger that," Jack agreed. "A if it's all the same to you, leave your badass girlfriend at home, oka "

"Don't be such a pussy, Jack,' Casey shot back with a grin. She stepped to the curb and the door c sed with a soft whoosh, but no more. With three quick strides she v s in the shadows, and within half a block she was taking the first alle she came to. She spared a glance over her shoulder as a parade of p ice cruisers filled the night with light and noise.

❖

Casey studied the lock for a bri moment and then pulled a square leather wallet from the inside pocke f her jacket. She popped the snap and considered the leads available her. The Schlage Camelot had a keypad, and if she couldn't short it, e couldn't pick the dead bolt with the tools she had with her.

"Shit."

The case disappeared back int er jacket and her eyes narrowed upon the keys. She was no longer u n the current models, but rolling through ten thousand combinations was not how she wanted to spend the rest of her evening. *I want to be inside*, she thought, *going through her things... without her permission.* Casey took the half step needed and leaned her shoulder against the door frame.

She felt very small at the thought and yet she had no idea how else she might find out what she wanted to know. She remembered very well what Malik had said earlier in the evening, and the fact that Finn had never violated the sanctity of her own personal space was suddenly a thorn in her side. She had never been that sort of thief and she knew it. Asher would be ashamed of her.

She ran a finger along the edge of the lock. *Finnegan.*

"Two."

Casey turned to her right and Finn stood at the top of the stairs, perhaps ten feet away.

She was badass up close, just as Jack had said, though he could not have seen how pale she was, or hear the exhaustion in that single word. Casey wanted to say something clever, but her pulse popped and her stomach flipped like a coin whose final landing face was still a mystery. She felt it in her legs as she pushed away from the door and stood on her own, a weak shiver in her muscles as if she'd just finished a run.

Finn approached and Casey's head tipped back, her eyes locking on to Finn's as she moved in that sleek way a cat does when they spot something tasty.

Finn invaded her space and stopped only when their clothes touched.

Casey lost sight of the details within the shadows but she could smell the remains of Finn's cologne, so faded that it was almost gone now, and the leather of her coat. The metallic scent of gunpowder was present, as well. She could smell the residue of Finn's weapon.

Casey's priorities changed in an instant, but should she ask, her advantage would be gone and Finn would know she was being watched. No matter what she might feel, the game was still in play and she had staked her future on the outcome.

Finn took hold of Casey's waist and it was all Casey could do not to react as she wanted, not to tip forward in a wave of heat and submission. She held to her mettle and Finn came to her, without invitation or hesitation. Finn's thighs brushed close and her mouth pushed through the loose curls of Casey's hair. "Two."

Finn's lips brushed against the lobe of Casey's right ear and Casey took hold of Finn's lapel with her right hand. With her left, Casey pressed the number two on the keypad.

"Another two, and a seven..." Finn's breath was warm against her neck. "Another seven. Two. Six..." Her lips skated over the soft skin behind Casey's ear, and Casey let out a strained breath, swallowed and licked her lips. "Three."

Casey saw the pattern and held her breath as her fingers completed the sequence without a prompt. *Seven. Two.*

The keypad turned green and the bolt slid open.

Casey closed her eyes as her hand hovered above the numbers. *Cassandra.*

Finn's hand slid to the small of Casey's back and her fingers dipped beneath the waist of Casey's jeans. Casey pulled her body against Finn's as her stomach filled with wings. She was afraid to look up, although she wasn't sure why. Finn's mouth swept lightly across her ear once more and Casey found her voice.

"That's either the most bizarely romantic thing that's ever happened to me...or I'm going to have to read up on the benefits of a restraining order."

Finn chuckled near her ear, the sound filled with appreciation. "Don't worry, I changed it yesterday. I expected you sooner, Casey Marinos."

Casey opened her eyes as her heart jackhammered and then her head fell back at the supple kiss along her jaw. Finn's whisper filled her head. "I've missed you."

Casey's hands moved of their own accord and sank within the strands of Finn's wild hair, Casey voicing a moan of profound and infinite satisfaction. Finn's hair was as soft as silk and honestly heavy, its blackness reaching out and pulling at everything within its immediate orbit, a celestial event all its own. It had been about twenty-four hours since Finn had last seen her, *Which isn't so long, maybe... though maybe it's been a lifetime. Because it feels like forever, since I've last been seen.*

She recognized the ironic amusement within her chest, a dark humor that was pointed squarely in her own direction. To be so enamored of another woman was way way beyond her current capacity for accepting new and exciting things, and she knew it. She couldn't help it, though, and she knew that, as well. *Fuck it.* Her voice, when it finally arrived, was as unburdened by caution as she could ever remember. "Finnegan, where in the hell have you been?" Her arms went about Finn's neck as Finn's lips covered hers, soft and wet with heat. She opened her mouth to Finn's tongue and Finn took what she offered.

Casey's sense of touch seemed to expand to its limits and then rupture, awakening in a rush of irresistible sensations. She could feel everything with a high intensity she hadn't expected, and all her fears fell before the flood, washed beneath it and swept away.

Her clothes were rough against her skin, out of place as they formed a barrier against Finn's body. She could feel the heat and strength of Finn's presence, her thighs pressing and the muscles of her arms. Finn's face was soft and her breasts were small but full, slightly above Casey's as Finn pulled her close. Finn's hands were filled with heat, her fingers opening as they slipped beneath the fabric of Casey's shirt.

Their mouths spoke with supple sounds, a language that the most primal part of her being understood with absolute clarity. Each breath that she pulled in through her nose was filled with Finn's scent, a unique fusion of life, leather, faded cologne, and sexual need. It soaked through Casey's tissues, and Finn's want was mirrored in the thick, heavy pulse that swelled through the flesh between her legs.

Finn leaned down as her hands moved with strength along Casey's butt and thighs, and Casey pulled in a quick breath as she opened her legs and Finn lifted her up. Casey dug her fingers into the thick leather at Finn's shoulders and leaned into the kiss, liking the change in angle as her back eased against the wall and Finn stepped between her legs.

Finn's pelvis pressed against her and Casey let out a gasp as she wrapped her legs around Finn's hips. Her thighs tightened and her muscles clenched down the length of her legs as she hooked one ankle beneath the other. She pulled her right hand back and took hold of Finn's face as she sealed their kiss. *Too far, too far, go back*, she thought in a panic and leaned back in. Her mouth brushed against Finn's lips as she spoke. "Open the door."

Finn reached with her right hand and Casey kissed her again, a thrill of excitement and arousal sparking through her body. They were moving and the air changed around her as they entered the loft and cleared the entrance, the heavy door swinging shut behind them. Finn's kiss was filled with soul, and a fierce need which Casey fed, her tongue going deep as her left hand reached over Finn's shoulder. She clutched at the leather beneath her palm and g⋯ bbed hold with a desperate grasp, the smooth, aged material submittin⋯ to her will.

"You taste…" Casey felt a bit ⋯zzy as she freed her mouth from Finn's. She ran her thumb along Finn⋯ lower lip and her thighs clenched at the slick remains of their kiss. He⋯ ex ached with a terrible, glorious weight. "Like whiskey and cherries.

"You taste like my dreams."

Casey searched Finn's eyes f⋯ a motive behind the words, or anything else that might disprove s⋯ ch a tenderly spoken admission, but she saw nothing other than a p⋯ sionate honesty that ripped right through her. She also saw somethi⋯ that wasn't right, though it had nothing to do with trust.

Her fingers trembled against ⋯he pliant skin of Finn's mouth and she almost laughed. She never ⋯embled. "I need to see you," she whispered. "I want to see your eyes ⋯etter, please."

Finn turned and they steppe⋯ around a table, or perhaps an ottoman, Casey wasn't entirely su⋯ and she really didn't care. Her feet touched the floor before Finn ⋯epped away, and Casey reached out with the unexpected need to sti⋯ be touching her, surprised by the flutter of panic within her chest. Fin⋯ ⋯eached back without looking and Casey grabbed hold of her hand.

Warm light surrounded them w⋯ ⋯ a click and Casey stepped close, her hands upon Finn's coat as Finn t⋯ ned. Her fingers slid along Finn's chest and then swept beneath the la⋯ ls, lifting the heavy leather. Finn shrugged and the coat piled onto the⋯ loor at their feet.

Casey stepped against her, lik⋯ g the silhouette of Finn's sports bra beneath the white of her T-shirt⋯ ⋯er touch was gentle upon Finn's cheek.

Finn's left eye held a hemorrh⋯ e of blood, as deep and bright as heart's blood as it spread out from th⋯ ⋯mber of her iris. Its presence was startling, and Casey's touch floated ⋯ove Finn's eyebrow. There were the smallest of stitches within the ⋯ ⋯ft hair, definitely three, perhaps four. It was good work, she could s⋯ that much, but the swollen flesh would be worse with the morning su⋯ .

She hadn't seen the punch, but⋯ he knew what had happened and the violence that Finn had encoun⋯ ⋯ed. She knew it and she would have to lie.

"Baby," she whispered, and fel⋯ ⋯n unexpected joy upon speaking the endearment.

A decent amount of dried bloo⋯ stained the front of Finn's white tee, and as Casey surveyed Finn's upper body, she saw the bruising on her left arm as well, the rise of blood beneath the skin from someone's violent handprint. She took off her own jacket and tossed it onto a nearby chair before she met Finn's gaze. "What else is there?"

"I'm all right, Casey, I promise."

"You don't look all right."

"I feel pretty good at the moment."

Casey favored her with an unguarded smile. "I won't ask about the other guy."

"That might be best," Finn agreed.

"You're a bloody boatload of trouble—I knew it when I first laid eyes on you."

"Maybe a dinghy full, but that's it."

Casey laughed softly. "How much have you had to drink?"

"Only a little bit."

"You don't really drink that much, do you." Casey was oddly certain of her words.

"Not really."

"If you think I'm going to take advantage of you, you're wrong." Casey's voice was filled with conviction, though her body had other ideas. *You're so full of shit, Marinos.*

Finn stepped close and slid her hands about Casey's waist. Her fingers pulled the rest of Casey's shirt free and slipped beneath to the skin. Finn kissed her and Casey went to her, her hands fisting hard in the stained cotton of Finn's tee. Finn's hand slid beneath the waistband of Casey's jeans and Casey caught her breath as Finn cupped her ass with strength, her mouth opening against Finn's.

Casey grabbed the back of Finn's neck. "If you start, I don't want any complaining later," she managed as Finn's hand moved up, and then slipped back down beneath her briefs. Her fingers opened on the heat of Casey's bare skin.

"I'm done with that."

Casey found it hard to breathe. "With what?"

"With waiting," Finn answered as she lifted her up and they moved. The wide couch was at Casey's back with a gentle drop and a whoosh of movement, and then Finn was above her.

"Oh, thank Christ," Casey moaned as she opened her legs and pulled Finn down.

Finn settled against her and her pelvis thrust as Casey lifted her hips in greeting. Her thighs tightened about Finn's and Finn kissed

her, Casey's hands greedy as they sl   l beneath Finn's tee. The muscles
of Finn's back moved against her   uch, and Casey moaned as Finn
opened her mouth farther.

Finn's hand went between them   nd Casey lifted from the cushions
in order to maintain their kiss, her   iirt open as she felt the touch of
Finn's fingers between her breasts.

The catch of her bra was relea   ed and Casey arched against her
as the heat of Finn's mouth closed u   on her left nipple. Casey let out a
harsh breath at the pressure and pull   f Finn's mouth, the fleeting touch
of her teeth, and the roughness of Fi   's tongue. Her legs tightened and
stretched out as a quiver of pleasu   shook along her clit, her hands
fisting in Finn's hair as her world wa   sent spinning beyond her control.

Finn felt the heat beneath he   hands and a thousand moments
collided within her thoughts. The t   te of her was overwhelming, the
tender flesh of Casey's nipple, tight   d hard beneath her tongue, it was
too much.

Long days spent beneath the   rench summer sun, days spent
wanting and watchful as she fell ir   ove. Her quiet calm at knowing
Casey was close and safe, just be   nd the darkness that seemed to
follow Finn like a fortune-teller's cu   se. All her bottled-up passion and
longing, it hurtled past her fears an   doubts and spilled over into their
new reality.

Finn lifted up and yanked at he   T-shirt and bra, desperate as they
slid up her chest, just far enough fo   vhat she needed.

"*Yes*, baby," Casey urged, and   ew her down once more.

Finn moaned as their breasts   ame together, her hips thrusting
smoothly as she reclaimed their ki   . Casey cried out within Finn's
mouth and submitted, her thighs tigl   ning around Finn as they moved.
Finn shifted her position and reache   etween them, her hand certain of
its course as she popped the button c   Casey's jeans. The zipper opened
as she slid her hand beneath Casey'   lothes and eased into the heart of
what she wanted.

Casey pulled back from their   ss and Finn's blood slowed, just
a little, as Casey held her face. Her   yes were dark and filled with so
much life and promise, Finn wasn't   uite sure what she could say that
would explain how she felt. The fev   within her blood ebbed, though,
and eased from its frenzy of want in   a stronger, even sweeter place.

"Casey," she whispered, and h   hand stilled within the heat and
silken hair.

Casey pushed up and kissed her.

Finn slid her fingers along the wet and swollen flesh and Casey cried out softly in response. The neck of Finn's T-shirt stretched and pulled and Finn felt her destiny slip to the side and fall.

Each breath that Casey took was sharp and quick through her nose as each pull of life raced downward. She clenched her muscles tightly and tried to stave it off, but the hard wave of pleasure that surged upward was desperate for release as Finn slid her touch inside. She cried out as Finn's fingers moved, her palm strong and persuasive against Casey's flesh in firm, quick strokes. It was too much and Casey's muscles stretched as everything tightened. "Finnegan," she said, and her voice broke upon the name.

Casey convulsed as she came, hard and fast, her cry of pleasure spent beside Finn's mouth as she lifted against the knowing touch. Her muscles closed around Finn's strong fingers and Finn's tongue was in her mouth. Casey was desperate for a breath as a second wave of pleasure crashed hard upon the heels of the first.

She pulled her mouth from Finn's with a gasp, the skin beneath her hands damp and dense with muscle as Casey arched and her body jerked, the abandon with which she felt her satisfaction crushing all other sensations until her need was satisfied.

Her chest filled with warmth as Finn kissed her and Casey responded, her arms holding on as tightly as she could as her tears welled up and slipped free.

Her body seemed to disappear into the cushions beneath her, and she felt her orgasm slip and vibrate into a low hum of luxury as Finn's hand slid along her belly. It was wet and hot and it caused a warm tremble along her spine.

She smiled against Finn's mouth, wrapped her legs about one of Finn's, and moved against her with a slow, sweet push that Finn returned. A small but potent aftershock quivered through her flesh and she opened her mouth against Finn's cheek. She let her lips linger against the soft skin of her new lover's face, though only for a moment. "Finnegan."

She dug her hands within Finn's hair and pulled her as close as she could. She sucked at Finn's earlobe and then let out a soft laugh of satisfaction, thankful for Finn's body on top of hers. Everything trembled upon the edge of forever, and she had no idea what that might mean. "Wherever have you been?"

"Casey." Finn considered the question as she drifted within the moment.

The taste of Casey's kiss was in her mouth. The quality of her flesh, and the soft, intimate texture, the hot milk that clung to her fingers, these things were hers now. Each sensation held its own distinctive force and throbbed within Finn's own flesh. The smell of their bodies together, and the subtle scent of spent pleasure. Casey's cries of satisfaction had been her doing, and it threw her senses into a place she had never been able to truly fathom or recover from easily. Perhaps because she had known so little of its power.

Finn was wet with need, and she hovered just beyond her own fulfillment as Casey pulled back and their eyes met.

The memory of the first gunshot filled Finn's head without warning, the cold echo a harsh counterpoint to the warm heartbeat that pumped within her chest. Her stitches seemed to burn with the recollection and her left ear rang oddly, still in pain. *Another half inch, and someone else would be holding you.*

"Finn?" Casey asked, and there was a keen edge of concern within her voice.

Finn reeled in her thoughts and tied them down. "I'm very tired."

Casey's eyes filled with warmth as she held Finn's face, and it was a balm against the new memories so near the surface. "I know," Casey whispered, and then kissed her, a tender kiss that lingered through the slowing of Finn's heartbeat. Casey's thumb trailed along Finn's lower lip, her eyes happy as they followed its progress. She whispered something that Finn couldn't hear.

"You won't leave?"

"No," Casey answered and guided her to the side with a gentle push. Finn tipped against the back of the couch and sank onto the cushions beneath them both, Casey moving with her and staying close. She pulled Finn's bra and T-shirt back down and smoothed at the abused material with the lift of a skeptical eyebrow. "We have unfinished business, you and I."

Finn struggled to keep her eyes open. She hadn't realized how much her head hurt.

"I want you inside me, Finnegan Starkweather, when you come." Casey's softly spoken words were filled with promise.

Finn's startled laughter bubbled upward and Casey's eyes lit up when the sound of it took flight in the air between them. "Casey," Finn said simply. *I love you.*

Their legs tangled together in an easy manner as Casey's mouth brushed against Finn's. A small thrill shuddered at the base of Finn's neck.

"Go to sleep, baby."

CHAPTER FIFTEEN

Casey moved through the loft in silence, her jeans low upon her hips and her button-down shirt untucked. Her socks slid along the hardwood floor, and she indulged the childish whim because she felt safe to do so.

The light within the loft was glorious, and what she hadn't seen the night before was exposed to her in all its wonder with the morning sun.

There were hundreds of books, books everywhere, old books and new books and books in glass cases. There were stacks of books and graphic novels, and comic books that appeared to be worthy of an appraisal. There was a signed book on a beautifully carved mantelpiece, *V* by Thomas Pynchon, signed, *To my Ailish, this is the proper shit, with love, Ruggles*. It was a British first edition.

"Ailish," Casey whispered and set it back down. She smiled that the mantelpiece was built around yet another bookcase.

There were pictures on the top shelf, and the photo of Finn as a teenager in a school baseball uniform filled her with pleasure. She ran her fingers along the glass for a moment and then set it back, picking up the one beside it. Finn in a football uniform. *Tight end, indeed.*

The picture farthest to the left was older, but the man who owned the space within the frame was a near carbon copy to Finn. His hair was just as black and just as out of control, but it was his eyes that caught her attention. They were the exact same amber color, deep and filled with the same vitality Casey had seen in Finn. He was rough around the edges and gorgeous and he could be no one else but her father. His soft, open expression showed his femininity, and he wore it as easily as his manhood. Casey wondered if he was an artist, for he looked the part. Finn walked between two worlds, as well, and though she did it with confidence and style, Casey suspected that Finn's neighborhood had been a rougher place to traverse.

She remembered Finn's touch inside her and she smiled an impish smile, entirely for her own benefit. She knew exactly what her fears were and they hadn't changed much since she had woken up, but she also hadn't felt so alive in years.

Casey spun upon the balls of her feet and walked toward the bank of windows on the west wall. There was a workout area in the corner, with free weights scattered upon the mat, weights that looked as if they were biding their time until they might cause the maximum amount of pain.

The ceiling was vaulted and finished, and the eggshell-colored fans that hung down complemented the color of the brick walls. There were stairs on the opposite end of the loft, and a full kitchen that flowed out from the space beneath them and into the living area.

She wondered about the bed upstairs, and the thought of sharing it with Finn made her stomach toss over in a lovely manner. That particular mystery, however, was not quite as tantalizing at the moment as how Finn came to be in possession of such an exquisite, expansive space. *Especially in one of the most miserly cities in the world, at least where real estate is concerned.*

Casey stopped at the french doors and considered the lock. The open air terrace just beyond offered a gorgeous view of the surrounding blocks.

"Casey."

Casey closed her eyes at the sound of Finn's voice. She licked her lips and smiled as her hair fell forward. A shimmy of pleasure moved through her stomach and deep into her thighs, and her nipples became hard. *This is just terrible, it really is…*

"I thought you had left."

Casey spun around.

Finn stood near the mantelpiece and she seemed a thousand miles away. Casey considered Finn's hair first, and then she went to her face, an unexpected wave of distress pushing back at her happiness as she closed the distance between them.

Casey's left hand took possession of a belt loop on Finn's jeans, while her right lifted in a confident manner. The backs of her fingers brushed against Finn's cheek, her touch careful upon the bruised flesh. Finn's eyebrow was swollen and so was the lid, though not enough to close her eye. The bleed had spread and Casey wanted none of it, because the stippling upon the skin and the crease within her eyebrow were decidedly *not* what she had thought they were in the late night shadows, with Finn's mouth on hers. It was not just a bruise.

Three shots, Casey reasoned. *Two men down, and the third shot... no, it was the first shot.*

"I thought you'd left." Finn smiled in a guileless manner.

"No," Casey answered with a grin of her own, unable to stop it. "I told you I wouldn't."

"I know."

"I know, but...?"

"But I'm sure you're busy," Finn replied with care.

"I'm sure I am."

Finn's eyes sparked. "Why are you mad?"

The real truth of Finn's injuries was new to her, and before she could put it into a neat little box and address the ramifications at a later date and time, reality popped her in the mouth with a closed fist. "Did you get shot in the head?"

Finn blinked at her, startled.

"You were shot in the fucking head, Finn," Casey accused with barely contained outrage. She stepped back to maintain a physical distance, if not perspective.

"Oh, well, wait now," Finn started. "I wasn't really—"

"I was *there*, Finn—I saw it." Casey interrupted. "And I don't care who you are or what you used to do, only a fool plays those kind of odds. Whatever that was, it was a total clusterfuck and you know it!"

"No, I didn't like it either," Finn agreed in a rational voice. "But I also wouldn't say I was shot in the head."

"No?" Casey fired back. "That not a gunshot wound?"

"Not exactly."

"Not exactly?"

"No."

"No?"

Finn's pleased expression was filled with unexpected warmth. "Stop repeating what I say, Marinos—

"I'm adding the question marks, Starkweather. You seem uncertain."

"O'Connell."

Casey started to speak and then stopped. "What?"

"My real name is O'Connell."

Casey considered the statement for a moment and then she was moving. "Oh, for fuck's sake, Finn." She brushed past her and stalked to the couch. "Do you think I give a damn what your real name is?" She slid across the floor and grabbed Finn's coat from where it had fallen the night before. She looked up as she dug within the inner pockets and her eyes narrowed in warning. "Although if you tell me your name isn't Finnegan? You better save last night in a special place, because you'll never get that close again."

Finn smiled. "No, that one's right."

Casey pulled the thick manila envelope free, dropped the duster, and ripped at the seal. "That's good. Moaning out the wrong name as I'm getting fucked has never been high on my list of things to do."

"Not much fun for the other person either, I suspect."

Casey smiled, the expression arriving completely against her will. The sound of traitorous laughter was in her voice, as well. "Don't even start."

The passports fell into her hand as she dropped the envelope.

They were American, and they were real, or they were the best damn forgeries she had ever seen. She did not have the impression, however, that the National Security Agency dealt in forged passports. "What sort of deal did you cut?" She tried to put the pieces together. The first passport was for Sahir Hamdan, and he was Syrian, as were the others. "What the hell are you doing, Finn?"

"Finishing a bargain I struck two years ago."

Casey studied her face with every ounce of deductive reasoning she could muster before she'd had her first cup of coffee. "Malik."

Finn nodded. "His cousin's family. They ran from Homs and wound up in Jordan. They fled without their papers and now they're in Zaatari, with no way out. His cousin, Sahir, was a teacher of Western poetry and literature. When the shabiha came for him, they ran." Finn gestured to the documents Casey held. "There's one for his wife, and one each for their three children. Those papers give them full political asylum. As of yesterday, they're official citizens of the United States of America."

Casey stared at her, uncertain of how she should proceed with this new information. "And you got shot in the head for these?"

"Only a little bit." Finn admitted. "I was more than content at the bookstore, debating the finer points of good literature, all while wanting you so badly that I popped something in the back of my brain. Something I'm fairly certain I'll need at a later date, by the way, but they called me. I thought the deal had died over a year ago, at least. It was the last call I ever expected. I jumped as high as they told me to—I admit it."

"Does Malik know what you were doing?" Casey asked, though she was fairly certain he had no idea. *He was too interested in looking out for your heart, Finn, instead of keeping your fine ass out of real trouble.*

Finn looked a bit sheepish. "N "

"Why you?"

"It was a crime of opportunity. if you will. I still had the contacts that would get me close." Finn made face of discontent as she debated her words. "Close to the guy you—'

"Ammon Richter?"

"Jesus." Finn frowned and her right shoulder came up slightly. "You're gonna get nailed if you aren careful."

Casey laughed. She'd had enough. *A fucking Boy Scout...sort of.* Casey considered the ways in which Finn had touched her the night before, and then she considered what might come next. *A fucking badass, sort of almost a Boy Scout... kay, not a Boy Scout at all. Jesus, we're never gonna get out of here in one piece.* She found the thought oddly pleasing as she let her eyes wander over her newly poured tall drink of water.

Finn's lips curled to the side in a sly grin that Casey had never seen from her before, and then she was on the move.

Finn's body language was likely a bit more mercenary than she understood it to be, but Casey had no plans to inform her of that fact. It was almost lupine in nature, and her natural fierceness could be seen even when it was not her dominant emotion. Casey's lips parted slightly as a spear of anticipation sliced through her.

"Has anyone ever told you how sweet your lower lip tastes?" Finn's voice was ever so soft as she stood but a few inches away.

"Don't change the subject," Casey managed.

"It tastes like plum brandy on a summer's night in June," Finn continued, ignoring her with a flash of rebellion in her eyes. "Slivovitz, made from the damson plums that grow in the hills, north of the White City. You may pick them early in the morning, in the spring..."

Finn took the papers from Casey and dropped them onto the couch. "But if you try to eat them from your hand?" Finn looked down into her eyes. "They're really very tart, and they'll make you sneeze, and you think at first, I will *never* eat these again, they're really quite awful...but their color is so rich and lavish, like velvet for your eyes, that you try again when no one is looking. But your second bite is still too sour, though a fraction less cruel for having taken the first."

Casey held her breath as Finn's index finger caressed a path from one side of her lower lip to the other. She felt it between her legs in no uncertain terms.

"But in June," Finn whispered, "their taste is the fermented sweetness of laughter, the laughter of the one lover you can never forget. The one whose name shall be whispered with your last breath. It lives in small glass cups, cups that were blown within a fire that burned a hundred years ago, cups that play an F-sharp in a D scale, when they touch in a toast meant for good fortune."

Casey felt the absence of Finn's brief touch like a physical blow.

"That, Cassandra Marinos, is how your lower lip tastes."

Casey regarded her for a seriously long time before she allowed the smile that fluttered within her chest to reach her lips. She had just been on the receiving end of a poem spun out of thin air, and she knew it. And though it certainly wasn't the first time a top had tried to charm her away from her own path, by God and sonny Jesus, it was the first time it had ever fucking worked. "I swear to God, Finnegan," Casey said in promise, "if you find me a decent cup of coffee and some real french toast?"

Finn leaned close, her eyes bright with laughter. "I'll find you these things, and you'll owe me nothing." Finn's hands slipped beneath Casey's shirt and pulled her close, her fingers opening upon Casey's skin. "For you have nothing to offer me that isn't already mine for the taking."

Casey moaned as Finn's tongue opened her mouth, though it wasn't long before she was laughing in their kiss. "You're still…in so much trouble…Finnegan Whoever."

"In a sticky wicket, eh?"

"A sticky something."

CHAPTER SIXTEEN

London
March 2010

"My friend," Asher said as he rolled his smoke, "you are not listening to me."

Finn glared at him with dark eyes. "I *am* listening."

Asher smiled. "Yes, that is what my Domino always says, after which she goes and does exactly what I told her not to do. She does it, I believe, because she does not like to be ruled by another person. Her freedom is everything, but she does not understand yet that freedom is not what she thinks it is. But you will do it, because it is your nature to do what you think is right."

Finn's expression softened when she smiled. "I'm not a fucking Boy Scout."

Asher chuckled. "No, not that."

"Listen, you told me that Ketri—"

"She has big brown eyes," Asher said, ignoring her. "And they have the power to sway, oh, my sweet Lord, it is very wonderful, and terrible at the same time. Such a beautiful woman, she has the power to destroy worlds."

Finn laughed. "Thankfully, none of them are yours. You're her papa."

Asher smiled and then sealed his cigarette, tacking it down with a smooth swipe and turn of his fingers. He set it between his lips and his gold Zippo pinged and ripped, its flame rising and lighting his smoke. "No, she is my Domino. Perhaps you, Finnegan Starkweather, she would be gentle with, but I cannot guarantee it."

Finn blushed and glanced down with a strange half smile. "I don't think I'm her type."

"I am betting you are everyone's type." Asher smiled when she looked up, clearly not understanding it was a compliment. "It means you are the sort of person people want around."

Finn shrugged and Asher extended the smoke to her. "Take this—I will make another."

Finn took it and brought it to her lips.

Asher scoffed and pulled a new paper from his pack. "Everyone thinks I am only so smart."

"A carefully cultivated ruse, in my opinion."

Asher smiled and bobbed his eyebrows, glancing up. "Will you just listen, then?" He stopped his smoke and tapped at his temple with a finger. "You must listen up here." He put his hand above his heart. "Do not listen here. Do you understand what I'm saying?"

"I understand," Finn answered quietly.

"Ketrin Arshavin is not a man you fuck with. He is not even a man you run over with your car, and then go back and shoot in the head just to be safe. Because he will get up, and he will remember who ran him over and shot him so rudely, and then he will proceed to crush you and all that you love. He is the man you run from at all costs."

"Then I don't know why we're even talking," Finn argued with a frown. "You said—"

"You were looking for the man responsible for the deaths at Badovinci. That man is Ketrin Arshavin."

Finn's expression was quick and curious. "You never have told me how you knew that, by the way. How did you know I was looking for the Butcher of Badovinci?"

"Many people are looking for the Butcher. Important people, yes?"

Finn sat back in her seat, her black wool jacket stark against the red vinyl of the booth. She wanted to trust him, he could see it, but she still wasn't sure. "Yes, which begs the question, why come looking for me? I'm no one, and we both know it."

Asher lit his smoke, then moved the ashtray to the middle of the table.

"Thomasino Lazarini would pay you some very serious money for the name you've given me for free. So I have to wonder, what is it you want from me in return?"

Asher watched as Finn took a drag on her smoke. She resembled a young Alain Delon, only just…now. He sniffed a gentle laugh. "Why are young people so suspicious?"

Finn's smile was beautiful, curving the left side of her lips. "Why don't you just answer the question?"

"Do you think I wish to be mixed up with organized crime?" Asher raised his eyebrows at her. "I have enough problems."

"His money is as good as any."

Asher scoffed. "Strange thing for a detective inspector of Interpol to say."

Finn shrugged. "Well, it is—good money, I mean."

"I would like you to do me a favor, okay?"

"What is it?"

"Not now, my friend, but later."

Finn's bright eyes sparked with interest.

"It is nothing illegal," Asher assured her. "I promise you that. I would not do that."

"And you'll give me Ketrin Arshavin?"

Her eyes had become hard, and he could almost feel her heartbeat push into a deeper, darker rhythm. "No, my lovely friend," he said and watched as her eyes showed subtle surprise. "Ketrin Arshavin may be the man responsible for the deaths at Badovinci, it's true, for it was his order that was carried out. But that was like ordering a steak for Ketrin—do you see what I mean?"

"No," Finn said softly, and he could see a touch of sorrow within her eyes now.

"He orders a steak, someone brings it, and he eats it." Asher picked a bit of tobacco from his tongue as he exhaled. "The empty plate goes back to the kitchen. He does not think of where the steak came from, or who cooked it just so. He does not think of the cow that dies, or the farmer who tended the cow for many years. It is just meat on a plate and it makes him happy, because someone brought him what he wanted. He thinks no more about it."

Finn took another drag on her smoke, leaned forward, and tapped the ashes into the ashtray. Her eyes were bright with unshed tears, and for a brief moment he could feel the heat of her anger. It was gone by the time she sat back again.

"But there is always a man who finds the place which makes the best steaks in town. And he watches the chef, to make sure he is skilled at his job. If the chef is not a good cook, this man will kill the chef and do it himself. Sometimes, he will go out and kill the cow himself, if need be, or the farmer, if he does not wish to give up his cow. This man likes to do these things, because the power he craves, is not the power of Ketrin Arshavin. Ketrin Arshavin is a good master, and this man loves him.

"He loves him for several reasons, but mostly, he loves Ketrin because Ketrin does not mind if he kills the chef for merely being a bad cook. And he approves if this man kills the farmer because the farmer did not respect Ketrin enough to give up his cow. All because Ketrin wanted a steak on his plate, which he would eat and forget about, until the next time he wants a steak."

Finn's hands sat upon the table as she watched her smoke burn to ash.

Asher took up his drink and sipped at the whiskey. Finn took a drag and then leaned forward and put it out.

When she looked up, he had no idea what she was going to say. "What did you do, James, to Ketrin Arshavin, that keeps you awake at night?"

Asher nodded and set his glass down, the ice clinking softly. It was a good question and an extremely keen observation. "How do you know it keeps me up at night?"

"Because I only ever see you in the dead of night."

Asher smiled at her. "I am an old thief—these are my office hours."

"How good a thief are you?"

The question surprised him. "There is only one better."

Finn smiled, her eyes alight. "Domino?"

Asher chuckled happily. "I cannot say."

"Do you have a picture of her?"

"Yes."

"May I see it?"

"No."

Her disappointment was obvious.

"A long time ago, I took something from Ketrin that was not mine to take."

Finn's expression changed in an instant. "You *stole* from him?"

"No, I did not." Asher put out his own smoke. He reached into his jacket almost at once and pulled out his tobacco. He remembered the drive through the woods beyond Baia Mare, and his hands shook as he rolled a new smoke, just a bit, though it was enough to make him frown as it happened. He sealed the smoke and put it between his lips. "It was not his, either. He was the real thief. I merely played a part in the liberation of…of his captive trea re." He shrugged and took a deep breath. "And that is all. It is a conve ation for another day, my friend."

"If I'm not looking for Ketrin rshavin, then who *am* I looking for?"

"You will owe me a favor, yes

Finn nodded. "Yes."

"I have your word?"

"Of course. I give you my wor "

"Petar Dimitrovich is his name f Ketrin lights a fire, Dimitrovich is the match."

Finn held his eyes as she sat ba again. He could see her thinking, and he was very curious as to what might be.

"He is the *true* Butcher of B lovinci, and he is the man who makes Ketrin Arshavin, who is alre y the most dangerous man I have ever known, untouchable."

"Do you know where he is?"

Asher did not think her questio was the question she truly wanted to ask. "At the moment? No," Asl r replied. "But I know he has a weakness for beautiful things. Pet loves to fill his emptiness with the ornaments and trinkets of cultur and refined people, even if those trinkets happen to be works of art. is a *penchant* he acquired from Ketrin, only I believe it is more of ? obsession with Petar. Ketrin has always wanted respectability and so al status. To be considered a man of great power, but also, a man of el gance. Petar is different."

"What does Petar want?" Fin s voice was a whisper. She was terribly vulnerable, and Asher rem nbered the night they had met. She was not yet beyond that place, here death might present a viable alternative to the pain she felt at eve moment.

"Petar wishes to have a soul."

"*Scheveningen* and *Nuenen*." ler amber eyes changed as she spoke of Van Gogh's stolen child n, and she understood what he meant—he could see it.

It was a respect that came n rally to her and he admired it. She would have made an exceptio l thief. "Have you ever been to Athens?" he asked. "It is very lovel this time of year, especially near the end of April." He reached into l jacket and pulled out his wallet. He placed ten euros on the table ? d a folded piece of paper. "You should go, my friend."

The intensity of Finn's gaze w almost eerie, and he stilled, his wallet halfway into his breast pocke nce more. "I use to read books," she said softly. The tears welled up, then slipped from her eyes. "That was my pursuit."

"And so now you are a hunter of men," Asher said in a hard but quiet voice. "What makes you think one pursuit is more worthy than the other?"

"Because they were only books."

"Then for now, you are on the right road." Asher let go of his wallet and it dropped to the bottom of his pocket. "One day, your loves will return to you. One night, when you cannot sleep, perhaps Charles Dickens will pay you a visit, and you will welcome him in, with his dirty London streets and long-haired thieves in overcoats."

She was surprised by his words, but not displeased.

"And do not forget, Finnegan Starkweather."

"Forget what?"

"That you owe me a favor. A promise."

She flicked the back of her hand across her cheek in annoyance. Her eyes were clear again. "I keep my promises."

Asher smiled. "I know that."

Finn's eyes were suspicious. "And how would you know that?"

"Do you remember the first girl you kissed?"

His question startled her completely, and seemed to shock her out of her darkness.

"Do you?"

Finn smiled and the inclination to do so appeared to be a complete revelation to her. Her eyes filled with a surprising abundance of warmth as she remembered—he could see it. "I don't know, old man, maybe *you're* the most dangerous person you know."

Asher laughed and then shrugged. "I am more hungry than I am old. Where are you taking me to eat?"

Finn's voice was filled with amusement. "Jesus, it's three in the morning."

"What kind of a cop are you, for fuck's sake?"

This time she did laugh. "A better one than I thought I'd be."

"I think you have a knack for things, yes. You should go into business for yourself. There are too many rules in your way."

Finn palmed the paper he had left on the table and slid from the booth. She waited for him as he inched his way out. "Don't break anything in your rush to get to the food."

Asher hissed at her. "Don't be wicked. You sound like my Domino."

"Do you like crepes?"

Asher stood up smoothly an   stared at her with a withering expression.

Finn chuckled as she slipped   ie paper into the front pocket of her jeans. "Whatever. I wouldn't sa   t was a stupid question, exactly."

"You see? I did not even hav   to speak. Your French is getting better."

"I'll have you know that I read   es Misérables in the original. It's prettier in French."

Asher rolled his eyes. "Yes, b   of course. When you're selling your teeth to pay for food, the lan   iage used to express such tragic irony should be very pretty."

Finn covered her mouth as the   iade their way toward the door of the nearly empty pub, looking dowi   s she laughed. "Jesus."

Asher smiled and set a hand o   ier shoulder. "Yes, I like crepes."

CHAPTER SEVENTEEN

Piraeus Port, Athens
April 2010

Ketrin Arshavin leaned back in the desk chair and the old spring beneath the wooden seat creaked in a slow manner. "You are not living up to your part of the bargain, Eric."

Eric Werner looked over the neatly ordered desk and took a deep, slow breath. His blue eyes were guarded, but Ketrin could see the wheels turning with thought. Eric's three piece suit was Italian, a satin steel gray that complemented his light coloring.

"I have provided you with a very lucrative business. I have advanced to you great monies, so you could provide the best experience, the best security, and the best of everything. In return, you provide for me either the items I would like from your auction, or the names I need, in order to procure those items for myself."

"Yes," Eric answered him. "I am aware of our deal."

"So what is the problem?"

"The problem is…" Eric paused to rearrange his words. "You see, Mr. Arshavin, it's very difficult to maintain a good reputation, and to keep the trust of both my customers and those that will provide them with their treasures…" Eric cleared his throat. "Let's say you purchase a Picasso at my auction. You pay an extreme amount of money, it's true, but a desired masterpiece is now in your possession. Pablo Picasso, he now hangs in your own private study. It is hard to put a value on such a thing. But you do, of course, because in order to possess such a treasure, you are required to hand over a fortune," Eric continued. "This fortune not only buys you your desired Picasso, but it guarantees you absolute anonymity and safe passage home with your purchase."

Ketrin narrowed his eyes at [E]ric Werner, the tightness of his [jaw] t[ight].

"But"—Eric opened his hands [as] he leaned forward in his chair— "much to your shock and dismay, [a] month later, perhaps two, a man breaks into your house and steals y[ou]r beautiful Picasso."

Ketrin said nothing in the si[len]ce that followed, and the man beside him stepped forward. "That [is] unfortunate," Petar Dimitrovich replied and a slow smile slipped acr[os]s his mouth.

"Yes," Eric agreed. "It is."

"But how can they go to the [po]lice to recoup their loss?" Petar inquired as he stepped about the d[es]k and sat on the corner closest to Eric's chair. He smoothed at his [c]risp blue suit and Ketrin smiled at Petar's expression. They both ad[mi]red Brooks Brothers, and Ketrin had always enjoyed Petar's impecca[bl]e appearance, for it reflected well upon his own reputation. His brown [h]air was a bit long at the moment, but it was slicked back nicely.

Eric cleared his throat quietly [a]nd sat back. "They cannot. And if there is talk that I have circulate[d] my list of buyers, the names of those who have attended a recent [au]ction, for example, such rumors will destroy our venture, and very q[u]ickly, I assure you." Eric glanced away from Petar, and Ketrin foun[d] the man's pleading expression somewhat disgusting. "I beg you, pl[ea]se, take better care from this day forward, or else this lovely well sh[all] run dry, and you will have very few opportunities in the coming yea[rs] to bolster your collection."

"Are you threatening me, Er[ic]?" Ketrin demanded and Petar stepped to his feet and looked dov[n] at their guest. Eric paled as he looked up in response to the appro[ac]h. "I believe Eric is threatening us, Petar."

"No," Eric said in a horrifie[d] voice. "No, I would never, Mr. Arshavin."

Ketrin laughed, liking Eric's c[ur]rent expression much better than his last.

The rotary phone that sat upo[n] the desk rang with a loud, old-fashioned bell and Petar picked it up[.] "Yes?"

Petar listened for just a few m[om]ents and then hung up before he stepped to the tall cabinet against th[e] west wall and opened its doors. The lights from six different securit[y] monitors flickered into the room and he studied each one before he p[ic]ked up the walkie-talkie handset next to the keyboard. "Dahvid?"

"Yes, sir?"

"Finish packing the trucks. We leave now. Let them come, and have your men deal with them once they are here. They could use the practice, and a statement should be made."

"Yes, sir."

Petar turned around. "Thank you for expressing your concerns, Eric. We will take what you've said under advisement."

Eric glanced at Ketrin and Ketrin stared back at him.

"If you will leave through the east door, just there"—Petar pointed to the opposite side of the room—"you should be away before they set up their perimeter."

Eric digested the words and then stood in a rush. "Who? Who is here?"

"The police, most likely Interpol, as well."

Eric turned his back without another word and walked away. Six or seven hurried steps and he was at the door across the narrow room, which he pulled open and passed through before Ketrin had decided which punishment would be most effective on their guest.

"Dahvid?" Petar said into the handset. "How long do we have?"

"Thirty minutes, maybe a little less. Your man called, and we picked them up en route."

Petar smiled, pleased that his spy had made a contribution. "Good. Leave the van on the street beyond the north entrance. We will leave from there."

❖

"Go! Go! Go!"

Finn grabbed her partner's shoulder and spun him into the corridor as splinters of wood cut through the air. She lifted her weapon, turned, and took her best guess. The short burst from her HK416 fired into the distance and she heard yelling, as well as a secondary burst of gunfire off to her left.

Her back hit the wall behind her and she looked to her right. Splash had lifted his goggles and his eyes were wild as he reloaded his weapon. "Fucking waiting for us."

"Is this the north corridor?" Finn searched the shadows beyond them both.

"I have no idea anymore," Splash answered and then laughed. "You're always a stickler for details, Dodger."

Finn touched her throat mike. "Where are we, please?"

"And you're too fucking nice.'

"There's no substitute for goo[d] [m]anners." Finn smiled.

Splash laughed and moved aro[un]d her. "Fuck it."

"North corridor, affirmative, D[od]ger."

"Splash!" Finn called out as [he] stepped around the corner and fired. She slid wide into the open as [h]e fell, and lifted her weapon. The sniper was on the upper level and [sh]e watched as he pulled the side bolt back on his weapon, the silenc[ed] barrel lifting up and to the side. She pulled the trigger and kept firin[g] The rifle fell, but that was all she saw before she ducked back and sl[id] to her knees beside her partner.

"Splash?"

Blood was spreading onto the [sm]ooth cement floor beneath them both.

Finn slung her HK over her sho[ul]der and opened her mike. "I need a medical evac at the north corridor [e]xit."

"Rodger that, Dodger." Comm[s] filled her head as she grabbed Splash by the shoulders of his vest, s[...]od, and pulled. "Main warehouse is being secured. Team one is movi[ng] in."

"A little fucking late." Finn's [v]oice was strained by her efforts and she was sucking air. Her adre[na]line had redlined, however, and she picked up speed. She could hea[r] he panic in her voice even as she heard James within her head. *If Ke[n] lights a fire, Dimitrovich is the match.* "How far am I from the offi[ce]?"

"Negative," comms responde[d] "Get to the evac point and then proceed."

Finn glanced over her shoul[de]r as she backpedaled and the corridor filled with light.

Her heart jumped into her thr[oa]t and she let go of Splash as her eyes tried to adjust. He fell against [h]er legs as she lifted her weapon and tried to turn. The hand was the[re], and she watched as it wrapped around the barrel of her HK like som[e] sort of alien creature. She pulled the trigger and the assault rifle fire[d t]oward the ceiling with a violent burst of sound.

There was a pop and a scream [...] sound within her head, like gears grinding and turning within an eng[ine] that wouldn't start. It began in her head, and then it spread, rattlin[g] through her chest and exploding deep into her legs.

Finn stared at the ceiling, the c[eme]nt floor cold against her body.

"Get the paintings, Dahvid."

Finn couldn't breathe but she [tri]ed to get up anyway. She was on fire. Everything was on fire. She heard the clatter, and the air rushed over her face and through her hair, cool, like she had dunked her head beneath the ice cold water from a hose. She watched as her helmet and goggles rolled away from her into the corridor. She felt the stock of the Sig Sauer within her right hand but it was caught. Something held it tight to her leg and she didn't understand what that could be.

"Would you like me to help?"

The voice was smooth and mocking, and yet there was an odd warmth to it. Finn's right shoulder fell back against the cement once more.

"Because I could help, if you…"

She stared at him and waited for him to finish.

He stared back, his brown hair falling forward as he stood over her. His eyes were wide and…and she couldn't tell what color they were. She thought they might be blue. He was like a ghost, as pale and pure as a silk sheet.

"Sweet boy?" There was denial as he took an awkward step back from her. "It's you," he said in a fractured breath. "It's *you*."

Finn ripped her weapon free despite its resistance, and she felt the pressure of the trigger beneath her finger. She pulled, and she kept pulling. There was a shout and more gunfire. Someone was screaming. She heard a rush of chatter through the comms. There was sunlight, and she saw a church with a narrow spire beneath a cloudy sky, held motionless in time within swirls of paint.

She tasted blood.

"Dodger?"

She opened her eyes, but she didn't recognize the face so close to her own.

"Stay with me, Dodger."

She tried to speak but she had no idea if she had.

"You hit somebody, yeah." The face smiled at her. "Stay with me now, okay?"

She felt a pull on her vest and then the pain hit.

It starts in Nuenen, in the Netherlands. It starts with a sketch of a church and a spire, and a young Vincent van Gogh, who had not yet discovered the joys of a colorful palette…

CHAPTER EIGHTEEN

San Francisco
Present day

Casey smiled as she swept the last of her butter fried baguette through her syrup. She felt unbelievably divine, and as she took the last bite, she let her lips linger along the tines before returning the fork to her plate. Finn was close to blushing. "Is this your favorite diner?"

As Finn glanced around, Casey noticed at least two dozen other patrons taking up space in their world. She didn't mind, exactly, but now that she'd eaten, she wanted to be back at Finn's loft. *In your bed, with you inside me, Finnegan O'Connell.* She shifted upon her seat and then crossed her legs with an inward laugh. *Dear God.*

"I haven't been here since I was a kid, actually."

Casey caught the odd wistful tone and she bobbed her boot forward beneath the table. The tap upon Finn's knee was gentle.

Finn smiled and turned back to her. "I remember the french toast as being very good."

"It was excellent," Casey agreed. "Thank you for breakfast."

"You're welcome," Finn said in a voice that gave Casey goose bumps.

Finn's wound was not as swollen as she expected it would be, but it bothered Casey on a terribly profound level. It didn't mar the emotions that were so thick within Finn's amber eyes, but it was obviously causing her pain. "Did you get something for that?"

Finn lifted her gaze from Casey's mouth and focused. "Hmm?"

Casey laughed. She was wet and everything throbbed and ached with the beat of her pulse, which wasn't doing her any favors as she stared into Finn's eyes. "Oh my God, do you even know how sexy you are?"

Finn hadn't touched her food. "I'm not even hungry."

Casey frowned. "Were you given something for the pain?" she asked again. She reached across the table. "Finn?"

Finn looked up from Casey's hand as it slid about hers. "That's not what I meant."

"What did you mean?"

"I was thinking about something else."

"What were you thinking about?"

"Something else." Finn's eyes seemed to catch fire.

Casey pushed her plate to the side and leaned forward. "Was it about putting your money where your mouth is?"

"I think I'll be putting my mouth there, too, just so you know."

Casey pulled the corner of her lower lip between her teeth for just an instant. "Are you always this naughty? Because if you are, I'm not sure we should be—"

"Cassandra Marinos?"

"Yes?"

"The only thought I've been able to keep in my head since I kissed you this morning is the thought that involves...well...We just need to go now, that's all there is to it."

"Finnegan," Casey said softly. "I want you, too."

"Because I'm going to do things to you that...that I really can't think about anymore, in such a public place, with someone's grandparents sitting over there enjoying the eggs Benedict and talking about the Blue Man Group show they saw in Orlando."

Casey laughed, but she was pushing from the booth before she even took another breath. By the time she stood, Finn was at the end of the table beside her and dropping cash onto the table.

❖

Casey let out a hard breath with each firm stroke, Finn's hands strong upon her hips. The sheets beneath her knees were soft and tangled and they called out to the reasonable part of her brain. They called out for good sense and quiet and the promise of dreams. The cock inside her filled her so deeply and so thoroughly, however, that she had stopped thinking completely. Her damp hair clung to her skin as Finn guided her movements, and Casey held her new lover's face. Her

mouth was open upon Finn's as she ᴏked into her eyes, but there were
no words she might've spoken that ᴠould do justice to anything that
was happening. As Finn thrust insidᴇ ᴚer, only her eyes spoke the truth.

She felt herself rising again a᷉ ᴉ she cried out, pushing her hips
forward as she leaned back for levᴇ ᴉge, the leather of Finn's harness
rough against the skin of her inner t ghs.

Finn's right arm went about thᴇ ᴍall of her back and took hold of
her. The bed was beneath her in a sᴍ ᴏth move and Finn's hips moved
between her legs. Casey's feet push ᴉ upon the bed and she clawed at
Finn's back and shoulders, wantinᴦ ᴏ mark her, wanting something,
anything, wanting everything, she ᴨ longer even knew.

Finn quickened her thrusts a᷉ ᴉ Casey tried to breathe, loving
Finn's weight on top of her, pinninᴦ her down as Finn's cock moved
inside her and Finn's tongue sparreᴅ with hers. A strong hand cupped
her left breast and then closed, her ᴀrdened, full nipple caught with
just the slightest touch of pain betᴠ ᴇen Finn's thumb and forefinger.
The first shudder rolled through hᴇ ᴉn response and her hands fisted
in Finn's hair, the cry she tried to ᴋ ᴉd back caught in her throat. Her
muscles shuddered and tightened a᷉ ᴅ she came and her furious spasm
caught Finn's thrust at its apex.

Casey tried to hold it, all the poᴡ ᴇr she felt inside, all the pleasure,
Finn's presence embedded so sweᴇᴛ and wild in the deepest, most
intimate part of her…but it rolled thᴦ ᴏugh her and she cried out, unable
to stop it.

Finn's lower body pushed, her ᴉᴉps thrusting in rapid, tight strokes
as she reached beneath and lifted Ca᷉ ᴇy up, just enough. Casey clung to
her, caught in the ebb of one wave ᴀᴅ the feverish rise of yet another.
She came again as Finn strained witᴨ ᴉn her arms, Finn's muscles taut as
she let out a ragged cry against Casᴇ ᴇ's neck.

Casey tightened her embrace a᷉ ᴅ held on with all the strength she
had left. There was only one thougᴨ ᴉ she recognized, and she listened
to it. *Don't let go.*

❖

Casey sat on Finn's thighs, bᴜᴛ a single button on her borrowed
shirt fastened beneath her breasts. Hᴇr smile was more than pleased as
she took hold of her hair and shook iᴛ ᴃack, combing her fingers through
it as best she could. "You fucked up ᴍy hair as well, O'Connell."

Finn returned Casey's smile as she shifted against the pillows at her back.

Casey spoke softly in French, enjoying the feel of the words upon her tongue.

Finn's lips reacted with an easy smile. "Oh, now I really only recognize that one thing."

Casey chuckled and pulled herself closer along Finn's thighs. She glanced across the bed at Finn's black leather harness and the rather lovely dark blue cock it still held. She met Finn's eyes. "I'd like to know where you learned to fuck like that, and if you tell me Paula the tennis pro, I will hunt her down and kill her on the spot, so please consider your answer carefully."

"Boston University," Finn answered and Casey laughed. "They concentrate extremely hard on the core skills."

Casey's amusement had a unique energy that Finn had not expected and it roused her in the quiet part of her thoughts that very few things in her life managed to touch. Casey reached up, her hand gentle as her thumb moved along Finn's left cheekbone. "How's your head, baby?"

"It's good."

Casey's eyes narrowed as she analyzed the answer. "I can't tell if you're lying or not."

Finn smiled. "It hurts."

The knowledge was clearly taken in and registered for future use. "You just gave away a tell," Casey whispered. "Have a care, Finnegan."

Finn savored the moment and the heat of Casey's body, the lovely weight upon her thighs and the touch against her cheek. Casey's expression was curious, but it was open and her guard was down. She was more alive than Finn could ever remember seeing her, and she was confident and strong in her satisfaction.

They shared a new intimacy that Finn had only known in her fantasies, though by design and discipline, those had been few in number. She held an unfair advantage over Casey, and to take that further could lead to trouble for even the most ethical of dreamers. Sometimes, though, in the deepest dreams of her sleep, Casey would appear. Finn couldn't help that.

"Finn?"

Finn pulled herself back.

Casey leaned forward and kissed her, holding her face with both hands. "You should say it," she whispered and Finn found her eyes with an unexpected jolt of emotion. Whatever it is, baby, just say it." Casey's hand pushed at Finn's hair. Are you going to confess?" Finn blinked the unexpected w ds. "Confess to what?"

"If I open your closet, are the going to be a hundred pictures of me stuck to the inside of the do r with Scotch tape?" Casey was trying hard not to smile. "Is there a s ine in here somewhere? Confess, O'Connell."

Finn chuckled happily. "Yes, a d there's a scrapbook, too. When I flip through the pages it's like slo motion porn. It's frustrating, but terribly hot all at the same time."

"I knew it," Casey said with l ghter. "You have that look about you."

"There's a look for that?"

Casey kissed her again and, w a deft twist of her body, pulled them both onto the sheets. Finn lan d between her legs for a moment and then she was rolled to the side, C sey certain of what she wanted as she broke away from their kiss. "Al ask"—Casey sat up and grabbed a pillow—"is that you light a candl nce a week."

Finn's head was lifted from the mattress with exquisite tenderness and the pillow was slipped beneath er. Casey leaned over her, pulled at the sheet, and covered them both she lay down along Finn's body.

"Do I have to say a prayer?"

Casey looked at her with supr ne skepticism, propped onto her right elbow. "Let's not piss off some e with the power to smite things, all right, darling?" She combed her l ir back with certain fingers. "And though I'm not all that sure what sn ing entails, it is not a verb I wish to encounter in a sentence where I'r featured in a prominent manner."

Finn laughed, thoroughly ench ited.

"I remember when the gods sn te poor Samantha Drake," Casey said in a rather pleasing Southern ac ent. "It really was a shame." She smiled down at Finn and Finn's hea skipped within her chest. Casey's expression lost its playful edge as s e slipped her leg between Finn's and leaned close. "And she was so g od-looking."

Finn held Casey's eyes and r nembered being inside her. She remembered the sweet and terrible hing, and the punishing pressure that had throbbed between her legs d begged for release. A knife like no other had danced along the tend edge of her swollen flesh. Each thrust had pushed her closer, each t ie she had buried her need in the woman she loved, the world beyond ad ceased to exist.

"Finn." Casey's voice was quiet and her tone was a touch off balance. "Baby, don't look at me like that."

Casey's fingers trembled—Finn could feel it. "Like what?" Casey settled tightly against her body and pulled the sheet up as she dropped away from Finn's line of sight. Her head felt good upon Finn's chest, as if it belonged there. It was a cliché, Finn knew it, but she happily accepted it.

"I'm going to look for that shrine in the morning," Casey warned her. "If you have any photos where the lighting is bad, or my ass isn't presented in the most pleasing manner, you will be in serious trouble."

Finn wrapped her arms about her. She had no desire to ever let go, but she tried not to hold on too tightly, either. "It's in my wallet, actually, and there's just that one extra-special black-and-white."

For a few seconds there was nothing, and then Casey's body shook with laughter. "If you think that bothers me, you haven't been paying attention."

CHAPTER NINETEEN

Near Bergerac, the Dordogne, France
December 2009

"Oncle?"

Asher looked over his right shoulder and across the back of the divan.

Casey stood beneath the smooth oak wood arch, her soft silk pajamas catching the warm light from the kitchen somewhere behind him. Her hair was down and slightly tousled, the loose curls looking the same to him as they had when she was a child.

"Are you well?"

Her lovely voice fell somewhere in between a whisper and a quiet plea for company. This was the same as well. "Yes, my Domino, I am very good."

She smiled and padded across the plush carpet. She grabbed a blanket from one of the chairs and walked around the couch until she could step on the cushions. Asher chuckled and lifted his arm out of the way.

She tucked against his side. "Do you like my house?" She threw part of the blanket over his legs and smiled when his strong arm hugged her shoulders. She laid her head at the crook of his neck. "I'll show you my boat tomorrow."

Asher was surprised. "A boat?"

"Yes."

"Good. A beautiful woman should have a boat."

"Why is that?"

"Because it shows that she has resources, and a mind of her own."

She laughed quietly. "I see."

"It felt like snow, earlier today."

"It did. Perhaps for Noel?"

"You have done very well for yourself, Domino. This place, it is beautiful, and the land, as well. I had not ever hoped for so much, years ago."

"Why not?"

"I don't know."

They were quiet for a time, and Asher thought about their first apartment in Rouen.

He had never been so terrified in all his life, of that he was still certain. He had left home at sixteen and he had not looked back for almost a decade. He had called his sister, Amelie, over the years, and they would talk, for she had always been the closest thing he had to a mother. As Casey had slept on the foldout bed, so small and quiet, tucked beneath the blankets he had bought, he had thought he would die of his fear.

But Amelie had taught him kindness above all, and a fierce independence that had shaped his life. *Take no shit from anyone, Asher. You will be your own man. A proud man, a good man. And if those bastards try and keep you down? If they try to crush you? Hurt them where it counts.* He wasn't sure if she would actually approve of his profession, but he thought she would not mind it so much, when she was alone with her thoughts. She would smile in satisfaction.

He had been so afraid during those first years, of being caught, or of reaching for too much, for Casey would have no place without him. She would have no one.

"I was terrified of being caught," he said at last. "Oh, it was terrible. Only small jobs made sense to me, until you were much older, but not then. Do you remember when I worked at that restaurant, in Rouen? It was a long time ago."

"You would bring home toasted bread and milk."

Asher smiled. "Yes. On wages."

Casey tipped her head back. "That Noel, it was my first, and you brought me my sweet little Magda."

Asher smiled, though the name caused his blood to give a push of brutal memory. Casey did not remember where the name came from, but he did. "That cat was almost the death of me. She would *pounce* at my legs in the morning and then run away. I know for certain, at least once I was given a heart attack. I was afraid I would fall on her and crush her, and then you would never forgive me. My God, for sure I thought she would find a corner an[d] giggle very tiny evil cat giggles, mocking me."

Casey laughed and tucked agai[n]st him farther.

"You have a new Magda?"

"I've been calling her Maggi[e] his time," Casey informed him. "She's still in bed. She loves to slee[p] beneath the covers."

Asher gave a small, satisfied [so]unt of acceptance. "And why is there no beautiful woman sleeping [b]eneath your covers? When will you find your love, Domino?"

Casey groaned and then turned [h]er face against his shirt, laughing. "You are terrible."

"No!" Asher laughed with her. You are too wonderful, Domino, to be alone."

"And so they come and stay, a[nd] then what? They will move my books about, and they will pin me [do]wn and take away my freedom. They will want me to change who I a[m], and most cannot be trusted with the truth of what I do, but yet they [w]ant the life that I lead as a result of it. A woman of resources, remem[be]r? Or they have not read a book in years and they think my love o[f t]hem is quaint, or an affectation. But I do not lack for company, Onc[e] I assure you. I am not lacking in companionship when I want it."

Asher sighed. "What about w[he]n you need it? When you need someone there for you?"

Casey was quiet and he waited [a] long time for her response. "I've not found that yet, no. I don't think [I] will."

"Why not?"

"I think I need a tall woman. A [wo]man who might make me laugh."

Asher was surprised by the s[ta]tement. "I met a tall woman in Paris, but a few weeks ago, now."

"Did you fall in love with her?[""]

Asher gave a gentle hiss. "No, [D]omino. She is your age, perhaps, and she is wild and strong." He co[ns]idered the truth of things. "And broken, too. She has nothing to lose [un]cle?"

Casey tipped her head back. "[Un]cle?"

"A woman like that...she has [al]l the freedom she will ever need. Too much," he whispered. "Perha[ps] too much freedom." He leaned away just a bit and met her eyes. "[To]o much freedom can make you careless, and extremely dangerous, [a]s well. Remember that, Domino. Sometimes, it is good to be tied to [so]meone. It makes you brave, and it makes you wise. Or at least, wiser than you were before. It is always better to fight for *someone*, rather than *something*."

Her eyes were filled with thought. She was trying to figure out where he was leading.

"But she is like you, maybe, a little bit. She leaves weeping women in her wake and does not look back."

Casey's brow went up and her eyes were filled with surprise. "What?"

"Yes, like you...but..."

"But what?"

He could hear her interest and curiosity. "But she is caught between two worlds. The world of men and the world of women." He turned his gaze back to the wide windows and found the trees beyond the pool. "What do you call such a woman?"

"Butch?"

"Yes, that's it."

"You're saying, you met a tall *butch* woman in Paris?"

Asher smiled but did not look at her. "Yes, I did. Paris welcomes everyone into her bed, we know this."

Casey clicked her tongue. "That's not what I meant, Oncle, and you know it."

"Don't worry. I'm not trying to...make you a date?"

"I think you would say, *fix me up*." Casey eyes were bright and quick.

"No." Asher sighed and settled back into the couch a bit farther. "I would not do that, fix you up. I would not presume such."

"Oh my God." Casey laughed.

Asher stared and her humor faded at his expression. "She is dangerous, Domino. That is not what I am doing."

"Okay," she whispered. Her eyes told him she saw him as no one else ever had. "But?"

Asher eased off from his warning—he couldn't help it. "But she is...she is like a Van Gogh. Thick ropes of brilliant color, smoothed by a sable brush. She is *magnifique*. Raw emotion that spills everywhere and screams out to the world, only it is in such a quiet voice."

Casey set her head upon his shoulder once more. "You should have been an artist, Oncle."

Asher considered her words. "You are right."

"I know."

"Would you like crepes before ou go back to bed?"

"Yes…I love you, Oncle."

"I love you, too."

It was a terribly long time b ore she spoke again and Asher thought she had fallen asleep, whicl atisfied.

"She sounds rather lovely," Ca y whispered.

His memories spiraled back in me as she fell asleep, and he was awake when the snow began to fall at, thick flakes that would never last once the sun came up.

Chapter Twenty

San Francisco
Present day

"My God, is this a first edition of *Alice's Adventures in Wonderland*?" Casey turned, the red clothbound book held with reverence as she looked across the loft.

Finn wore an ancient faded pair of Levi's and a faded navy Foo Fighters T-shirt as she stood at the stove, the handle of a pan in one hand and a spatula in the other. "No, technically it's the second," Finn answered with a pleased smile. "Dodgson didn't like the illustrations in the first edition, and neither did the artist, so they stopped the run and made that one."

Casey ran her fingers over the gold stamp on the front cover. "Where did you get it?"

"My grandmother gave it to me when I was twelve."

Casey noted the slight shift in tone and put the book back on the shelf. She was completely relaxed, every muscle in her body limber and soft with satisfaction and ease. It was a strange feeling, actually, and one she only truly encountered when she was at home. She wore a pair of Finn's pajamas, the plaid flannel rolled up several times at the cuffs, fluffy white socks, and one of Finn's white T-shirts soft from the wash. She had no idea what time it was and she didn't care. It was dark and well past midnight from the feel of it.

Finn was awake, but dazed and sleepy, though not so sleepy that she couldn't keep her word. Casey smiled as she moved toward the kitchen counter. Finn had put her mouth just about everywhere and Casey felt a bit dazed herself.

"What are you making?"

"Sit down and I'll show you."

Casey chuckled and spun the middle stool before she hopped onto the seat. "You didn't tell me you could cook."

Finn turned and slid a plate across the counter. "That's an extremely generous description of my skills."

Casey stared at the plate in surprise as Finn placed silverware and a bowl of freshly mashed raspberries and sauce beside it. "You made me crepes?"

"You don't like—"

"Stop," Casey interrupted with smile. "I love them."

"At two in the morning they seem to be good choice."

Casey rolled the top crepe. "You seem to be up a lot at two in the morning." Casey set the food down and braced her hands on the edge of the counter. She lifted herself up and leaned across, careful of the plate. Finn met her halfway and Casey kissed her, tasting her tongue for just a moment. "I can't believe you made me crepes."

Finn stepped to the fridge and opened the door. "I've got orange juice, Guinness, some sort of carbonated water I don't remember buying, that was probably bottled in Cleveland...and a bottle of..."

Casey bit into the crepe and before her first bite was fully consumed, her mouth filled with memories. Lovely memories that were heavy with longing. Memories that she had placed to the side, not because they were unimportant, but because they were still so overwhelming.

"A bottle of...Coche-Dury Corton-Charlemagne Grand Cru? Finn turned with the bottle in hand. Did I say that right?"

Casey looked up from her plate.

"Not so good?" Finn nodded toward Casey's plate.

"No," Casey whispered, and then spoke in French.

Finn smiled at her.

"No, baby, they taste like a memory," Casey translated. "A very good memory, actually."

The question within Finn's eyes disappeared and was replaced by a depth of warmth, and something else, something Casey wasn't quite sure she understood. Her attention shifted to the wine bottle in Finn's hand, a bit startled. "What did you say that was?"

Finn checked the label again. "Coche-Dury...Corton-Charle—"

"Charlemagne Grand *Cru*? For the love of all that's *holy*, Finnegan." Casey groaned. "Give me that!"

Finn laughed and took a careful step. "Will it go well with crepes? Because it has a price, you know."

Casey laughed happily. "If that's what I think it is, it will go well with anything. Name your price, O'Connell."

"Forgive me."

Casey's smile faded and her attention shifted gears in the blink of an eye. Finn's voice was quiet, but it was filled with all sorts of things. Too many things, actually, for Casey to decipher on the spot. "Forgive you for what?" Casey asked, uncertain of what she would do if she received an answer she didn't like. *Am I going to walk out? Can I leave without touching you again, Finn? Would I even be able to do that, at this point?*

"Please forgive me for scaring you, that night at the Campton. I know that was a part of your evening, the fear of who I might be and what I might want from you. That you had somehow been exposed. It was a consequence of the truth, but I couldn't see any way around it. I'm sorry for that."

It was the last thing Casey expected, quite frankly, and she felt the blush swarm within her chest and blossom upward. She had felt a rush of fear, it was true, but it wasn't as Finn thought. She moved her plate aside and the bowl of raspberries, and then she lifted herself up with an agile twist and sat on the counter. She spun about and, with a quick push, slid across the smooth marble surface.

Finn's expression was pleased as Casey fisted her left hand within Finn's T-shirt and pulled her lover between her legs. Finn's skin was soft beneath her hands as she held her face. "Set the bottle down, please."

Finn obeyed and Casey let her eyes wander. She pushed her hand into the heavy strands of Finn's hair, her fingers opening slowly and enjoying it. "I don't know what to make of you," she confessed. She tightened her legs around Finn's waist and pulled her flush against the counter, hooking her ankles together in order to hold Finn secure.

"Why?"

Casey smiled. "You're not like any top I've ever met."

"Have you met a lot of us, then?"

"I've met a lot of *them*."

"Where do I fit in?"

Casey laughed within her throat, the sound filled with delight. "You don't. You're a different animal altogether."

"Oh."

"And why *is* that?"

"Why is what?"

"How is it that you're you? Was there something in the water when you were a child?"

"Ambiguous modifiers, mostly which I was told to spoon out before I drank my fill."

Casey accepted her answer with amusement. "Why did you give me a 1947 Cheval Blanc?"

Finn's eyes flared with surprise and she tried to step back.

Casey tightened her legs and pulled her back. "I'll slide right off the counter if you keep going, baby. You'll be surprised, and you'll be too late to catch me. I'll fall backward and hit my head on this rather expensive-looking marble. You'll have to rush me to the hospital." Casey smiled when Finn did and she enjoyed the heat that colored Finn's cheeks. "It'll be a whole scene filled with guilt and remorse and tears."

Finn took a deep breath and lifted her gaze.

"Or you could just answer the question."

Finn's mouth was a glorious, reluctant pout that was worthy of even the most beautiful Frenchwoman. A Frenchwoman who was clearly not getting what she wanted. *Or she's caught within her own trap,* Casey thought with affection. *God, you're fucking beautiful, Finnegan O'Connell.* Casey leaned down and kissed her, savoring Finn's full mouth and coaxing her face upward. She let Finn open her mouth and take control of the kiss, though only for a moment before she pulled back. Her thighs tightened of their own volition, the pulse that moved through her flesh, an ache that made her want to stretch and laugh with righteousness. The physical pleasure she had felt and continued to feel within Finn's presence was off the charts and she wanted more. *So much more.* "Did you steal it, perhaps?"

"I did not steal it, actually, though I sort of wanted to."

Casey chuckled. "Then why didn't you?"

"I'm not as coordinated as I may appear to be."

"Why did you give me a 1947 Cheval Blanc, Finnegan O'Connell?"

Casey saw the struggle in her eyes, she saw it as plain as day. She saw it as if Finn's two angels, one nice, and one not so nice, were engaged in a rather uncivilized and unscheduled bout of fisticuffs. It was outrageously sexy.

"Because..."

"Because why, baby?" Casey's whisper accompanied her thumb

as she trailed it across the softness of Finn's lower lip. She kissed the lip
slowly, letting it slip away from her mouth at the last moment.
"Because I wanted to give you something special. Something no
one else had ever given you."
Casey felt just a tad short of breath at the tenderness of Finn's
answer and she lifted her eyes to Finn's.
"Something no one else ever would."
Casey had heard enough, but she asked anyway. "Why?"
"Because I didn't think this moment, right now, would ever
happen."
Casey wrapped her arms about Finn's neck and kissed her
completely. She pulled herself from the counter and Finn's hands
slipped beneath her thighs as Finn stepped back. Casey's tongue
explored with need, not just want, engaging and searching. Finn moved
backward for a few steps and then started forward around the counter,
held captive by the kiss.
Casey pulled back, breathless. "Can you get up the stairs like
this?"
"Like what?"
"With a lustful succubus, trying to pull the soul from the very
depths of your body." Casey laughed as Finn stepped to the right.
"Because that's exactly what you make me want to do."
Finn's eyes were bright as she tightened her hold. "Not if you
make me laugh, I can't."
"Succubi?"
Finn stretched carefully around a chair. "Don't do it."
"Succuba?"
"Fucking Latin."
Casey laughed and then kissed her again. Her hands disappeared
in Finn's hair, and she felt the entire world was hers to do with as she
wished. She didn't care if they made it upstairs or not.

❖

Casey lay tucked along Finn's right side, her right leg hooked
over Finn's. Heat still poured from her body, and for the moment, the
stillness that possessed them both was the sweetest thing that the gods
had ever made. Finn could feel every breath Casey took, as Casey's
breasts were pressed against her. The heat from her sex was wet against
Finn's thigh, and her right arm was draped in exhaustion across Finn's

stomach. Finn was sore, but she wa gloriously spent, her flesh sated and still humming slightly with satis action.

"When I was fifteen, or maybe ixteen..." Finn closed her eyes at the sou d of Casey's voice. It was a little rough, but it was low and filled with ntimacy.

"There was a girl I would see i the Montparnasse, usually along the Rue Gassendi. She ran with a cr wd of older artists, mostly young men, and she had this way about he that drove me crazy, but I didn't know what it was exactly. I mean, s e was a butch, and I loved that." The touch of Casey's hand moved u on Finn's stomach. "But I didn't really understand what that meant, at least, what it meant to me. I was always much too nervous to a roach her." Finn heard the brief smile. "She was always *way* out of y league. Tough and distant, and she had this leather jacket that was vell, it was just the best thing in the world."

Casey lifted her face a bit. "H name was Rian Devons. A few years later, when I knew better abo what I wanted—I mean, when I knew what I needed—I went looki for her, in the Montparnasse. It was foolish, I know, but—"

"It wasn't foolish," Finn disagr d. She still wore her harness, and the cock it held lay heavy against he leg.

"Anyway"—Casey's hand slid the center of Finn's body—"she never strayed very far, apparently. I vas terrified, but I wanted to talk with her." Casey caressed the unders le of Finn's left breast, her fingers straying to the hardened nipple. "W n I finally found some of the old crowd that she use to run with, they ld me she'd killed herself, just a year or so after I had left Paris."

Finn closed her eyes.

"I don't know what this is, Fir egan, not exactly." Casey shifted onto her elbow. The touch upon Fir 's face was delicate and yet Finn could feel it deep within her stomacl "But I want us both to have what we want, what we need."

Finn saw the edges of Casey's prehension within the warmth of her eyes. "Don't be afraid, Cassanc Marinos," she whispered. "I'm the woman I was meant to be...and am neither caught where I don't belong, nor am I running from who am. I'm not saying I haven't had my moments, especially when I wa young. I was filled with rage just walking down the street, but not so uch anymore."

"Not so much anymore," Ca y echoed softly and her eyes

traveled slowly down Finn's body, as did her hand. Finn felt the touch upon her scars, filled with tenderness. "Baby, what happened here?" Finn tried hard not to see his face again, as he stood over her. "Someone tried to kill me." Casey's touch stilled.

Finn moved her hand up the soft skin of Casey's back, her fingers opening within the wide, messy curls. Casey caught her breath and her head tipped back as Finn closed her hand. Finn watched as Casey's eyes fluttered shut, the soft, damp hair within her fingers as close to unearthly as Finn thought she might ever feel.

Casey's touch upon her belly changed, her fingernails dancing upon Finn's skin. Finn guided her gently and Casey submitted, her eyes still shut as her full lips skated along Finn's cheek. Finn's lips pushed within her curls.

Finn could feel Casey's nipples harden and press against her, the flesh between her own legs alive with the soft pleasure of the moment and clenching with renewed need. "But I'm right here," she whispered. "With you, as it should be."

Casey was breathing hard, her arm going about Finn's ribs as she tried to move. Finn held her in place though, and again, Casey obeyed. Her forehead pressed against Finn's neck and Finn felt Casey's hips push against her.

Finn slid her hand on Casey's right thigh, and her touch slipped along the underside and between her legs. Casey let out a soft sound and she let Finn draw her leg higher, Finn's fingers gliding through the heat and silk of Casey's arousal. Casey moaned and thrust against her as Finn stroked her slowly and noted with wonder all the changes that Casey's body went through.

Casey moaned again and pressed harder as she began to lose her restraint. "*Finn.*"

Finn's heart stabbed within her chest and she felt the bite at her neck as she pulled Casey's leg across her body. She rolled with the movement and Casey opened beneath her as Finn guided her cock. Casey caught her breath as Finn entered her, her hands grasping at Finn's shoulders.

Finn thrust her hips slowly as she braced above her. "Open your eyes."

Casey complied and Finn let out a quick breath, pulled within their brightness. She kept her strokes slow but firm as she leaned down, and her mouth brushed against Casey's as she spoke. "Is this…what you want, baby?"

Casey pushed up and kissed her. "*More.*"

"Answer me, Casey."

"Yes, yes, yes, *please*, Finn."

"It's what I want, too," Finn whispered as Casey's hands grasped at her neck and pulled. "But not just this."

"Everything," Casey said with jagged breath.

"Yes, everything."

Casey's mouth was impatient and Finn obliged her, kissing her deeply and with all the love she had within her. It mattered, that she loved her beyond all good sense, and Finn knew it. With each touch and each movement, she tried to convey all she felt, and all she knew to be true. She understood there would be a reckoning with the past. She knew that all too well. But for now, and for as long as she had Casey in her arms, nothing else mattered.

She was swollen, and with each sure stroke, a wave of pleasure poured along her clit, the leather of her harness tight and smooth against her pulsing flesh. The muscles of her thighs and butt tightened, and with each push, Casey's nails dug at her arms. Her breath began to change, and the cadence of her pulse and the sounds that Casey made as she rose within her passion.

Finn responded to her urgency and Casey cried out as she turned from their kiss. Finn felt the pull within her hair, and she felt her lover come, caught within the tightness of Casey's flesh.

It was her name spoken in that low, aching voice that pushed Finn over the edge. Her name in Casey's mouth, voiced in the heat of her pleasure, with Casey's arms and legs wrapped around her. Her name, as Casey arched against her, followed by that beautiful sound from the back of her throat that Finn already craved.

Finn held her own cry within her throat as she came and hid her face against Casey's neck, breathing in her scent and drowning beneath its lovely weight.

CHAPTER TWENTY-ONE

"No," Casey said quietly into her phone, looking out across the city. The air was cold as it curled around the building, but she liked it, at least for the moment. "Is he okay?"

"He's fine. He's got a brand-new setup, with new computers and everything a paranoid boy genius could want," Jack answered her. "How are *you*?"

Casey smiled, ducked her head, and let her hair hide her expression as she walked along the waist-high brick wall that surrounded the terrace. She knew he couldn't see her, but she hid anyway. "Everything's okay, Jack, really. Just make sure Colin has whatever he needs. I'm going to have a few more things for him before the auction."

"Are we still in the game, then?"

"Of course," Casey answered and her voice sounded more confident than she felt. "She's after one of the buyers, not the bounty on the Rembrandt."

"And she told you this?"

Casey turned, but the glare along the loft windows did not afford her much insight into what Finnegan might be doing. "No. Malik Kaseem did."

"Out of the goodness of his heart?"

Casey smiled. "Yes, actually, that's exactly why he told me."

Jack laughed. "It's a little cold this time of year for swimming in the deep end, kiddo. But I'm with you, just like always."

"I won't mess it up, I promise."

"She hasn't shot anyone since I saw her last, has she?"

"Fuck off, Jack."

His chuckle turned wicked. "That's my girl."

"I'll call you when I get back to the hotel."

"Tonight is good, yeah."

A jagged bolt of irritation shot through Casey's chest and she turned. "Listen, Jack, maybe you think you have the right to—"

"Stop."

They were both silent for several seconds.

"I didn't mean anything by it, Casey. I wasn't telling you what to do, I'm just worried."

"Haven't you always gotten paid?" Casey asked, and though her tone was much sharper than she intended, she couldn't seem to stop it. "When that painting hits the block, you'll have more money than you'll fucking know what to do with, all right?"

"I didn't mean about the money—"

Casey closed her eyes.

"Shake it off, kiddo, and call me when you get back. I'll bring you some shitty coffee."

Casey opened her mouth to apologize, but he'd hung up.

She shut her phone off with a curse, slid it into the front pocket of her jeans, and stared at her reflection in the window.

He was worried about her, and by all accounts, she should be worried, as well. She wasn't, though, and she had no explanation for it except that she'd been right. Or at least she was right today, in what she'd said several days ago. She knew Finn.

She didn't know her as she wanted to, or as she should, but she knew enough. She didn't know her as she needed to, and need was the proper word. It was in her bones, an emotional longing she hadn't counted on. Even now, Finn felt too far away.

They had eaten an exquisite breakfast in an out-of-the-way restaurant, sitting close in a back corner booth meant for at least half a dozen people. The lighting had been low and they had sipped hot Bai Mudan tea that was fragrant and golden and tasted like an exotic distillation of an unknown fruit. They had walked through an inner courtyard of market stands and booths on their way back to the loft, and Finn had bought her a silver charm she liked, which was now safe within her pocket. It had all been terribly normal and she had loved it.

She hadn't thought once about the auction, or the fact that what Finn wanted was most likely at odds with what she herself wanted. Whether or not those two conflicting goals would destroy each other remained to be seen.

She needed more information and she was loath to try to get it.
Her phone rang in her pocket and she jumped a bit before she
grabbed it.

"Yes?"

"Are you coming inside?"

Casey smiled and looked at the windows again. "What's in it for
me?"

There was silence.

"Finn?"

"I'm just trying to decide how dirty my original answer actually
was, compared to the one that came after it."

"Don't you think I should be the judge of that?"

"Maybe. Are you any good at that sort of thing?"

Casey laughed. "I'm not sure that's a gauntlet you want to be
throwing down, O'Connell. You have no idea the sort of insanity that
will follow."

"I may not know much, but I know crazy. I could probably hold
my own."

"There would have to be a prize involved," Casey responded as
she moved to the door and pulled it open. "I mean, when I leave you in
the dust, I should receive some sort of trophy or medal for my efforts."

Finn smiled as the door closed behind her and Casey moved
through the loft. Finn pocketed her phone. "I could have a nice plaque
made up for you, put your name on it and stuff."

Casey felt her eyes flare as she stowed her phone, as well. "Stuff?"

Finn stood by the couch and chairs and Casey stopped when she
was but a few inches away from her. She could feel the heat from Finn's
body.

"How about," Finn said quietly, "we play a different game."

Finn's eyes were bright but they had taken on a serious expression.
The bleed in her eye had receded somewhat, and though the bruising on
her face was still spotty, the color seemed to have settled into a softer
version of its former self. Casey was somewhat startled by just how
relieved she was.

"Does this game have rules?" She had reached out and taken
Finn's hand and she'd only just realized it.

"It does."

"And they are?"

"You ask a question…and I answer it."

Casey blinked, truly thrown.

Finn pulled her forward and kissed her lips, the gesture lush and filled with subtle promise. "Come and sit down."

Casey let herself be led and she sat on the couch as Finn took the closest chair. Her mind was suddenly racing and she tried to slow it down.

"There are some things I'm not going to tell you," Finn explained as she leaned forward, her elbows on her knees. She was holding tight to her left hand and it was a nervous gesture Casey had not seen from her before. "Because I don't think it's safe, but I—"

"What is it that you want from me, Finn?" Casey blurted out, unable to stop the words. Finn smiled even as Casey frowned. "I'm sorry, baby, but I just…"

She would have to give up Mac if she went further, and she had already decided against that. No one should be punished for trying to be a good friend, and she wasn't going to be the one who threw him under the bus. She had never had a lot of friends, and her respect for such an endeavor had always been at a premium.

So she waited.

❖

Finn contemplated the question from several different angles, and none of them offered her the satisfaction she was looking for. She could tell the truth, but what was the truth? What was the whole truth when she stood above it all and considered the entire painting, and not just the brushstrokes of her favorite portion of the canvas?

For years, what she had wanted had always been extremely clear. She wanted justice, and she wanted revenge. Those two things, however, had turned out to be very complicated goals when put together on the same plate.

Casey's eyes were suddenly sharp and clear. "We could dance around it, if you'd like," she offered. "We could ignore it, or you could just tell me what you want."

"What if there's more than one answer to that?"

"Let's start with the most important one, then," Casey suggested and did not look away.

Finn could see that she was vulnerable. It was in the way she held her shoulders, and though her gaze was steady, Casey was somewhat out of her element, and it showed. That Casey allowed that to happen, that she felt safe enough to expose herself in such a way... *Please don't let me fuck this up,* Finn begged of anyone who might be listening.

She chose to address what she assumed was Casey's most pressing concern. "Am I after the bounty on your Rembrandt?"

Casey's expression wavered for a moment and then recovered. "Are you?"

"No."

"Do you think I have something else, then?"

"Yes," Finn answered and couldn't help but smile a little. "But I don't want him."

Casey leaned back slightly. It took her longer than Finn expected to find her voice. When the seconds continued to tick by, Finn almost reached out, but she stiffened against it.

"Him?" Casey asked at last.

"Vincent's road is different than mine, and for now, he may go where he sees fit."

Casey's eyes flashed and widened and the faintest blush of color rose along her neck. Finn watched as she tamed her distress, which was most likely considerable, and then Casey set about moving the pieces on her board. She adjusted and pulled back, she regrouped. She would take a new line of action and Finn had no idea what that might be.

"Do you think those are the most important questions to me, at this moment?"

"I'm not sure," Finn replied. "But if they're not, they sure as hell should be."

Casey laughed. She leaned back against the couch and crossed her legs in a casual manner. Her hair tumbled forward when she looked down, and she tucked a portion of the loose blond curls behind her right ear. It was a gesture that Finn recognized. Her words had hurt, and she hadn't meant them to.

"Or I could tell you..." Finn pushed against the resistance that bloomed through her chest, and the fear that flowered from it. The strange beauty of it burned like the kiss from a God, blessing and cursing her at the same time. *And so what does it matter, in the end, if you're too damned frightened to reap the rewards of such a kiss? Either you reach the sun and rise into the pantheon, or you fall from the stars upon wings of molten wax. Either way, at least it's a brave end.*

"Or I could tell you I love you, Casey," she said quietly and as bravely as she could. "Because I do I'm in love with you, Cassandra Marinos."

As far as Finn could tell, Casey had no reaction to her confession.

❖

Casey closed her eyes at the sound of Finn's voice and tried desperately to will her heart into an even tempo.

Within those rare words Casey heard a world of promise, and a stunning amount of danger. She heard need and desire and honesty, and fear beneath it all, quietly forgiving her as if Finn's heart had already admitted defeat. And she heard her own restraint fall and shatter, as if it were a fine china plate that had slipped from her hand.

"The way that came about, I don't like it," Finn went on. "It gives me an unfair advantage. The balance of power between us, it's all wrong."

Casey couldn't help but smile, knowing that her hair would hide it.

No woman she had ever been with had given up such an advantage so freely. No one had ever complained about being on top. She had been burned years ago by that lack of equilibrium, by handing her power over because it sated the needs of her physical desires. But life wasn't lived in the bedroom, and no matter what pleasure she might have received, it did not equal the freedom she had given up. It had taken years to understand the balance she needed in order to be happy, though mostly what she had learned was that she couldn't do it on her own.

Those lessons had all led to a dead end, and a decision that had ruled her heart for the next decade. Never again. *And none of it equaled what I feel with you, my sweet Finn and last night, I don't even know where to put that. Where do I put it? Your need so deep inside me, and my need to have you there, and whatever that was that happened when they met.*

Casey had not lost her voice in years, but at the moment, she had no idea where it had gone. Finn was in love with her.

"You can learn quite a bit from watching someone." Finn's voice was tinged with regret, but her tone was nothing short of tender. "What toothpaste you use, or the sort of lovers you take, though I've always thought they couldn't give you what you want. I know you like to drive faster than you should, and you like to read in the sun with your cat nearby. I know odd and curious things that have no real weight, because they have no context within the reality of your presence. But having that advantage is wrong, no matter how basic those things may be. It's wrong on so many levels, Casey, now that I've held you."

Casey pulled in a very careful breath and let it out slowly.

"And my reasons for having done it, they were righteous when I started down this road, but now I don't know anymore...Now it's just..."

Casey lifted her eyes at last and she found Finn waiting for her. "Just what?"

Finn opened her hands, her eyes filled with an emotion that Casey didn't recognize. "All I really want is you, Casey, and that fucks everything up in my head. And all I can think now is that my means to an end...I have been *so* less than honorable."

Casey couldn't help but smile. She remembered what Malik had said. "Finnegan."

"And the thought that I might put you in danger somehow because of what I want from all this? The fact that our imbalance, it can only hurt you? I can live with a lot of pain, Casey. I've done it for most of my life. But not that."

"Finnegan."

"If I've just said something that didn't make sense, you should know I can fix that."

Casey laughed softly. She had never even considered a conversation such as they were having, much less making sense of one. She'd had no idea when she'd finished talking to Jack that she would be given exactly what she needed. It was new, clean territory, and despite all the questions still left to answer, she wanted to stake her claim to a nice, new piece of life. A life not too far from the shade of the adrenaline rush she enjoyed, but still within easy walking distance of happiness. "I'm less than honorable. Let's not compare suits of armor at this point."

The frown on Finn's face was quite lovely. "You're not dishonorable. Your profession is considered less than honest, it's true. It walks a rather fine line at times, but I think that has very little to do with who you are as a human being."

"And you can tell that from my toothpaste?"

Finn's eyes sparked. "No, I have empirical evidence, thank you very much. But to be fair, perhaps it's just a guess. You should know, however, that I'm extremely good at those."

Casey remembered Malik once more. "You're good at the magical big picture, is that it?"

Finn thought about the comment and then her eyes narrowed slightly before she pushed up from her chair and walked to the kitchen. Casey wanted to touch her. She had no control over that desire, at least not yet. Perhaps the price wasn't high enough at the moment for her to find a way to rein it in, but she didn't know for sure. Finn turned from the fridge and let the door close as she set two bottles of Guinness onto the counter. She twisted off a top and pushed one of the bottles to the opposite edge.

"I have a proposition for you."

Casey stood up and joined her. "Does it involve touching you? Because I can't seem to get a handle on that one, and it's trampling about on all my fine, expensive china."

Finn smiled and Casey saw the beginnings of a blush. It was an interesting addition to what she was coming to learn about her new lover, and it pleased her. "Not at the moment, no."

"That's too bad," Casey responded and took a long drink. "Because there's a few—" She stopped when Finn held up her hand. "All right, what's your proposition?"

"Even the scales. Let's play. You ask, and I'll answer."

"What's off-limits?"

"I'll let you know if I hear it. You have your plans and I have mine. Maybe everything will get blown all to hell, I don't know."

"This is crazy."

"Maybe, but I can't walk away. Not from what I need to do, and not from you, I can't. I love you, Casey. You burn right through the fucking heart of me."

Finn admitted it so openly that Casey felt a bit dizzy. She set her hand on the counter for balance.

"I'd like to give you what knowledge I can, and I guess you can do what you want with it. I owe you that. But even if I didn't owe you, I'd give you those words. They're yours now, and maybe one day, you'll remember that I gave them to you."

Casey's blood rushed in her ears.

"I have a debt to pay, and if I can't settle that debt, I'm not sure we'll ever have a chance. There's thirty-odd years' worth of things I don't know about you, Casey, and I'd like to. I have a head start on that and it isn't fair, so ask me whatever it is you need to know, because when you're done? I'm going to take you up those stairs and I'm going to find that place inside you where all your pleasure and all your secret desires live…and then I'm gonna break down the door and wait for you to do what you need to do."

Casey tipped her head back, just a bit, just enough for her to acknowledge she was in the most serious trouble of her life. She fought to find her voice. "Which is what?"

"Invite me in."

Casey turned away, unable to hold Finn's gaze. She drank instead. She took a long drink, two, three, and then four deep swallows. "Stop talking, please."

"Okay."

Casey set the bottle down and it was too loud, the clack of the heavy glass against the marble filling the space between them. "No one ever says things." Casey felt the belch rise and she let it past her lips with care. Her stomach was suddenly a mess and she had downed almost her entire bottle without thinking better of it. "No one ever says things like that, Finn, just so you know."

"Like what?"

"Like *that*, at least not that I've encountered."

"You don't like it?"

Casey took her bottle up and drank what remained before setting it down once more, this time with a lighter touch. "I fucking like it a lot, actually, but it's freaking me out."

Finn's smile was a rogue's smile as she held out her own beer. "Maybe this will help."

Casey took it with a look of challenge. It set her mind back on track just a bit and she seized the opportunity. "I can drink you under the table, O'Connell, and you know it."

"I know it, you're right."

"I can ask anything I want?"

"I'll let you know if it's off-limits."

It was an interesting proposition, and if she asked the right questions, she might find out what she needed anyway. Malik had given up more than his fair share, and without knowing he'd done it. *Or maybe he did know*, she thought. *And maybe I shouldn't even give a shit who says what, as long as I fly out of here with what I came for.* And then she wondered what that might be, exactly, as she stood on the edge of Finn's kitchen, caught within an unexpected affair that seemed to be leaving her best kept fantasies in the dust, and her own plans somewhat in jeopardy. Whoever Finn was after wanted Vincent, and

Finn was leaving him in play as bait t was a smart move. It's what she would've done.

"I won't lie," Finn added.

"How would I know if you had -I mean *really*," Casey countered.

"If I can't tell you the truth, I w n't answer the question."

"Fair enough," Casey agreed.

She wanted information, and e was wet with desire, as well. Those two things appeared to be o opposite ends of a spectrum she wasn't certain she could even track, uch less gauge what her best play might be. And she didn't really wan o play anymore, if she was going to be truly honest with herself. *Perh s I should ask, how fast can you get that fine and lovely ass of yours a flight of stairs?*

Casey stepped away from the c unter and moved in a slow circle as she considered the amount of trus she'd just been given. She would start with the basics, *and we'll see i 'm half as clever as I think I am.*

CHAPTER TWENTY-TWO

"How did you get this loft?"

Finn's smile was slow but it was genuine. "It was my grandfather's. He taught at the San Francisco Conservatory of Music. He bought it in 1953 with the money he made from his tour of Western Europe and a run of shows in New York City. My grandmother taught at Boston College at the time. He had horrible stage fright, though, and after playing Carnegie Hall he couldn't take it anymore. My grandmother said what he really hated was the tux." Finn's expression was filled with warmth. "They came here in 1955 and stayed until my father got married. They moved back to Boston, but he kept the building."

"Your grandfather played at Carnegie Hall?" It was the last thing Casey had expected to hear. "What did he play?"

"Rachmaninoff's Concerto number two."

Casey smiled. "No, I meant what instrument. The piano, then?"

"Ah, yes, but he played the cello, as well." Finn pointed across the loft. "That one over there, actually."

Casey glanced over her shoulder and found the case standing among several stacks of books. She hadn't noticed it before. "What did your grandmother teach?"

"Literature."

"Of course she did."

Finn picked up one of the bottle caps and moved it through her fingers as if it were a casino chip, with ease and a now familiar playfulness.

"Where did you study, and what?"

"Boston College—I got a tuition break because of my grandmother. I had a double major in art history and literature."

Casey moved deeper into the ft. "And you wound up working for Interpol?"

"For a time, yes."

"And how did *that* happen?" Casey asked, trying to find the thread. She turned back to the kitc n as she took a drink. Finn was considering several answers, she c ld see it. One of them was the truth and the others were lies. "Wait, she said, handing Finn a reprieve. "What else?"

"What else what?"

"You have more diplomas on t wall somewhere, I can feel it."

"I studied for one year at the lassachusetts College of Art and Design for my MFA," Finn answere as she looked down at the bottle cap. She pulled it into her palm a l closed her hand. "But I didn't finish."

"Why not?"

Finn didn't answer, nor did she ook up.

It was a source of pain, but th e was more to it than a thwarted ambition, Casey could see that uch. Something had happened, something that had changed her cou e.

"There was death in the family

Casey turned to the mantel a considered Finn's word choice. She walked to the pictures and set l r Guinness upon the smooth oak finish before she picked up the firs photo. "Is this your father?" She knew it was. There was no one else could be.

"Yes."

Casey looked back across the l t. "What's his name?"

"Ian. His name was Ian O'Con ell."

Was.

Casey set the frame down anc picked up another. The choice to move on was easy enough. She dic 't wish to cause her pain, and in fact, that was the last thing she wo ld ever want. She knew that and acknowledged it easily enough. And inn was putting herself in harm's way. "You didn't tell me you played aseball as well as football."

"I wasn't very good at baseball

Casey smiled in disagreement "I don't know, I'd say you look pretty damn hot in the uniform. It c uldn't have been all that bad for you, what with that one special che leader who followed you around everywhere, pining for you." Casey felt pleased at the thought, and a bit jealous, too. "Good Christ, that happened, didn't it." It wasn't a question.

"It's a good picture."

Casey turned at the softly spoken words, only to find Finn but a few feet away.

"But you should look again, and tell me what you see."

Casey let out a cautious breath at the timbre of Finn's voice. "It's okay, baby, I have other questions." Finn took the last few steps until their bodies touched. "Finn, you don't—"

Finn leaned down and kissed her, and Casey felt the warmth of Finn's mouth and the sweetness of her tongue, touched with the taste of Irish stout. Casey arched against her and her body reacted, the heavy ache between her legs intensifying. It was close to pain and she opened her mouth in invitation. Finn pulled her closer and obliged, right before she pulled back.

That pleasing, tender moment after their kiss was a new sensation for Casey, and her eyes drifted from Finn's, only to find her lover's mouth. They went astray from the world in the best possible way, and though there was an edge of fear to the profound connection Casey felt to her, it was an exhilarating and lush tapestry to be wrapped in.

"Look again, my love."

Casey swallowed and looked at the photo, feeling the heat of Finn's spoken endearment.

She saw Finn's wild black hair and her full lips. She saw the cheekbones and the strong shoulders, and those amber-colored eyes, filled with laughter that had been caught in the midst of a happy moment. A forgotten joy lost to the passage of time.

Casey's heart skipped oddly and she touched the glass in reaction, the fingers of her left hand tracing over the face before her. The cheekbones were sharper and the eyebrows were a bit thicker. And the nose was longer, though not by too much. The hair appeared soft upon the upper lip, barely there at all, really, the reluctant and stubborn growth of a boy's first mustache.

"His name was Declan."

Casey closed her eyes.

"Baseball moves too slowly for me," Finn explained. "But Declan loved it. I was the older one, by almost nineteen minutes."

"Finn."

"We have years between us now, and I'm still not sure sometimes if that's real."

Casey placed the picture on the mantel with exquisite care before she turned and set her hand upon Finn's chest. She stared at the collar of Finn's shirt as she tried to chart h[er] way beyond the knowledge she'd just been given. This wasn't what s[he] 'd expected, either, and it pushed her with desperate hands before sh[e] [c]ould think straight "What about your mother, where's your mother, [I] [a]n?"

"I don't know where she is," [a]ctually." Finn's tone was oddly curious. "Her family lives in New [Y]ork, real blue blood types. She's probably there, if she's still alive. S[he] left when we were ten years old and never came back."

Casey regretted the question, [bu]t neither could she take it back. "Finn, I'm sorry. I'm sorry I asked. [s]houldn't have."

"But your questions are fair, C[as]ey," Finn contradicted her. "And even if they weren't, you have the ri[ght] [i]t to ask them. I'm not hiding any of this—it's just not something I us[ua]lly lead with."

"How does any of this comp[ar]e to what brand of toothpaste I use?" Casey took a step back. She f[elt] as if she'd sullied something, as if she had thrown something away [th]at she could never get back. She wasn't sure why, or what that woul[d] [b]e, but she didn't like the feeling.

"I don't actually know what to[ ] hpaste you use," Finn said with a sheepish grin. "I was trying to make[ ] point. And you didn't ask me the most important question."

Casey wiped her palms on her j[ea]ns and took a deep breath. "What question is that?"

"Do I play?"

Casey didn't understand. "Play[ ]"

Finn moved away from her a[nd] stepped between the stacks of books. The cello case swung free w[it]h surprising ease as Finn turned back around. "Ask me."

Casey let out a startled laugh. "[If] you tell me you can play that, I'll be forced to say something we'll pr[ob]ably *both* regret."

Finn chuckled, and from the s[ou]nd, she was nothing but charmed by her words. "I find that hard to be[lie]ve, at least at the moment." Finn took a seat on the nearest chair. "A[nd] besides, I'm a fan of regretful things." Finn opened the case. "Not [th]at they happen, but that they give you the chance to make things right[ ]"

Casey was about to reply, but [a] wordless sound popped from her throat instead.

It could only be a Stradivari[us], Casey could see it within the cello's very structure. The varnish [wa]s ancient, a golden tint showing through the deep but faded red stain[ ] [i]t was solid, though, and the lines were flawless. There was an old gouge upon the left edge, but it had been smoothed down by a careful hand and the passing of years. The most interesting feature of all, was a puncture just to the left of the strings but far enough beneath the f-hole that the grain had never split, and if she didn't miss her guess, it was a bullet hole. "How old is that thing, and is it what it looks like?"

"No, it's a Guarneri. It was made in 1722, in Florence." Finn's grin was stunning. "It was given to my grandfather O'Connell just after the war, in a small town north of Salerno, along with a few other things." She set the cello between her legs. "This chair is wrong but it'll do. Are you going to ask?"

"Is that a bullet hole?"

"It is." There was a childlike joy in Finn's expression. "An Italian partisan named Pietro Gallo shot the Nazi who was playing it at the time. It went through the other side and took him in the thigh. After which, of course, Pietro adjusted his aim and shot him some more."

Casey was enchanted by the whole damn thing. "I love that you know his name."

"Pietro was the son of a rich man, and my grandfather helped him retake the town where he was from, San Michele di Serino. His entire family was gone, and it was his mother who played. A few days after the fighting was done, my grandfather tuned it and he played for Pietro, who wept for the loss of his mother. He gave it to my grandfather and kissed him on both cheeks, and told him that forever and always our family would be welcome in his home. He said, *Your blood is my blood, you are the brother of my heart. We are brothers now.* And he meant it."

"Did your grandfather ever go back?"

Finn's eyes were filled with pleasure. "Yes, we did."

"Jesus, Finn." Casey laughed. "You tell a damn good story, I have to say."

"It's the way Grandfather Pietro told it."

Grandfather Pietro, Casey thought with delighted resignation. *Richard Burton in a fucking rowboat, I am so in over my head.* "I'm about to say something we'll both regret, again."

"Listen, Marinos, I can't sit here all day," Finn shot back, though her expression said otherwise. She lifted an eyebrow and waited.

"Will you play for me?"

The deep sound that filled the loft as Finn drew the bow across the strings sent a shiver along Casey[...] spine. The sound was dense and filled with color, something liquid i[...] its depths that defied recognition as it tried to seep within her blood. [...]ly shit.

Finn tuned the cello with ease, [...] er hands certain of the task. "Just a taste, baby," Finn per[...]aded beneath the layered sound. "For my lover."

Casey was startled by the wor[...], or perhaps it was the way they were spoken. *She loves me*...And th[...] just like that, Bach's Cello Suite no. 1 filled the air.

Casey had heard it before, m[...]y times, actually. She had even heard Mischa Maisky play it in Rom[...] the night after she had pilfered a rather lovely teardrop diamond from[...]he Contessa Carlotta La Franchi. The opera house in Rome had no e[...]al in her mind, though standing in Finn's loft as Finn tilted her head[...]her eyes closed as Bach rose and filled the space between them, Case[...]reconsidered. She was good, too. Casey didn't know the particulars c[...]such things, but she suspected if Finn were playing in the Teatro de[...]'Opera di Roma, she would not have been out of place. Casey kn[...]/ she was biased, but it did not change her opinion.

A sweet transformation took pl[...]e as Finn's left hand fingered the strings, and her upper body moved [...]t times with her bow, a dance of clean, quick strokes that tilted one w[...]/ and then the other, her shoulders back. Casey saw the delicate sadnes[...]slip away, and though she wasn't quite sure what replaced it, she coul[...]eel the energy around her change. It was marvelous to stand before the[...]vave and let it wash over her.

Casey followed the movemer[...]as it progressed and the music surrounded her like a pool of light[...]Finn's bow pulling a playfulness from the notes that most likely had [...]t been intended, though it was an unexpected gift regardless of Bach[...]intentions. She had never heard Bach played in such a manner, and [...]startled her in the best possible way.

The bow descended along the[...]strings and Finn pulled free, the hum of what was yet to be left to p[...]se in the air around them. Finn's face was quiet for a moment and th[...]touched with amusement. "That wasn't the whole prelude, but it's b[...]n a while." She scratched at her thick hair and the bow bobbed behin[...]her head. "That could've been *so* much uglier, I promise you."

Casey saw everything she need[...]to see as Finn glanced up, clearly nervous of the reception she woul[...]receive. There was an unspoken apology in her eyes.

Whatever Finn's objective was, and whatever prize she was chasing, Casey no longer gave a damn. There would be answers soon enough for everyone, she was certain of that much, at least. "Don't you dare apologize...Finnegan Whoever."

Finn pulled the cello onto her left thigh with a practiced move. Casey started at the top button and moved downward, opening her shirt at a leisurely pace.

"I should practice more." Finn placed the bow within the case and undid the endpin with a knowing twist of her hand. "I usually...don't."

"When?" Casey asked, unwilling to accept the evasion. She undid the last button and let her shirt fall open. "When do you play?"

Finn set the cello into its case with care and lifted the lid over. "When I have dreams that keep me awake."

Casey undid the button of her jeans. "You should play when you're happy."

"I just did." Finn smiled as she looked up.

Casey was extremely pleased as Finn's eyes darkened and changed course within the span of a heartbeat. She leaned over and untied the laces of her left boot, and then her right, taking a small step back as she pushed free of first one and then the other. "I just realized that I've been asking all the wrong questions."

"So ask the right one."

Casey could feel her breasts become heavy, and her nipples hardened beneath the fabric of her bra. "How fast can you get that fine and lovely ass of yours up a flight of stairs?" Casey's hand slid beneath her jeans and briefs. "Because I have something that needs your attention."

Finn stood up in a fluid move.

Casey stepped to the side with a quick dodge of movement, but Finn still caught her and pulled her close. Casey laughed, and the sound filled her with as much happiness as Finn's mouth did, as it opened against hers and kissed her. She slid her hands within Finn's hair. "I'm going to make a complete mess of you—you know that, right?"

Finn lifted her up. "You already have."

Casey let out a gasp as she wrapped her legs about Finn's hips.

The books stacked upon one of the low bookcases scattered and fell to the floor, and Casey found herself perched on top of it, with Finn's hips pressed between her legs.

Casey's hands were gentle as she touched Finn's face. "Are you kicking in the door?"

Finn kissed her again, and then her words moved in a soft breath against Casey's ear. "I can't find the well."

Casey wrapped her arms about Finn's strong shoulders and held tight as she tucked her face against Finn's neck. She breathed in her scent. "I want you in my mouth," she declared. "Make the world go away now, please."

Finn's touch moved up the skin of Casey's back, filled with heat. "Stay the night."

"Yes," Casey answered and pulled back, though only to kiss Finn's pliant lips. "Yes."

"I'll take you where you need go in the morning." Finn's eyes held a savage need that shadowed her vulnerability. It was a combination that could not be denied. "I'll tell you everything, Casey, I promise... but just, just wake up with me."

Casey pushed Finn's hair back with a tender hand. "Yes. Yes, baby, I promise."

CHAPTER TWENTY-THREE

Badovinci, Serbia
September 2005

Asher stumbled across the threshold and then straightened up as his boots stuck to the thick carpet. His shoulders went back and he turned his head beneath the heavy canvas hood. His heart was racing and he could still feel the hand upon the center of his back.

He was just one bad decision away from being shot in the head and he knew it, but a part of him began to bargain anyway that it might be worth it. He'd had enough.

"Wait in here." The hand disappeared from his back. "Sit. Don't touch things. Petar won't like it."

Asher reached up and yanked the hood off as the door slammed behind him, and the sound held an odd finality that made his heart thud. He took several steps into the room before he stopped, looked over his left shoulder, and waited. He stood completely still for almost a minute, and then he took a deep breath as he surveyed the room.

It was a study of sorts, with shelves lining the wall on his left, and darker shadows with unknown spaces along the right. There was a window behind a huge desk at the opposite end of the room, but there was a massive, heavy curtain pulled over it. The fabric was red, and velvet from the looks of it, and one of the two green-shaded banker's lamps on the desk cast a strange glow that seemed to sink into the folds and disappear.

Asher reached within his jacket and pulled out his tobacco pouch and paper. His hands worked out of habit, and the comforting routine allowed his mind to catch up. He pulled a paper free with the touch of his lower lip and set about his task. He straightened the paper and portioned out the tobacco. He closed the pouch and slipped it back in his jacket, and his hands were steady as he prepared the perfect smoke.

He set the tightly rolled cigarette between his lips and stepped farther into the room, for his eyes had adjusted to the light and he was eager to take in all that he could. His gold Zippo flicked open with a ping, and the wheel scraped beneath his thumb as he closed his eyes against the momentary flame.

The books to his left were thick and bound in dark leather. Some were French and some were Russian. He recognized Tolstoy and Pasternak, and Hugo, as well as Rudyard Kipling, who seemed out of place. They seemed untouched, and when he ran his finger along the shelf beneath them there was a heavy layer of dust.

He walked along the shelves until he was beside the desk. It was somewhat cluttered, but it was orderly clutter, as such things go. There were multiple ledgers and unopened mail, all neatly stacked. There were several ashtrays, and the smell of old smoke hung in the air. He tapped his cigarette in the nearest one and eyed the phone before he looked away.

There were paintings stacked on end leaning against the bookshelves, and he glanced at the door before he leaned over. He placed his smoke between his lips before he touched the first frame, which was a heavy, scrolled oak.

It was a Kandinsky, and Asher's brow went up in curiosity as he tipped it forward in order to get at the next one. Peter Paul Rubens and a Joan Miró. Asher dropped to a knee and reached toward the desk where he put his cigarette out in the ashtray. That such paintings were stacked in a dark library that smelled of smoke, open to the changes in temperature and humidity, made his upper lip twitch with annoyance.

His attention shifted to the second stack of paintings. There were four of them, but his hand stopped in midair as he stared at the first one.

It had no frame, and you could see the darkness of the paint as it tipped about the edges, thick and as carefully painted as the rest. He pored over the image and he went to both knees before it, noting the soot and the damage to the lower left side of the canvas. He fumbled for his lighter and brought it forth again, the Zippo's flame rising on command.

Asher's right hand trembled as it hovered above the canvas. The thick rolls of paint reached out to him and the tips of his fingers whisked above them in a lover's caress.

"I think it's real."

Asher's shoulders jerked and his heart seized hard as the lighter fell from his fingers.

He grabbed at it with both hands from where it burned on the carpet and snapped it shut as he pushed to his feet. He blinked into the darkness across the room as he backed into the shelves. His fists were at his waist, ready to do what he could if he had to. He was damn good in a fight, always had been.

"I'm sorry…I didn't mean to scare you."

"Who is there?" Asher asked in a breathless voice.

Someone coughed and Asher heard the rattle and clink of metal but a moment later.

"Do you…do you have water?"

Asher took a step away from the shelves. He squinted into the heavy shadows. "Step into the light."

He heard the quiet clatter of metal once more, and then, "I can't."

Asher heard the sadness and the pain in the man's voice, and he moved slowly into the room. He didn't know if it was a mistake, but he followed his instincts and took a chance. "You know Van Gogh?"

The rattle came again, and Asher recognized it this time. It was the sound of captivity. He had been in his fair share of police stations.

"I know history."

Asher glanced to his left and then stepped to the desk. He pulled the chain on the second lamp, and the shadows that swamped the far side of the room were pushed back just enough.

Asher's stomach clenched and he felt a grimace flip over his expression. He looked at the door and did not move as he calculated the odds. It didn't matter, though, and he knew it.

He crossed what remained of the distance between him and his unexpected companion and knelt down before the wooden chair. He reached out with care and a good deal of caution.

The man was handcuffed at the wrists to the curving wood, his arms lax and weak upon the armrests. He was wet, his jeans damp and his shirt soaked through. His fingers hung useless but his knuckles were bruised and bloodied. He had gotten his licks in, for if Asher didn't miss his guess, there were broken knuckles, as well. The button-down shirt was filthy and stained with blood, both old and new.

The man's shoulders were caved in and his head lolled forward.

Asher held his chin with his left hand and, with a gentle touch, slid the fingers of his right into the man's hair. It was thick, and as black as pitch.

The man tipped back and Ashe looked into his eyes. He'd been beaten, his left eye)ruised and almost swollen shut. There was a deep cut across the brid; of his nose, and his lips had been split, his lower one swollen and cro(ed as it seemed to pull toward his strong chin. He was very young, ar Asher could feel the wet within his heavy hair, though whether it w ; blood or sweat he couldn't tell. He assumed it was both.

"My friend," Asher said gently 'I am here." The young man smiled and th blood moved along his teeth. "I think the painting is real."

Asher returned the smile, a s (and terrible feeling within his stomach. He brought his right han(down and held the young man's face. "It may be," he replied. "But i vould be a miracle if it was."

The young man took a deep l eath and Asher watched as tears slipped from his eyes and ran down is cheeks. "I'm very thirsty."

"Yes," Asher agreed. There w: something inexplicably familiar in the man's appearance, though he ouldn't say what it was. Even in such an altered and broken state, he)uld feel it. Something was there, he *knew* it, and it rang within his he l like a clarion bell. "I'll find you water, yes, but…what is your name, ly friend?"

"Declan. My name is Declan (Connell."

Chapter Twenty-four

San Francisco
Present day

Finn tried to open her eyes.

"*Finn.*"

The music she heard was the sarabande from Bach's Suite no. 4 for cello, and it moved through her body like a river of ice. The harsh, bright light that poured down from above scattered when her eyes fluttered open, unable to withstand the warm light of the bedside lamp.

They hung in the balance, together, as they always had. And so she waited for him.

"Baby, take a breath."

The hand upon her face was a familiar whisper and she let it turn her head.

Casey greeted her with a tender smile. "Hi, baby...just breathe."

Finn took a breath and blinked, the air rushing into her lungs. The tears rolled back along her temples and she understood where she was. She understood, as well, that Declan would never catch up.

Casey's hair tumbled about her face and she pushed a long curling strand behind her right ear as she leaned in. The kiss beside Finn's mouth was supple and warm, and it sent a shudder of sweetness through Finn's chest that pushed back at the cold.

"I'm glad you're awake now." Casey's right hand moved along Finn's neck as she spoke, her touch as quiet and soft as her voice was. "I was missing you."

Finn could feel Casey's naked body along her own, the heat of it, and her strong presence as it spilled over with warmth. Casey's touch moved with slow confidence down the center of her chest and Finn took another deep breath. Casey's manicu ed nails were light for a heartbeat upon the underside of Finn's left bro st, and then the softness returned as her caress moved to Finn's stoma n.

"Cassandra Marinos."

Casey stilled completely, and r what felt like forever, she held Finn's eyes.

Casey reached for the sheet a l the soft cotton billowed out as she shifted and moved in a sleek ma ner. Finn let out a breath as Casey straddled her, her weight a much nec ed anchor that held Finn in place.

Casey's hands traveled over Fii 's breasts and then along her ribs, her fingers opening as her touch ex ored. Each caress had a purpose and Finn's body reacted, her tight muscles easing as Casey leaned forward.

Casey took ownership of Fi 's lips, and Finn was helpless against the softness, against the tast of her and the texture of Casey's tongue when it found her own. Case 's gentle fingers were in her hair, pushing and then pulling back alor her scalp as Finn slid her hands upon Casey's thighs. Finn's heart wa pounding within her chest as she tried to remember the word she wan d. None of her words were where they should be.

"What is it, baby?"

Casey's hands were hot agaii her cheeks and her eyes were bright.

"Slivovitz," Finn whispered, a d her heart was pounding for an entirely new reason when Casey sn led with delight. Finn could feel the blood again, pushing through l r veins. She was alive. She was alive, and her love was here.

"How is it you're so charming

Finn felt the last of her tears s le free and Casey kissed her, her breath a balm against Finn's bruisec kin.

"I'm going to do things to yc now." Casey's whisper invaded her head, the words like an entirely ew dream that danced along her earlobe. "And then we're going to back to sleep, together. Do you see, baby?"

Finn felt the ache of arousal tween her legs, her flesh heavy with it. Her grip upon Casey's waist ghtened and her hips shifted with a slow push.

Casey bit at her lower lip with a smile. "Will you let me please you, Daddy?"

Finn let out a breath of surprise

"What?" Casey teased. "After tonight, Finnegan Starkweather O'Connell Whoever, if you're not my Daddy, I won't *ever* be having one."

"No."

"No?"

"No, I mean…" Finn fought for what she wanted to say. "No one's ever asked me that before."

Casey drew her nails over Finn's breasts, lightly, but not so lightly that Finn didn't feel the repercussions of it. The muscles in her thighs and buttocks tightened and Casey's hands dropped to the bed on each side of her as she leaned down.

"Good," she whispered. "They weren't meant for you. They were fools, and they weren't good enough for you."

Casey's eyes were fierce, almost angry, and Finn fell all over again.

"Tell me to make you come, Finnegan."

Finn could hear the intense need in Casey's voice, and her stomach flipped over in a rather elaborate manner. The sensation poured into her thighs and the flesh between her legs clenched. "Tell me." Casey leaned in and kissed her with just a touch of force. "Tell me, Daddy, please." Her next kiss was deeper, potent with desire and impatience. "Tell me you want my mouth on you. Say it, Daddy, *please*."

"I want your mouth on me." Finn's voice was rough, though her lips were wet from the attention. She could feel her pulse move through them and they felt lush with life.

"Yes, baby."

In an agile move Casey parted Finn's legs and her own body settled between them. Finn sucked in her breath as Casey's mouth found her right nipple.

Beneath the touch of Casey's tongue and the caress of her hands, Finn's thoughts faltered, uncertain of what was real, and what might be a dream. Casey lifted up and her stomach stroked against the wetness of Finn's flesh.

She shuddered with pleasure as Casey indulged her need. Casey kissed Finn with an open mouth, and she pulled at Finn's skin, leisurely but with purpose, marking Finn's body as she pressed between her legs. When Finn moaned, Casey trailed her nails along her ribs until Finn's body jerked beneath the touch and her hips pushed from the bed.

Finn's hand delved into Casey's hair and tightened, and Casey turned her face, patient as Finn trembled.

"I love you," Finn whispered a l let her go.

Casey's mouth resumed its e loration, and when she stopped at Finn's belly and kissed her scar tears of surprise welled up and slipped from Finn's eyes. "Only me." Casey's weight s fted and her touch moved upon Finn's inner thighs. "Only me, baby lo you hear?" Finn's back arched when Cas 's mouth took possession of her sex, her hands finding the sheet ben th them and pulling.

❖

Casey sat on the edge of the be and looked down at Finn.

She was sleeping hard, and fr n her serene expression, she was not bothered by dreams of any sort, nuch less bad ones. Her skin had a soft shine to it and her muscles se ned spent and pliable. The sheet was at her lower back and Casey re ched out and lifted the edge. The cotton slid easily and Casey laid it Finn's shoulders, noting the pink scratches she had left upon her back

I hadn't known I could do tha sweet Finnegan, Casey thought. Her fingers were like a breeze as t y moved through Finn's tumble of hair. It wasn't enough though an so she pressed farther, the strands dense and familiar within her hand. *'ve longed for that abandon. I've longed for that...for you.*

The bruise around Finn's left e was dark in the low light, and there was still the small stain of n v blood along her eyebrow. She remembered the heat of it against he face, unable to pull away for they had been too far gone, both upon th edge of the abyss. Casey's desire had become clean and savage in nn's absence, locked away and biding its time. Finn had alluded to much, and she'd been right. That Finn had matched that passion so n urally—it frightened her now, as it hadn't the night before.

She had no idea what would h pen next. She had no idea where they would end. Perhaps they wou l just end, and that would be it. The moment she walked out that d r, the wheels of the world would turn again, and they would spin like fucking freight train. Where that would leave Finn's heart, she had n idea. Where it might leave hers, she didn't dare speculate, not yet. aybe when their game was over, they could meet again and none of i vould matter.

Casey closed her eyes.

She had showered and used Fir 's towels and the toothbrush Finn had given her. Her body felt utterly consumed, and in a way she had never experienced before. It was sublime and overwhelming at the same time, though she had stayed focused on what needed to be done.

She had dressed quickly, putting on Finn's Foo Fighters tee beneath her own shirt. It smelled of Finn and her faded cologne, and it was sinfully soft from wear and countless washings. It belonged to Casey now. She did not even question the taking of it.

If she waited for Finn to wake up, she would never leave. She knew it. She had promised and she had meant it, at least when she had spoken the words.

She hadn't known what would come after, though. She hadn't realized how far she had fallen, nor how deep the rabbit hole had gone. But now she found herself sitting at the bottom and looking up, with no sunlight in sight.

Tears fell when she opened her eyes. "I'm sorry," she confessed, so softly that only Finn's books gave witness to her words. Her throat was brutally tight. "I'm so sorry."

She did not look back as she moved like a ghost from the bedroom, accepting she might never return. For the next thirty years, just as Finn had said, she wanted to explore all there was to discover, or at least give it a shot, but those years would not start today.

As she descended the stairs and moved past the kitchen, she reached out and palmed Finn's abandoned bottle cap from the counter.

She grabbed her jacket and punched in the code for the door, and then her hand trembled above the handle.

The echo of Bach's cello suite moved through her like a wave of color, red with passion and blue with whispers meant only for her. Finn's promise against her ear as they lay spent and tangled, the only two people on earth. *I love you.*

Casey's determination faltered. *I'll tell you everything, I promise.*

She turned the handle with a violent grip, knowing somehow that whatever Finn would tell her would ruin all her plans.

Once on the other side, she waited for the lock to catch and the dead bolt to reset, and then she took the stairs, her feet moving fast as her right hand slid along the rail. The crimped edges of the bottle cap dug into the palm of her left hand, the fist she made unable to tighten any farther. It was the only thing that kept her from running like a complete fool when she hit the street.

CHAPTER T\ ENTY-FIVE

Casey heard the music float around er and she pulled herself through the fog in order to reach it. Her har pushed through the covers until she found her phone. "Yeah…"

"Jesus." There was laughter. ' ough night, or the best night of your life?"

Casey rubbed at her eyes and oked at her phone. The face that greeted her pushed her toward reali , despite that she hadn't meant to accept a video call. "Jack."

"The one and only. I'm almost iere."

"Coffee?"

"Yes, there is. I even went to S rbucks for you."

Casey flopped back onto the p low and dropped the phone. Her muscles, maybe even her very bones were still in a dream state and she closed her eyes. She felt Finn's mou i against the side of her neck and Finn's lips were soft with new sec ts. She was pulled back beneath the covers by the heat of Finn's bod and her stomach gave a pleasing flutter. She spoke softly to her lover Do I have to get up?"

There was a long pause and the Jack's quiet voice. "I could work the lock, but then I'd spill your mas vely expensive drink."

Casey's eyes shot open and sh blinked at the ceiling. A rush of adrenaline pushed through her che as her brain caught up, and she looked to her left to find only pillows She drew in a deep breath through her nose and let it out through her nouth before she gave herself a mental shake and grabbed the phor again. "I'll get it," she said and hung up as she threw off the covers id got out of bed.

She slid the phone onto the ta le as she passed, her dishes still there from earlier in the day. She c nbed at her hair with her fingers and walked to the door as her musc s began to wake up. She flipped the security bar, turned the dead bolt, and opened the door with a hard pull.

Blackjack Vermillion handed her a Venti coffee with a smile. "I like the shirt."

Casey looked down. "So do I," she replied and turned her back. "What time is it?"

"Almost three." He closed the door behind him.

"Did you get what I asked for?"

"Some of it. Colin sent you some files, too, but he's still digging. He told me to tell you if he winds up at a black site somewhere in Poland, you're next on his list."

Casey smiled as she set her coffee on the table. She walked into the bathroom and the door swung behind her. "If he winds up at a black site in Poland"—her voice was raised in order to reach the outer room— "I'm sure I'll be the least of his problems." She sat down and reached for the toilet paper. "And that's aside from the fact that I obviously paid him too much and would require a refund."

"What does any of this have to do with Sir Jeffery Wilkinson?" Jack asked. "Nothing has changed. He's still in town, and he's still willing to pay a bloody fortune for anything Van Gogh, according to Eric. The only thing we have to worry about is if he has a fucking heart attack when he sees it. Or if he has enough money to outbid everyone else, once they realize what it is."

"Someone else wants a Vincent just as badly." Casey stood, flushed the toilet, and stepped to the sink to wash her hands.

Jack grunted from the other room, unconvinced.

"I need to find out who's going to be there." Casey grabbed her pajama bottoms from the hook on the back of the door and stepped into the soft cotton. They weren't as plush as Finn's had been, but she moved past the thought. "I don't think we're in trouble." Casey opened the door and returned to the main room where she retrieved her coffee. "But someone else sure as hell is. Let's hope it's not Eric's mystery buyer."

"I'm not buying his spiel about that one, and besides, all we have to do is get Vincent to the party. We don't even have to be there, really. I mean, it's not actually required of you."

"I'll be there." Casey sat down. "And I'm going to watch as Eric personally transfers all that money into my account. I don't trust him, Jack, not on this one. Not one goddamn bit."

Jack leaned his elbows on the table, his eyes sharp and clear in their assessment of her. He had moved the dishes aside and placed her computer in front of her chair. "Have you spoken with him?"

"Not yet, no. Maybe I'll buy something small and play the good little heiress, dipping her toe in the dark rivers of sin. No one will know who I am, and I can keep an eye on things."

Jack sighed and leaned back in his chair, taking a sip of his coffee as Casey began to type. "So you're absolutely certain she's after one of the buyers?"

"Yes."

"Not the Rembrandt?"

"No."

"So she's been following you order to get to the auction. That makes sense." Jack was clearly no saying what he wanted, and she knew it.

Casey sipped at her coffee an set it aside. "I'm giving you a bonus for the mocha." She almost si hed. "Thank you."

"Does she know about Vincent

Oh, well, there's a nice healt piece of it, Casey thought, but didn't answer his question.

"If she does, Casey, that chan s the game. We need to pull up stakes." His voice slipped into a ne that betrayed his underlying anxiety and she didn't really blame l n. "We'll take a hit on the payoff, but you are *way* too close to this w for us to get out clean. This isn't just some run-of-the-mill Van G gh, not that such a category even exists. This is it, Casey. Once it's s n? It's *the* Van Gogh. Wilkinson might be the odds-on favorite to wa away with it, but if she wanted *him,* she certainly didn't need you o he auction to find him. Sir Jeffrey is right out in the open. That means ere's someone else she's looking for and Vincent is the bait. Whether s Eric's mystery man or not, that puts us right in the middle of some ne else's play. That's not a good place to be, kiddo, especially if you n't trust Eric to protect us."

"This is just getting harder, Jac all of it. The sale is *here,* the sale is *now.* Once it's made and Eric tran ers the money, whatever is going on behind the scenes is no concern ours." She returned her attention to the screen, knowing there was a sperate edge to her voice. "I just want it gone. I want it out of my life. et it be someone else's problem." She covered her eyes with a hand d tried to banish the last of her sleep. "Why didn't Asher sell it, Ja ? He let it sit there for years in Mabelle's attic, for God's sake. And ow did he even get it there? Yes, Mabelle's is the safest place in the world, but why *here?* It doesn't make sense. We have a safe house in London, and in Paris, as well. Unless he found it here in the States, he would've had to smuggle it halfway across the world. I mean, what the hell was he doing?"

"Maybe that's the question of the day, you know? Not to mention that if *that* was hanging on someone's wall as their own little war trophy and fuck-you to the world, they might be wanting it back. If Starkweather knows it's here, Casey, she's probably not the only one, because I'm pretty sure she's not on Eric's invitation list."

Casey smiled at that. "No, I don't think she is."

She had wondered about a connection between Finn and Eric, more than once. Now it seemed foolish. *Although, none of this explains the convenience of everything happening in your own backyard, my sweet Finnegan. I'm still missing a piece of your puzzle.*

It had been damn good business for Eric to acquiesce to her subtle request as to a preferred venue for the sale. She was bringing a Van Gogh to the party and so it was more than wise to play nice. When she had wistfully talked about the San Francisco shopping and the nightlife, he had listened, and no doubt, he had agreed with her. As far as Casey knew, however, no one had *ever* dictated the terms or circumstances of an auction to Eric Werner. Her relief had been immense—she had to admit it. The thought of trying to move the painting back overseas and through the increased customs scrutiny, or even just across the country, had made her want to destroy the damn thing herself before she took such a risk. The inherent and unnecessary dangers involved with such an endeavor had never been a part of her practice.

"The auction is tomorrow night, kiddo. Eric's rules say he takes possession of all items for sale by eight in the morning, the day of. Either we get the painting ready tonight for delivery, or we pull up stakes and drift."

"I want it gone, Jack. Let's just do it and take our shot at the big score." The words made Casey feel exhausted. "I'd like to live my life and never look back. So could you, for all of your chop shop mayhem and pissing around."

Jack smiled. "Are you sure about this?"

"Yeah, I'm sure."

"All right. Let's do it."

Colin's files began to download and Casey took up her coffee again. She leaned back in her chair, an odd mirror to Jack's position. "What? You've changed your mind already?"

"No, it's just…you look different, from when I saw you last."

Casey made a sound of annoyance. "Like I've seen the light?"

"No," Jack shot back. "You loo..."

Cassie waited, but he didn't finish. She looked away and her gaze fell to the bed across the room. Her bed was empty. *Just like my promises.* "I look good."

"You do," he said, and there was satisfaction in his voice. "You look as right as fucking rain, if you want the truth." He took a drink. "Strange how that can happen, just like that."

Cassie stared at the bed. "Are you going to tell me about one of your wives now?"

Jack's chuckle eased her just a bit. It always did. "No, I never married Sabine."

Cassie turned, surprised. He'd had four wives so far, and none of them was named Sabine. "Sabine?"

Jack contemplated his coffee and fiddled with the lid. "Yeah, Sabine. I always thought it was a pretty name."

"It is. It's a beautiful name."

He wiped at the coffee lid with his thumb and straightened it just how he wanted it. "The best damn twenty-six days and thirteen hours of my life."

"You didn't ask her to marry you?"

"No." His smile was filled with regret. "She was too good for me, you know?"

Casey frowned. "No, Jack, I don't know that, and I don't believe it."

"All I'm saying is, don't run if you don't have to. It's not worth it, no matter what's going on with all this Van Gogh bullshit."

"I'm not running anywhere."

"No yet, maybe," Jack continued with his thought. "But it'll come. I don't know when, but there'll be a moment. You'll be walking away with every intention of going back. Maybe you'll be going out for coffee, or food, or whatever, and then it hits you, and you'll panic, and you'll run. It's what we're good at. It's what we do."

Casey returned to her computer screen. "Maybe."

She should have said something. She should've woken Finn up. She should've kissed her, and touched her one last time before the game started in earnest. It was a fact, and her guilt and grief were already a throbbing ache within her chest.

She thought of the devastation in Finn's eyes as she had fought her way free of her nightmares, and the relief that had replaced it when

Finn had understood where she was. Casey remembered the love she had heard in the softly spoken sound of her name. She hadn't known her name could sound like that.

She remembered the taste of Finn's body and the joy that had sent her spilling into the unknown when she had made Finn come. The sounds that Finn had made drifted through Casey's head, and her body reacted to the memory—she couldn't stop it. There was suddenly heat and need as she felt the ghost of Finn's hand tremble within her hair and take hold.

"Hey."

Casey looked across the table.

"Are you okay?"

Casey's face felt hot and she regarded her expensive coffee. "I already ran, Jack. It doesn't matter now."

"Well, you didn't run very far."

"How far did *you* go?" Casey's tone was filled with sudden anger.

"Thailand."

Casey blinked at him and then laughed. "Jesus, Jack, what the hell?"

"I was young."

Casey sighed and pushed at her thoughts, willing them into order. She took several long drinks of her coffee, even though it was still a bit hot. "I wish I smoked," she whispered and sat up in her chair. She had never realized how calming it had been to watch Asher roll one of his cigarettes, not until he was gone at least. She longed for that feeling of peace again, and to have him near. His presence had made everything all right, always.

"No, you don't," Jack responded. "You'd have to stand out front on the street. People throw loose change. It hurts."

Casey chuckled as she opened her downloads folder.

"Pick up some dinner and go back, Casey. Knock on the door and wait for it to open. When it does? Tell her you're bloody well sorry. Just ask her what's going on. Maybe she'll tell you."

I'll tell you everything, Casey, I promise.

Casey didn't want to know, and she had accepted that fact with both resignation and a touch of disgrace. Finn's goal was beyond the banality of money, whatever it was, and Casey had known this morning that she would give in, even if Finn never asked her to. It didn't matter what it might be, she'd give in. *Hell, Finn, I couldn't resist you after five minutes, much less the last four days. I would've just handed it all away, all the freedom and safety the Vincent will bring. Where would that leave me?*

"And what if you're wrong, Jack?"

His expression was somewhat annoyed as he grabbed his coffee and sat back. "And just for the record, if you really think that we can't trust Eric? We should go elsewhere.

"Eric is a fierce enemy to have. It isn't like it used to be, Jack. We'd be pinched within six months, that's my guess. And hitting the open market goes against one of the two things that Asher told me I should *never* do, and I never have, and I've never been caught. Always have a middleman who's more dangerous than the buyer."

"What was the second thing?"

"Don't shit where you eat."

Jack laughed and put his feet on the table. "So how's that one working out?"

Casey smiled—she couldn't help it. He was right. "Better than you'd think." She felt the weight of right down to the floor.

His laugh turned into his trademark giggle. "Don't be such a pussy, Casey."

"You think I was kidding about getting caught?"

"I think you're scared."

Casey's eyes narrowed. "Of going back?"

"Yes."

"You're wrong."

"No, I'm not. I was terrified, and I never mustered up the balls to make it right. It's a decision I regret very day, right when I wake up… and she's not there."

Casey searched through her downloads folder and tried to ignore him. She was hanging on by a thread as it was. "Badovinci," she said as she copied each of Colin's folders and arranged them on her desktop. "Why does that sound so familiar?"

"Jesus Christ," Jack said in a breath. "What are you looking at, Casey?"

Casey's hand upon the mouse stilled and she looked across the table. "Colin's files."

"What the fuck does Badovinci have to do with Finnegan Starkweather?"

Casey remained very still and tried to assess his reaction. His tone was dark and it held a touch of honest-to-God fear. She'd never heard Jack afraid of anything. "Should I know what this means, Jack?"

He seemed to debate his words before proceeding. "Badovinci, Serbia, maybe eleven years ago? That's where Thomasino Lazarini's daughter was murdered, along with seven other people. Some say it was a botched kidnapping attempt, and some say it *was* a kidnapping, and Lazarini just flat out refused to pay the ransom." Jack pulled his feet from the table, turned in his chair, and faced her. His expression was not a comfortable one. "I don't believe he would've done that, though, but whatever happened, it didn't end well for a lot of people."

Casey felt her anxiety rise at Jack's words, and an odd chill skated along the back of her neck, tickling over the surface of her scalp. She didn't understand why she hadn't recognized the name. As Jack spoke, she began to remember, disturbed by the fact that she needed his prompt to do so. A surge of discomfort began to roll through her stomach, and all she knew was that she wanted to be with Finn. She wanted her near, more than she could possibly put into words.

"Interpol was called in by the Serbian police, and UN investigators, too, I think. That's when they were trying so hard to join the EU, and everything was a total cluster all the way around. The Italian *Guardia di Finanza* investigated things, which wasn't a surprise, really, considering the amount of power the Lazarini family has. There turned out to be a lot more bodies buried at Badovinci than just those connected with Isabella Lazarini, and they figured it was a dumping ground for someone, during and after the Balkan Wars. They never did find out who that someone was. They've called him the Badovinci Butcher ever since."

Casey studied the lines on Jack's face as she tried to slow her breathing. She was looking at his chin when she asked her question. She forced her voice out, as if it were a car that had stalled and she had to use all her strength in order to push it onto the shoulder of the road. "Who do they think it was?"

"The talk has always been Ketrin Arshavin, but no one has ever gone on record with that." Jack made a face of complete distaste. "No one wants to die in little pieces scattered about Europe."

Casey returned to her computer and clicked on the first file. The page blossomed onto her screen and she began to scroll through a copy of the official confidential Interpol report. "I should remember this," she whispered as she skimmed through the pages. "This isn't something that I would ever forget." Casey felt as if the floor had tipped beneath her. "I should…"

A cold ribbon of emotion slithered around her spine and punched its way through her rib cage, leaving splinters in its wake as she let out a harsh, startled sound. Her shoulders pulled in as her body instinctively made itself as small as possible without her conscious consent.

"Casey?"

Casey heard his voice, but she couldn't quite process what her response should be.

"Hey, Casey."

She wanted to pull her gaze away from the photos, but she couldn't do it. She wanted them burned clean from her mind.

"*Casey.*" Jack's voice held clear authority over the moment.

Jack was blurred within her sight, and he seemed to waver and tip as her tears spilled over and slid down her cheeks. Her touch left the mouse and she placed her hands together in her lap. The shocking, brutal certainty of what she had seen was followed by a wave of relief so profound and immeasurable, that for a few seconds, she wasn't sure what might happen. No doubt she would be damned for it.

"It's okay," Jack offered. "Whatever it is."

"I know what she wants," Casey said and let out a breath of startled, distressed laughter. She could not undo what she saw, and she could never make it right. Her voice sounded terribly strange to her ears, as if she had spoken from another spot within the room. As if she were standing beside her empty bed. "I understand now."

"That's good, Casey." Jack's voice was soothing. "Is it okay to tell me?"

Casey nodded and she wiped at her eyes. She reached out and closed her laptop, slowly and with great care, so as not to upset the delicate balance of fate. "She wants revenge."

Belgrade, Serbia
September 2005

Finn stared at the side of the computer monitor as the noise from the police station washed over her. She could smell cigarette smoke and it was harsh to her nose, a stale scent that was nothing like the sweet cigars they smoked on the patios in San Michele. The lights were bright and she felt ill, as if she were floating slightly above her chair. It was a dizziness that invaded all her senses, and if she moved her head too fast, her stomach lurched.

There were voices on the phones, and she could understand very little of what they said. She had recognized three different languages so far, and when a phone rang, the old-fashioned sound rattled inside her skull as if she were being pelted with rocks.

There were black uniforms and blue uniforms, and the gray-green of the Italian police. She could smell burned coffee beneath the smoke, and some sort of sausage, perhaps, from someone's lunch. It was a pungent and yet somehow flat scent.

Her eyes moved slowly to the right and she stared at the inspector in front of her.

He had turned from his computer and he was speaking, but she didn't care what he might be saying. He leaned forward in his chair and set his elbows on the desk.

Finn closed her eyes against his words.

She saw the shackle wounds on Declan's wrists, and his broken hands. She saw the burn marks along his ribs and the bruises that trailed down his thighs like theater paint. She saw his face again, battered and split and devoid of life, and the divot in his forehead where the bullet had entered at last.

Finn opened her eyes.

The fingers that snapped in front of her face seemed to move in slow motion and she felt her stomach roll.

The inspector held out a pen and waited.

Finn took the pen and watched as he slid several papers across the desk.

"Sign, please."

The inspector sat back with an odd look on his face and then he pushed away from the desk in order to stand.

A familiar scent invaded Finn's nose and she felt the heat of another person against her right shoulder. She hadn't realized how cold she was until that moment. Her toes burned with cold within her shoes and her hand could barely hold the pen. She trembled and it shimmied outward as her thighs shook.

The soft silk of hair brushed against her cheek and it smelled faintly of sweet grass and summer grapes. It was a clean, fresh scent. It was a woman's scent.

The hand that touched her cheek was tender. "It's okay, Finn, everything's going to be okay. Just sign the papers, sweetie, and we can go." The heat of her voice drifted down the side of Finn's neck.

Finn looked down at the desk.

"Just write your name at the bottom, and we can go outside and stand in the sun. Please, Finn, we ⟨ca⟩n't be in here anymore, but you have to help me."

Finn blinked at the forms an⟨d⟩ suddenly she understood. They wouldn't let her take Declan home, ⟨a⟩nd they wouldn't let her take his things, even what little there was to ⟨cl⟩aim, if she didn't sign her name.

"Sign them, Finnegan, and w⟨e⟩ won't ever have to come back here—I swear to God. I'll get you ⟨ou⟩t of here. I'll get us both out of here."

Finn signed the papers.

CHAPTER TWENTY-SIX

San Francisco
Present day

Finn looked out onto the city and though the afternoon sun was still bright, the breeze was cold and damp as it tried to snake beneath her leather duster. The view was not the best in the city, but it was achingly familiar, and the neighborhood was one that she loved. It was a good place to get her mind right, before she did what was necessary.

She felt the weight of the Kevlar vest she wore and the smooth sleeves of the tactical compression shirt beneath it. She wore a black button-down shirt over both and she was as protected as she could be, without drawing undue attention to herself. Her jeans were dark and heavy over her boots, and she could feel the weapons she wore. A Walther PPK on the back of each hip, and a Sig Sauer P250 strapped beneath her left arm. The hideout holster on her left ankle held a Bersa Thunder 380.

It all seemed foolish and extreme and yet she knew exactly what she was doing. She would have never in a million years expected to be good at such things, but they came as naturally to her as reciting a page of poetry. Poetry had been more Declan's love than hers, but she had held her own.

She took a deep, clean breath and closed her eyes.

She had waited her whole life for Casey, and she had been right to do so. She had even known it in Monte Carlo, though she hadn't known who Casey was at the time. She hadn't known anything at all, except that they belonged together. Finnegan's radar, Declan had called it, and Finn had never really formed a logical argument to dispute his claim.

The magical big picture, Malik was ond of saying, and she had never disputed his words, either.

She didn't know what it was 1 the end, only that Declan had something to do with it, and he'd 1 .d his own version of it. He had always known what the next pitch v uld be.

She had woken up alone, and tl ugh the reality of what that meant had blistered its way through the h irt of her, she understood why it had happened. It didn't make it hur iny less, but there was an honest symmetry to it. She had never wan d a head start, but circumstances had pushed her down that path wit very little say in the matter. She had always been out in front, and ie had never expected Casey to overcome the distance between th(i in so short a time. She hadn't expected anything, actually, though ie had wished for the world.

She had gambled everything at Ketrin Arshavin would come for his trophy, and she could think f only one last move that might lead her to his door while leaving (isey completely absent from the equation. One last move that would low her to keep her promise.

If it doesn't kill me first.

She could feel the presence of ie ocean in the distance, and she could feel the presence of Petar Dir trovich, as well. She hadn't been wrong, and neither had Asher James

Finn opened her eyes, turned, nd walked toward the patio door with a rather insolent smile. "I'm ot to sell my teeth, old man."

Athens
April 2010

"*The doctor seemed especially tr(bled by the fact of the robbery having been unexpected, and attem, ed in the night-time; as if it were the established custom of gentleme* ...Good Lord, my friend, I have never seen so many commas." Ashe frowned and cleared his throat in order to properly deepen his voice a he read aloud from *Oliver Twist*. "*As if it were the established custom f gentlemen in the housebreaking way to transact business at noon, nd to make an appointment, by the twopenny post, a day or two pr ious.*" Asher considered what he had just read and then gave a snoi of agreement. "They are always surprised, it's true. Dickens was not /rong."

Asher's heart gave a thud as F1 iegan opened her eyes.

The hospital room was quiet it for the hum of the monitors,

which were not that loud. The heating unit on the outside wall beneath the fourth-story window was the loudest thing of all, but Asher had learned to tune it out over the past three nights. The clinic on the outskirts of Athens was a good one, and though he was not a wanted man, he had entered through a back stairwell from the basement and kept Finn company without anyone being the wiser. The nurse would check on her patient at the top of each hour, though before that happened, he would make himself scarce while wearing counterfeit credentials.

The clinic security was better than most, and there were guards in the lobby who would verify and provide identification badges for each visitor. Asher had purchased what he needed the evening he had arrived, all for the price of four or five drinks, one hundred euros, and three hours of listening to an orderly complain about living with his mother. It was a sticky situation that involved a basement and a cat, and Asher had listened with true empathy. He knew about cats.

Asher stood up and leaned over the bed, his hand gentle as he slipped it beneath hers. "My friend!" His voice was low but filled with pleasure as he greeted her. As far as he could tell from her medical chart, she had been unconscious since her surgeries, the day of her arrival. It was the first time she had been awake within his presence. "It is very good to see you."

Her eyes were confused.

"You are in a clinic outside of Athens. You were shot in the belly, two times." Asher's voice was clear and firm, but still filled with happiness. "It was bad, but you'll be fine."

Finn's grip tightened around his thumb. It was not much, almost nothing, really, but it was enough for him.

Asher nodded. "Yes. It was a mess, from what the papers say. Your partner, he is well. He was shot in the shoulder and neck, but the angle of the bullet was good for him. It missed the important things, lucky for him. He is just down the hall from you, right now," he explained. "I have seen his wife in the café downstairs. She likes to talk." Asher smiled. "She is a nicely proportioned woman, I have to say."

Finn closed her eyes and Asher could see the left side of her mouth turn up.

He stepped closer and, with great caution, sat upon the edge of the bed. Finn showed no discomfort in reaction and Asher was relieved. "I think you must leave your job now, after this, Finnegan. We will find another way."

Finn opened her eyes.

"I do not like it, and I think you can do better for yourself." Her eyes were thick with medication, but he could see her surprise. She was listening.

"They are too vulnerable to the grift, do you understand? You are not safe there." Asher's voice was convinced. "I believe that you were betrayed in some way. You may call it a hunch, if you like, but I have my sources, as well." He was talking too much, he knew it, but his fear for her was finally finding an outlet. "And, you know, I see these bounties, and it is a lot of money for the taking. Why should you do these things for wages, when you could make yourself a rich woman? And you would still be in the hunt. There would be no rules, only the ones you choose to follow."

Asher sat beside her for a long time then and held her hand. He was extremely distressed and he was afraid it would show. When she squeezed his thumb once again, he leaned forward.

"I will."

Asher smiled, but he could see the bargain within her lovely eyes. "But?"

Finn licked her lips and swallowed. "Domino."

Asher was surprised. "Ah, yes...what of my Domino, sweet Finnegan?"

The expression within her gaze was decidedly certain and he recognized it. "She was the treasure you took from Ketrin."

Asher stared, thrown for a loop by her words.

"Your name...isn't just James." She could barely manage a smile, but she tried. "It's Asher. Asher James."

Asher let out a puff of breath and his hand tightened on hers. It was the last thing he'd expected from her, though in the end, he was not all that surprised. She was a woman with both practical and dangerous skills, and they were painted through her character with the heavy, rich colors of her humor and melancholy. It was a magnificent combination.

"I remember."

Asher held her gaze for a long time and she did not look away, nor did she drift off to sleep. It was an effort for her to stay with him and he could see it. "As I remember you..." His sudden smile could not be stopped. "I have been waiting for Ian O'Connell's daughter to arrive. I am glad you are here now."

"You shouldn't have—" Pain washed through her expression and she closed her eyes. It passed, but when she looked at him again, her strength was gone and her hand was lax within his. "Asked me that question."

Asher laughed softly and leaned down farther, even as he lifted her hand. He kissed the back of it with all the affection he felt for her. "But I am French, my friend. Such a question cannot be avoided forever."

CHAPTER TWENTY-SEVEN

Novi Sad, Socialist Federal Republic of Yugoslavia
June 1986

Finnegan sat in the long grass on the hill and looked down at the road. The man had walked around the car several times and he had leaned down beneath the hood more than that. He had fidgeted with the engine inside and he had thrown his tools, and then he had picked them up and put them back in the bag where they lived. He had smoked five cigarettes and he'd used bad language, as well. She didn't know what he said, exactly, but she knew it wasn't good.

"What are you looking at?"

Finn looked over her left shoulder and smiled at her brother. "There's a man down there on the road. His car doesn't work."

Declan wore faded jeans and a red and blue plaid shirt, the flannel worn and soft. His black hair was a mess and he had a juice stain around his lips. She did, too, though, so it was okay. Declan sat down next to her and pulled his right foot back, his knee coming up. He leaned over and retied his shoe, the black Converse covered with dirt. "Dad said to come to the grove for lunch."

"Okay."

They sat there, though, and time went by. The man below rolled another cigarette and lit it with a match that he shook out and dropped on the road before stomping on it with his boot.

"Who's in the car?"

"Somebody small."

Declan reached over and fixed Finn's collar, which was turned under.

"Hey."

They turned as one.

Ian O'Connell smiled and came to a stop as he looked at his children.

If Finn's hair hadn't been a bit longer than Declan's, he would've had a hard time telling them apart, and he knew and understood them better than anyone else on earth. The novelty of that difficulty wouldn't last long, once Declan hit his growth spurt, and so Ian enjoyed the beauty of it. "What's going on?"

"There's a man down there on the road," Finn began.

"Whose car doesn't work," Declan finished.

Ian stepped up behind his children and set his hands on his hips. He watched the man smoke his cigarette for several moments, taking his measure as the man stared beneath the hood of the old Renault. "Did you think to help him out?"

"I can't fix a car just yet," Finn answered. "I'm sorry to say."

Ian smiled and tried not to laugh at her tone, which was drier than a bone left in the desert sun for years on end. There was not an ounce of meanness in it, no matter how hard you might look for it, only wry amusement. It was a tone that was much too old for all her eight years, but it belonged to her regardless. It was her mother's, as well, and it was Finn's inheritance. "Declan, go back and fetch Papa Aedan. He's good with cars."

Declan pushed to his feet, spun about, and broke into a sprint with a smile.

Ian stepped up beside his daughter and held out his hand. "Shall we introduce ourselves, my darling satirical child?"

Finn grabbed his hand and pulled herself up. She leaned against him. "You're gonna give me some sort of a complex."

Ian chuckled. "Do you even know what that means?"

"Grandma says I'll need therapy for it, whatever it is."

Ian considered her statement and nodded. "Probably."

He gave her hand a pull and they started down the small hill.

"Do I have to go to class for that?"

"For what?"

"Therapy."

Ian smiled, a bit surprised. "No, sweetie, I'm sorry. Don't worry. I'll stop giving you a complex."

"Maybe you could just give Declan one."

Ian held back his laughter once again. "I'll see what I can do."

The man turned from his car as they approached, and he was

startled, seemingly out of his eleme as he took a small step back. He dropped his cigarette and used his l ot to put it out. When he looked up, he had recovered and his smile s emed cautious but genuine.

"Do you need some help?" Ia said as they neared. He noticed the blond-haired girl in the front se "Go see." Ian swung Finn's arm forward with his, and Finn let go of s hand and hurried to the car. She took hold of the small bit of window hat was still rolled up and looked into the car.

"You speak English?"

The man spoke with a heavy F nch accent, but his pronunciation was clear and precise. Ian stepped fc ward and extended his right hand. "Yes. My name is Ian O'Connell, by vay of Boston. We're American."

"Asher James." The man respc ded with an easier smile than his first one, and his blue eyes were fill l with relief. "Thank you. Thank you for coming down." Asher gestu d to the path they'd taken. "This car is a beauty, though she is old. A uck hit us a few weeks ago," He turned to the engine. "We stayed to t it fixed, but now, she is not the same."

"Dad?"

Ian glanced at Finn and then rned back to Asher. He pointed toward the front seat of the car. "Is i okay?"

"Ah!" Asher nodded. "Yes, of urse, yes."

Finn let go of the window, tu ned the handle of the door, and pulled it open.

"Your daughter?"

"No." Asher stepped a bit clos "My niece, Cassandra. My sister and her husband, they were killed an accident, not long ago. My other sister has three children of he own, and so we are going there. We are going home."

"I'm sorry for your loss, Mr. Ja es."

"Thank you." Asher watched t front seat of the car with a close eye. "It wasn't good." His tense e ression seemed to ease when he saw his niece. "And Cassandra, she ...it just wasn't good, that is all. Call me Asher, please."

"Well, Asher," Ian said with a grin and extended his hand once more. "Though it's been a rough y so far, welcome to the Ailish Orchard."

Asher chuckled and shook his nd again. "Thank you, Ian, thank you. We are not far from Belgrade, s?"

"In the hills to the north, a fe hours away. As for your car, my father's coming to help, and he's very good with engines. He can fix anything."

Asher's eyes went wide. "A mechanic?"

Ian tipped his hand back and forth. "Sort of, pretty close to that. I'm sure he can fix it if we have the parts."

Asher took in his words and then looked down for a moment. "Ah, yes." He looked up and Ian saw such a wave of relief in his expression, he thought the man might cry. He appeared to be worn out, worried, and just plainly at the end of his rope. "Yes, this would be good. We have been traveling a long time, it seems, just so we may get home. It will be good, to feel France beneath my feet."

"Are you hungry?" Asher was surprised by the question and Ian took a chance. "Listen, we're having some food, back over the hill. You and Cassandra, come back with us and eat. Take a rest for a bit. My father will take a look at your car. It makes him extremely happy to fix things, you have no idea." Ian rolled his eyes a bit in amusement. "We can eat and drink some cider. You and I can have a smoke or two. We're spending the day in the sun, planning for the harvest. Come and join us. You'll be on your way home in no time."

Asher seemed a bit uncertain and he looked away.

Ian followed his gaze.

"Is that your boy?"

Ian considered Finn as she stood next to Cassandra—the girl had gotten out of the car. Cassandra was shorter and very skinny in a pale green dress and pink windbreaker, but she seemed healthy. Her hair was a dark blond and her eyes were clear and sharp. Her eyes were, in fact, very intelligent as she gazed back at him, and Ian felt that she sized him up in an extremely shrewd and efficient manner. She held on to a rather sad-looking stuffed cat, hugging it to her chest with her left arm.

"That's my daughter, Finnegan. Although I'm not sure she's made up her mind about that."

Asher chuckled and Ian found the timbre and feeling behind it free of suspicion, or at least he hoped so. Asher met his eyes. "About what?"

"About who she needs to be."

Asher's eyes filled with warmth. "Ah yes, a tomboy, in English?"

Ian realized at once that it more than satisfied. "Yes."

"My God, she looks just like you."

"Wait until you see my other one."

Cassandra turned her head and considered Finn, her eyes still piercing as Finn looked back at her. Finn tipped to her left just a tad, and whispered something that Ian c[ou]ldn't hear. She did not look away and Ian gave her credit for that, an[d] for the playful, open expression she wore. There were very few thi[ng]s that intimidated his Finnegan. He had the feeling that such an attr[ib]ute was going to come in handy, and he watched as she used it to bo[lst]er whatever spell her charm was weaving.

Cassandra tilted her head as Ia[n] and Asher watched, and then she reached out and slipped her small h[a]nd in Finn's. She turned back to them both with a fierce, unyielding [ex]pression.

Ian looked at Asher with a slig[h]t turn of his head. "I guess that's settled."

Asher's eyes were bright. "Yes

CHAPTER TWENTY-EIGHT

San Francisco
Present day

Casey was already stepping from the cherry-red GTO as it jerked to a stop. Her Docs hit the pavement and she leaned back down. "Are you sure you're good with this?"

"Yeah, it's a good plan, Casey. I'll take care of my end."

"Meet me back here, unless I call you," she confirmed. "Ten o'clock sharp, don't be late."

"I'll be here."

Casey pushed the door shut and faced the door of Finn's building as Jack gunned the GTO and swung away from the curb.

Casey couldn't help but remember how she'd felt that morning, as she acknowledged her current emotions. Her fear had intensified a hundredfold, but it was a righteous fear, and not born of weakness. As she hurried to the door she admitted to herself that even though her reasons for running had been valid on some level, she had betrayed herself as much as she had betrayed Finn.

Asher's words were bold within her thoughts, and for the first time, she truly understood them. Not the simplistic message on the surface, but the sacrifice implied underneath. *It's always better to fight for* someone, *rather than something.*

She worked the dead bolt with a set of heavy leads in about seven seconds and swung the door open. She took the stairs two at a time, and before she could even take a deep breath, she stood before Finnegan's door.

Casey punched the keys that would spell out her name, uncertain if Finn had changed the code. The bolt slid with a satisfying pop, however, and Casey shoved into the loft. "Finn?"

The early evening shadows filled the space, and what little light from the street did reach the loft struggled against the shades that had been drawn. The door closed behind her and Casey took several steps into the silence.

Finn's energy was gone, she could feel that at once, and though she hadn't known her for long, she knew Finn's presence. She knew it and she understood it. She knew it as surely as she knew Finn's kiss, or the feel of her body, or the dreamy influence of that heavy hair sifting through her hands. She knew her. As she stood alone in the quiet, Casey understood that, as well.

She held the weight of Finn's heart within her care, and it was a gift she had never expected to be given. She had paid close attention, and even though she'd been careless in the end, she knew what she had. She had known it from their first kiss. She had known it when Finn had spoken her name, still caught within the tatters of her dark dreams. Casey could guess what those dreams had been now, and that knowledge pulled at the loose thread of her composure. Her anger had been building since she'd opened Cin's files, and it was only getting worse.

She knew the feel of an empty house, and despite the indifferent aura of the loft, she found herself rushing anyway, around the couch and chairs and up the stairs. The small hallway that led past the bathroom and into the bedroom was dark, and she flicked the light switch as she passed beneath the arch.

The bedroom filled with light.

"Finn?"

Her chest tightened as the memories rose up, and the image of her lover peacefully asleep beneath her couch, just that morning, took her back until she bumped against the wall. It was suddenly hard to breathe, faced with yet another empty bed.

Cassandra Marinos.

Casey closed her eyes as the heated feel of Finn's body spun her thoughts in a cruel manner. Finn's tender but firm hands, and the soft sheet against her face as Finn pulled her back. The touch of Finn's breasts, pressed against her back and then gone. The luxury of Finn's mouth, her kisses like drops of fire between her shoulders, their skin slick with sweat and passion as Finn moved inside her. She'd been taken over that edge she always craved, with the added ecstasy of Finn's promise in her ear. *I love you.*

Love.

They had been bathed in it, as they lay together and spoke softly, and Finn had laughed freely as Casey had joked and held her close. Casey remembered very well what she'd thought at that moment, as she had teased her lover. *I'm never letting you go, Finnegan, not ever.*

Love.

Not so easy to come by and even harder to keep. She had felt it, but she hadn't said it. And she had let Finn go all too easily.

"*Fuck.*" Casey's voice ripped against her throat, and the sound of her fear drew out like a blade through the empty room.

She stepped away from the wall and moved into the room as she pushed her hair back. Her hands lingered at the back of her neck, and she could hear Bach in her head as she tried to break free before it all slipped away.

Never panic, Domino, there's always a way out. If you panic, you're trapped. If you let your fear knock you over? Everything will crash down around you, one thing after the other, click, click, click. Then you will have nothing. Don't panic.

Asher's voice rose from her deepest memories, and it brought with it a wave of calm that washed over everything. Casey exhaled slowly and dug in the front pocket of her jeans. She pulled out a hair band and tied her hair at her nape before she looked about the room.

For the most part, things were as she had last seen them, though their dishes had been taken care of, and the books had been straightened on the side table. The bed was made and she could see where Finn had sat to put her boots on.

Casey moved about the bed and eyed the picture-perfect ripple of fabric. *Or perhaps you only sat, my sweet Finnegan.* Casey turned around.

Three steps took her to the armoire and she opened the doors.

All the clothes rested to the right of center along the clothes rod and Casey shoved them against the side panel before she dropped to a knee. The bottom drawer was a facade, and so she slid her touch along the underside of the lip. Her fingers caught upon the catch, she pressed, and the base of the armoire gave a muffled pop as the latch was freed. She found the tab in the back corner and swung the false bottom on its hinge.

The vault safe greeted her with lence and she took several steady breaths, long and easy until her pu e obeyed. She rubbed her hands together to warm them, and to cen r her sense of touch as she took another deep breath.

She set her right hand upon th lial and her left on the surface of the safe, her fingers spread wide u n the textured steel. She closed her eyes, spun the dial, and let the tu iblers play out. She picked up the wheels, and the sound they made f ed her head like a favorite song. She needed only the music in order remember the words.

Her fingers moved on instinc the forefinger of her left hand giving a soft tap when the grind of wheel spoke to her. The fingers of her right turned the dial with a d t touch. *Four, no, five wheels…a National, a trip and gap with a fenc* ..

The first wheel caught and sh reversed the dial, the drive cam turning within the spindle until the s ond notch caught. She tipped her head a bit at the shift in sound, repea ng the process, adjusting the turn of the dial as each wheel caught ar the notches lined up. The fence fell into the gap from the gravity o ts own weight and Casey pulled the handle.

The heavy door lifted open and he contents of the long vault were revealed.

Casey recognized what she saw nd she tried to move her thoughts around the panic that flared within h chest. She pushed to her feet and backed away until the bed forced he to sit.

She had not expected to see tha even though she should have.

Her phone was in her hand ; she slipped along the smooth bedcovers, dropped to the floor, and rought her knees up.

Finn's voicemail greeting was hort and to the point and it was painful to hear her voice.

"Finnegan." Casey cleared her iroat.

Say it.

"Finn…baby, it's Casey."

Say it.

"I think I know what's going o and…"

Coward.

"You need to call me back now as soon as you get this."

I love you, Finn.

"I'm so very sorry about this n irning, I didn't…I didn't mean to do that, Finnegan, but I got scared.' The shadows in the armoire were ominous, so she looked down. She c vered her eyes with her left hand.

"Finn," she whispered. "We're kind of perfect for each other, aren't we?"

Say it.

"I didn't…I didn't really know that could happen—I mean, people say it can, I know." Casey wiped at her cheeks. "Like in the movies, I guess, but I'm way too old for fairy tales." She smiled through the embarrassment she felt. "And I never wanted that, anyway."

When you've had enough, Domino, you've had enough. Each morning you wake up, and you get out of your bed, but if you're too afraid of what comes next? That life is not for our kind. We know when to say enough. We know the joy of embracing the unknown, yes? We do not wear suits and ties and sit in rooms without windows. We take what we want and live in the sun, even when times are hard.

"I love you, Finn." Casey gave her the words and it was wonderful. "Don't do anything crazy, okay? Just call me back because…because I love you." Casey wiped at her cheeks again and smiled, startled. "And just so you know, it feels really good to say that, and I didn't know it would."

She sat in the silence and refused to hang up, knowing that Finn's phone was in one of her pockets, warmed by the heat of her body. "Just come home, because I'm here, okay?"

Casey's heart gave a thud as she heard the front door close, muffled through the distance and the floor beneath her.

Casey moved as if she had wings, along the hallway and down the stairs as she searched through the shadows of the first floor. She slowed in surprise and took the last few steps with care. Malik stood beside the couch.

"She's not here?" he asked.

Casey put her thoughts in order and stacked her chips for the game. It was a fierce blow, to see Malik instead of Finn. "No."

"Why are you here, then?"

"Because I'm looking for my lover," Casey answered and her voice held a cold edge. It felt good to release some portion of her anger and fear, even though he didn't deserve it. Or maybe he did.

"I'm not sure what's going on," Malik confessed. "I can't find her and she won't answer her phone. How did you get in?"

"I was given the code. How did *you* get in?"

"She texted me when she changed it, in case of an emergency."

"Did you let her go alone?"

Malik frowned. "When? Today?"

"Did she go to Belgrade alone ' Casey demanded as she moved into the living room. "Was she all al ıe for that?"

Several emotions moved throu h Malik's expression that Casey didn't recognize, though one of th n, she assumed, was regret. *Or maybe it's shame.* She didn't know ıim well enough yet and he was decidedly on his guard.

"She didn't tell me, Casey." It /as regret, she could hear it. "We were at MassArt together and then he was just gone. I didn't know until she'd come home."

"Who allowed that to happen?' :asey moved around the chair. He took a small step back as she approz ıed. "Who let her do that?"

"There was no one else," Malil ınswered quietly. "She didn't tell her grandparents until she'd returne . Her grandfather wasn't well at all, and their dad was gone."

"I saw." Casey's voice was rou ı. "I saw the photos."

"I'm sorry you saw that. Finr vould never want that, not ever. Neither would I, not now. Not befor either."

"Before what?" He could see , and Casey understood that she would never be able to hide such a ı ıng. It wasn't something that was meant to be hidden.

"Before you fell in love with h ."

"At first, I thought…" She cou ın't say it. "Even though it didn't make sense."

"I know."

"Is that who you're after? The an who did that?"

"Petar Dimitrovich," Malik nswered. "His name is Petar Dimitrovich. He was a Russian mer nary, until he started working for a man named Ketrin Arshavin. Din rovich is his man, his general of sorts."

"Ketrin Arshavin." The name ?ld a good deal of power, Casey could feel it. "The Butcher of Bado\ ıci."

"Yes." Malik's gaze was perc(tive and he noted the leap she'd taken. "She almost had him in Gr :ce, a little over five years ago. Finn was part of a raid outside Athe , but it all went bad. Dimitrovich had been tipped off that they wer coming. It was a mess and her partner went down. She was draggir him free when their egress route collapsed." Malik's expression was ı ıubled. "When she turned around, Dimitrovich was there. He shot he twice in the stomach. Ballistics matched the bullets."

Casey stepped away from him, alked to the couch, and sat down.

She remembered the heavy texture of Finn's scars beneath her fingers, and how Finn had caught her breath when she had kissed them.

"The gun that killed Declan, and Isabella Lazarini, was the gun he shot Finn with."

Casey assimilated the information as quickly as she could, but her brain wasn't quite up to speed yet. "What does all this have to do with me?" She felt extremely small for asking, but she needed to know. "I'll take you to the auction, Malik—I don't care what it costs me. Whatever she needs, I'll do it. But there's an empty gun safe upstairs, and so I think we have a more immediate concern on our hands."

Malik sat in the chair Finn had last occupied. "She's been trying to protect you."

Casey shook her head. "From *what*? I'm not involved in this really, except for…"

"She's convinced you have something he wants, and she's right, isn't she."

"Yes, but"—Casey felt her focus shift—"once it's seen, Malik, everyone there will want it. At that point, it will go to the buyer who's willing to give up everything they've got, in order to get it. There will be men there with centuries of wealth behind them. No matter how much power Arshavin has, he's going up against pockets that will *never* be empty. They just have to choose how deeply they wish to dig."

"In a perfect world, he doesn't have to win, he just has to show up. Finn has been worried that he'll get what he wants without even doing that."

"If he wants the painting, he has to."

"Casey, Ketrin Arshavin is the man who bankrolls Eric Werner, and he always has been. If what you have is as valuable as you say it is, then I doubt very much it will ever make it to the auction. I think Finn has been right to be worried about your safety."

Casey leaned back, shocked by what he said.

"If Arshavin wants what you have, he'll take it, and kill anyone who gets in his way. He's been running this grift with Werner for many years, according to Finn, and she's pretty certain that you're next in line."

Casey struggled to find her voice. "Why are you telling me this now, when you refused to tell me before?"

"Because if I can't find her, and you can't find her? Something big happened, something that changed her course. And that means she's in the wind, without backup."

"How?" Casey felt a wicked j t of adrenaline at his words, and her head began to clear in record tir . *I'm what happened to you. You and I are what happened. We're* v *at happened that changed your* course. She needed to find the patt n within Finn's actions, in order to chart a course to where Finn wou be. "How did she find out about all this, about Arshavin and Eric? A ut *me*? Why on earth would she spend all this time watching over so eone she had never even met?"

"Did you know a man named / her James?"

Casey stared at him in disbe ef, but her adrenaline was well on its way to doing a fine job, and ith Asher's name floating in the air between them, it exploded thro h every cell in her body. For a moment she couldn't move, but the again she didn't have to for her deductive reasoning skills to shift to overdrive and fly through the crowded intersection.

"Do you know who he was?"

Casey laughed as she stepp d into a brave new world of possibilities. Her chest filled with stunning, familiar warmth. "My missing piece of the puzzle."

"What is?"

"My beautiful Finnegan is Ash 's Paris Van Gogh."

Chapter Twenty-nine

"May I sit down?" Finn asked.

The muzzle of the Beretta was pushed behind her right ear and Finn's shoulder came up as he rapped the end of the barrel against her skull. "Shut up."

The office was huge, with art that was hung at the perfect height, impeccably spaced and coordinated. There were a few bookshelves as well, but the room was not overcrowded by any means. The lamplight was golden and the windows behind an obscenely large desk let in what little remaining daylight there was. The glass was spotless and Finn knew they afforded a rather lovely view of the estate grounds, should one get close enough to look through them. The room was decorated in a flawless manner—not too much, but just enough elegant flair to announce the wealth and power one would be dealing with.

"I don't see why I can't sit down."

The guard stepped closer to her and leaned in. "Are you fucking stupid, or what?"

Finn smiled. "What."

His eyes narrowed. "What?"

"I have to pee."

He was surprised by her response and Finn turned smoothly with a high, hard shrug of her right shoulder. She hooked her right arm over his left elbow and used her body as a brace. He let out a shout of pain and the weapon went off behind her back as his elbow popped out of joint. Finn spun with the attack, swiped the Beretta from his hand before he dropped it, and came back around in a tight swirl of movement.

He was on his knees and tippe back as she leaned in and rapped him on the forehead with the end his own gun. It made a dense, hollow sound and he flinched in pai "It sort of hurts, doesn't it?" "Finnegan, darling, don't play ith your food."

Finn stood up straight and fou the side door, though Theresina Lazarini was already halfway to he desk before Finn could smile at her.

She was dressed in Versace, w ch had always been her designer of choice, black on black, with he ong dark hair pulled back from her face in a heavy ponytail. Finn asn't sure if the fabric was silk, but her blouse and wide-legged sla s hung upon her lean frame with sophistication and chic. She droppe everal file folders onto the corner of her desk and then turned.

Finn gestured with the gun, a ding to the general area behind her. "That wasn't actually my fault, the way."

Theresina held her smile back vith no small amount of effort— Finn could see it.

The guard cradled his left arm gainst his side as he struggled to his feet.

"Lucky for you he's left-hande ."

Finn gave a laugh. "I know, rig t?"

"I'm sorry, Ms. Lazarini," the ard said in a tight voice. "It was my mistake."

"It's all right, Enzo," Theresi responded and walked over to him. She was barefoot as she padde across the thick rug. She touched his right shoulder and then held out er hand to Finn. "Give me that."

Finn handed her the gun.

"Go and see Mary," she order . "It's going to hurt, but I'd say you've earned it."

He nodded and glanced at Finn efore he obeyed.

Theresina walked back to the sk and set the Beretta on top of the file folders, and though she lool d calm and collected, Finn could see the tightness of her shoulders a he debated within her head what would happen next. Her eyes were f used somewhere on the desk, but Finn couldn't tell where, and she su posed it didn't matter. She heard Enzo leave and the door close behi her, and when it did, Theresina looked up.

There were tears in her eyes and they fell when she smiled.

"Hello, Finn."

Finn remembered the last time they had seen each other. "The dark rose of San Michele...Hello, Sina."

The raw emotions within Theresina's expression flared in her eyes. She let out a quiet laugh, wiped at her cheeks, and considered. "No one's called me that since you."

"That seems like a terrible shame."

"You're lucky Enzo didn't drag your dead body in here." Her eyes had cleared somewhat and she had found her balance. "If my father sees you, you're a dead woman. My next task of the day will be finding somewhere obscure and out of the way where they won't find your body for months, maybe even years."

"That seems like a shame, too."

Theresina chuckled. "Jesus, Finnegan."

"You look really good, Sina." Theresina had always been beautiful, but she had aged into her looks with a power and grace that had been missing when they were young.

"So do you."

"How is your father, anyway? I read that he wasn't well, and since then, there's been nothing to read." Finn took a step closer to her, and then another. "That was a nice job, by the way."

"It turns out I'm a natural." Sina took a small step away from the desk and into the room. "When Paolo died, Papà thought I was too weak."

"I could've told him how wrong he was, if he wouldn't have shot me in the head first."

"That would be a deterrent, it's true."

Finn smiled and took the last few steps. Her thumb wiped at Sina's cheek. "I never got the chance to thank you for that day," Finn whispered. "*Grazie*, Sina."

Sina went to her and Finn felt the strength of the arms that embraced her shoulders and neck. Finn lifted her from the floor and held on tight, just long enough for them both to remember. Sina kissed her cheek with warm lips and Finn set her down.

"Why are you here, my old friend?" Sina grabbed the edge of the vest at Finn's right shoulder, her touch pushing against Finn's jacket and shirt in order to take hold. She gave it a good tug. "Smart."

Finn could feel the raw dominance of a gaze that was used to bringing powerful men to their knees. That was different, as well. "Because he's here, now, in San Francisco."

Sina's green eyes were quick, [bu]t she was cautious. "Who? Who is here?"

"The man who killed Declan a[nd] Isabella."

The warmth left her gaze and [sh]e let go of Finn's vest. "How do you know this?"

"Does the name Eric Werner ri[ng] any bells?"

Sina made a face of annoyance. [Y]es, I know him, and his auctions. He's contacted us. When he has a s[ale], we take our cut for protection. He's asked for our permission to ho[ld] one of his *art* parties, if you will, this next February. I've even purcha[se]d a few items in the past, though he was in New York at the time."

"Did you know he's in town ri[gh]t now?"

"No, I didn't."

"And that within a few days, h[e']ll be hosting one of his parties?"

Sina said nothing, nor did her [ex]pression betray a reaction.

"Perhaps you don't know abou[t t]his particular sale because Eric's operation is funded by Ketrin Arsh[av]in, and it always has been. And Arshavin is in town because there['s] something on the block that he wants very badly. Badly enough t[o r]esurface and play nice with the other children until he can get his h[an]ds on it."

Sina's face was still calm as [sh]e turned and moved around the desk. She sat in her chair and crosse[d] her legs. "Sit, please."

Finn took the offer and sat in t[he] chair to her left.

"Arshavin is a competitor, yes[. A]nd he has been no friend to my family, it's true. But it's a free coun[tr]y, and I would not impinge upon his right to travel where he wants. N[o] one is looking for a war, least of all the Lazarini family."

Finn remained silent as she eas[ed] her shoulders against the chair.

"We don't have the power we [o]nce did, Finn, I'm sorry to say. When Paolo died, my father was alr[ea]dy ill. This was hidden from me, and before I could take the reins, t[he] damage had already been done. He was never the same after Isabel[la]'s murder, and then Paolo." She looked at her desk and leaned forw[ar]d. She picked up a thick stack of papers. "This is what we are now.["]She dropped them and they slid across the desk blotter. "Are you t[ell]ing me Ketrin Arshavin was the man behind the kidnapping of my [Oz]zy, and our people?" Her voice had softened. "And sweet Declan?"

"Yes."

"Do you have proof of this?"

"Yes."

"May I have it?"

"I can only give you my word. It's the truth—you have my oath on it."

They stared at one another while a clock ticked on one of the shelves, and then Sina made a face that Finn remembered fairly well. She was pissed.

"Goddammit, Finnegan." Her chair spun to the right as she got to her feet. "You're the *only* person that has ever worked for—you know that, right? Even Paolo took you at your word."

Finn stood up and pulled the shirt from her jeans. She lifted her vest and undershirt and bared her scars, and Sina looked. "The man who shot me used the same gun that was used to kill both Declan and Isabella."

Sina lifted her eyes to Finn's, startled.

"It was confirmed by ballistics at Interpol. I can get you copies, if you really think you need more paperwork. And that's aside from the fact that he thought I was Declan when he did it."

Sina's expression wavered and her voice slipped into a whisper. "Finn."

Finn gave her vest a yank and tucked in her shirt with quick hands. "That man works for Ketrin Arshavin, who gave the order at Badovinci. The man who tried to take what is yours and destroy your family in the bargain."

"There's always been talk that it was Ketrin." Sina's voice was quiet, but there was an old and bitter rage within her tone. "I've never stopped looking for proof, Finn—you should know that."

"I do know it, and I've never thought otherwise. We just went about it differently."

Sina considered the words and gave a small smile. "I'll have to tell my father. Something like this, I can't keep it from him. It would cause bad blood, and no matter what, he's still Thomasino Lazarini."

"Then do it."

"What do you need?"

"If you can't find Arshavin for me, then I need you to find Eric Werner."

"That might be easier than you'd think," Sina told her. "If Arshavin is already here, and we don't know about it, the number of rocks he can hide under is fewer than he'd like."

Finn's blood was already up, bu her heartbeat kicked into a higher gear as Sina walked behind her desk gain and grabbed the phone. Her wait was but a few seconds.

"Matteo? I need you to find m⟨ ⟩ phone—" Sina's gaze lifted and she stared across the room, to a poi beyond Finn. The color drained from her face and her eyes widened

Finn let out a slow sigh of res nation. "Oh, man…this is gonna hurt."

"Papà, no!"

Finn turned around. A disheve d old man in a rumpled bathrobe stood in the doorway, and she coul smell the clean scent of Casey's hair, which she thought was strange but a really nice bonus all things considered.

"Papà!"

The bullet took Finn right in th chest.

CHAPTER THIRTY

San Michele di Serino, Italy
June 2005

Finn looked down at the diamond ring as it sat, nestled and perfect in its black velvet box. It was a rock, to be sure, but it had style, and the facets pulled the light within and threw it back again with gusto. The lines of the gold band were elegant and sleek, with two smaller rubies in the setting, one on each side of the diamond. They flowed down and tapered before the band narrowed, as if they had magically blossomed in the only place they could have.

"Do you think she'll like it?"

Finn looked up and met her brother's eyes. His hair was long and it had started to curl at the ends as it framed his face and fell about his neck, and he had a tan already, which set his eyes on fire. He sported a day's worth of facial hair and he appeared to be an entire truckload of trouble.

They sat atop the stone wall that ran along the southern end of the Gallo estate, and the hills in the distance were crowded with cypress and cedar trees. The long grass moved like water in the breeze, and if you sat there long enough, you would swear it was. This was one of Finn's favorite places on the estate, and with the sun in its golden hour, there was no place on earth she would rather be.

"Finn, come on."

Finnegan smiled. "It's really nice."

"*Nice?*"

"Pretty?"

"It's *pretty?*"

"It's very, well, engagementy? Declan's eyes were growing (rker by the second. "That's not even a fucking word." He reached (t and fixed her collar, which had turned under.

Finn chuckled. "Dec, it's freak ιg beautiful. I mean, what would you like me to say?"

"Would it be a ring *you* would ve to your girl?"

Finn's smile deepened. "Yes. Y ;, I would."

Declan laughed a wicked lau ι that was all his own, and he plucked the box from her hands. "I' giving it to her tonight."

"Safety first. Wear a condom,) ung man."

Declan giggled and leaned, a l his right shoulder pushed into Finn's left. "Knock it off."

"I'm serious, actually." Finn br ;hed her hand against his arm and he met her eyes. "The only thing anding between you and a total beating is Theresina. You know tha right? Her father is going to go insane when he finds out, and you' be lucky if he doesn't shoot you with that shotgun he carries arou . If Isabella winds up pregnant before the wedding? God help us al '

"He looks like a character fro *The Godfather*. He even has the hat and suspenders."

Finn reached out and lightly s ιpped his face. It wasn't enough to hurt, but it surprised him. "That r ιn is the father of the woman you love. The woman you wish to marry ιnd have children with. He's also the head of one of the most powerf families in Italy, and the both of you are finally going to have to deal ⁄ith that. One word from him and I could find you facedown in a ditcl ιomewhere. If you're going to do this, Declan, show him the respect I deserves. Because regardless of whether you do actually respect hin he's damn sure going to ask you for it. And if he senses you don't? H ll tear you and Isabella apart, and he has the means to do it."

Declan listened—she could se it in his eyes. She could also see that she had properly freaked him o , which was fine with her.

"I will. I'm sorry I said that."

"Don't be sorry." Finn leaned ⁊ver and kissed his cheek. "Just remember what I said and do what m telling you. And don't *ever* do that *Godfather* thing again. You'll re ret it forever, trust me."

He gave a nod. "I heard you."

Finn narrowed her eyes a bit. ' ut what aren't you telling me?"

"Oh, well...I was wondering iι ou could, ah, take care—"

"You haven't told Pietro."

Declan cringed.

Finn groaned and looked away from him. "Jesus, I'm not gonna do it."

"But you're so much better with him than I am."

"That's just because…"

Declan laughed. "Because why?"

"Just."

"Because you're tougher than I am, that's why."

"No, I'm not."

"You are, just admit it, Finn. Oh!" Declan pointed toward Pietro Gallo's ancestral home in the distance, just as the massive rectangular villa caught the late afternoon sun. The dun-colored stone seemed to be on fire with light, a fertile gold and a lazy-hued orange. The flat black of the shutters and wrought-iron balconies soaked it in, and the contrast presented a stunning portrait of seventeenth-century Italian architecture. The blue sky behind it was streaked with pink, and the red clay tiles of the roof turned dark and precise. "Postcard."

"The only thing missing is a young peasant woman drawing water from the well—"

"In order to bathe her chubby, rosy-cheeked babes."

Finn laughed happily.

"Renaissance." Declan smiled, pleased that he had made her laugh. "But listen," he began again. His eyes scanned the back road that led around Pietro's land, toward San Michele di Serino. "You know, I'm not the one who sneaks out at all hours with cousin Marco and gets into fights that the old men in town talk about for a week."

Finn's shoulder came up slightly. "Jesus."

"And I'm sure as hell not the one who steals Pietro's GTB Coupe with Marco—*again* with Marco—and drives it into Rome without permission. I don't know how many women you guys went through this last time, but I've never seen the old man look so fucking proud in his life."

Finn looked down at the long wheat-colored grass between her dangling feet, embarrassed. Her lips puffed out and her entire body was blushing, she knew it. *Fucking Marco.*

"Do you know what he said to me?"

Finn closed her eyes.

"Declan, my little man, are you like my Finnegan? Is that why you—"

Finn threw her head back and laughed. She met his eyes with her own fire. "He did *not* say that, and don't you fucking lie about it."

Declan laughed, as well. "I'm just saying. He can't get mad at you."

"And why would that possibly be the case? Don't be ridiculous."

Declan's right hand took hold of her left and he laced his fingers between hers. "Because you're Finnegan."

"That makes no sense."

"Not to you."

"There was only one girl in Rome."

"I don't believe you."

Finn leaned over and put her head on his shoulder. "It's true. Marco likes to talk."

"He adores you."

"I can be crazy with him."

"I know. I like that."

"You're not mad?"

"God, no." Declan laughed quietly. "I have a lot more free time now."

"Asshole."

Declan leaned down and tried to see her eyes. "You can be hard to keep up with, Finn."

She thought about his words, and she knew they were true. "I'm sorry, Dec."

"Don't be sorry," he replied in a quiet voice, just for her. "I know you're angry. I *know* it, Finn. Not just about Dad, but...but about where your place is. You've always worried more about that than I have."

Finn let out a faint snort of laughter. "That's because I'm a butch lesbian, Declan, who'd rather fight my way out of a dress shop than ever consider actually *wearing* a dress."

Declan chuckled and the sound was warmhearted and familiar. "I would *so* pay to see that. You know that, right?"

"You should've come to Rome with us, then."

"Don't tease me, and that *is* what I meant, by the way."

"What?"

"About you. I meant, I don't worry as much about your place in the world as you do."

"This should be good."

"The things that scare you are definitely not the concerns of most people. When you move through the world, you're Finnegan, you know? And if someone wants to fuck with you, they usually think three or four times before making their move. And it's not because they know you, it's because of the way you stand. You're not scared of them."

"I'm not scared of an ass kicking, so no."

"But you're scared of someone believing that you're less deserving than everyone else, because you're a butch lesbian who's willing to fight her way out of a fucking dress shop."

Finn laughed. "Thank you, Dr. Adler, for that insightful analysis of my inferiority issues."

"That, my darling, is not what I was saying, either."

"What if Thomasino says no?"

His hand tightened around hers and she returned the pressure. "Then I guess we'll find another way to be together."

"Don't run. It'll be too dangerous for her, for the both of you."

"If we run from him, Finn, we won't ever run from you. Not ever. I promise."

Finn looked into the distance and saw the car approaching along the back road to the estate. It was a black convertible Alfa Romeo, with a badass white racing stripe that ran up the hood and down the back. "I think your ride's here." She sat up, and he let go of her hand as he pushed from the wall. "Declan?"

He shoved the ring box into the pocket of his faded Levi's and looked up at her.

"Dad would be so very proud of you. You know that, right?"

"I hope so."

"You know how I know?"

He considered her question. "How?"

"Because *I'm* so very proud of you, and he liked you a hell of a lot more than I do."

Declan's smile lit up his face. "You'll find her, you know."

Finn's brow went up a bit. "Find who?"

"Your girl," he answered. "I just saw it now, like it was the next pitch. She'll be a curveball, and she'll bend away from you, but that's just because she's scared. She'll come back around, so, you know, don't be mad at her. Be extra sweet to her instead, okay? Make her smile."

CHAPTER THIRTY-ONE

San Francisco
Present day

Casey walked to the kitchen and opened the fridge, which was empty but for the beer and the leftover Champagne Grand Cru.

She stared at the emptiness of and immediately pushed back at the fear. They had gone to a twenty-four-hour bodega the night before and bought fresh fruit and warm Greek bread, and a cake that had tasted like heaven.

Finn had emptied her fridge.

Casey let the door close and turned back into the loft. *Pick up your phone, my love.*

"So who was he?" Malik asked again as he walked to the counter.

"Asher James was the man who raised me. My parents were killed when I was three, maybe four, Asher was never sure," Casey explained. "He claimed he was my uncle, but there were things that never added up, and by the time I was old enough to understand, I didn't care. He was the best man I've ever known, and we were a family, and we loved each other. The home I was in before that, when he found me, I don't remember it well, if at all. We never spoke of it."

"It was Asher James who led Finn to Dimitrovich and Arshavin, and to you, I suppose."

"No," Casey said quietly and looked to her left. "He wouldn't have done that to me."

Casey took a step to the side and grabbed up the envelope that sat atop the marble counter. Her name was on it, written in dark blue ink. She assumed it was Finn's handwriting, but she realized she had never actually seen Finn's handwriting.

Casey's fingertips drifted over the letters. *I'm going to fix that, baby, you'll see.* She slipped a finger beneath the flap and it popped open. Casey's hands trembled as she pulled a folded piece of paper from the envelope and flipped it open. Finn's penmanship was lovely and Casey felt like crying all over again.

Dear Cassandra Marinos,
I couldn't wait for you to get back with the coffee—I'm sorry. I hope you're not mad.
The box that Johann is holding is for you, from your Papa.

Casey lifted her eyes and found Finn's cello case across the room, braced across the arms of the chair Finn had occupied when she had so easily opened the doors of Casey's heart. The doors Casey hadn't even known were there, much less locked so tightly. On top of the case, a black lacquered box waited with patience, as it must have waited for years now, since Asher's death, waiting for her arrival. She returned to her letter.

I knew Asher James, and he was my dear friend. I'm sorry I didn't tell you. I was a coward. But from your first smile, that smile that was given only to me, I've been trying to find you again. And once I did, well, I've been terrified you would slip away, as you did one night in Monte Carlo. It turns out, while I was searching for three different women, all of them were actually you. And you should know I can explain that later, if you'd like.
Asher never gave you up, but then, you already know that. It turns out he didn't have to, for I have a long memory. Long enough for all of us, I suppose.
I made a promise that I have to keep. I made several promises, actually. If things go smoothly with the first two, I'd like to keep the third, which I made to you. I'd like to tell you everything.
And I must ask you again to please forgive me, my love.
Forgive me for not being here to kiss you upon your return. The taste of plums cooked in sugar and distilled wine are but a shadow of the sweetness contained upon your lips.

And I will give this up for no on... but should you find my love
lacking in something that you ... ed.
I love you, Casey. I hav ... no words to describe how
much. Declan would find that e ... remely amusing, just so you
know.

With all my heart, I rema... only yours,
Finnegan O'Connell

Postscriptum: I also like sun...ts and long walks on the
beach, if this turns out to be yo... thing.
Postquam post scriptum: Here ... the picture from my wallet.
The light is perfect, but I can't ...e your ass in this one.

Casey let out a breath of laught... and wiped at her eyes before she pulled the photo from the envelope. ...he stared at it for a long moment, and then she laughed again.

"What is it?"

"You need to answer a few que...ions for me, Malik, all right?"

"Yeah, I can do that, but"—... gestured toward the photo she held—"what *is* it?"

Casey pulled the photo and the ...tter to her chest with both hands. She knew he would never take th...n away, but she felt possessive regardless. She had never actuall... received a love letter before. *Finnegan O'Connell, I'm going to ...ake a complete mess of your fine ass.*

Casey smiled. "It's a picture of ...ny damn cat."

❖

"Finnegan?"

Finn sucked in a huge breath, ...inked, and then released a groan of pain. "Holy *shit*."

Theresina Lazarini smiled dow... at her and touched her face. "That was truly fucking balls out, Finn, I l...ve to say it."

Finn grimaced, shifted her shou...ers, and took another deep breath. She wheezed slightly and her left k...e came up as she coughed from deep within her chest. Theresina's ...nd was on her shoulder and held her secure. Finn took another breath... ut the urge to cough was gone.

"You've been out for a little while. I think you should breathe through your nose."

"Is that going to help?"

Sina smiled. "I have no idea."

"So I'm not dead?"

"No."

"Am I on the floor?"

"Yes."

"Is he still here?"

"No. I told him you were dead and he went back to bed."

Finn blinked a few times. "That's nice...did you give him a cookie?"

"I sent Mary up with coffee and biscuits, smart-ass."

"Ms. Lazarini? You have a phone call on your reserved line," a voice interrupted.

"Don't move yet, Finn, okay?"

"But I still have to pee."

Sina smiled as she got to her feet. "Shut up." She held out her hand as her secretary stepped forward and handed her the cell. "This is Theresina Lazarini."

Finn considered the area that was currently experiencing pain to be about the size of a cast-iron frying pan, with the handle reaching down toward her belly button. She wasn't sure what that was about, but she wasn't enjoying it. Sina turned around smoothly and looked down at her with a surprised, intense look.

Finn stared back at her and breathed through her nose.

"How did you get this number?"

Finn frowned, but Sina ignored her while she listened. She smiled in a lovely manner and stepped back to her desk. "No, I can assure you that's not the case, but I understand your concern."

Finn leaned to the left a little and used her elbow to push herself up, letting out a hiss at the discomfort. She looked down and pulled at her shirt. The top three buttons were already undone and she ran her hand over the surface of her vest.

Sina picked up a pen and began to write. "Yes, I can make that. I was already on my way out, in just a bit."

Finn pried the bullet from the vest and looked at it. *How's that for a souvenir, old man?*

"No, actually, I'm looking forward to it."

Finn slipped the bullet into the front pocket of her jeans and looked up at Sina. "I wasn't kidding about having to use the bathroom."

"I'll see you there." Sina hung up and held the phone out. Her secretary, a rather good-looking blond man in a finely tailored Italian suit, stepped forward and took it from her hand. "Thank you, Matteo."

"They're bringing the car around."

"And Bennet?"

"He says they're a go."

"Thank you, Matteo. If you could wait until I return, before retiring for the evening?"

"Of course, Ms. Lazarini. I hope all goes well," Matteo responded before he turned around and walked from the room. He closed the door behind him.

Sina crouched and balanced on the balls of her bare feet, her elbows resting on her knees as she looked Finn in the eyes. "You were right, Finn. He's here."

"Tell me."

Chapter Thirty-two

Paris
August 2013

Asher laughed into the phone. "Did you write it down or not?"

"Listen, old man," Finn said on the other end. "I think I can remember an address. Text it to me, if you're worried about it."

"For the love of God, man!" Asher barked, annoyed, and then he laughed.

Finn was laughing, as well. "I know, I know, you only text Domino, I remember. Sixteen twenty, Rue de Plaisance, the top floor. Montparnasse. Did I get it right?"

"Yes. Call if you get lost."

"For the love of God."

Asher chuckled happily. "And bring me something to eat."

"You're like a bottomless pit."

Asher nodded. "I am glad you are in town, my friend. We have much to speak of, and I have information for you that you should know. It is important."

"How important?"

"I'm going to take a nap for an hour. I will decide when I wake up."

"All right. I'll be there as soon as I can."

"Until then, Finnegan O'Connell," he said with affection. "Don't forget the food."

He could hear Finn's smile when she spoke. "I won't...hey!"

"What, what?"

"I've missed you. And besides that, you're the only person I like who stays up later than I do. It's a hardship—you have no idea."

Asher smiled and looked down t his shoes as he sat upon the side of the bed. He had not expected to re for her as much as he did. He had not counted on that. He shoulc ve known, though. He should've remembered. "Yes, I have missed y , too, my friend. And I *have* been up late. I've been working a new jol '

"Oh God, don't tell me anythir ," she said with a knowing laugh. "I'll have a stroke, old man, and the you'll be sorry. See you in a bit."

"Yes, have a care."

"Wait, I've changed my mind. Vhat's the job? Are you involved with a beautiful Frenchwoman v io needs something shiny and expensive liberated from the safe in er closet?"

"No, it is too late. Now you v ll never know." Asher looked at the screen and hung up as he laughe to himself, setting the phone on the bedside table beside his tobacc , papers, and lighter. He kicked off his shoes, rolled onto the bed, a l groaned with satisfaction as he pulled the heavy quilt over. He shift l around a bit and kicked his feet for more space beneath the quilt. H pulled at the foam pillow which he had paid much too much for, anc hen the bed seemed to accept his weight and sink down in all the righ places.

Asher smiled.

His beautiful Finnegan was (her way, and she would bring him food that would make his m(th water. She always found the best food. They were nearing the e1 of their quest—he could feel it. There was a deep pleasure in that k owledge, like no other. He could finally make things right, and perha it would help Finnegan gain her freedom. And he would see his Don no, in just two weeks' time. They were going to Provence, and if he c ild survive the drive in her Aston Martin, they would sit in the sun an it would be like the old days. He would tell her about Madame Cruey and her Cartier jewels. He could wear his Armani and dance with a l autiful woman.

Asher opened his eyes and oked at the ceiling, pleasantly surprised. "At this moment, I lack f nothing."

❖

As quietly as she could, Finn et the heavy bag of food on the landing beyond Asher's front door, hich was open to the hallway by several inches.

She had felt it, coming up the s irs, like a smell that would not go away. It had tickled at the back of he nose and throat and made the hair on the back of her neck stand up. Her adrenaline had kicked in without conscious thought and her body had reacted in a practiced manner. She gave her shoulders a smooth roll and stepped to the door. The wood was cold beneath her hand and she pushed it slowly, just a few more inches. The movement was blessedly silent and her eyes focused as the front room was revealed.

There was a broken lamp on the floor near the top of the room, where the windows faced the street, and the television lay facedown beside it.

She reached for her Walther at the back of her right hip, but it wasn't there. The snarl that turned her lips was quick and she adjusted her thinking accordingly. She could smell the cologne, and though it wasn't cheap, it wasn't right. Asher would never wear something so gaudy.

She pushed the door open and waited, but there was no retaliation for the intrusion. She scanned the space with quick eyes and stepped over the threshold.

There was a dead man on the kitchen floor, and a second one crumpled near the wall of bookshelves, directly to her right. The carpet beneath him was soaked with blood and she stepped around it before she knelt down. Her hand searched for a pulse, though she knew he was dead, there was too much blood. The apartment was revealed to her from a new angle.

The bedroom doorway was on the opposite side of the small flat and there was a light on.

There was also a blood trail along the hardwood floor. She stripped the weapon from the man beside her and stood.

The man in the kitchen was lying faceup and she stopped at the edge of the carpet. There was shattered glass on the floor, and broken plates, and blood that had pooled and spread out beneath the body. It was a forensics nightmare and she avoided it completely. He'd been stabbed multiple times—she didn't need to take his pulse. There was a silver .45 caliber on the floor near the edge of the carpet, but she didn't pick it up.

Finn raised the Sig as she moved toward the bedroom. She took a breath, waited, and then called out softly. "Asher?"

"Ah...*Finn.*"

Finn followed the blood trail to the door and leaned her left shoulder against the frame as she looked into the room.

Asher leaned against a chair near the end of the bed and his shirt was soaked with blood, which he had tried to stop with a quilt.

Her heart rate spiked at the si it of him. "How many, please?" Her voice broke on the words.

Asher gave a pained smile. "Ju …the two."

Finn shoved the gun beneath h(jeans at the small of her back and moved across the room. She slid up 1 her knees and caught him as he tipped to the side.

"Jesus, old man…" The quilt t it he held to his chest was soaked with the warmth of his blood and it oated her fingers. "I didn't know we were having company. I need t see," she said and put her hand over his.

"No, no." His voice was wet, s could hear it. "You don't need… to see."

Finn shifted his weight and gr bed for her phone.

"No!"

Finn leaned down as he pulled er hand to his chest and trapped her phone against the quilt. "Asher, lease now, let me do what needs to be done."

"They were Ketrin's men."

Finn looked to the doorway on istinct.

"They will find you."

Finn turned back to him and 1 t the fevered warmth of his face against hers. "It's all right, Asher, lon't care. Let them come." Her voice did not sound like her own. ' ie strength of his right hand was beyond what she thought it could be and he would not let go.

"Listen. Listen to me."

"Let go of my hand."

"Ketrin murdered Domino's pa nts. He slaughtered them both, in a barn behind his house, in Baia Mai ." He coughed and Finn tightened her arm about him. She felt the fai spray of blood upon the back of her left hand, still held by his. "The had a secret…that he wanted."

"*Jesus*," Finn said. "Asher, ple e."

"She was there, and he kept l after…waiting for her to grow. She was only a child."

Finn closed her eyes.

"She does not remember."

Some part of Finn's mind still orked. "The orchard."

"Yes, we were running…and y ir papa, he saved our lives."

Finn pulled at her hand but e did not let go. "Give me the goddamn phone, Asher."

"Let me confess!"

Finn's heart stopped at the raw power in his voice, and then started once again within a sway of dread. She had always known there was something, but she had always been too scared to ask. She liked him too damn much, and he had saved her life.

"I was there…"

"Don't say it."

"I was there…at Badovinci."

Finn pulled him close and shut her eyes, pressing her face to his. "No, don't—stop it, Finnegan…stop."

"Asher," Finn whispered beside his ear, "what have you done?"

"The man in the kitchen is Pavel Arshavin. He is the dumbest man I have ever fucking met…but he is Ketrin's blood. I was caught, just outside of Prague, and taken to Ketrin. He liked me, I don't know why. Maybe…"

"Stop talking, old man," Finn begged in a desperate whisper. "Please."

"Because I paid my debt. I think." Asher's tone was almost curious, despite the deep rattle in his lungs. "Perhaps…I was the only one to ever pay him back. And he must've known that I took his treasure. He must have. Who else would it have been?"

Finn turned her eyes to the bedroom window. The lights from street played off the green curtains, and she wondered what time it was. They would never arrive in time to stop it.

"They put me in the wrong room, I think, and I saw…I saw your Declan."

Finn stared at their hands, still held together with strength atop the bloody quilt.

"He was wounded, but…but he was the boy who took the pictures that day. He was the boy who told me you would—" Asher coughed and Finn moved with him, holding him until the spasms passed. "I recognized Ian in him."

"He took wonderful pictures," Finn whispered.

"He told me to run, but he would not come with me. He would not leave his wife."

You did it, little brother. Finn's tears fell. *You married the girl of your dreams.*

Asher turned his head and met her eyes. "It was not too hard to get out. I was surprised by that…I called the police and waited."

"But they never came."

"No. No one came but Ketrin's men. I ran farther, and I stole a car. In Loznica I was able to call L[ ]n, and I spoke to a man, he was from—"

"Interpol."

"Yes."

Finn nodded and leaned close. You did good, old man…You did good."

"But it was too late." Tears slip[ ]ed from his eyes. "Please forgive me, but I could not carry him, and h[ ]would not come."

His words rang true. Declan w[ ]uld never have left Isabella. Not ever. "I forgive you."

Asher closed his eyes and sque[ ]zed her hand. "I took a painting."

"What?"

"Declan, he told me to take it. [ ]e said, it would be his revenge… He said that I *must* take it. That I ha[ ]no choice."

Finn stared at him, afraid to br[ ]the.

"It is…*Painter on the Road*"-[ ]Asher licked his lips with blood and opened his eyes to hers—"*to Ta*[ ]*scon.*"

Finn stared at him, speechless.

"Yes." Asher tried to smile. "[ ]ly lovely Finnegan, I knew you would know."

"It can't be."

"It is real, and there is proof…[ ]nd my Domino will have it soon. She will try to sell it and run away f[ ]m all this."

"I'll find her, Asher, I promise.

"Eric Werner was there, at Ba[ ]ovinci…I heard his voice, when they brought me into the building[ ]He is not a brave man, and his voice…" Asher made a strained fac[ ]. "So high pitched, I heard him. Find him. She will sell the painting[ ]through him…but he is Ketrin's man." Asher moved and Finn tipped[ ]back as he let go of her hand and grabbed her jacket. "He still looks f[ ]her!"

"I need her full name."

"No."

"Asher, *please*, I can't find her[ ]ithout it."

"What sort of…fucking cop ar[ ]you?"

Finn lifted her phone and he hit[ ]er wrist with unexpected strength. The phone clattered to the floor and[ ]id away from them both.

He grabbed her jacket and j[ ]ked her back. "I cannot betray her, Finnegan. You must find her.][ ]nd my Domino." He pulled in a wheezing breath. "I have fixed it, a[ ]best I could. They will come to *you*, Finnegan, all of them…if my Domino…if she stays true to her course."

Finn grabbed his wrist with an iron grip.

"You gave your word. Protect her." Finn turned her head at the distant sound of sirens, but Asher's bloody laughter brought her back. "You will fall in love, I think, with my Domino."

"I'm already half in love with her," Finn admitted and smiled at him. "For all the good it will do me, you crazy old man."

"You may be…surprised."

"They're coming now, Asher. It's gonna be okay."

"Take the box in the closet—it is for my girl…and take with you what is mine."

Asher began to ease within her arms and Finn pulled him higher. "No. No, don't go."

"Kill them with Pavel's silver gun." Asher's voice was thick, but he laughed. The blood gurgled in his lungs and throat and he let go of her jacket as it slid down his chin.

"Asher?" Finn gave him a gentle shake, but she could see him leaving her. His eyes were wrong, they were completely wrong. Finn leaned close and whispered fiercely in his ear. "We love you, Asher James. We *love* you."

"*Run…*"

CHAPTER THIRTY-THREE

San Francisco
Present day

Casey watched as Theresina Lazari was shown into the back room of the Darjeeling Tea House by the owner, Duval Fararr. Duval was an old friend from Provence, and she had helped finance his venture in the States as repayment for an old favor. The Tea House was a fortress and it was also a well-known meeting place for Mabelle Babineaux and her clientele. More than one deal had gone down here, and a few of them had even gone well. But none, as far as Casey knew, had ever gone south.

Casey tried not to smile as Blackjack Vermillion held out his hand and helped her from her chair like a proper gentleman.

"How do you like my change in plans so far?"

Jack's expression remained neutral, but his eyes were bright. "You sure know how to show a guy a good time, I'll say that much."

Theresina was dressed in black Versace, and the long silk jacket she wore swished around her calves in a gorgeous flow of fabric. Her hair was thick and straight as it fell loose about her shoulders, and her eyes were focused and clear.

The man who walked behind her was bigger than Jack, and his suit was cut to fit his overabundance of muscles and the weapons he wore, both of which were on display despite the suit. Casey was fairly certain Blackjack could take him, though she heard Jack make a small, disgruntled sound behind her.

Theresina approached without pause and held out her hand. "I'm Theresina Lazarini."

Casey shook her hand. "Samantha Drake."

"Your call was unexpected, Ms. Drake," Theresina said with a curious smile. "Especially on my private line."

"Shall we sit?" Casey asked and gestured to the table. Casey waited for Theresina to take her chair before she herself sat.

"I would like to—"

"Have you seen Finnegan O'Connell?" Casey asked, interrupting her. It was a mistake, but she couldn't stop it.

There had been only two options for Finn, and neither of them had pleased Casey in the least. Finn needed to find Eric Werner, or she needed to find Arshavin, and the opportunities that would help her achieve either were extremely limited.

Theresina started to answer, and then she smiled and changed her course. "Who *are* you, Ms. Drake, if you don't mind my asking first?"

Casey considered the question, which she had already known was coming, and just as earlier in the evening, she was uncertain of her answer.

She was a thief and she was an orphan. She hadn't always been either, but Asher had saved her from pretty much everything, and what he hadn't saved her from, he had given her. But then he had died, and she'd been left alone once more. She was rich—she was that—and that made her a free woman of means. She had taken lovers when she wanted and she had traveled the world. She had eaten the best food, and savored the best wines, including a 1947 Cheval Blanc. She had heard Dame Marta Barchelini perform Puccini at the Teatro dell'Opera di Roma, and she had watched Eyjafjallajökull erupt in Iceland amidst a snowstorm.

There were so many beautiful and amazing things that she had experienced over the years, but what did they add up to when the final count was taken? She had either been alone, or with a lover who'd been a distraction from that loneliness, though nothing more. She had shared her life with Asher, and those times were embedded in her heart, but it wasn't the same. He had tried to tell her as much, that night years ago in the Dordogne, but she had shrugged it off.

There was really only one answer to that question. "I don't know yet."

Theresina's mask of cool slipped as a touch of surprise brightened her eyes.

"But I know..." Casey looked down at her hands as they sat on the table. *Finnegan. And I know exactly who I am when I'm with her, and I like that person very much. When I'm with her, I am Cassandra Marinos, and there's nowhere to run..and better yet, I have no desire to.*

"What do you know?"

Casey smiled at the true interest she heard and she looked up. "I know I'm Finnegan's lover, and that without her, nothing I could tell you makes much sense. And I can really think of anything, either, that's worth all that much if she's not with me. And while those things are new to my reality, that doesn't make them any less true. And I know that both Finn and your family lost something extremely precious at the hands of Ketrin Arshavin."

Her words were met with silence though it was far from indifferent.

"Finn is trying to protect me from Arshavin because I have something he wants very badly. I think she's going to come to you for help."

"To me?"

"Yes," Casey answered. "Is it true that your father once swore vengeance against her?"

"Yes, that's true."

"And he told her she should never set foot in Italy again?"

"Yes, something like that was said."

"Are these things still non-negotiable?"

Theresina let out a breath of surprised laughter. "Well, I suppose that would depend."

"On what?"

"On what's being offered to appease my father's desire for vengeance. There is no price that may be placed on the pain my sister's death has caused our family."

"Of course not," Casey said with genuine respect. "And I would never think that, much less suggest such a thing."

Theresina leaned back in her chair just a bit. "But my father is old, Ms. Drake, and he's very tired. And while the loss of Isabella still haunts his thoughts, in my opinion I believe he would welcome an opportunity for closure. Nothing will bring her back, but at this point, a suitable rapprochement is a desirable alternative to further violence."

"Would I speak to your father about this?"

Theresina smiled. "No, actually you would speak to me."

Casey held Theresina's gaze and made her call, for she didn't believe Theresina lied. Casey felt that she was hiding something, but since she had no idea what that something was, she'd have to let it ride. "Are you familiar with the works of Vincent van Gogh?"

❖

The night air was cold as they stepped onto the sidewalk and Theresina Lazarini stopped at the curb within a swirl of silk, her sleek black limousine catching the light as it sat waiting for her return.

"It was a pleasure doing business with you, Ms. Drake," Theresina said with a smile and held out her right hand. "An unexpected one, but a delight, nonetheless."

Casey shook her hand. "You'll let me know if she shows up?"

"Of course. But let me drop you off, won't you? The Lazarini offices are not far from here, and we might as well finalize the transfer of funds this evening. I'm sure you'd like to know that such a significant amount is firmly in your accounts."

Jack stepped forward and Casey glanced at him. *Oh God, don't do it, Jack.*

"I've got that taken care of, Sina, but thanks for the offer. We can follow you."

Theresina shifted her gaze to Jack, and though at first her look was cool and surprised, her eyes warmed as she looked him up and down.

Richard Burton in a wheelbarrow, we're all gonna fucking die.

"That's my ride, over there," Jack said with a smooth grin.

Theresina turned and then laughed out loud, the jet-black Ferrari 458 Italia looking like a New Age God beneath the glow of the neon lights from the Tea Shop. She turned back to him. "Are you joking?"

"I never joke about cars."

"That's yours?"

"For the moment it is."

Theresina's eyes flashed. "Get in the limo, Samantha. I think I'll take a ride with…?"

Jack stepped forward and extended his right hand to her. "Blackjack Vermillion."

Theresina shook his hand, the motion slow and filled with questions, as was her expression. "I'll ride with Blackjack Vermillion."

"Ms. Lazarini, I don't think that's—"

Her man stopped speaking when she looked at him. "Follow Bennet, and we'll follow you, does that seem fair, Danilo?"

"Of course, Ms. Lazarini."

"I'll be safe with you, Mr. Ver⟨ llion, will I not?"

Jack smiled yet again. "Call m⟨ Blackjack, please. And I suppose that would all depend on your point⟨ f view."

"Get the door for Ms. Drake, ⟨ nilo."

Theresina stepped aside as Dar⟨ o shifted his graceful bulk around and opened the door for her. Casey⟨ used for just a moment and then she stepped forward. If Jack wound⟨ ⟩ with a bullet in his head, at least he would go out as he lived. *Just⟨ ke my Asher,* she thought, *killed while his house was being robbed, f⟨ fuck's sake. And God damn it all to hell.*

"Would you like to drive?" Ca⟨ y heard Jack offer as she stepped into the limo.

Casey slid onto the seat and⟨ he door closed, and while she wondered, she was somewhat relieve⟨ that she couldn't hear Theresina's response. She looked to her right, c⟨ ght by the shift of the faint blue light within the car.

Finn pulled at her leather dus⟨ · just a bit and stretched her left leg out.

She was dozing, perhaps, Case⟨ wasn't sure, but she looked tired and so it made sense. Her hair was⟨ heavy, lovely mess, and Casey caught her breath when Finn's head⟨ bbed forward slightly, only to be jerked back as she fought to wake u⟨

Casey's body came alive, every⟨ it of it, and she remembered their first kiss on the street, and the quie⟨ perfection of finding what she'd always been looking for.

Finn's eyes opened and she ⟨ nked at the privacy screen that shielded them from the driver. The ⟨ nt door closed with a slight, dull sound, and the engine turned over⟨ ith an equally muted hum. Finn looked out her window. "Where are ⟨ e?"

"Just outside of the Darjeeli⟨ Tea House," Casey answered softly. The car pulled away from t⟨ curb and onto the street. "Or at least we were." She could sense the⟨ ange in Finn's energy, and as the last thread of her composure stretch⟨ l out before her, she cut it. She'd had enough. "You should really che⟨ your phone messages, Finnegan Whoever."

Finn shifted, and even within t⟨ odd low light of the limo, Casey could feel the heat and warmth of th⟨ se amber eyes.

"What are you doing he—"

"I love you, Finnegan."

Finn stared at her for what seemed like three years, twelve days, and fourteen hours. With change. "What?"

Casey smiled at the startled whisper. "I said, I love you, Finnegan."

"I don't know how you—"

Casey moved smoothly across the seat, swung her left leg over Finn's, and straddled her lover. Finn's skin felt extremely warm beneath her hands and Casey tipped Finn's face up as she kissed her.

Finn's mouth was hot and lush and Finn opened to her without reservation. Casey raked her left hand through Finn's hair as she tasted her, her tongue caressing Finn's with a possessiveness she'd never really experienced before. And it felt good. It felt very good, and the rest of her body reacted to the pleasure of it.

Finn took hold of her waist and Casey tipped her head back to take a breath. "You need to listen to your phone messages."

"Did you leave me a message?"

"I did."

"What did it say?"

"I just told you."

Casey kissed her again, pulling both of Finn's lips between her own and then tasting the bottom one for the pure enjoyment of it. She moved her mouth along Finn's jaw and then kissed her neck. Finn's scent filled her nose and she felt the ache between her legs intensify.

"Which...what, which part?"

"What part?"

"I don't know, say it again."

"I love you."

"My phone's not working."

Casey came back up and kissed her again. "I'm sorry I broke my promise, baby."

Finn's tongue was in her mouth and her muscles happily surrendered as Finn's arms went about her.

"It's...okay. I love you, Casey."

Casey smiled and pulled back, her mouth clinging to Finn's. "I know, I'm so sorry."

"I missed your face."

"I'm not sure I approve of you carrying a picture of my cat around, and not me."

"She's a very beautiful cat."

"She'll keep your feet warm, if you'd like to..."

"Like to what?"

"Why doesn't your phone worl ?"

"I fell on it."

"You fell on your phone?"

The car turned to the left a l Casey smiled as Finn's arms strengthened around her to keep her rom tipping.

"Yes."

"Why?"

Finn's eyes were alive with the ght, but she didn't answer.

"Finnegan?"

"I got shot."

Casey stared at her and then l ined back. Finn's arms loosened but did not leave her as Casey sat n Finn's thighs and checked her over. Her hands pushed beneath the houlders of Finn's jacket and she searched, her fingers exploring alon the soft material of Finn's shirt.

"I have my vest on."

"I can see that." Casey met Finn s eyes before undoing the buttons of Finn's shirt. The material of the est was dented squarely between Finn's breasts and Casey's fingerti skated over the defect. "Is that why your skin is so hot?"

"It's okay, baby, I promise. I'l have another bruise, that's all. It just really hurts."

Casey didn't like it. "How bad

"It's gonna be a beauty."

Casey sighed. "You don't seem oo upset by that."

"That's because I'm not dead.'

"Yes." Casey refused to even to :h that particular thought. "That's a good point."

Finn smiled. "How did you fin me?"

"Malik isn't as tough as you re, remember? He talked and I listened. You didn't have a lot of op ns."

"Did you open Asher's box?"

Casey heard it in her voice and she touched Finn's face. She had loved him. There would be more to eir story, she knew that, but Finn had loved Asher. *And he loved you too, I think, my sweet Finnegan. How could he not? He finally had h. very own Van Gogh.*

Finn's eyes were bright with ui hed tears. "I never looked inside, Casey, I promise."

"I know that," she whispered. didn't open it yet. I was waiting for you."

Finn's expression was tender, but her voice was strong. "I have something I need to do first—I can't change that. And you can't come with me."

"I know that, too." Casey kissed her. "I know, baby, but you can't leave me behind anymore, either, okay?"

"But I..."

Casey knew for a fact that Finn's mouth tasted sweet, she knew it, but she didn't remember it quite like this. It scrambled her thoughts.

"What?"

"Nothing."

"I love you, Finn," Casey confessed again on a hushed breath.

"Baby?" Her lips sought her lover's. "Who shot you?"

"Thomasino Lazarini."

Casey stopped in midkiss and met Finn's eyes. She waited for the rest.

"But on the bright side, he thinks I'm dead now."

"Why is that a bright side?"

"Well, it sort of frees me up, I guess, for a few things I couldn't do before, though it's a long story...What's the matter?"

Casey slipped her arms about Finn's neck. She held on tight as she turned her face, and she let the touch of Finn's hair soothe her. It didn't take very long at all. "Theresina Lazarini just took us for about seventy-five million dollars."

There was a long pause before Finn spoke. "*How* much?"

CHAPTER THIRTY-FOUR

The driveway curved slightly and the shrubbery that lined it was incredibly well-kept. The lawn was thick and lush, and the lights from the huge brick house were bright. Finn stopped just beyond their reach.

She reached into her inner coat pocket and pulled out a pouch of tobacco and a packet of papers, and she proceeded to roll a cigarette, just as she had seen Asher do a hundred times. She remembered the first time she had seen him, in the hills of Novi Sad, and how he had put all his energy into the artful task before he had gone back to his worries. She understood now why he had done it, and she smiled as she tucked the tobacco pouch back in her jacket. She brought the smoke to her tongue and sealed it.

They had all been together that day, and the memory held more meaning now than it ever had. It was an odd moment in time, when pretty much everyone she had ever loved had been in the same place at the same time.

She watched the two guards as they talked by the wide front doors, at their leisure and somewhat animated. She heard a laugh in the distance as she raised Asher's gold lighter.

The Zippo pinged open and the guards turned at the sound, silent as the wheel scraped beneath her thumb and its flame rose.

She drew on the smoke, flipped the lighter shut, and slipped it back in the pocket of her jeans, where it came to rest beside Thomasino Lazarini's bullet.

She walked into the light and one of the guards came down from the stairs. His suit was good, it was t   he, but the AR-15 assault rifle that hung from his right shoulder appeared to be top-notch. He held up his left hand as he came down the drive "No, you wait there."

His head popped back with a sharp jerk and he crumpled to the ground.

The guard who had remained by the doors went for the weapon at his belt.

His head snapped back and he spun to the left, fell, and slid down the stairs. His gun was still in its holster as Finn walked up the steps.

She noted the blood spray on the door and along the bricks as she turned upon the landing. She didn't like it, but it didn't bother her that much, either. Badovinci held a price, and sooner or later they would all have to pay it.

Nicola Bennet and Danilo Abruzzio walked out of the darkness, and Sina's head of security handed his silenced rifle to Danilo as they approached. Finn took a drag on her smoke and then flicked it down onto the walk as Bennet drew the 9 mm at his hip. He gave her a clipped wave of permission.

Finn spun around and turned the handle on the door as she pulled the silenced Walther from her right hip.

The man who sat near the bottom of the stairs flipped a page of his magazine. "It's not time yet." His Russian accent was thick and he sighed as he sat back. "Assholes."

Finn took the final step, placed her silenced Walther beneath his chin, and tilted his head back with it. "Where is Petar Dimitrovich?"

He stared at her with a shocked expression, but she could also see that he debated what his reaction should be.

"Either *we* can kill you, or Petar will pay you for your services later. You could take your chances, if you like. It's up to you."

"He is upstairs. Go right. There is a big, um"—he searched for the word—"office room at the end of the hall. Very big."

"Is there a porch?"

He narrowed his eyes a bit.

"A balcony? Ah, *balkon*?"

"Yes."

"Where is Ketrin Arshavin?"

"In his bed. There are two rooms, with the big one. He sleeps in one. Petar goes in the other, but he does not sleep."

Finn considered his unexpected statement. "Why not?"

The man held her gaze for several seconds. "He waits for someone, I think, to come."

Finn smiled as all her pain rose up in a slow burn of rage. "And so here I am."

She took a step back and Benn[...]t appeared on her right, lean and dapper looking in his three-piece [...]it. "We'll clear the downstairs, O'Connell. Go."

Finn started up the stairs to the [...]uted pop of Bennet's weapon.

She remembered the day she [...]had played the sarabande from Bach's Suite no. 4 for cello, with [...]ly Declan to bear witness. They had sat barefoot in the backyard, a[...]he house in Boston, and Declan had convinced her she could do it. [...]e had laughed and he had taken her by the shoulders, and he had tol[...]her to stop thinking. *Don't think. Don't think. Just do. Close your eye[...]nd play it.*

As she moved down the hallw[...], Finn lifted her weapon.

The guard who sat beside the d[...]rs glanced up from his phone and her first shot took him in the chest, [...]s did her second. She was at the double doors before the blood bega[...]o seep through his shirt.

Declan had sat on his knees i[...]silence and believed in her. And he'd been right.

Finn opened the door and step[...]d in to the room.

Petar Dimitrovich sat on a long [...]ather sofa, with a book in his left hand. His expression was startled a[...] Finn watched as the color in his face drained away.

He was in a basic blue sweate[...]ut it was made of fine wool, and his slacks were navy. He wore brow[...]xfords, but his socks were white, his right leg hooked casually over [...]s left knee. His brown hair was slicked back, but it had fallen forwa[...] a bit, no doubt as he had read.

He stared at her, and Finn loo[...]d down the sight of her Walther as she moved deeper into the room. [...]e was adjusting to his new reality and she let him. He exhaled a long, s[...]w breath, and then his expression cleared. "I knew you would come."

His voice was fuller than she r[...]nembered, but there was still that strange, warm mocking tone in his [...]rds.

"May I stand?"

"Go ahead," Finn answered, [...]nd she willed her voice to be stronger.

He stood in a single fluid mo[...]ment and closed his book with a snap. He smiled at her. "I have t[...]ught about, for many years now, those words...his last words."

Finn's legs began to tremble. [...]ler body wasn't doing the most efficient job of containing either her [...]sh of emotions, or the adrenaline that pumped through her system. He[...] hand was steady, though.

The sound of automatic gunfire echoed from somewhere beneath them and Petar's eyes twitched to his left. There was shouting, and the sound of a handgun—two, three, four shots—and then silence.

Petar laughed. "Should I tell you what they were?"

Finn pulled the trigger.

CHAPTER THIRTY-FIVE

"It'll be okay, Casey."

Casey did not respond and Jac s comment did nothing to soothe her.

They sat in the back seat of Thresina Lazarini's black SUV, and Casey leaned hard into the far corner. Her legs were crossed and so were her arms, and she stared out the window into the surrounding darkness.

She'd been in Amsterdam when she'd received word of Asher's death. A mutual friend had called her, one of Asher's old cohorts and most trusted friends, though by the time he had reached her she'd been much too late for anything but tears. He'd told her that Asher's death had been suspicious, and though the apartment had been robbed, the police had serious questions, for there were two dead bodies other than his. He told her to stay away, and that he would contact her again when it was safe. Six months later, she'd received a package in the post at her Paris apartment. An apartment she owned as Marie Ann Broussard.

His ashes had sat upon the mantel in the Dordogne ever since, above the hearth where he'd made the fire each Noel and they had toasted with smooth French brandy another successful year of living life on their own terms. In the house where they had last opened presents, and watched old movies, just as they had always done. She had not eaten crepes again until Finn had made them for her.

Ketrin Arshavin.

The photos Colin had sent were brutal, and the images of Declan's body had been not only shocking, but tragic, and in the purest sense of the word. In that first instant of recognition, she had seen Finn. In the next, she had seen the truth.

Casey's heartbeat quickened and the gloom beyond the road

seemed to move of its own accord. She had watched Finn walk down the driveway and disappear into the darkness, the night closing between them as if it were a weathered barn door that would creak upon rusted hinges. She had watched, completely helpless to stop it, and that was all it took.

"Casey, are you all right?"

She reached for her voice and found it waiting for her. "I'm all right, Jack."

The memories had come flooding back, as imperfect and incomplete as they were, distorted by the years. They were the memories of a child, but they held a power she could not deny.

Gunfire popped in the distance and Casey flinched.

Ketrin Arshavin.

He had been an old man who would follow her about the house—when she would look up, he would be there. He was like a bear, and she had always wondered when he would finally grab her and take her into the trees. He had seemed to sense her presence and she would walk as silently as she could, so as not to disturb him. She had refused to speak, knowing he would hear her, and come for her, and take her into the house in back, between the red cedars.

She thought he could smell her, as well, for bears had a wonderful sense of smell, and he looked as if he could, as if he would, as if she made him hungry.

"She's a badass, remember?" Jack's voice was almost a whisper and she didn't blame him for it. The night was watching. "And this time she has backup."

Casey closed her eyes. "I know."

Her kitten was small and always in danger, and she would not let her loose, especially at night. He could not steal her away if she did not let Naamah go.

The silence had returned and she could hear the low talk of Theresina's men, who had been left behind to guard the cars.

Pavel, she remembered Pavel. She remembered hiding from him, for he would shout and scream and grab her arms. He had even tried to take Naamah once and throw her into the fire, but Magda had stopped him and he had beaten her for it. They had fought in the kitchen, where Pavel would taunt them with food. She and Naamah were always hungry, and Pavel smelled of perfume and bacon. Sharp smells, strange smells.

Casey opened her eyes. *Magda.*

She felt the tremble within he whole body, as if she were cold right down to her bones.

She remembered being in the ilver car and driving away from the cold light of the house, the empt light that never changed. And she remembered how scared she was. It ad been so very long since she'd been in a car.

It will be all right, little one, yo will see. We'll have an adventure, you and I, yes? Asher had spoken in ʒentle voice, and she had watched him as they drove, the trees crowdir the road as they went.

He was soft looking but his hai s were strong on the wheel of the silver car, pretty even. His brown co was soft, too, and warm looking. She had wondered if he had any brea in his pockets and whether or not he would share it with her. She had vondered if the bear in the house that they left behind was after him oo. Bears could eat a lot, really, and he would be pretty tasty becaus he smelled really nice. He would probably taste good to a bear.

A single gunshot echoed in the istance and Casey let out a harsh breath. The tears slipped down her ɪeeks and she reached out with a jerk of movement for the door hand .

"Finn."

CHAPTER THIRTY-SIX

The bullet took Dimitrovich in the right shoulder, and he twisted and hit the floor.

Finn holstered the Walther and pulled the Sig Sauer from beneath her left arm as she walked toward him.

The last time she had spoken to Declan, he had called her from Paris, and his voice had been filled with happiness. She had heard Isabella in the background, talking of the perfect dress. He told her that he had sat along the Seine, where Hemingway had once sat, and she had laughed.

Petar got to his knees and then his feet, and he stumbled forward. He shoved at the balcony doors and they rattled open as he walked awkwardly into the night air. His right arm hung useless and his sleeve was soaked with blood. He let out a bark of sound, and Finn took note of his Luger on the table beside the sofa as she passed.

Finn's arm came up and the second bullet took off the top of his left ear, maybe more.

The report of the weapon filled the room as she stepped onto the balcony.

Petar bent at the waist and spun in a tight circle. He took several steps before he stood up straight. The left side of his face was covered with blood and Finn could see the pain within his eyes, even though he smiled. "You must...you must want to know."

Finn felt her voice rise up. "*I made up rhymes in dark and scary places, and like a lyre I plucked the tired laces...of my worn out shoes, one foot beneath my heart.*"

Petar Dimitrovich stared at her, his eyes filling with shock. He took a step back from her, not because he had to, but because he was frightened. In that moment, he knew [t]hat he was going to die, she could see it. "But it was…" His expressio[n] turned and she could see his rage at being denied. "But you weren't t[h]re."

Finn said nothing and he be[ga]n to panic somewhat. He had absolutely no control over the mom[en]t and he had no idea what to do about it.

"It was his favorite poem, that[] all." Pietro had been right. Justice w[o]uld never be enough.

"No, actually, it wasn't."

Finn pulled the trigger, dead [ce]nter of her target, and she kept pulling until she had emptied the c[li]p into his torso. He was pushed back by the force of it, his arms swi[n]ging out as he went.

Finn stopped and watched as [he] teetered, strangely enough, still standing as he tried to suck in a last[] useless breath of air.

She lowered her weapon and t[oo]k the final few steps of Declan's revenge.

Her boot hit him in the ches[t a]nd he flipped over the balcony railing and fell.

Finn heard him hit, but she he[ld] her ground and remembered the weight and warmth of Declan's arm[] thrown about her shoulders. She felt his laughter vibrate in her ches[t] and she could see him as he ran barefoot through the grass.

She stepped to the stone railin[g a]nd surveyed the patio below.

The blood of Petar Dimitrovi[c] was splashed on the flat bricks around his broken body, and as Fin[] stared down at him, a fresh pool began to spread. She turned away [a]s she popped the empty clip from the Sig and dropped it in her jacket [po]cket.

"It was mine."

She grabbed a new clip as she [st]epped through the balcony doors and she shoved it in as she checke[d] the bedroom doors. She stopped where Petar Dimitrovich had stood [on]ly a few moments before.

"Who are you?" the old man i[n] he bedroom doorway demanded.

Ketrin Arshavin didn't look as [Ga]sher had once described him, not really, not anymore. He was very sq[ua]re, it was true, but his white hair was a bit wild about his head and h[] shoulders were somewhat drawn in. He had lost muscle mass and we[] ht from his younger days, and as he stood in the doorway he seemed [un]steady on his feet.

His eyes, however, were as sh[] thought they would be, cold, and sinister with loathing for the world a[ro]und him. His hand also appeared to be extremely steady as he leveled a blue steel .45 caliber directly at her head.

"Where is Petar? What is all this shooting?"

Finn said nothing, uncertain of what she *could* say. She was looking at the boogeyman, and the creature from beneath the bed. She was looking at the man who had finally run the nimble Asher James to ground, a beautiful fox caught by Ketrin's hounds. He had gazed down from his rotting throne and fed her beautiful Declan and sweet Isabella to his monster, Dimitrovich. He had destroyed Thomasino Lazarini in one fell swoop, though he hadn't known it. He was the cruel, pitiless man who had butchered Casey's parents, and then stolen their child.

Casey had kissed her not half an hour ago, and there had been a brutal fear in her eyes. But Casey had let her go anyway, and she had even managed a careful smile and a firm nod of her head. Casey hadn't known how brave she was actually being, but Finn would not forget it.

"I will kill you, make no mistake," Ketrin said.

Finn took a chance. "I'm the one who has your treasure. The one Asher James stole from you."

Ketrin's eyes narrowed.

"I'm the one who keeps the memories."

"Asher James is dead. Pavel killed him."

"Asher is the one who sent me."

Ketrin's heated stare wavered, and he lowered the gun just a bit. "You have the girl? Does she have my key?"

"Ketrin?" A woman's voice spoke from the bedroom.

His attention shifted back to the bedroom and the gun lowered to his side.

"Ask her where Petar is."

Finn raised her weapon and took aim as she moved quietly along the sofa. She had no idea who was in the bedroom, but the voice was definitely a woman's.

Ketrin turned back to Finn and he appeared confused, his cold loathing replaced by disorder and uncertainty. "Where is Petar?"

"Petar is dead." Finn would never lie about that. She couldn't. Finn saw Bennet at the top of the stairs and Sina was but a step behind.

"Give me the gun, darling, and we'll get your treasure," the woman promised him.

Ketrin held out the gun and Finn adjusted her aim as the woman came into view. She was older, but he was in good shape, her dress formfitting and made of a beautiful dark green wool. Her blond hair was pinned atop her head with an expert twist, and she stepped close to him and took the gun.

"Put it down, please," Finn ordered in a quiet voice.

The woman held the gun by the barrel and patted Ketrin on the chest. "Wait here for me, all right, darling?" She regarded Finn with interest. "Is Petar Dimitrovich truly dead?"

Finn lowered her arms a bit, which shifted her aim to the floor at the woman's feet. "It's all right, Bennet, come ahead."

Bennet entered the room and Sina followed. Sina stopped about ten feet through the door as Bennet and Danilo moved about the space in an efficient manner. Danilo gave a clipped wave to Bennet before he disappeared into the second bedroom.

Finn met Sina's eyes, then Sina turned the other way and said, "Ketrin Arshavin?"

"Yes?"

"I am Theresina Lazarini, the daughter of Thomasino Lazarini."

"Yes," Ketrin said simply. "I remember you. You were the bitch I couldn't get to."

The room was quiet for a long time and Sina did not look away from him, not even for a heartbeat. When Danilo reappeared from the second bedroom, Sina finally turned her attention to the woman. "Who are you?"

"I am Magda Sokolov."

"Magda, step out of the doorway, please," Sina ordered in an icy voice and Magda obeyed. Sina held up Pavel Arshavin's silver-plated, dragon-etched .45 pistol with red maple wood stocks. Bennet took Magda by the arm and seized Ketrin weapon. "Do you recognize this gun, Ketrin?"

"That is my son's gun. Do you now where he is?"

"Yes, I do."

Finn felt sick to her stomach and there was a bitter taste in her mouth. "Sina?"

Sina met Finn's eyes. "Are you okay?"

"Where is she?"

"She's at the gates, by the road still." Sina's expression softened, and she even smiled a little. "Why don't you go and see your girl, Finn, and I'll finish up here, all right?"

Finn lowered her gun completely and walked away. "Good-bye, Sina."

"Hey?"

Finn stopped in the doorway.

"Thank you, Finnegan O'Connell." Sina's green eyes reminded her again of that day, all those years ago. Theresina Lazarini had been the only one there for her when she had claimed Declan's body. "Maybe I'll see you both around San Michele, sometime soon."

"That would be nice." Finn's voice was hoarse as she turned her back. She put one foot in front of the other, and she walked away.

Finn was at the bottom of the stairs when she heard Pavel Arshavin's gun go off, and it sounded like a cannon as it filled her head with an incredible weight.

A huge hand grabbed her by the left arm and her vision blurred as she tried to adjust. She was about to fall from the last steps, but she was taken by both arms and set squarely onto her feet.

"Here," he said, and took the Sig from her hand. He lifted her coat. "Arm up." Finn lifted her left arm and the Sig was placed back in its holster. "There ya go."

Finn studied his face and tried to place him.

"Enzo, remember?"

Finn let out a surprised breath. "I'm sorry about that."

He shrugged. "I was being a dick. I've had worse. Are you gonna be sick?"

"I don't know."

"Yeah, well, your pick-up sticks man from the balcony made Carlo puke on his shoes." He faced her toward the front doors. "Fresh air. Go find it."

She's at the gates, by the road still.

"Thank you, Enzo."

"You're welcome."

The body was gone from the front steps, and as she took the stairs to the drive, the pavement was clear until it met the night and she could no longer see. Her legs felt like lead as she walked, but she kept moving forward. She would always look back, she accepted that, but not at this place. This moment would become a ghost, and then perhaps, nothing at all. It would become a corner that her memories would move around and brush past, on their way to someplace clean.

Finn's eyes adjusted to the changes around her, and as she moved farther from the lights of the house, ᴉe could see more of the winding drive as it stretched out before her. ᴉhe silhouette in her path seemed to rise up from the blacktop and she ᴉt out a breath that stole away the last of her strength.

❖

Casey's stride lengthened whᴇ Finn stopped, and Casey could hear Asher's voice within her heaᴅ *What about when you need it? When you need someone there for y* ᴉ?

Casey came to a stop before ᴇr lover, and though she wanted desperately to feel Finn's arms aroᴜ ᴅd her, she did not take that last step. Finn appeared as young and fᴦ gile as Casey had ever seen her, caught in the ebb of a rage that had ᴉsted for more than a decade. And yet Casey knew the strength that wᴀ there, and the untamed passion. She wasn't sure if she had ever encoᴜ ᴛtered such determination before, either, but then again, how long had ᴉinn been looking for her, as well? She could finally give Asher ᴛᴇ answer he'd been longing for. *Yes, Papa, I have that now, too. You ᴡere right.*

Finn's expression was quiet as ᴛᴉᴇ shadows played across her face. "Cassandra Marinos."

Casey swallowed through the tᴉ htness of her throat. "Is it done?" "Yes."

She reached out and took Finn ᴉ hand.

Finn's skin was cold, but it wᴏᴜ ᴉld warm up soon enough. There was a tremble in Finn's fingers anᴅ ᴉo Casey stepped closer, pulling Finn's hand to her chest. She held iᴛ ᴛhere with strength and certainty. "Would you like to come home witl ᴉe now?"

Finn held her eyes for a long tiᴍ ᴇ and then she smiled the smallest of smiles. "Yes."

Casey pulled her with a gentle ᴉg.

Finn walked beside her and ᴄ sey saw Jack by the limo as he talked with the driver.

Jack motioned her forward as ᴉ opened the back door of the limo and Casey walked them to the long ᴄar within a wash of relief. When they had crossed the road, she turneᴅ ᴉinn at her shoulders and slid her right hand into Finn's hair, guiding ᴉ r lover as she got into the car.

"He'll take you back to the lofᴉ ᴉ

Casey touched Jack's face. "Tᴉ nk you, Jack."

He smiled. "Sure thing, kiddo. ᴉet her outta here."

The door was shut behind her, and Casey slid along the leather seat until she was able to pull Finn into her arms.

The tenderness of their kiss broke Casey's heart at last, but the loving warmth of Finn's mouth upon her own gave her the courage she needed as she pulled Finn onto her lap. Finn turned and surrendered within the warm embrace, and this time, Casey did not let go.

CHAPTER THIRTY-SEVEN

Casey sat crossed-legged on the bed and watched her lover sleep, and though she had waited for Finn earlier in the day, her willpower had finally run out and she had opened Asher's box.

The latch had been easy, for the replica Houdini lock that held it secure had been the first victory of her childhood training. That Asher had kept it had caused a few tears, but they were good tears. It was a memory she had lost along the way and now it was hers again.

The black lacquer box had been filled with photos. Photos that Casey remembered and photos she hadn't known existed. School photos and photos of Asher as a young man. Photos of their first trip to the coast, and Asher in his Armani suit. There was even one with Amelie, Asher's beloved sister and Casey had stared at it for a long time. She had met Amelie several times, and each time, Amelie had kissed Casey's cheeks and hugged her so thoroughly that Casey thought she would pop. But it had felt good, too. Good and right, and as it should be.

They had made macarons that day, Amelie and Asher, and they had laughed as the music had played. They had danced about the kitchen, and Amelie had told her about the day Asher had climbed to the top of the house and she'd been forced to fetch him back down. It had been a splendid day, and it was the last time they had seen Amelie alive. Her funeral was one of the first and only times that she had seen Asher openly weep, and she had stayed close to him for nearly a year afterward, so he would know he was not alone. They would never be alone again, as long as they had each other.

Naamah had been tucked into the box, and if a portion of Casey's memories had not already returned to her earlier in the evening, she wasn't sure how she might've reacted.

The cat was tattered and torn and her fur was beaten down, but she was still blue, and she still held Casey's secrets within her black button eyes. She had cried quietly for Naamah, and for the lost girl she had been so long ago. And while she held her oldest friend, she had felt the key that was pushed deep within the stuffing of one of Naamah's legs. She had no idea what lock it would open, or what treasure it might reveal, but it was a tarnished brass mystery that still caught the light when she held it up.

There were a dozen names upon a heavy piece of paper that was sealed in an envelope, and there had been other photos, as well, tucked in a tall, narrow book about Secretariat. The book had made her smile when she saw it, and she noted how the pages were worn down, and almost I every page was marked with notes. The notes made no sense to her. Many of them appeared to be in a code of sorts, though she had no idea what that code might be.

The black-and-white photos tucked within the pages of the book had revealed to her yet another incredible, stunning mystery, and a memory that she could not quite grasp, no matter how hard she reached for it. Though perhaps, she would find some of her answers in the morning, when the woman she loved woke up beside her. The wonder of that, of being in love and loved in return, defied description, or at least her ability to put those feelings into words. But add to it what those photos contained, and her world had been tipped on its axis.

"Asher's Van Gogh," she whispered aloud and Finn turned onto her side and faced Casey.

It was an invitation and Casey gladly accepted. She put the box and its mysteries on the bedside table, and then she climbed beneath the sheet and woven blanket. She tucked in as close to Finn as she possibly could and Finn's left arm took hold of her.

Casey's tears came again and she pulled her arms in as she yielded to the quiet strength of the woman who held her, even while she slept. She had no explanation for the capricious whims of fate, or the secretive workings of the world, nor could her logic illuminate the broken clock of her memories. But she did know that in this particular instance, it didn't matter.

CHAPTER TH◦RTY-EIGHT

Novi Sad, Socialist Federal Republi◦ of Yugoslavia
June 1986

Asher shook Ian's hand. His grip wa◦ perhaps too tight, but he couldn't help it. "It is too much. I may not ◦ the best man in the world, but I cannot take so much." He held out ◦e roll of bills that Ian had given him. It was a bit more than a thou◦ ◦nd dollars in American money. With the exchange rate at the mom◦ ◦t, he could almost double that if he worked the system.

"I will not take it back. That w◦ ◦ld be bad luck."

"I cannot thank you enough, m◦ friend, truly. I will pay you back. I swear it."

Ian smiled. "And that would br◦ k my heart. Use that money to get home. Use it for food, and for a warn◦ r coat for Cassandra. It's summer, I know, but sometimes the nights ge◦ cold. Finn gets cold. Use it to fix the car if my father's repairs aren't a◦ perfect as he says they are."

Asher laughed in a quiet mann◦ ◦.

"Or use it to help you get a fresl◦ ◦tart, once you're back in France."

Asher didn't know what to say◦ ◦ot to any of it. He had never been on the receiving end of such a gift ◦fore. "I can work. I am good at many things."

"Taking care of a child, it can hange your plans in a heartbeat. Just take the money, Asher. Perha◦ she will stay with Amelie, but perhaps she'll go with you. She see◦ ◦ fairly attached."

"You will see." Asher was cert◦ ◦ of his words. The sun had gone down and they needed to be on the r◦ d. "I will find a way to repay you. Somehow. Someday, perhaps."

Ian agreed with a nod and held out his hand again. "All right. Someday."

Asher shook it. "Does she really seem to like me?"

"Yes, she does, and quite a lot, from what I can tell."

Asher turned, and both he and Ian watched as Cassandra stood beside Finn. They had towed the Renault up to the house, where Ian's father had worked his considerable magic on all sorts of mechanical injuries. He had fixed Asher's silver angel until she purred like a brand-new car, and Asher could have wept.

Finn held Cassandra's stuffed cat and scratched at the ears, and though it was something simple, Casey seemed enchanted by the entire scenario. Casey had smiled only at Finn, and when Finn whispered to the stuffed cat, as if she shared a secret, Casey's eyes became full and a smile slipped quickly across her lips.

Asher's voice was soft. "Today, it is the first I have seen her even smile."

"Mister Asher?"

Declan slid to a stop and Asher reached out and steadied him. "You are too fast to be a human being." Asher laughed. "You must be a superhero, like in the comics."

Declan's smile lit up his entire face. "I'm faster than Finn."

"I believe it."

Declan held out an envelope. "These are the pictures I took. Mama Ailish helped me with them, so you could take them with you."

Asher blinked and took the envelope with a careful hand. Declan had been taking pictures all day with a beat-up Kodak camera, and Asher had no idea what moments he might've caught with his keen eye. Ian's mother was a photographer of sorts, from what he could tell, and she took great pride in her grandson's skill. It was a lovely gift and completely unexpected. "Declan." Asher noted the pride on Ian's face, and he had to take a moment before he spoke again. "You are a true gentleman, Declan, thank you for your kindness."

"Did Cassandra speak to you, Declan?" Ian asked. "Or to Finn?"

"No." Declan put his hands on his hips as he tried to stand taller. "But she likes Finn an awful lot, and Finn likes to make her smile."

"Go get the food from Mama Ailish, okay?" Ian put a hand on his son's shoulder. "It'll be good for the road and Casey might get hungry. And the blankets, too."

"Yes, sir."

Asher watched the boy run toward the house again. "You have a fine family, Ian."

"So do you."

Finn handed Casey's kitten back to her and Casey took a small step closer as she reached out with her free hand, pulling at Finn's shirt. When Finn leaned down, Asher thought that Casey would speak, but Casey lifted onto the tips of her toes and kissed her instead.

It was a small, soft kiss upon the mouth, but it was sweet, and when Finn stepped back, there was a look on her face that Asher remembered very well. His own first kiss seemed a lifetime ago, though he had never forgotten the magic of that moment.

Ian laughed softly and Cassandra walked away from Finn without a word. Asher waited as she approached him with a strange sort of confidence. When she reached him, she slipped her hand within his and stood close.

Asher leaned over at the waist and Casey's big brown eyes stared into his own. He had dared to hope that she would've spoken to another child, and Ian's Finnegan was most certainly a charmer. Perhaps it was not meant to be. Perhaps she would never speak. Perhaps there would be no King of Thieves. "Are you ready to go home, Cassandra?"

Asher's heart let loose with a flutter at the unexpected warmth and emotion that swirled up within her eyes. The open display of feelings was new to them both and he held his breath.

"Yes, Oncle."

CHAPTER THIRTY-NINE

Near Bergerac, the Dordogne, France
Present day

Casey dropped her backpack to the floor, walked to the window, and pushed the shutters open to the late afternoon breeze. The trees were still full and there was a pleasant rustle of leaves as she looked down the hill. The afternoon sun hit the back of her house and the bank of windows was set ablaze by the angle of golden light. The maples had come in nicely, and from a distance, her land was absolutely beautiful.

She heard Finn's boots on the wooden floor behind her and she spun around. Finn wore her faded Levi's and a navy-colored button-down that hung untucked beneath Asher's battered and yet still lovely brown leather jacket. Finn had given over the jacket, which she had carefully stored, and Casey had promptly given it right back to her. Finn's eyes had filled with tears as she smiled, and when she had shrugged into it, it was quite clear that it belonged exactly where it was. Her bruises were healed and the stitches had come out, and as Finn stood before her, she appeared to be as guilty as original sin.

Casey could not have been more in love with her if she'd tried. "So this is where you watched me from?"

"Mostly. You can't see the river from here, or your boat."

Casey nodded and stepped to her right. The laptops were stored neatly but there was a pile of books on the corner of the table, and a surveillance scope the size of which she'd never seen before. She touched the scope and eyed her lover. "This is very nice."

Finn's lips puffed out as she exhaled.

"It's okay." Casey grinned and walked to the bed. "No, it's good."

She bent over and pushed her hands onto the mattress. It was soft, but it creaked slightly. Casey pulled at the slightly rumpled blanket and straightened it out with a flick of her fingers. "Is this where you slept then, Finnegan O'Connell?"

"Yes."

"Is it soft?"

"It's not too bad." Finn's voice was quiet. "It creaks a bit."

There was a small light on the bedside table but nothing else, and Casey opened the drawer and then shut it. She turned back and stood up straight. "So when you went to bed, did you..." She tried very hard not to smile, but the blush that moved along Finn's neck and over her jaw was fairly spectacular. "Did you think of me, while you touched yourself?"

Finn didn't answer her.

Casey smiled at last as she put her hands into the back pockets of her jeans.

Finn was still so fragile in many ways, and perhaps she was finally grieving for Declan in a way that her rage had not allowed before. It was a startling thing to be given access to, Finn's vulnerability, and it was a heady gift that Casey did not take for granted. She had let go once before and it had almost been the end of her. She wouldn't make the same mistake twice.

It had been a long time since she had been needed by someone, and Finn let her inside without a second thought. She had realized quite quickly that there was no greater work of art she might have stolen than Finn's heart. "You did, didn't you, Finnegan."

Finn still wouldn't answer her.

"Come on, O'Connell, give it up. I mean, there were plenty of times I went swimming this past summer, and more than once without a suit."

"I know that. I remember that."

Casey held her lover's eyes. Her clothes were pulled tight across her breasts and she could feel her nipples press against her bra and the white blouse she wore beneath her green leather. It was a terrible thing to want someone so badly, at all times, and yet it was fucking glorious in every way. "Finnegan."

"Okay, but just...just a couple times."

"A couple of times?" Casey repeated. "Define that, please."

"More than once." There was actually a touch of laughter in Finn's voice. "Less than two hundred and fifty-six. Not a lot."

Casey laughed. "Is that just a random number? Or does that mean your definition of *a lot* means two hundred and fifty-seven? Because you really should be specific with this one. It's going to matter."

"It is?"

"It might."

"How?"

"Was it just one fantasy, or did you mix it up? Did you enjoy a nice variety of things?"

Finn took a step back from the end of the bed and shifted her weight as she shoved her hands into the pockets of her jeans.

"Are you counting them?" Casey asked softly.

Finn's eyes began to change. It was subtle, but the rest of Casey's body felt the effects of the shift. Casey went to her and when she was close enough, she grabbed Finn's shirt and pulled.

Finn took a step.

Casey felt the power of their attraction within her thighs and the flesh between her legs filled with heat. "Can you hear me?" Casey whispered as softly as she possibly could.

Finn leaned closer.

"Tell me, Daddy...did you have your cock in any of these fantasies?"

Finn closed her eyes and Casey was a bit startled at the unexpected tremble in Finn's shoulders. She was walking a rather lovely edge and she wondered just how quickly things were about to progress. They hadn't really touched each other since...well, for almost nine thousand kilometers. *For the love of God, that won't be happening again.*

"Did you lie beneath the covers and imagine being inside me?"

Finn was closer yet again, though Casey hadn't moved. Finn's subtle cologne was a now familiar scent and she found herself trying not to lean forward.

"Was the house quiet..." The lure of Finn's hair was too close and Casey swallowed and licked her lips. That such loveliness existed in the world had never occurred to her until Finn. "When you touched yourself?" She felt Finn's breath against her cheek, and then the heat of her lover's face, so close, too close, not close enough. "Did I make you wet, my love?"

"Casey."

"Did the bed creak beneath you, Daddy?" Casey's breath was quick now, and she could picture Finn naked beneath the covers as she fantasized, as she made herself come. Fantasies about her, even as she herself had...*As I pleasured yself, in the house down the hill, now have.* "Did it turn you on more?"

Finn's hand slid along her wa[ ]st and Casey closed her eyes as she tipped forward. Her forehead la[ ]ded against Finn's chest and she pulled at her lower lip with her teet[ ] She turned her head to the side. "Goddammit."

"What?" Finn asked in a whisp[ ]r.

"This whole scene..." Casey's [ ]nd found its way into Finn's hair. She took hold and pulled Finn's m[ ]uth to hers. Their kiss was filled with passion and Finn's hands slippe[ ] around her, even as Casey pulled her mouth away. "I wanted to give y[ ]u your fantasy."

"I approve of your plan, yes."

Casey kissed her again and Fi[ ]n pulled her up and close. Their kiss became hot-blooded and deep [ ]d everything changed within an instant. Casey moaned and pulled [ ]ck, even though her arms were fierce about Finn's neck and should[ ]s. "But now..."

"Now?"

"Yes."

"What about now?"

"I can give you maybe thirty se[ ]onds, at best. You drive me crazy, Finn, I can't help it, I really can't."

Finn's eyes were a dusky amb[ ], and Casey saw within them the next thirty years that Finn had spok[ ] of. Finn's slow smile was filled with delight. "That was number sev[ ]nteen, actually, so I think you're golden."

Finn walked her sideways an[ ] Casey laughed happily as they tumbled onto the bed.

About the Author

Shea Godfrey is an artist and writer working and living in the Midwest. While her education is in journalism and photography, she has spent most of her career in 3-D animation and design.

You may write to her at sheagodfreymail@gmail.com.

Books Available From Bold Strokes Books

A More Perfect Union by Carsen Taite. Major Zoey Granger and DC fixer Rook Daniels risk their reputations for a chance at true love while dealing with a scandal that threatens to rock the military. (978-1-62639-754-5)

Arrival by Gun Brooke. The spaceship *Pathfinder* reaches its passengers' new homeworld where danger lurks in the shadows while Pamas Seclan disembarks and finds unexpected love in young science genius Darmiya Do Voy. (978-1-62639-859-7)

Captain's Choice by VK Powell. Architect Kerstin Anthony's life is going to plan until Bennett Carlyle, the first girl she ever kissed, is assigned to her latest and most important project, a police district substation. (978-1-62639-997-6)

Falling Into Her by Erin Zak. Pam Phillips, widow at the age of forty, meets Kathryn Hawthorne, local Chicago celebrity, and it changes her life forever—in ways she hadn't even considered possible. (978-1-63555-092-4)

Hookin' Up by MJ Williamz. Will Leah get what she needs from casual hookups or will she see the love she desires right in front of her? (978-1-63555-051-1)

King of Thieves by Shea Godfrey. When art thief Casey Marinos meets bounty hunter Finnegan Starkweather, the crimes of the past just might set the stage for a payoff worth more than she ever dreamed possible. (978-1-63555-007-8)

Lucy's Chance by Jackie D. As a serial killer haunts the streets, Lucy tries to stitch up old wounds with her first love in the wake of a small town's rapid descent into chaos. (978-1-63555-027-6)

Right Here, Right Now by Georgia Beers. When Alicia Wright moves into the office next door to Lacey Chamberlain's accounting firm, Lacey is about to find out that sometimes the last person you want is exactly the person you need. (978-1-63555-154-9)

Strictly Need to Know by MB Aus... ... Covert operator Maji Rios will do whatever she must to complete ... r mission, but saving a gorgeous stranger from Russian mobsters w... not in her plans. (978-1-63555-114-3)

Tailor-Made by Yolanda Wallace. T... ...or Grace Henderson doesn't date clients, but when she meets gender- ...nding model Dakota Lane, she's tempted to throw all the rules out th... window. (978-1-63555-081-8)

Time Will Tell by M. Ullrich. W... ... the ability to time travel, Eva Caldwell will have to decide betwe... ...n having it all and erasing it all. (978-1-63555-088-7)

Change in Time by Robyn Nyx. V... ...rking in the past is hell on your future. The Extractor series: Book T... o. (978-1-62639-880-1)

Love After Hours by Radclyffe. ...When Gina Antonelli agrees to renovate Carrie Longmire's new ho... ...se, she doesn't welcome Carrie's overtures at friendship or her ow... unexpected attraction. A Rivers Community Novel. (978-1-63555-0...)-0)

Nantucket Rose by CF Frizzell. M... ...ggie Jordan can't wait to convert a historic Nantucket home into a B... .B, but doesn't expect to fall for mariner Ellis Chilton, who has mo... claim to the house than Maggie realizes. (978-1-63555-056-6)

Picture Perfect by Lisa Moreau. F... ...lling in love wasn't supposed to be part of the stakes for Olive and ...abby, rival photographers in the competition of a lifetime. (978-1-62... ...39-975-4)

Set the Stage by Karis Walsh. Actr... s Emilie Danvers takes the stage again in Ashland, Oregon, little real... ...ing that landscaper Arden Philips is about to offer her a very personal ...omantic lead role. (978-1-63555-087-0)

Strike a Match by Fiona Riley. W... ...n their attempts at matchmaking fizzle out, firefighter Sasha and ... ...luctant millionairess Abby find themselves turning to each other t... strike a perfect match. (978-1-62639-999-0)

The Price of Cash by Ashley Bartlett. Cash Braddock is doing her best to keep her business afloat, stay out of jail, and avoid Detective Kallen. It's not working. (978-1-62639-708-8)

Under Her Wing by Ronica Black. At Angel's Wings Rescue, dogs are usually the ones saved, but when quiet Kassandra Haden meets outspoken owner Jayden Beaumont, the two stubborn women just might end up saving each other. (978-1-63555-077-1)

Underwater Vibes by Mickey Brent. When Hélène, a translator in Brussels, Belgium, meets Sylvie, a young Greek photographer and swim coach, unsettling feelings hijack Hélène's mind and body—even her poems. (978-1-63555-002-3)

A Date to Die by Anne Laughlin. Someone is killing people close to Detective Kay Adler, who must look to her own troubled past for a suspect. There she finds more than one person seeking revenge against her. (978-1- 63555-023-8)

Captured Soul by Laydin Michaels. Can Kadence Munroe save the woman she loves from a twisted killer, or will she lose her to a collector of souls? (978-1-62639-915-0)

Dawn's New Day by TJ Thomas. Can Dawn Oliver and Cam Cooper, two women who have loved and lost, open their hearts to love again? (978-1-63555-072-6)

Definite Possibility by Maggie Cummings. Sam Miller is just out for good times, but Lucy Weston makes her realize happily ever after is a definite possibility. (978-1-62639-909-9)

Eyes Like Those by Melissa Brayden. Isabel Chase and Taylor Andrews struggle between love and ambition from the writers' room on one of Hollywood's hottest TV shows. (978-1-63555-012-2)

Heart's Orders by Jaycie Morrison. Helen Tucker and Tee Owens escape hardscrabble lives to careers in the Women's Army Corps, but more than their hearts are at risk as friendship blossoms into love. (978-1-63555-073-3)

KING OF THIEVES

By the Author

Nightshade

Blackstone

King of Thieves